THE FOLDS

THE FOLDS

*Everyone has their dying day...
some happen to know when*

by CLINT TOWNSEND

Tate Publishing *& Enterprises*

The Folds
Copyright © 2007 by Uno Tejano, L.L.C. All rights reserved.

This title is also available as a Tate Out Loud product. Visit www.tatepublishing.com for more information.

No part of this publication may be reproduced, stored in a retrieval system or transmitted in any way by any means, electronic, mechanical, photocopy, recording or otherwise without the prior permission of the author except as provided by USA copyright law.

Scripture quotations marked "kjv" are taken from the Holy Bible, King James Version, Cambridge, 1769. Used by permission. All rights reserved.

This novel is a work of fiction. Names, descriptions, entities and incidents included in the story are products of the author's imagination. Any resemblance to actual persons, events and entities is entirely coincidental.

The opinions expressed by the author are not necessarily those of Tate Publishing, LLC.

Published by Tate Publishing & Enterprises, LLC
127 E. Trade Center Terrace | Mustang, Oklahoma 73064 USA
1.888.361.9473 | www.tatepublishing.com

Tate Publishing is committed to excellence in the publishing industry. The company reflects the philosophy established by the founders, based on Psalm 68:11,
"The Lord gave the word and great was the company of those who published it."

Book design copyright © 2007 by Tate Publishing, LLC. All rights reserved.
Cover design by Janae J. Glass
Interior design by Nathan Harmony

Published in the United States of America

ISBN: 978-1-60462-291-1
1. Fiction
2. Action & Adventure
14.06.05

I would like to thank my Lord and Savior, Jesus Christ, for breathing the life of this story into my heart. For Mom, Dad, Kim, and Emilie to whom I thank for their unending support, love, and encouragement

Acknowledgments

I would like to thank the following for their assistance and guidance during the writing process:

Maj. Stanley Clark; Texas Dept. of Public Safety, Dallas, Texas
Dr. Lee Brock; McKinney, Texas
Steven Brock; Austin, Texas
Kathy Quinonez; Tulsa, Oklahoma
Michelle Denham; Levelland, Texas
Mike and Tracy Brock; Dallas, Texas
Leon and Emily; Blanchard, Oklahoma
Brad Lacey; Bonham, Texas
Brett and Toni Brock; Garland, Texas
Jennifer Maya; El Paso, Texas
Pastor Raymond Simms; Blanchard, Oklahoma

Table of Contents

The Game of Their Lives

- 13 -

The Lord's Day

- 20 -

BBQ and Horseshoes

- 29 -

Monday Morning

- 38 -

100 Years at the VFW

- 45 -

Saturday, Superman and Fishing

- 49 -

Wishes

- 57 -

Requiem
- 82 -

October
- 87 -

The Fold
- 94 -

'Tis the Season
- 101 -

Fold #2
- 108 -

And So It Begins
- 119 -

1988
- 128 -

1993
- 131 -

1999
- 132 -

Just One of Many
- 134 -

The Catalyst
- 137 -

Secrets Revealed
- 142 -

A Personal Resurrection
- 145 -

A Not So Joyous Reunion
- 153 -

The Morning After
- 159 -

The Homecoming
- 162 -

Prove It to Me
- 166 -

A Prophecy Fulfilled
- 179 -

Digging Up the Past
- 181 -

An Unwelcome Visitor
- 185 -

Third Time's a Charmer
- 189 -

Oil and Water
- 192 -

All Old Things are Made New
- 201 -

Another Door Closes
- 211 -

It's Okay to Let Go
- 222 -

History Repeats Itself
- 228 -

Behind the Eight Ball

- 232 -

Testing the Hypothesis

- 239 -

Scars in the Heart

- 250 -

Ghosts from the Past

- 257 -

And All Flesh Shall be Made New

- 272 -

The Game of Their Lives

Late summer. Texas, 1978. The sun rested on the tops of the trees in the early evening sky. Like a faded bulb on a weathered strand of Christmas lights, it shone through the branches, bathing all in a soft, red glow. While standing in line at the refreshment stand, Tommy could see the fresh popcorn flowing like a waterfall over the hopper and onto the perforated base. The white heat lamp made the salt crystals look like dancing snowflakes as a young girl shook the large blue canister of Morton's, stirring the kernels with her spatula. Another woman took a small pan from an old stovetop in the corner and poured melted sweet butter over the tops of the bags of popcorn before handing them to the hungry spectators. Tommy hurriedly recited the snack order in his head while trying to watch the game from the back of the line. Danny Lee Albright, Tommy and Sarah's boy, was third down in the line-up following Billy Williams and Daryl Wilke. As he slowly and impatiently inched his way to the counter of the snack bar, Tommy overlooked the three baseball fields, drew a deep breath and reminisced about how good it used to feel when he and his friends played ball together in the thick, still summer air at this very same park. Now, Tommy's son, Danny, and the sons of all his friends played together.

Tommy hollered out his order as the lines of anxious customers voiced their objections for such a long list of food and taking so much time. He then walked slowly, cautiously, and way overloaded toward the bleachers, looking all around as he crept so as to not have anyone enter his personal and unbalanced space.

"All right, all right, all right!" Tommy announced, as he stepped slow and wide onto the first step of the aluminum bleachers. "Hot stuff! Coming through! Official police business! One side!" Like a waiter, he repeated the orders as he passed out the food, climbing one step at a time. "Jason, two hotdogs; Monica, Sugar Babies and Coke; Doc, Baby Ruth and Coke and Miss Holly get da Big Hunk and DP. Case and Terri, popcorn and DP's; Miss Joellen and John, DP's and Reese's times two. Sarah?"

Tommy looked up expecting to see his wife in the stands. Not seeing her or having his call answered, he called again, "Sarah?!"

Looking across to the visiting team bleachers, Sarah Albright stood at the rail of the walkway talking with a couple of friends. "Sarah!" he hollered, holding up her food. "I'm eatin' three hot hotdogs in five seconds if ya ain't over here in two!" Tommy barked.

Sarah waved back in acknowledgement as Tommy squirted a dash of mustard into his mouth before cramming in one of the hotdogs.

Jason Wilke leaned in as Tommy sat to join him, "How much we owe ya, Tommy?"

"Nuttin,' it was from Sarah's purse," he mumbled through his food. The two men then toasted each other with a chuckle.

They had always been together: Tommy, Ron, John, Jason, and Casey. They had lived there all of their lives and had remained the best of friends. Most children from small towns do. Sarah, with her brood of friends: Terri, Holly, Joey, and Monica, had done the same. All ten were friends from elementary school throughout junior high, enjoying 4-H, student council, sports, and church together. Slowly but surely, all ten friends had become couples by their freshmen and sophomore years of high school.

Tommy was the eldest of the five boys and, while growing up, had naturally assumed the role of leader at an early age. Now at thirty-five years, he stood six-foot-four, weighed in at two-hundred-forty pounds, and cut quite an imposing figure to both friend and foe… whether in or out of uniform. But with slightly curly, blond hair, blue eyes, tanned smooth skin, a great smile, and more than an adequate amount of muscle, Tommy was also easy on the eyes and hearts of the local women.

Just as Danny Lee's team took position in the "on deck" and batter's box for the bottom of the first inning, Sarah quickly made her way from the visiting team bleachers to the home team stands to join her husband and friends.

"Where is he?" Sarah asked, not looking at Tommy as she, too, crammed a hotdog in her mouth, squirting mustard in afterwards. "Is he up?" she mumbled.

"Nah, he's third down behind Billy and Daryl," Tommy pointed out as pieces of hotdog flew from his mouth. He took a drink of Sarah's Dr. Pepper and turned to address the group of men. "Now, if y'all come over next Saturday around five am," he hypothesized, "technically, we should be able to load everything in the boats and fit everyone in the Jeep and Jimmy. I'm thinking we should be at Texoma 'round noon."

Before anyone in the group could respond, Terri and Casey Williams stood and screamed for their eight-year-old boy. Billy Williams strolled out to the batter's box, awkwardly swinging a bat that, if stood on end, was sure to be as tall if not taller than he.

"C'mon, Billy! Get a hit! Easy stuff! Take your time!" the prideful duo hollered. Billy, the youngest and smallest of the boys, with bright strawberry red hair and freckles, wore a uniform whose pants, hat and shirt literally swallowed him. He glanced towards the stands where his mom and dad were standing, waving excitedly. Casey clenched his fists to his son in confidence.

"Get up!" Terri commanded, frogging Tommy in the back of the shoulder. "C'mon!" she demanded while motioning for the others to get up and show their support. Tommy, Sarah, and the other husbands and wives slowly stood to clap and cheer for the ever-hopeful runt.

"C'mon! Get a hit, son! Jus' like at home!" Casey could be heard from all over the park as he shouted. Billy lifted the gargantuan bat, letting it rest it on his shoulder as he looked for the batting signal from his third base coach, Pastor Mike Cregan.

"I hope he hits it!" Terri squeaked under her breath, grabbing Casey's arm.

"He will, he will," Casey replied, patting her hand. "We been practicing every night this week!"

At the bottom half of the first inning, on the opening pitch, Billy closed his eyes, stuck his tongue out of the corner of his mouth, and took a big swing. He made contact and lightly lobbed the ball over the third baseman's head. Billy stood shocked for a moment as both Terri and Casey jumped up and ecstatically screamed, "Run! Run!"

Billy looked to Pastor Mike who leapt for joy and motioned for him to run to first base. Lost in the amazement of actually getting a hit, he unknowingly took the bat with him and made a mad, unbalanced dash to first base. He barely reached the bag before the throw from the shallows of left field was caught. Billy dropped the bat just outside the baseline and thrust his fists in the air. The small boy's excited, wide-eyed jubilance amused the spectators from both sides of the field as they all laughed and applauded enthusiastically.

As the others sat down and adjusted themselves, Terri and Casey remained standing, clapping, cheering and yelling. Billy stood on first base, pulling up his oversized pants while waving wildly to his mom and dad.

All eyes then turned to home plate as Daryl Wilke stepped into the batter's box. Daryl was second only to Danny Lee in age and size. John and Joey Wilke clapped and whistled for their boy as he swung his bat a few times.

Tommy turned to his father, Johnny Lee, and asked, "Daddy, you wan' come out to th' lake next Saturday w' me and the boys? Be just like old times!"

John joined in on the plead, "C'mon, Johnny Lee! Doc says he can out-fish you any day."

Ron Hall, with a self-titled a.k.a. of "Doctor Fish," was supposedly the master of bass fishing and catfish frying. He also claimed that he could "pull 'em out of the water and just keep on a' pulling." Upon overhearing John's comment, Ron stood for all to see and began performing an energetic charade of casting his line. Immediately pretending to catch a "big one," he leaned back and put on a show complete with grunts, whoops, and sound effects of a reel zipping with the weight of his prize-winning imaginary catch. Doc played his part quite convincingly.

As the friends clapped and laughed at the performance in the stands, Johnny Lee shook his head at Ron and then informed John, "You know he brags just to hear himself talk!"

Ron, with arms out-stretched as if he were holding a "whopper of a fish," leaned back and proclaimed, "It ain't bragging when it's the truth! All I gotta do is yell, 'Doc's here!' and they just jump outta the water!" Ron leaned over and shook hands with Johnny Lee as all had a good laugh.

Holly Hall, with a not-so-amazed look on her face, commented to her husband, "You *do* know you're pathetic, right?" then kissed him.

Daryl got a base hit that flew between first and second base. Billy scurried to second base, struggling to keep a hand on his pants and beat the throw from right field as Daryl easily reached first. Both boys were safe. John and Joey clapped and hugged each other as John reached down between the bleachers to pull a cold bottle of Shiner beer from his cooler.

"Okay now," Jason began, leaning in between Johnny and Tommy. "We have Danny Lee, Tommy Lee and Johnny Lee. What's with the 'Lee'?" he asked.

Tommy, without taking his eyes off the field, turned his head to Johnny Lee and asked, "You wanna get that one, Daddy?" Tommy then stood as Danny Lee stepped into the batter's box. Sarah joined Tommy and discovered that they were the only ones standing for the team. The score was two to zero in the bottom half of the first inning with Danny's team down.

Tommy clapped nervously, hollering out, "C'mon, Superman! Here we go! Out of the park! Make him throw it to ya!"

As he approached the plate, Danny looked up at his grandfather, Johnny Lee, who nodded and winked in confident approval.

Without taking his eyes off Danny, Johnny began his explanation to Jason. "Well, my great-granddad was the first of our family to come to Texas in the early 1860's. His name was Glenard Lee. He married a Cherokee girl, Mabel, and was registered in the Daws Land Act of 1887."

All stop talking and watched intensely as Danny's first pitch came in low and fast to the outside. Danny gave a mighty swing, but only made contact with the air.

Johnny continued to explain, "So, to honor him, we made it a tradition to give every newborn the middle name of 'Lee.' Boy or girl, you're gonna get 'Lee' for a middle name."

Tommy continued standing, slowly rocking his hips back and forth in anticipation, clapping and calling out, "Good eye! Good eye! Take your time, Superman!"

A loud crack broke the still air, ringing throughout the park. Danny got a hit. A *big* hit. The ball went deep into left field, near the fence.

"HOO!" Tommy screamed, thrusting his fists in the air. Both sections of bleachers stood to witness the spectacle.

The bench in the dugout cleared as twelve prepubescent boys came to life and let loose with a high-pitched barrage of indiscernible cheers. All eyes watched intently as the new, white leather Rawlings baseball fell just inside the base line.

"That's it! Go!" Tommy muttered to himself as he made his way down the stands through the crowd of friends and families. "Go! Go! Danny, go! All the way, don't stop!" Tommy yelled.

Daryl caught up with Billy and his pants as they rounded third while Danny headed for second base. He paused at second to see where the ball was as Tommy yelled impatiently, "Don't look at the ball. Listen to Mike!" Pastor Cregan motioned for Danny to come to third because the ball had been wildly thrown over the second baseman's head.

"Go! Go! Go!" Pastor Mike leapt and shouted while frantically circling his arms.

"Fly, Superman! Fly!" Tommy blared, grabbing the chain link fence behind home plate for stability as he jumped up and down. The first baseman caught the overthrow from left field and shot it to the third baseman. Danny dove hands and head first, sliding hard into the dirt.

The third baseman's reach wasn't quite long enough; the ball skipped out of the base line once again and bounced off the chain link fence toward left field. Billy struggled to stay clothed as he crossed home plate, coming close to being run over by Daryl as he, too, scored safely, then turned to watch the drama unfold.

Pastor Mike, Tommy and the entire home team section of bleachers yelled out, "Run!" as Danny scampered to his feet and dashed for home. Without missing a beat, the left fielder ran to the fence, bent down in mid-stride and scooped up the ball with his right hand.

Like a slow-motion scene from a movie, he lunged out with his left leg and hurled the ball with all his might towards home plate. Danny slid safely into home with the catcher still standing above him, his glove empty.

Tommy jumped, screamed, clapped, whistled, and hollered as he knocked the bags of popcorn out of his friend's hands. Danny's teammates poured out of the dugout and dog-piling their conquering hero. Tommy and Sarah hugged each other as all the other parents clapped and cheered for the team.

There were few joyful noises emanating from the visiting team's dugout or stands.

Danny and the boys made their way back into the dugout, jumping and squealing in front of their friends and family. As he strutted past the chain link backstop, Danny searched the stands for his grandfather. His face beamed with pride as Johnny Lee again clenched his fist, winked, and nodded his approval.

Danny spied Jessica Renee Holder standing at the fence and paused for a moment to smile. She blushed, smiled broadly and then ran to meet her parents who were waiting near the concession stand.

After the game, Tommy, Sarah, Johnny, and the other parents huddled by the bottom of the bleachers to enjoy their beers in the shadows. The boys, in their own huddle, each put a gloved hand in the middle of the circle and chanted, "Two, four, six, eight! Who do we appreciate? Bears! Bears! Bears!"

The fifteen battle-weary warriors then darted past their cheering parents with blurts of, "Hi, Mom!" and, "Did you see me, Dad?" and raced to be first in line for their victory snow cones and sodas.

Pastor Mike approached the group of proud parents who offered up a thunderous round of applause for his efforts. He bowed and waved and whispered an overly dramatic, "Thank you! Thank you!"

The Lord's Day

Sunday morning. At ten o'clock they started coming in and went directly to "their seats" in the congregation, the same seats they had occupied for years. It was an unwritten seating chart, but everybody knew where everyone sat and respected that for each other. The elders traditionally stood at both sides of the double doors leading into the sanctuary, greeting church members, and, while shaking hands, dispensed smiles and poorly copied news bulletins printed on pastel pink and yellow paper.

The new wing of the church, consisting of ten rooms for Bible school and a nursery, was added on two years ago and construction on the sanctuary extension was to start at the beginning of next spring. Hanging on the foyer walls were several of the original glass plate negatives showing the small church being built in certain stages back in 1884. Included with the plates was a fine copy of one of the original deeds to the church property signed by Glenard Lee Albright, Levi Holder, Jeffrey Childress, and Austin Collard. All four men were instrumental in establishing the town, its civil offices and government. Glenard Lee, Tommy's great-great-granddad, was the first elder of the church. Jeffrey Childress, Sarah's great-great-granddad, helped establish the school, becoming the first principal, then later the superintendent.

The sanctuary consisted of three sections of fifteen pews, with each pew holding anywhere from ten to twelve people. At the front of the pews, a one-step platform of thick burgundy carpet spread out the width of the hall. A mixed choir, forty-two voices strong, sat on three rows of chairs behind a podium along with four wing chairs, two on each side of the podium. Pastors Raymond Brock and Mike Cregan, the youth minister and sometimes baseball coach, sat on one side of the podium. On the other side of the podium sat elder Celton Tartt and the music director, Clinton Brown.

The town was to celebrate its centennial at the end of the July; the schools, city offices, businesses, and public service departments all planned special celebrations throughout the month. The First Baptist Church chose to recognize those who had dedicated their lives to law enforcement and public safety by inviting all those who were currently serving, or who had served in the past, to wear their uniforms to the services.

Tommy, Sarah, and Danny Lee arrived fifteen minutes after ten and spent the first five in the foyer. Tommy and Danny shook hands and spoke with the elders while Sarah complimented dresses and hair. Tommy's uniform, as well as Sarah's, was pressed with stiff creases. His light gray felt hat rested forward and low on his head. The trousers and shirt, both dark brown with blue and red stripes on the sleeve and outer pant seam, were perfectly aligned. Sarah's skirt's and shirt's were consistently and immaculately clean. The couple's shoes, both as dark as ebony, shone brilliantly from freshly applied, melted carnauba wax.

They all talked it over, waited for each other to graduate college, and in 1966, Tommy, Sarah, John, Jason, Ron, and Casey all joined the Texas Department of Public Safety. They all elected to train for, and aspired to become, Texas DPS Troopers. It was a perfect plan. What better way to ensure the security of their friendships and ties than for all to live in the same work area and have the same holidays?

Tommy and Sarah were the first to marry in June, 1960, right after their high school graduation. In the fall of that year, both enrolled at the University of Texas where Tommy majored in political science and graduated with a 3.72. Sarah graduated fourth in her class with a degree in elementary education, a 3.96 and made the Dean's List. They worked the weekends and drove to Austin everyday.

John and Joey married that same June summer night in 1960 immediately after Tommy and Sarah's wedding, followed by Ron and Holly in October, Jason and Monica in November and Casey and Terri in December. John and Joey had broken up for a couple of months prior to graduating, but while attending the wedding for Tommy and Sarah as a bridesmaid and groomsmen, the two were so overcome with emotion, they came to realize that they truly loved each other.

At the reception, during a slow dance, John pulled away from Joey crying, "I don't ever want to be without you." "Oh, baby!" Joey cooed and stroked his cheek. At that moment, the Spirit came over John and he got down on his knee in the middle of the dance floor to propose. She immediately said yes and leapt into his arms before he could even complete his proposal.

Not wanting to wait any longer, they asked Pastor Cregan to marry them right then and there in the dance hall after marrying Tommy and Sarah only hours earlier. The two asked Tommy and Sarah to be their maid of honor and best man. John didn't have a ring at the moment, so Mrs. Wilke, John's mother, with tears in her eyes, took off her ring, handed it to John, hugged him and kissed Joey.

"Can't have my new daughter come into the family with no ring!" she choked, as she walked off the dance floor. All in attendance clapped and had a good laugh. Joey stood for an awkward moment with no ring to give John. Sarah leaned back to look at Tommy and nodded her head toward Joey. Tommy then took off his wedding band and handed it to Joey. Looking at John, Tommy said, "Better not lose it!" The young couple stumbled through their vows and kissed each other. The rest of the reception went great. Tommy and Sarah were the first to have a child, Danny Lee, in July 1968. By the early fall of 1970, all five couples had one child, and all were boys. Terri and Casey's boy, Billy, was the last and the smallest. Born eight weeks premature, his lungs hadn't fully developed and so had to stay in the pediatric ward of the hospital for an additional five weeks to put on weight.

Ron and Holly were the first interracially mixed couple in town. Ron's parents moved from Corpus Christi when he was entering first grade and almost immediately became Tommy's best friend. Tommy and Ron met long before Casey, John, and Jason's parents moved into the area. Ron was one of only a handful of black children growing up in town. He and Holly's boy, Bobby, had beautiful olive skin, was smart, athletic, and full of energy. With Ron being a DPS Trooper and Holly the being the first female high school principal, not too many remarks were made about Bobby's mixed blood.

Upon entering the sanctuary, Tommy, Sarah, and Danny saw that their friends were already there. All the boys rushed from their seats to greet Danny, who then turned to Tommy for approval to be dismissed. With a nod, all five young men quickly scurried to the front of the pews for the prayer offering with Pastor Cregan. The men tipped their hats to one another with smiles and winks, looking each other over in their dress uniforms. The girls huddled at the end of one pew to firm up plans Ladies Bible Study at Monica's house. The guest house would rotate every Monday night for the ladies and every Tuesday the men would do the same.

Jason, not the most socially gracious of the bunch, called across the room, "Tuesday night at my place guys … second Corinthians. Read up!" Tommy, Ron, John, and Casey needed not to look around to see who was speaking. They just knew.

Pastor Brock approached the podium and requested, "Could we please get all the children to come join Pastor Cregan and myself for the morning prayer?" A swarm of children rushed the stage to see who would sit closest to Pastor Cregan. Mike Cregan, tall and thin with tan skin, blond hair, green eyes, straight teeth and simple words, sat upon the steps with the children.

"All right! What do we have here today?" he asked. "Hoowee! I see some buckles have been shined up! I see some pretty new dresses; some new boots." The parents smiled and laughed as some of the smaller children stood up to show off their nice clothes.

At that very moment, the doors to the sanctuary opened wide as Mr. and Mrs. Holder attempted to quietly take their seats. Jessica was close behind but did not join her mother and father. She darted to the front of the stage and tried to squeeze her way in between Danny and Daryl.

"Maybe someone needs to get a new clock or watch?" Mike said jokingly to the children. Both he and the congregation laughed as Danny softly nudged Jessica, who nudged back. "Okay now, how 'bout we all join hands and, Billy, will you lead us in a prayer?" The congregation then stood and extended their hands across the aisles as all the children did the same. Billy looked to Mike for when to speak, and after a moment, was given a wink and nod to begin.

"Dear God," the boy began, "Thank you for this day, thank you for our mommies and daddies and our teachers. Thanks for our horses and our daddies' work. Thank you for letting me hit the ball yesterday and letting us win." It was all that anyone could do to not burst out laughing with joy at the simple prayer, but Billy continued, "Thank you, Lord, for your son, Jesus Christ."

The entire church resonated with a strong, "Amen!"

The children then scrambled to their respective lines for Sunday School. Once in line, some children waved to their parents as their teachers led them out into the hall of the new wing of classrooms. Clinton Brown rose from his chair and motioned for the choir to stand. They, along with the congregation, belted out "How Great Thou Art" as the children marched out of the sanctuary into the hall.

"Man, am I glad we don't have to stay in there the whole time. My mom can't sing a lick!" Jessica stated thankfully as she, Danny and Daryl entered the hallway. "You think you got it bad? My dad thinks he's Frankie Valie and tries to sing everything high like mom!" Daryl added. The children peeled off into their classrooms, and for the next hour Danny, Daryl, Jessica, Jimmy, Billy, and Bobby would listen to Pastor Mike Cregan teach them the word of God.

As the children entered their room, Pastor Mike was waiting at the front of the class next to the podium and chalkboard. He wore a plastic helmet with horns sticking out the sides, a breastplate, and was armed with a plastic shield and spear. The children began to jump and scream at the sight of Mike dressed up like a warrior, crowding to touch and investigate his weaponry. He even had a red cape. Danny and Jimmy started to chant, "Evil Knievil! Evil Knievil!" and the lot joined in.

Pastor Brock, who more closely resembled a young, stocky version of Sigmund Freud, once again stood at the podium in the sanctuary. With a quick glance about the room and a strong voice, he stated, "Thank you, Clinton, and thank you, members of the choir, for the uplifting song. And we want to thank you for coming to worship the Lord with us this morning as we near the day of celebration for our town's centennial. We're also giving thanks and praise today to those who serve and sacrifice themselves, their time and their lives, to ensure our community remains a haven where we can openly and earnestly pursue our faith. To express our love for God, free from persecution."

"If you have your Bible with you this morning and would like to read along," Pastor Brock continued, "we will be reading the word of God from the book of Ephesians, chapter six … Ephesians, chapter six … and will begin with verse eleven." The turning pages of the congregation's Bibles broke the stillness in the sanctuary. Casey fumbled through his Bible two times and still couldn't seem find the chapter, even though the pages were clearly tabbed with abbreviations. Terri, frustrated at having to watch and listen to her disoriented husband flip back and forth, grabbed the large Bible and turned almost immediately to the page.

"Men's Bible class!" she mumbled under her breath, smirking, and finished with, "Can't even say Bible!"

Pastor Brock and Pastor Cregan typically planned their Sunday sermons and lessons each week to mirror one another so that parents could discuss with their children what was talked about in their class and follow up with the lesson throughout the next week.

Mike, after convincing the children to sit down, turned to the chalkboard and asked, "How do we know when we're being tempted to do something wrong? Or when our faith is being tested?" All was quiet behind him as he continued writing, "How do we protect ourselves from temptation and be not led away from God and His love?" Mike wrote out the name, "Ephesians." The children looked at him with almost no expression of interest in the lesson, but more in amazement at the costume.

"Because the devil is mean!" said little April Patterson.

"Well, that's the start of it." Mike answered.

Back in the church, Pastor Brock asked, "How do the servants in our community stay spiritually sharp? To not get pulled into depression, drugs and drinking with all that they encounter? How do they hold steadfast in their faith?" He would address one side of the congregation, then the other, constantly moving his eyes from one person to the next, smiling.

"You know, sometimes it's hard to know when we're being tempted." Mike said to the restless pod. "In Ephesians chapter six we're encouraged to 'put on the whole armor of God,'" he then stated, slowly spinning in a circle, showing all of his armor. "The whole armour of God," he repeated. "What does that mean to ya'll? Jessica, does that mean you need to wear a helmet everyday to school?" he asked. The children turned to Jessica and laughed, pointing and holding their hands to their mouths. "Danny?" Mike asked with more volume, "Do you need to carry a shield to baseball practice?" Bobby and Jimmy poked and pinched Danny. "Daryl, when you ride your horse do you carry a spear?" Mike tried to stop smiling as he questioned.

"Yeah!" Billy jokingly blurted out, "Just like an Indian!"

"We are told to 'Put on the whole armour of God,'" Pastor Brock quoted, paused, then continued, "'That ye may be able to stand against the wiles of the devil ... for we wrestle not against flesh and blood, but against principalities ... against powers ... against the rulers of the darkness of this world ... against spiritual wickedness in high places.'" (Eph. 6:11 kjv) He had memorized the verse and paced his words as he slowly walked about the stage, testifying.

"Wherefore take unto you the whole armor of God," Mike read aloud from his Bible. Before class, Mike wrote out the verse on a big, flip-over tablet that he mounted on an easel by the chalkboard. "C'mon, ya'll. Say it with me louder," he urged.

Slowly, with some fumbling, the children began to read aloud, "That ye may be able to withstand in the evil day, and having done all, to stand."

"Stand therefore," the congregation chanted to Pastor Brock, "Having your loins girt about with truth, and having on the breastplate of righteousness; and your feet shod with the preparation of the gospel of peace ... "

Mike stood with a pointer, slowly underlining each word so that no one would get lost as they learned the word of God, "Above all, taking the shield of faith, wherewith ye shall be able to quench all the fiery darts of the wicked ... "

Sarah and Tommy squeezed their intertwined fingers as they read with their friends in the pews, "And take the helmet of salvation, and the sword of the Spirit, which is the word of God." With the verses now over, the church grew silent—waiting. Pastor Brock, with a shine in his eye and love in his heart, returned to the podium.

The shepherd of the church looked to his sheep and repeated, "The whole armor of God, ladies and gentlemen, to protect our hearts, our minds, our spirit and our souls … so as to better serve the Lord."

The services ended promptly at eleven thirty and at eleven thirty-one, the side doors to the new wing were blown off their hinges as the young boys and girls flooded out onto the covered circular driveway, screaming as they rushed to meet their parents or race their way to the new playground. Complete with slides, swings, a jungle gym, rope bridges, and tire ladders, the ability to dilute the restlessness in the children after class was an idea embraced by almost all parishioners. The proud parents of the most recent crop of newborns, however, followed moments later, coming out into the blinding, late morning July sun, only to find themselves immediately consumed by friends and grand parents, desiring nothing else than to hold, kiss, and pat the tiny ones.

While Tommy and Sarah shook hands and mingled with the hoard, some men and women peeled off to either side of the covered porch to smoke. The women stuck close to the courtyard, standing in the shade, fanning themselves with their bulletins, while the men stood out in the sun near the parking blocks, puffing their pipes and cigars, talking about their work week and their crops. The mix of DPS, police, fire, and emergency personnel interspersed within the crowd made the whole event look like some type of political rally or major emergency—minus of course the sirens.

Down near the front slope of the church property, Danny and Jessica approached the pond of rain run-off. The two walked silently for a moment at the edge of the clear water before Danny stopped to pick up a rock and skip it across the pond.

"That was a great hit you made yesterday!" Jessica shyly admitted, trying not to let Danny see her smile.

"Thanks" he said, lowly, "Dad and Granddad been practicing wit' me at night after chores."

"I think you're the best one on your team!" she again complimented. Jessica was wearing her new, white linen, sleeveless summer dress that Mrs. Holder made, complete with a ruffled print of tiny bluebonnets on the shoulder straps, neck, and hemlines. She wore white sandals and had her hair pulled back in a tight ponytail, held in place with ribbons of white and dark blue. Her tan skin and sun bleached hair paired perfectly with her eyes. Danny strut about like Apollo in his pressed Wranglers and yellow button up; his white, wide-brimmed straw hat barely covered his curly, blond hair.

Like Gary Cooper to Grace Kelly, Danny asked, "You goin' to the dance Friday at the VFW?" not at all looking at Jessica as she crouched in the long grass at the edge of the pond.

"Yeah," she answered, her eyes fixed on the reflection of the clouds on the water, "I think my mom and dad wanna go for a while." From the top of the hill Mr. Holder blasted a short, high-pitched whistle. The starry-eyed youngsters stopped and turned to look up the hill at Mr. and Mrs. Holder waving Jessica in. "I guess I gotta go," she mourned, shrugging her shoulders as she kicked at the grass. Danny stood silent for a moment with his hands on his hips before adding, "I think were gonna go to the dance, too!" Jessica lowered her head down to the side and brightly smiled to herself at the idea of Danny being at the dance. The young sprite suddenly turned and darted across the grassy hill. Just like the night before at the baseball game, and many times prior, she paused to look at Danny once more before skipping away on the clouds to her waiting parents.

BBQ and Horseshoes

Tommy, Sarah, and Danny arrived back at home from church around twelve-thirty. Tommy pulled his midnight blue 1978 GMC Jimmy into the gravel driveway of the two-story, white wood panel house built by Sarah's grandparents, Jeffrey and Sally Childress, in 1888. The meticulously-kept house stood as a testament to the love and dedication of not only Tommy and Sarah, but those family members who pioneered this community and region.

The trio entered the spacious home, then proceeded to climb the carpeted stairs to their respective rooms. Danny's room was immediately to the left at the top of the landing with a three-quarter bath next to it. A small guest room, used by Sarah as a workroom, was to the right of the bathroom with she and Tommy's room at the end of the hall. The house was originally built with four small bedrooms upstairs with a larger master bedroom downstairs. But when Danny was born, Tommy and Sarah decided to take down the wall separating the third and fourth bedrooms, built a new bathroom and moved everything upstairs, leaving the old master bedroom to become their new office and study. To get to Tommy and Sarah's room, one had to pass through a hall where there was no more than one square inch of visible drywall space due to Sarah's hanging of the family tree in pictures. They were all there: the moms and dads, grandparents, aunts and uncles, cousins, nieces and nephews. And like the house, the pictures silently bid them goodbye each morning and at night, welcomed them back in constant, quiet love.

Danny entered his room to change clothes from church, which was actually more like throwing his clothes on the floor. Even though only worn for two hours, heconsidered the clothing dirty and tossed them about them about as he stripped.

From down the hall Sarah, called from her closet, "Danny? I want you to hang your pants and shirt! We just had them cleaned and pressed!" He begrudgingly untangled his wadded up Wranglers, folded them over a cardboard hanger, then wedged himself between the bed and wall to find the yellow shirt he threw across the room.

"Dano?" Tommy called out while putting his uniform away. "I want you to get your stall cleaned up 'fore supper!"

"Dad!" Danny lamented, slumping back on the bed in his underwear and socks, rolling his eyes.

"We're having supper 'round four-thirty," Tommy bellowed, then continued "'N your granddaddy will be here 'round four!"

Danny flopped back on his bed, looking up at his ceiling. He had always embraced his family's ties to law enforcement, but last year, after turning nine, his pride in his grandfather and father culminated in an equally strong interest and admiration for Gene Autry and Superman. Like a star in the sky, the law of the west was captured in the persona of Autry. With his white hat and clean, soft mannerism, he reminded Danny of his grandfather. But on the other end of the spectrum was his father and the fantasy of law enforcement, personified by the image of Superman. Like the stripes on his uniform, both Tommy and Superman wore red and blue. They were both very brave, told the truth and always got their man. Danny's room had grown into nothing short of a shrine of posters, banners, comics, pajamas, robes, hats, shirts, and nightlights of his two heroes.

Tommy entered his closet as a barefooted Sarah exited hers, buttoning a light blouse over faded blue jeans with frayed leg bottoms and holes in the knees. Tommy came back out and turned on the record player, spinning an old thirty-three of Frank Sinatra. "Old Blue Eyes" belted out "You Make Me Feel So Young" as Tommy sang along, swinging his hips and snapping his fingers, then glided back into the walk-in closet. Sarah sat on the edge of the bed, putting on her socks and boots as her husband bellowed loudly and out of key.

Danny sprang to life upon hearing the song down the hall and yanked down the pants he just hung moments ago, breaking the cardboard hanger, then pulled down a different, freshly laundered shirt. As he pulled up his pants, one thought ran through his mind: Jessica.

Tommy emerged from his walk-in closet wearing only his hat, holster, boots, and striped boxers. Sarah was taken back at the sight of her husband and laughed out loud as he began to serenade her. After a few moments though, she smiled like a schoolgirl, all a giddy with her first crush as she watched Tommy dance in his underwear. She pranced over to the dresser, took a dried rose from a vase and placed it in her mouth. Sarah began to slowly unbutton her blouse as she rocked her hips and strutted to the beat of the music towards Tommy. He took her by the hand, reeled her in and dipped her.

It was at that moment the two wanna-be teenagers stopped to acknowledge a nine-year-old cowboy standing in the doorway. Tommy raised Sarah to her feet; she quickly took the rose from her mouth and darted toward the bathroom to button her shirt. "You need to knock, young man!" Tommy snorted.

"The door was open!" Danny exclaimed in his own self-defense. "Besides, I'm not the one dancing around in my underwear eating dead roses!"

"What your father is trying to say," Sarah interjected, as she exited from the closet, fully dressed, "is that you need to be more respectful of people's privacy."

"What are ya dressed up for again?" Tommy asked, pulling a t-shirt over his head.

"Well?" Danny began to plea, "I was just thinking … can I go ask Jessica to come over for supper?"

"Now?" Sarah asked. "Why didn't you ask us earlier when we were all at church?"

"I didn't think about it at the time. Please?" Danny begged, butting out his chin.

"Funny how you 'just thought' of this as soon as I asked you to clean your stalls!" Tommy snapped.

Sarah went about and tidied up the room as she explained, "Well, son, it's almost one; by the time you saddle up and ride over there it'll be two, two fifteen. You gotta talk to Mr. Holder, get her saddled and ride back. By that time it'll be four or four-thirty. It'll be time for supper, your granddad will have been here already, and you're stalls won't be cleaned out!" Both parents stood silently for a moment to see Danny's reaction.

"Well, maybe ... " Danny started to respond, but was cut off by Sarah.

"Then it won't be 'til next weekend that you'll have the extra time to ... well, no, never mind that 'cuz you'll be ... " A pillow flew across the room and hit Sarah in the head "Hey!" she snapped.

"What your mother is trying to say, is that you need to think about what you're doin,' get your chores taken care of early in the week, and not wait until the last minute!" Tommy ordered, glaring at Sarah. "You got two hours. Ya hear?! Two hours!" Tommy finally declared. Danny turned and bolted down the hall without saying a word as Tommy hollered, "You talk to her daddy first!"

"I will!" Danny shouted, leaping down multiple stairs at a time.

Tommy and Sarah watched from their bedroom window as the excited boy ran to Tommy's patrol car, opened the passenger door and reached into the glove compartment for his father's bottle of Stetson cologne. "Don't use it all!" Tommy bellowed from the second floor. Danny looked up and smiled, splashed on some cologne, slammed the car door and zipped across the front yard to the stables. "Go get her, Casanova!" Tommy chuckled.

"Are ya just trying to blow his surprise?" Tommy interrogated.

"I'm sorry, I didn't think about it" Sarah meekly answered.

"I don't want him to think anything is going on next weekend and comments like that will only get him goin'!"

"I'm sorry, baby. I just didn't know you were so sly and foxy!" she said, crawling on the bed on her hands and knees.

"You know I'm foxy!" Tommy grinned, "I'm a sly, foxy fox!"

"Oh yeah? Just how foxy are you?" she asked seductively, wrapping her arms around Tommy's waist. Tommy kissed his wife passionately. They broke their kiss and turned in unison as they heard the door to the barn swing open. They then dashed to and leaned out the window and watched the barn door. After a brief moment, the sound of horse hoofs and braying echoed from the stalls. Danny emerged from the barn into the bright sunlight and led the horse to the water trough. He let the horse drink for a couple of seconds, then turned around and began a slow gallop through the young cotton bowls.

Tommy stood Sarah up and whispered in her ear, pulling her backwards towards the bed "How long for him to get there and back?"

"Oh … " Sarah hypothesized as her husband kissed her neck, "maybe two and a half hours."

"And how long 'fore you need to start getting supper ready?" he breathed heavily as he unbuttoned her shirt.

Closing her eyes in sweet anticipation, Sarah softly replied, "Two hours and fifteen minutes." Tommy playfully pushed Sarah onto the bed and slowly climbed up on her.

"Ya think your daddy would mind PB and J's, Pringles, and hot Dr. Peppers?" she joked as Tommy kissed her stomach. "Nah, I think he's probl'y tired of the Sunday feasts." The two rolled on the bed laughing and kissing.

Two hours later, Sarah hurriedly finished setting up the table in the backyard under the shade of the large oak trees. Half an hour earlier, while slipping his pants on, Tommy phoned in an order to The Longhorn Ranch House for some ribs, chopped brisket, honey baked beans with jalapenos, cornbread and potato salad. Sarah rushed outside with a vase of flowers in one hand and place settings in the other. She looked up to see Tommy flying down to the easement road with a billowing cloud of dust is in tow. Not too far behind him were Johnny Lee and Doris, early for lunch. From the right side of the barn, Danny Lee and Jessica came trotting, also early.

Sarah quickly added a full cup of sugar to two gallon jugs of sun tea that sat on the picnic table. After coming to a skidding stop in the gravel driveway, Tommy jumped out with plastic bags, Styrofoam cups, and aluminum pans. The recently physically satisfied couple was now in a panic. They frantically struggled to get lunch set for six as the grandparents and kids arrived prematurely.

No better way to spend a Sunday afternoon then to be under the blue Texas sky, blanketed by the shade of an oak with the slightest breeze whipping through the leaves.

"That's good ribbin.' Good ribbin'!" Johnny Lee complimented.

"Mm, Mm!" Doris hummed with her mouth full.

"I'd take a couple more, if you please?" Johnny requested and began to pass his plate down to Tommy.

"Oh, gee, Daddy," Tommy lamented. "I only cooked enough for today, what with such a busy week comin' up and all."

"We didn't think you'd eat so much." Sarah offered.

"Oh, that's all right." Johnny smiled, taking his plate back. He glanced at the grill with its cover still on, undisturbed. Tommy glanced behind him to see what his father was looking at. Johnny winked at Tommy, who then smiled to himself, knowing that he'd been caught lying.

"So, did ya have to go 'tend the fields'?" Johnny snickered. Both men had a laugh, but were quickly slapped or pinched by their wives.

"Why did your mom and grandma hit Tommy and Johnny?" Jessica whispered to Danny.

"I dunno?" he answered, confused. "Daddy told me we don't have to work the field for two more weeks."

Johnny and Tommy spent the rest of the afternoon with Jessica and Danny, working on cutting and racing their horses in the barrels, while Sarah and Doris passed their time talking over coffee on the patio. In the early evening, just before dusk, Johnny and Jessica challenged Tommy and Danny to a game of horseshoes. Jessica, a mean shoe thrower for her age, quickly landed a ringer and a leaner, bruising Danny's pride.

Tommy, with his trademark Shiner in hand, spoke up after another round of tosses, "Danny, you 'n Jess better get saddled up and git her on home. Coyotes will be out soon."

"I don' care 'bout no coyotes! I ain't scared of nuthin!" Danny puffed. Jessica stopped her throw to hear the conversation.

"Didn't say you were scared, but you got a young lady to take care of tonight and I'm more worried about what her daddy thinks of a $10,000 dollar cuttin' horse walking out in the dark with coyotes runnin' round! C'mon! Saddle up!" Tommy gently ordered before turning with Johnny to head to the porch. Danny and Jessica begrudgingly tossed their shoes into the sand before heading to the stables. The two men came to rest on the porch rail, joining their wives, and gazed out at the large red setting sun.

Danny and Jessica emerged from the barn, leading their mounts, then climbed into their saddles. "G'nite, Mr. and Mrs. Albright. Thanks,

Tommy. Thank you for dinner, Sarah!" Jessica hollered, waving. Danny also waived, moping.

"Dear, sweet, courageous son of mine … fare thee well as you travel the hostile lands on your arduous journey, guiding the fair Jessica along the way," Tommy rattled off. Sarah slapped her sarcastic husband on the shoulder. "What?! He knows I'm kidding." The two couples watched as the young cowboy and his girl trot down the gravel road. "Look kinda familiar?" Tommy asked as he wrapped his arms around Sarah.

"Yup!" Johnny interjected, then kissed Doris on the head.

One hour later, at the Holder home, by the moonlight and one solitary yellow flood lamp, Jessica and Danny slowly walked their horses to the stable. Danny tied his horse to the split rail fence while Jessica walked hers into the stall to take off the saddle. Danny helped to put away the tack and brushed the back of the sweaty mare; Jessica fetched some corn and alfalfa.

The two had just exited the barn when they heard Mr. Holder's distinct whistle. It was time for Jessica to go in. While standing in the shadows, Jessica quietly asked, "So, ya'll going to the fair on Saturday?"

"Yeah," Danny whispered, "and they also wanna go to the dance on Friday."

Jessica paused briefly, then informed her beau, "I think my mom and dad wanna go to the dance, too." Another but longer whistle pierced the still darkness. Jessica peeked around the corner and saw her dad standing on the porch.

"I'll see ya tomorrow." Danny mumbled as he climbed into the saddle. Jessica stood in silence as he trotted by. He stopped and circled back to Jessica and dismounted. "Um," he stammered shyly, "you can be with me at the dance … if you want to." He lunged forward in a swell of confidence and kissed Jessica's cheek. Danny quickly hopped back into the saddle and galloped away under the full moonlight. The young Romeo turned to look once more at his golden girl before breaking into a full run. Jessica held her hand to her cheek, smiled and skipped her way to the house.

While walking his horse into the driveway of his parent's house, Danny heard some coyotes in the cotton fields, just yards away. It was then that he noticed the house and barn, usually lit up at night, were completely dark with the exception of one dim light bulb above the back porch door that flickered off and on. The wind had suddenly picked up and like a wisp of smoke, one long, thin cloud was spreading itself in front of the large, pale yellow moon. The stars shone brightly; Danny heard himself breathing heavily as he stood alone in the dark.

He led his horse to the barn, but was more mindful now to look all around as he crept. Danny tied his horse off to the fence while still in the light of the porch, removed the saddle then slowly swung open the large wooden door. The old, painted hinge creaked to life with the weight of the wood. A large, ominous, black void greeted him as the sounds of something moving around in the straw filled his ears. He lowered the saddle down his left leg to rest on the ground, then rubbed his right hand on the wall to find the light switch and gave it a flick. The damp and musty stable remained dark. Danny poked his head around the door frame and stood on his tip toes. From the other end of the long stable he could see the moon and stars shining through one small window above his father's work bench. He rubbed his eyes to help adjust to the dark and timidly scooted in. When almost to the edge of the bench, he reached out and searched the blackness for the dangling string to turn on the work light.

From the top of the storage lockers came a deep, guttural growl followed by something heavy landing in front of him. Danny turned with a jump to face the beast in the dark while his hands waved aimlessly above him, trying to find the string. Suddenly, a bright light illuminated a distorted face that twisted with a loud, wicked groan like that of a wounded animal. Danny sprinted to the other end of the barn, tripping over his saddle in the process, all the while screaming, "Mom! Dad! Mom! Dad!" Tommy turned off his flashlight and quickly followed Danny, unable to control his laughter.

"Ain't afraid of nuttin,' are ya?!" he called out to his son between laughs.

Tommy and Sarah knelt beside Danny's bed and listened to his short prayer, "And God bless Mom and Dad n' Grandpa and Grandma, and Jessica. In Jesus' name, amen."

"Amen," the couple echoed in closing.

"You are such a good boy!" Sarah stated, kissing her son's head. "How did you get to be so good?" she asked.

"He got it from his daddy!" Tommy answered.

"I said 'good' not 'goofy,'" Sarah quipped.

"Oh, so you think it's funny to insult the old man?" he grinned.

Sarah and Danny curled up in the sheets as Tommy slowly crouched down and held his hands in the air. "Well, maybe it's time you both had a visit from Tommy Claws!" he exclaimed, then jumped on the bed, pinching their knees between his thumb and middle finger. The two screamed simultaneously with laughter and pain.

Sarah broke free and ran down the hall but not before shrieking "Goodnight, Danny, I love you!"

Tommy, in his best Hitler style voice, pointed sharply and blared out, "All rrrright now! Evyvone vill listen to mi." Danny tucked his head under his sheets with the exception of his eyes. Even though his mouth was hidden by the sheet, Danny's eyes gave it away that he was happy and smiling. "No playink!" Adolph resumed. "No laffink! Unt you! You fill slip heah! Unt … not mek a pip!" The perfect boy lowered the sheet from his face. Tommy sat on the edge of the bed for a moment and stroked his son's hair, rubbing his forehead with his large hand. "D'jyu know I'm proud of you?" he asked, leaning on his elbow across Danny's stomach. "My boy! The big man! Hittin' home runs for all the girls to see!"

Danny sat up and gave five to Tommy, then proudly exclaimed, "Maaaan, am I good!"

"Listen," Tommy softly instructed. "I want for you and me to spend a little more time together. Some things I wanna talk to you about."

"Dad, I know about that kinda stuff!" Danny said, embarrassed, but smiling.

"Well, I know you seen a lot of things," Tommy admitted, "and maybe you know more than I think you do. Maybe I need some advice from you? Hmm?" he suggested. "I just wanna talk to you about the man you're becoming and the man you're gonna wanna be someday. Like your granddad. Okay?" Danny nodded in agreement. "Now get to sleep, we all got a busy week," Tommy instructed before leaving the room. Danny looked to the doorway as the light was turned off and heard his father say, just like he did every night, "I love you." Danny curled up on his side for a moment then rolled onto his back. Minutes later, Danny was quiet and motionless, flying with Superman and riding his horse with Gene.

Monday Morning

Monday morning, 5 a.m. The water pipes that ran through the old thin walls separating the bathroom from Danny's room, gurgled to life. Danny was once again roused from a deep sleep upon hearing the vibrating pipes as the water made its way up from the basement and passed through the shower and sinker valves in his mother and father's bathroom.

He laid motionless and tried to go back to sleep, but to no avail. Once a month, all DPS troopers gathered at their district headquarters for a mandatory meeting. The meetings started at seven a.m. and it was at the very least a forty minute drive to the city. So, every four weeks, Danny couldn't help but wake up early with Tommy and Sarah.

After a few minutes, the pipes stopped their rattling and Danny's room slowly began to fill with the dim purple light from the oncoming sunrise. Something caught Danny's attention. He realized that the sound of vibrating pipes had been replaced with that of soft voices, speaking simultaneously.

Danny crawled out of bed onto his hands and knees and slowly inched his way across the creaky wooden floor. He placed his ear against the metal grate of the heater vent. The voices were coming from his parent's room.

He gently turned the bronze handle and gingerly opened his door. The glow of his parent's bedroom light could be seen underneath their door. He quickly tiptoed down the hall and put his head to the floor to see if there was any movement inside. He tenderly nudged their door with a muffled groan of the hinge. The night stand lights were on and both closet doors pulled almost completely to with Tommy and Sarah inside each. Danny approached his father's door; he curiously watched Tommy in the morning ritual of polishing his belt and holster. As he polished the leather to a fine luster he recited, "The Lord is my shepherd; I shall not want, He maketh me to lie down in green pastures: he leadeth me beside the still waters … "

As Danny listened, another voice could be heard chanting from inside his mother's closet. Walking a few feet to Sarah's door, he pressed his ear to the frame, struggling to hear what she was saying. Sarah, too, was reciting, "Our father, who art in heaven, Hallowed be Thy Name. Thy kingdom come, Thy will be done, on Earth as it is in Heaven."

Danny stood between the closet doorways, listening to the two prayers of his parents. In unison they proclaimed their faith and requested strength along with guidance and wisdom. Like a tennis match, both Tommy and Sarah, unknowingly returned each other's volleys of prayer:

"He restoreth my soul: He leadeth me in the paths of righteousness for His name's sake."

"Give us this day our daily bread. Forgive us our trespasses, as we forgive those who trespass against us. And lead us not into temptation."

"Though I walk through the valley of the shadow of death, I will fear no evil: for Thou art with me; Thy rod and Thy staff they comfort me."

"But deliver us from evil. For Thine is the kingdom, and the power … "

"Thou preparest a table for me in the presence of mine enemies: Thou annointest my head with oil … "

" … and the glory."

"My cup runneth over."

"For ever and ever."

"Surely goodness and mercy shall follow me all the days of my life: and I will dwell in the house of the Lord … "

"Amen."

" … forever." Tommy inserted the last of the six bullets in his revolver and commented, "The whole armor of God."

A few minutes later, Tommy and Sarah offered their morning goodbyes and kisses to Danny, who, by that time, had quickly made his way back to bed, faking his sleep. Tommy started down the stairs as Sarah backed out of the room. Danny rolled over and whispered "I love you, Momma."

"I love you too," Sarah whispered, "Make sure you get yourself up to the bus on time for day care at the church. Your daddy and I won't be here to take ya. Okay?"

"Okay," Danny answered groggily. Sarah headed downstairs and out the door. Danny sat up in his bed, leaned over to his window and pulled back the blind to watch his mom and dad pull out of the driveway into the early morning sunrise.

Sergeant Scott Huddleston was the epitome of a Texas law enforcement officer. Standing six-foot-three and weighing two-hundred-forty pounds, he was a man's man: an excellent marksman with a revolver, even more deadly with a rifle and scope, a rancher, a former boxer, and football player. Scott was seventeen when he first parachuted into Germany during World War II and by eighteen had seen more than his fair share of the darker side of life. He commanded respect when he spoke. His word was always the last word, his word was the law and he knew the law backwards and forwards. Scott finished his officers training in Austin an astounding five weeks prior to the rest of his class. He now served as a district sergeant for the Texas Department of Public Safety and oversaw the commanding lieutenants for each of the county precincts in his district. So, once a month he scheduled a "meeting of the minds" to discuss news in the Texas DPS, Texas law and the like.

The meeting room seated around a hundred. Traditionally, Tommy, Jason, Ron, John, Casey and other officers from their county would all sit together. Officers from other counties did the same. The meeting was nearing its end and from the podium in the front of the room, Sergeant Huddleston blasted, "All right, you brainless imps, last thing. Listen up. I want you to meet your new on staff investigator, Cleo Farley. He'll be working with the DPS through the apprenticeship services of the Texas Rangers." Tommy and the boys sat up straight to see to whom he was referring. "Specifically," Sgt. Huddleston continued, "Mr. Farley will be working in conjunction with local and county law enforcement agencies representing the counties of Van Zandt, Henderson, Anderson, Navarro,

Kaufman, and Dallas. Cleo finished his fast track for training in Austin recently. He's a native Texan, graduated in December with honors, receiving master's degrees from UT in both criminal science and behavioral neuroscience. Behavioral Neuroscience? What the blazes is that?"

The room grew deathly silent as Sgt. Huddleston glanced up over his glasses to the front desk, waiting for a response. Tommy and the boys watched Cleo Farley nervously rise from his seat and turn to the crowd of stern faced strangers. Cleo stood silently for a moment, the focal point of a predominantly white group, minus Ron, before turning back to Sgt. Huddleston. "It's the study of how and why the brain likes what it does and how and why it helps in determining what we do and don't do." Cleo timidly responded, "Why someone will like candy, some like the color yellow or a particular singer, a place. How a time of year or season relates to someone's intellectual creativity and activity or their psychological dormancy. It's a new thought process on the ideas of thought … and I think it has a promising application to the intervention of and reduction of crime." The silence was maddening.

Sgt. Huddleston, Tommy, Ron, and the other DPS officers sat with blank expressions on their faces, as if waiting for some type of real, human explanation of what was just said. Embarrassed, Cleo slowly took his seat and exhaled a deep breathe of regret.

"So, Mister Farley … " Sgt. Huddleston queried, "How do you like to be addressed ? Farley? Cleo? Mr. Farley?"

"Butch … It's Butch, sir." he replied flatly.

"Butch, huh? That's quite a departure from the actual, isn't it?" Sgt. Huddleston retorted.

"Yes, sir." Butch agreed, "But I feel comfortable wearin' it just the same."

"Well, you ladies make yourself presentable and welcome the detective. Show him how we do things downtown. Dismissed!" the sergeant bellowed. The room was suddenly a burst with the sounds of scooting desks and chairs while bodies hurried to leave. Butch remained seated, smiling to himself in silent anticipation while placing the last of his paperwork in his satchel. When he finally stood to turn and greet the members of his new family, he became disheartened as the last few officers shuffled out the door. Butch stood alone.

Butch left the meeting room to enter the main hallway of the local

HQ. When he approached a group of troopers gathered at the vending machines, Butch smiled, straightened himself and prepared to speak. The confidence on his face once again faded as the officers looked him up and down, then turned away in quiet disapproval.

A boisterous "Tommy Lee Albright!" and a slap on the shoulder brought Butch back to life as Tommy entered the hallway from the men's restroom. Butch, startled and taken aback, extended his hand to the tall, blond, brazen Tommy, "Farley. Cleo Farley."

"Butch though, right?" Tommy confirmed.

"Butch. Yes … yes … 'Scuse me. Right." he replied, lost for a moment

"Cleo? Where'd that come from?" Tommy asked as the two strut down the hall. A warm smile finally graced Butch's face as the anvil was ever so slightly lifted off his shoulders.

"Aw," Butch reluctantly explained, "Mom and Dad thought it'd be nice to name me after my great granddad. Didn't go over so well in junior high … not the most masculine of names, you know. It's like being named Percival or Felix." Butch laughed out loud at the mere pronouncing of the names.

Tommy stopped in mid stride, turned to Butch and declared, "My great uncle's name was Percival, God rest his soul!"

"I … I'm sorry … I didn't mean to … " Butch stumbled on his words as Tommy leaned over and began to laugh, pushing his hand against Butch's side for support. "I … I … I'm," Tommy imitated, perpetuating his own laughter. Butch was only ever so slightly amused. The two continued walking.

"Well, puke, how'd ya like Austin?" Tommy asked.

"Puke?" Butch replied.

"Yeah, Puke. The new guy; freshman; green guy; rookie; bottom man on the totem pole."

"Um, training was good. It was pretty intense though, trying to think about how to apply all that I just got through learning in school. Like this one time … "

"Yeah, basic was tough, for a while." Tommy interrupted. "But, you get used to the format in a couple o' weeks then it lightens up some." The two men stopped at the end of the hall near the men's and women's locker rooms. "You been assigned to a district supervisor yet?" Tommy inquired.

"Uh, I, uh, I'm supposed to meet with Huddleston later today to find out." Butch answered.

"Well, if you need anything or have any questions, give me a holler. All right?" Tommy extend his hand and firmly shook Butch's.

"Yeah … sure. I'll give you a shout. Thanks." Tommy turned to enter the men's locker room. Butch again stood alone in the empty hall.

"Oh, hey!" Tommy called, lunging out from the locker room door and slapping Butch on the shoulder again, "You gonna do fine. Nice to meet ya!"

Before he even reached his friends in the back of the locker room, Tommy loudly alerted all of his coming, "All right, boys, feast your eyes on this." As he entered the row of benches and lockers, he opened a legal manila envelope, turned it upside down and started shaking out its contents. John, Ron, Jason, and Casey all gathered in close to see what the hubbub was about. A plastic bag slowly emerged from the paper envelope containing a rare Superman comic. A number three issue to be exact. Like Jason holding his prized golden fleece, Tommy held up the red and blue super hero in his original plastic sheath.

"Whoo! Oh, yeah! Whoa! Slick stuff, chief!" and "Where'd ya get that?" emanated from the curious quartet.

"Big D a couple of months ago," Tommy answered with wild-eyed pride as he displayed the invaluable digest. Like a group of little boys, all the grown men clambered to see the cover. "They been holdin' it for me." Tommy continued, "Sarah and I been saving for a few months to get it. Cost an arm and a leg, but it'll be worth more in the future."

"When ya gonna give it to him?" John asked.

"Oh, prob'ly Saturday 'for we head to Texoma," he answered. After contemplating his words, Tommy continued, "And I was thinkin' … why don't we have the boys come with us?"

"Awwww! Tommy! What?" The foursome groaned in disbelief.

"You know this is the only time for all us to be together!?" Casey blasted.

"Casey … " Tommy lamented while shaking his head. "You sound just like Sarah! 'You know this is our only time to be alone'!"

"You know what I mean!" Casey exclaimed. "C'mon! This is prob'ly gonna be the last fishing trip of the year for all of us!"

"That's why it's all the more special," Tommy interjected. "It'll be all the boys' first time with us and be on Danny's birthday. How old were we when we on our first trips? Ten? Eleven? Well, they're about that age now 'n they're want'n to go fishing. And all the boys can go with all their daddies at one time." The four grown men began to resemble sulking teenagers not getting their way.

"Ya said anything yet to Sarah or Danny?" Jason grunted, slumping against the locker.

"Not to Danny," Tommy answered. "I wanted to check wit ya'll first, but Sarah knows what I wanna do. Well?"

"Now that means we gotta behave!" John quipped as he stood up. "An' I don' wanna behave. I been planning for months on not behaving.' I really need to not behave!"

"So, are we supposed to just bring 'em with us to your house on Saturday?" Ron chimed in.

Tommy looked at his lifelong friends and with a large white toothed grin answered simply, "Yup!"

The plan was in motion.

100 Years at the VFW

Friday night, July twenty-second. The stars were just beginning to shine in the purple eastern sky as the sun neared the western horizon, hanging low, wide, and dark orange. The smell of smoked brisket and ribs floated above the sounds of hundreds of children playing in the park next to the old, domed corrugated metal VFW hall. Fireflies skimmed the surface of the stock pond while mockingbirds sang from the trees.

Inside the hall, the centennial celebration dance was in full swing. Tommy, Sarah, their friends and almost the entire town populace crammed themselves into the local landmark. The town folk feasted on a spread of red beans and rice, brisket, ribs, potato salad, jalapeno cornbread and homemade tortillas. To drive another nail in the coffin, large hand-sewn dish towels covered up two tables worth of home made apple cobblers, velvet cakes, pecan pies and chilled canisters of ice cream. The masses sipped cold, sweet sun tea and Shiner Bock as they listened to Lynnly Ives and her band.

Tommy was his usual self in a crowd: the center of attention, telling stories, and being the practical joker. Tommy stood as he finished telling the one about pulling over a drunk driver. Demonstrating with his own beer in hand, he reenacted the scene "So he falls out of the driver's door, can't stand, can't focus on where *I'm* standing, can barely say nothing.' He moved to the front then slides down the tire well, looks up at me with this confused look and says, 'You can't site me. This ain't even my car!'" The cluster of ten friends all laughed, taking swigs of their beers.

Just about that time, Lynnly hollered to the crowd, "How ya'll like the Cotton Eyed Joe?" The benches and tables cleared as hundreds of patriotic, well-soused Texans took to the plank wood dance floor. The fiddle player chopped out a continuous choo-choo rhythm, waiting for more to pack the square. Tommy and the boys didn't even put their beers down as they grabbed their wives and bullied themselves through the energetic mass.

The song started out slowly, but quickly picked up speed. The ten friends, along with all in attendance, were happy to be dancing arm and arm, kicking and yelling, sweating and laughing, as they struggled to keep up with one another. The song soon ended, and Lynnly and her band were immediately bombarded by a roaring applause.

"Thanks, ya'll!" She gratefully stated, "We gonna tune up and slow things down a little."

Ron threw Tommy over his shoulder, spinning him around while Tommy, continued to sing "What you say? One more time!"

The two buddies laughed and spilled their beers as Sarah called out over the noise, "Tommy? Tommy Lee!"

"Yeah, baby?" Tommy answered, dismounting Ron's shoulder.

"Now what you say, baby? One more time!" Tommy sang with a seductive smile, shaking his hips and placing his roaming hands on Sarah's waist.

"Hon!" she firmly stated, brushing his hands off her hips. "The waltz is about to start, can 'ya dance with Grandma?"

"Sarah!" Tommy shriveled with a moan.

"Please?" she pleaded. "She never gets to dance anymore, and all the men who are her age … well … can't. It would give her such a thrill! This night ain't ever gonna come again for her. Please, baby?"

Tommy looked his wife squarely in the face and made the deal, "One dance!" Sarah clapped to herself, quietly. "One. That's it!' he firmly stated.

"One dance!" Sarah repeated. "One dance and I'll keep one cold for ya," she added.

"She better not try to kiss or pinch me!" Tommy warned with a grin.

"You leave that to me!" she whispered seductively in his ear. Sarah kissed her husband's neck and tenderly declared "I love you, baby!" before giving him a slap on the rear to send him on his way.

"I love you, baby!" he replied over his shoulder, weaving his way through the partially cleared floor.

Tommy worked his way over to Sarah's great-grandmother, Marguerite. She and her other senior friends sat near the back wall at a large round table, trying to talk over the noise. Tommy strutted to the table, extended his arms and crooned out with a long Texas drawl, "Ladies, ladies, laaaaddies!"

"Woo, woo! Arrest me! I'm guilty! Take me away!" the table of senior's replied. "My, my!" he exclaimed. "So many attractive offers from so many young fillies. How 'bout you, Marguerite?" He sauntered over to Marguerite's side of the table, pleading his case as he approached her, "I know I'm prob'ly just another face in the crowd to you, but it would be a mighty honor if you would dance with me."

"Go on! Go on!" Marguerite's friends encouraged. "How often do you have a chance like this? What're ya waitin' for?"

"Well?" Tommy pushed, holding his hand out.

Marguerite pondered a moment then reluctantly gave in, with a smile, "Okay. Maybe just one."

Tommy helped the great-grandmother of ninety-three years to her feet then escorted her to the dance floor. The guitar and fiddle were just leading into a waltz that was written by Lynnly for her grandmothers. Sarah rushed to the side of the dance floor to watch and stood in amazement of how gracefully her grandmother still moved. After the first verse the other couples took notice and pulled themselves to the side to watch Tommy and Marguerite. Sarah could hardly hold back her tears of joy and love for her husband and grandmother.

Marguerite was all smiles as she floated across the weathered plank wood. She looked at Tommy's face and suddenly all became a blur as visions of she and her husband, Ernest, dancing together flooded her mind. Years ago, because they lived so far out of town, Marguerite and Ernest would go on group dates with their friends. They would all park their vehicles in a circle, turn on their headlights, crank up the radios, and dance together under the wide Texas sky with the stars looking down on them.

The music slowed down a bit, drawing to a close when Tommy lightly leaned Marguerite back for a small dip. Lynnly, the band members, Sarah and the crowd of onlookers applauded generously for the couple as they exited the dance floor.

"Who's up for some fireworks?!" came a voice over the loud speakers as the large, sliding side doors opened to the grassy slope on the west side of the metal building. Sarah and Terri went to help Marguerite to a chair on the covered patio. Tommy and the others wandered out into the early night air as the raspy speakers blared out, "The Eyes of Texas are Upon You." It warmed Marguerite's heart to see all the children running around the edge of the pond, waving their sparklers before the big show started. Holly, Joey and Monica, along with the assistants for the nursing home, escorted the remaining seniors to their chairs under the awning to watch the fireworks.

A loud crack pierced the mild hum of casual conversations as the first of many rose clusters flew into the air, exploding in a sprinkling of blue that turned red, then white. The "Yellow Rose of Texas" began to play over the speakers; cheering, laughter, screaming children and applause could be heard for miles around. A couple of explosions later, Sarah joined Tommy and their friends at the top of the rise and wrapped her arms around his waist. She leaned into his ear and whispered, "I love you. You make me so … " then buried her head into his shoulder, crying with joy. Tommy turned to respond, but instead remained silent and stroked her head as he watched the fire in the sky.

Danny and Jessica were walking in the playground just as the fireworks began. They climbed the ladder into the enclosed landing of the tall rocket slide. Danny then shimmied through the rails and onto the top of the capsule. Like a true gentleman, he extended his hand to help Jessica. The two sat quietly, side by side under the full moon, the stars of Texas and the eyes of God. Danny reached out and placed his hand on Jessica's. Jessica smiled and closed her eyes.

Saturday, Superman, and Fishing

Five a.m., Saturday, July twenty-third, 1978. Just seven hours ago the whole town was whooping it up at the VFW. Now, Tommy, Sarah, their friends and boys were busy loading up for the first all-man, two and a half retreat to Lake Texoma. Since Sarah assisted with the dispatch and scheduling of the officers, it was easy for her to get all the men's territories covered for the long weekend away.

Tommy and Sarah's home more closely resembled a war zone than a house. In the garage and driveway there appeared to be enough trucks, boats, and camping gear to sustain New York during a nuclear holocaust.

Joey stood at the kitchen island and sorted through the seemingly unending supply of grocery bags that Terri and Sarah brought in from the garage. As she threw another empty brown paper bag on the floor, Joey called out, "Sarah? Do you want me to put all the meats into one cooler and dairy in another?" Sarah did not reply. While unpacking one full Piggly Wiggly sack of wieners, Joey asked herself, "How many hotdogs can five men and five boys eat in forty-eight hours?" Sarah peeked her head around the door frame then stealthily tiptoed directly behind

Joey. "*Sarah!*" Joey yelled again "What do you ... " then turned to see Sarah standing directly behind her. "Oooohhh!" Joey screamed and dropped to her knees, covering her eyes.

"Separate!" Sarah playfully answered.

"I can't believe you! *Augh!*" Joey grunted, red and shaking. She proceeded to pick up the packages of wieners as Sarah laughed out loud and bent down to help. "I hate being scared! You've known that for thirty years!" she exclaimed, slamming the wieners into the cooler, "You just ... stand there and scare me! Ugh!"

"I'm so glad some things never change!" Sarah stated evilly. "Otherwise I would never have had so many years of fun at your expense." she admitted, placing a kiss on her friend's cheek.

Joey retorted with her traditional and sarcastic, "Nuh nuh nuh!"

Terri and Casey sat out in the middle of the driveway in folding aluminum chairs. Stacked between them were cases of Shiner Bock, some water, and one case of Dr. Pepper. Terri compared the large stack of beer with that of the short stack of soft drinks and water. As she pulled the plastic rings off the cans she softly suggested, "Case, don't you think you should have gotten more sodas or water?"

"Nah!" Casey refuted, "Sodas and water are for the boys." With a slap to the side of a rather large cooler not yet filled halfway with beer, Casey added "We got our own cooler." He then nonchalantly returned to unpacking more cans.

"You amaze me!" Terri snapped before rising to walk away, throwing her stack of plastic rings at Casey.

"What?" he asked, confused. "They got plenty o' DP!" Terri was already into the garage as he thought out loud to himself and opened a can of warm Shiner, "How much Dr. Pepper can five boys drink in two days?"

Tommy, John, Monica, and Holly were all in the living room. The two men sat in the middle of the floor with their fishing tackle scattered everywhere. Both had been prepping their rods and reels for two hours already as the girls began to pack the necessary toiletries and first aid supplies.

Tommy asked John, "Did you get the licenses?" while reeling in new line on one rods.

Monica handed Holly items to pack and called their name out loud as she marked them off the checklist, "Toilet paper, paper towels, batteries, mosquito repellent, band aids, sunscreen, medical kit, tooth paste … "

"Good God, ya'll!" John exclaimed. "We ain' gonna be out there but all of two and a half days!" John rolled his eyes to Tommy before answering, "Nah. I figured we can stop either in Gordonville or Dennison for the licenses. They're cheaper there."

"What're ya'll thinkin's gonna happen? Tommy asked with a slightly devilish smile. "We gonna be fishin,' sleeping, and eatin'! That's it! Were going to Texoma. Tex-o-mah! It's not like we're gonna be searching for a lost civilization. We do know what we're doing."

Holly, with one hand on her hip, pointed a finger at Tommy and exclaimed, "You never know what's gonna happen! Any one of ya'll can have an accident at any time. You could run up on someone who might be hurt and need your help!"

The two emergency nurses continued their packing when John decided to chime in with his two bits, "When we was kids we didn't have to worry 'bout skin repellent, band aids, 'n sun block. We just got up 'n went. Got hurt? Rub some dirt on it and get on with it!"

"Yeah!" Tommy agreed, with a nod of his head, smiling. "When Daddy was a kid, he'd just get his pole 'n take off with a Sears and Roebuck catalogue and look, we all turned out okay?"

Monica elected to take her turn in the great debate, "Well, that just goes to show how lucky you are you didn't have any accidents out there by yourselves!"

"Accidents!" Tommy scoffed, "Man, I busted so many bones ropin,' playin' football, fishin.' Accidents gon' happen. So just accept it and then keep on fishin'! Helps you enjoy it all the more. It's like a war wound or a trophy!"

"Amen!" John praised.

"You survived it!" Tommy continued. "It's like when a woman gives birth. It hurts, but you keep on pushing and pushing, and you get a baby, so you love your baby, even though it hurt some. We men get hurt just as bad! And just keep on fishin.' Cuz we love our fishin'!" The two men extended their hands and gave each other five, laughing.

"You two are pathetic!" Monica complained, "I can't believe … "

"You can't talk to them." Holly interjected smartly, "They prob'ly don't even recognize us. They have their beer, fishing poles, guns, axes, and fire." The two women then threw a couple of rolls of toilet tissue in defiance at the unruly men as they left the living room.

Before exiting, Monica added an insult, "Bunch of Neanderthal cavemen!" Tommy and John grunted and shook their fishing poles over their heads in playful retaliation.

In the kitchen, Joey, looking confused, peeked into one of the coolers and asked Sarah, "Did we get enough meat? I thought I only saw wieners and steaks!"

Sarah searched through the remaining grocery bags with Joey then stated, "I thought Ron was supposed to get chicken." She took a few steps to the garage door and shouted, "Holly?" "Yeah?" she answered, handing supplies to Jason who was standing in the boat.

"Did Ron get the chicken?" Sarah asked. Ron, who was then leaning over the passenger side back seat of his car, backed up and struggled to lift a large cooler out of the car, leaning back from the weight.

"Oh! I got the chicken!" he proclaimed loudly. It took Ron and Holly both to lift the large cooler of chicken into the boat to Jason. The weight of the cooler, along with the rest of the camping materials, was enough to make the hitch of the boat rise a bit into the air. Jason quickly grabbed the rail to steady himself. Laughingly he asked Ron and Holly, "Think we got enough or do we just need a bigger boat?"

Terri leaned into the living room from the kitchen doorway to John and Tommy and suggested, "Shouldn't one of ya'll be checking the boys' packing?" Both men raised their heads and screeched at Terri. Terri shook her hands in front of her and mumbled to herself in irritation before climbing the stairs to Danny's room. As she approached the top of the landing, she could hear the boys wrestling around. She sneakily peaked her head in and was unable to find the floor from all the sleeping bags, blankets, clothes, hats, shoes, duffle bags, and suitcases.

She marched back down the stairs into the kitchen and with a disgusted look on her face, testified, "I can't believe this morning! I don't know why we married any of them!" Stopping dead in her tracks, she stood in amazement at the sight of the kitchen island covered with bags and coolers and asked, "My gosh! Who are they feeding?"

"It's always like this." Sarah admitted lightly, "You're just never here to see it. Here's how it works," she explained as she stacked the food by the door. "They leave ya'll, come here, then I deal with 'em 'til it's time to go. But you know what?" Sarah questioned softly, leaning in to the other girls with a sly grin, "There will be absolutely no men or boys around for almost three days." The five women glanced at each other, smiling broadly. At that moment, Casey, Ron, and Jason emerged from the garage. As they entered the kitchen, the women suddenly stopped their talking and stood upright. The three men looked at them curiously, silently, as they passed on through to the living room. No sooner were all five men in the living room when they heard the women again whisper something then laugh out loud.

"Oh no!" Casey grumbled, "They're planning something!"

"I don't wanna know what it is," Ron added. "I'm just glad to be leaving."

"You 'n me both," Jason quipped. The five boys finally come down stairs, dragging their luggage and sleeping bags behind them as they filed out. Danny lead the group to the kitchen garage door, put his two bags and pillow on the floor, then made a U-turn to head back to his bedroom. The other impressionable boys followed their leaders example by throwing their belongings in a pile, then attempted to pass their mothers with not so much as a word.

"Whoa, whoa, whoa!" Jason howled to the line of anxious young men, placing his foot on the stairs to block their path. "What do ya think your doin'?" he asked.

"Giving you our stuff to put in the boat!" Daryl answered meekly.

"You're big boys now, you pack your own," Ron commanded, crossing his arms. "Do ya think I pack Tommy's clothes or roll up Doc's sleeping bag?" Casey inquired. The boys looked at their dads with questionable faces and big eyes.

"Get your stuff on up and out to the second boat!" John ordered. The five sloths reluctantly and sluggishly gathered their belongings and headed out to the garage.

"First boat is food and drinks!" Tommy bellowed.

The boys sluggishly to the two tightly-packed vehicles and boats. "Man, I'm telling you." Danny predicted, "They're gonna make us do everything for the whole weekend!"

"The whole weekend?" Billy asked, as he and the boys tossed their luggage into the first boat on top of the food, ignoring what Tommy told them not just two minutes ago.

"Chop the wood! Get me a beer!" Daryl demanded as he flung his bag on top of the chips and bread. "Make the fire! Get us a beer! Clean the fish! Get me a beer! I can just hear it!" he added with an aggravated climax.

Tommy gathered his friends close to him in the living room, and under his breath excitedly declared, "Man, we ain't gonna have t' lift a finger the whole weekend!"

Holly announced with a giggle to all the women, "I'm not cleaning a thing 'til Monday night."

Billy kicked at the gravel in the driveway leading up to the concrete and whined "Well, maybe we can go out exploring on our own and not have to do so much?"

"You dork!" Danny snapped, "You know how big Texoma is?"

Sarah entered the living room and took Tommy to the side. "You wanna do this now, so we can get some stuff organized around here?"

"Yeah, might as well." Tommy agreed, looking out the window, "It's gettin' light outside."

"You think our dads are gonna just let us loose?" Jimmy asked Bobby. "'Sideways, we'll be on the boats most the time. I wanna go fishing too, but, man! I don't wanna be with my dad all weekend! He'll just gimme more chores to do than I already have!"

"Danny?" Sarah shouted from the garage kitchen door. "You and the boys come in here for a sec!" Judging from the tone in Sarah's voice and sensing trouble, the intimidated cluster hesitated to move.

"C'mon!" she demanded. Danny slowly led the brood of slugs through the kitchen to the living room. His eyes burst open wide with surprise as he was greeted by all the parents standing behind Tommy and Sarah in the middle of the room. Sarah held a birthday cake, all decked out with lit candles and plastic cowboys on horses stuck into the icing. The adults started singing "Happy Birthday" to Danny as he approached the cake.

The song ended and amidst the clapping and whistles, shouts of "The Big Man! Ten years old! Whooo!" and "Girls beware!" rang out. Danny leaned over the cake, took a deep breath and with one burst, easily snuffed out all ten candles.

"My little boy … getting to be a big man!" Tommy proclaimed as he swept Danny up tightly in his arms. Just as Tommy set him down, Danny received a barrage of pats on the back from his friends, kisses and hugs from the mothers while the men take took turns spanking, nuggying and giving tiny Indian rope burns to the proud boy.

Tommy led Danny to his arm chair, sat him down and enthusiastically began his presentation, "All right now! Ya ready?" he asked, clasping his hands together then sliding them back and forth to raise the level of excitement. "You gotta close your eyes on this one!" Tommy demanded as he crept to the hall closet. Danny closed his eyes slightly and Ron quickly barked, "Ah! Shut those eyes!" All of the boys placed their hands on Danny's face to keep him from peeking. Tommy gently walked over to Danny and the boys, paused, then softly said "Okay." Danny's friends removed their hands from his face, allowing him to open his eyes. Tommy stood in front of Danny with an envelope in one hand and a gun in the other. "All right now!" he stated, "This is the first gun your granddad ever had. He gave it to me when I was your age. Now he and I want you to have it. He couldn't be here this morning, but he wanted me to give it to you." Danny's eyes popped open as Tommy placed the shiny, well-oiled and kept .22 rifle in his hands. "We'll all go out shootin' sometime and I'll teach ya how to use it safely and to take care of it."

A barely audible "Wow!" was the only word to escape Danny's mouth.

"One more!" Tommy stated. Casey leaned in and took the gun away while Joey held the cleaning case that went with it. "Your mom and I wanted to get you something … that'll last a long time; something that will truly make you happy." He softly placed the large envelope in Danny's hands.

Sarah came to Tommy's side and added, "We think that maybe one day this'll be one of your dearest possessions. So, we hope you like it!" She then leaned over and kissed her son's head. "Happy Birthday."

Danny gazed about the room as his friends scooted in closer to see, "Go on! What ya waitin' for?" Jason urged. Danny untied the string then turned the envelope upside down, giving it a little jiggle. The men looked at Tommy who, by this point, could barely contain his excitement. Another shake of the envelope and out slid the Superman comic book. Danny held it upright and stared for a moment with a blank expression on his face.

"It's very rare and worth some money now," Tommy informed. "But who knows what it'll be worth twenty in years? The store clerk said maybe one to three thousand dollars." Danny jumped up past his friends and into his daddy's arms, wrapping himself around his waist and neck.

"I love you!' he mumbled into his father's shoulder.

"Oh! I love you too! You're *my* superman!"

"We both love you!" Sarah confirmed as she rubbed her son's back.

"And boys, I'm sorry to say but I've got some bad news," Tommy announced, lowering Danny. "We're not going to Texoma this morning!" The boys, mothers, and fathers were immediately transformed into statuesque figures complete with dropped jaws, bulging eyes and panic stricken faces. "Because," he further explained, looking at his watch "in a little over two hours, at nine o'clock ... Superman's gonna be at the Radio Active comic store in the city ... and you're all gonna go meet him!"

Sarah and the other parents exhaled a deep, genuine sigh of relief and held their ears as the five Clark Kent wannabe's jumped up and down, squealing with girlish excitement.

Meanwhile ...

Wishes

One hour away in the city, in a dingy, gray, broken down house on the south side of town, Brooke and Dale lay on a sheetless, cigarette and beer stained mattress and box spring, listening to Led Zeppelin. Dale, twenty-one, with slicked back hair and ratty clothes, was smoking a joint while his eight-month-pregnant girlfriend, Brooke, thumbed through the latest issue of Better Homes and Gardens. The tiny, two-room shack, with its ripped window screens and peeling, splintering front door, was not only typical of the area they lived in, but also very revealing as to the character traits and qualities of those who dwelled inside.

Dale's car sat in the driveway, leaning to the side with its hood up. The engine had problems, the rear tires were flat and was in desperate need of new brakes. Brooke, then only seventeen, didn't graduate from high school, nor did she work. She spent half of her time living at home with her mother when their relationship was on good terms. Whenever the rapport with her mother would sour, she would then move back in with Dale. Brooke's forgiving heart and love for Dale constantly overrode all logic and her ability to make the right decisions for their unborn baby.

While looking over her magazine, Brooke lightly scratched at Dale's arm and asked, "Hon, don't you gotta work today?"

Dale tried to talk while holding back a deep hit from his joint, but spurted out a weak "Nah!" as he choked. "Don't need me today, it's Saturday. Nobody takes in a car on a Saturday to be worked on." Dale exhaled completely and finished with a belittling, "What are ya? Stupid?"

"Wow, look at this, baby!" Brooke exclaimed, with a slap of the magazine on Dale's stomach. "That's where I'm gonna live one day! California or L.A." She bobbed up and down on her knees excitedly while pointing to a white, two-story house overlooking the Pacific Ocean.

"California?" Dale asked dully to the starry-eyed dreamer.

"Why not?" Brooke defended. "Prettier then flat, crap grass Texas!"

Brooke stood up on the mattresses and peered out the window at Dale's backyard. The enthusiastic optimism on her face was suddenly wiped away as she gazed upon the reality of brown, faded wood fences, and dried, yellow grass. "There's no mountains! No ocean!" She complained.

"Corpus, Galveston, Houston … " Dale listed out loud, counting on his fingers sarcastically. "Well, there ain't no Hi-Way Number One overlooking the ocean with big trees 'n cliffs." Brooke whined. She stepped down off the bed and stomped to the musty, dark bathroom in a huff. "I want our baby to live in a nice house!" she implored while going to the restroom. She closed the fantasy on a high pitched "With a white fence an' a swing!" The commode flushed and Brooke emerged, still pleading her case "I just wanna get away!"

Dale hesitated then offered an insincere quick fix, "We can go on a vacation!?" to which Brooke replied with a frog punch to his shoulder.

"Ow!" he complained.

The phone rang, startling Dale who leapt off the bed to answer it. "Hurry! Turn down the music!" he snapped.

"Why do I … ?" she started to ask.

"Shut up and just do it!" he shouted. "Sshhh! Ssshhh!" Dale patted his hand down as he picked up the receiver. "Hello?" he grunted, struggling to make himself talk with a moan. "Yeah, it's me. Nah … I'm not doing so good. I dunno just sore throat and feel pretty hot. Yeah, I was gonna call but, I jus' been so sick." Brooke marched directly beside Dale and put her hands on her hips, glaring and breathing heavily. "Late yesterday afternoon, I think. No, I don't think I can." Dale winked with a smile and tried to take Brooke's hand. "I don't got enough money for a doctor. But I'll be there Monday. I know I'll be fine by then!" Brooke pulled back and turned away in disgust at Dale's lying; he walked into the hall away from Brooke's judgmental eyes. "I'm what? You're kidding?!" Dale yelled, his voice getting clearer as he spoke. "For a couple of hours on a Saturday? Man! I do everything you ask me to! I'm sick for once and you … Hello? Hello!? Screw you then!" he roared, then threw the phone into the drywall, adding to his ongoing collection of large holes.

"You were supposed to work today, weren't you?!" Brooke scolded sternly from the bedroom.

"It was an option," Dale whimpered back, reluctant to enter the room. "He asked if I wanted some overtime, so I said maybe." He sheepishly presented himself and leaned against the door frame.

"Maybe?" Brooke questioned angrily, lying on the bed, looking at the ceiling. She lay still for a moment then continued her persecution and blasted Dale, "You can get time and a half on a Saturday and you say 'maybe'?" Brooke's rage surfaced quickly, "We need the money!" she shouted while exhibiting her full belly. "This baby is coming in four weeks and we don't even have a bed yet! Your car is falling apart, and you tell him maybe? Then you lie to him?" Dale's lack of rebuttal and eye contact were not very reassuring. "Did you get fired?" she asked, yet Dale said nothing. "Did … you … get … fired?!"

"It was a dead end job anyhow!" Dale asserted. "We don't need him!"

"What am I supposed to do?" Brooke asked anxiously, changing her emotions from anger and irritation to worry and panic. "I can't work! I'm scared! I don't want my baby to grow up the way I did!" The young couple stared at each other from across the room. "Don't you want this baby?" she asked.

"Sure I do, sure I do!" Dale softly stated with a light, reassuring chuckle. He employed the use of his typical hypnotic mind tricks and hissed a lifeless "I love you so much! Just be patient with me … we'll be okay … you'll see!"

"How can you say that? You lay here getting stoned, then get fired and tell me to be patient? Patient for what?"

Dale changed his approach, "Do you wanna get outta here? Get away from your mom?"

"Well, yeah, but … " Brooke answered, confused.

"No! No buts!" he interjected, "Do you wanna leave with me?

Now? Leave this stupid town and go down to Mexico or up to Canada? California? Maybe live in the mountains?" The genuine smile in Dales face was quickly replaced with a sick, distorted face the likes of which Brooke had never seen before.

Brooke's heart and mind began to fill with doubt, confusion and nervousness. Unsteadily she asked, "What are you talking 'bout?"

"Do you love me ... and want what's best for our kid?" Dale asked, low, slow and evilly as he painfully squeezed her shoulders.

Tommy slowly backed the restored 1941 Series Sixty-One Cadillac out of the small work barn. The engine hummed with a soft, smooth, low rumble as the dark green body and tan roof reflected the early morning, summer sun. Tommy and Johnny Lee spent over two years of weekends, long nights and summer and winter vacations overhauling the engine, re-fabricating the interior and patching the dented and rusted body.

"All right, ya'll! C'mon, git in!" Tommy hollered out the window to the young pack. The back doors opened and, with the exception of Danny Lee, all the boys packed into the backseat. Danny jumped into the front seat next to Tommy. Sarah sauntered over to the driver's side window and knelt down to eye level with Tommy as he started calculating. "We'll be there in about forty-five minutes ... probably have to wait in line a good hour ... then hop on back here. It's almost seven now, so that'll be ... "

"Eleven-thirty or twelve," she quickly answered.

"Man, you're good!" Tommy grinned. "Give me some sugar!" With that, he pulled on Sarah's neck and kisses her. The boys groaned and made puking and retching noises at the mere sight of adults kissing.

"C'mon, Dad!" Danny nagged with a tug at Tommy's shoulder. "Let's go! He's gonna be gone by the time we get there!" With a deep breath Tommy pulled away from Sarah and rolled his eyes.

The young lads rolled down their windows and chanted, "Superman! Superman! Superman!" as they bounced on the back bench seat.

"Augh! All right! We're going!" Tommy howled in frustration. "The comic store's not goin' anywhere!" With tiny hands waving out of every window, the large green Cadillac pulled out of the gravel driveway onto the local farm road.

Instinctively, John and Jason both reached into one of the ice chests in the boat and pulled out a cold Shiner as the car full of children sped away. "What?" John asked, realizing that both he and Jason were on the receiving end of evil eyes from Joey and Monica.

"Are you kidding?" Brooke exclaimed, flustered. "You know how much trouble we can get into?"

"That's only if we get caught!" Dale reassured her. "We'll be out of town before they even know who to look for! I run in, get the money, we get out of town and they waste their time lookin' here. It's perfect!" he explained, almost professionally and nonchalantly while slithering his arms around the mother-to-be's waist. Brooke contemplated the risks involved as Dale continued his artificial testimonial, "I love you so much and want everything to be perfect. I don't want to be without you."

"I'm just so scared … " she confessed timidly.

After a brief moment of silence Dale coldly lied, "Me too!"

The full pink and orange sun was beginning to peak through the tops of the trees as Tommy and the boys journeyed to the city to start off the fun filled weekend. Danny sat in front on his knees with his back turned to the dashboard. The five musketeers' boisterous conversation was interrupted by Tommy's confirmation, "Yep! We'll meet Superman then head out for the best fishin' in Texas!" The back seat quartet pulled themselves up to the front seat to hear Tommy, "Ya'lls daddies and I been goin' to Texoma since we was ya'lls' age."

"Who's the best fisherman?" Bobby asked. "Dad says he was always better 'n you!"

"Doc is … " Tommy began to testify and hesitated for effect, "Doc has … and always will be … the best fisher of all us."

"See?" Bobby touted. "I told you my daddy was best!" and pointed to his chest.

"What about my dad?" Daryl asked anxiously. "Is he good?"

"Daryl?" Tommy said apologetically. "Your daddy couldn't catch a fish if it walked on two legs and laid itself down in the pan." The youngsters laughed and pointed their fingers at Daryl.

"Shut up!" Daryl demanded as he punched Jimmy in the arm.

"But I'll give him this," Tommy interrupted, looking at Daryl in the rear view mirror, "He's a mean cook!" A broad smile washed over Daryl's face as Tommy expressed his admiration, "We'd catch and clean all day and your daddy would batter 'em up with a little cornmeal 'n lemon ... fry 'em up just right! Do up a little tater and okra and ... man ... alive!" Tommy winked, "Your dad is an excellent outdoorsman!"

"What about my dad, Tommy?" little Billy Williams squeaked, standing on the hump in the floorboard.

"I hate to disappoint you, but, your dad is just so goofy lookin' I think he scares all the fish away." Tommy joked. Billy slumped back in the seat with a frown. His little chin quivered while his friends laughed at him.

"Hey?" Tommy warmly called, finding the boy in the rearview mirror, "Your daddy taught me everything I know and then some." he confided, reaching his hand back to shake Billy's. "Your daddy's a great fisher!" Billy smiled broadly to his friends and resumed his place on the hump.

While changing into a different shirt, Dale instructed Brooke on what to do as he led her though the unkempt and disorganized house, "Go on and get what you wan' take wit' ya, 'cuz we ain't comin' back!" Brooke stopped in the living room and gazed all about. Dale went into the kitchen in search of a bottle of Dr. Pepper. "We're startin' over!" he yelled, crouched down in front of the refrigerator door. "A whole new life!" Dale sauntered back to the living room and impatiently ordered Brooke, "Gimme your keys 'n I'll go fill the car up." She looked up at him, confused, "I'll be right back, okay? C'mon. Gimme ten minutes." He kissed her forehead and quickly walked to the door.

"I love ... " she tried to say as the door slammed shut on her words.

"So, who else do you boys like besides Superman?" Tommy asked.

His ears resonated with torrential screams of, "Green Lantern! Batman! Spiderman!" The quintet then started shouting over each other to see who was the quickest at calling off the coolest of heroes, "The Hulk! Captain America! Iron Man! Fantastic Four! Thor!"

"What about villains? Who do ya'll like?" he regrettably inquired.

Again the shouting and screaming ensued, "Juggernaut! Magneto! The Joker! The Riddler! The Penguin! Lex Luthor! Dr. Octopus! The Green Goblin!"

"You know being a trooper is almost like being a superhero?" Tommy stated factually. The boys laughed and ridiculed Tommy. "No, no, no! Think about it!" he challenged, "We chase the bad guys, we got fast cars, got almost any kind a gun you could want like on 'S.W.A.T. ... '"

Now he really had their attention and was immediately rewarded with, "Really? No way! Cool! Ever shoot one?"

Dale sat parked by the curb in Brooke's car, impatiently honking the horn as she struggled to close and lock the splintering front door. The frustrated pregnant girl turned with a shrug to Dale, "Leave it! We ain't comin back!" he yelled from the car. Brooke looked around to see if anyone was watching, and picked up the garbage sack containing her only worldly possessions. She then slowly and awkwardly waddled to the car. She flung the large bag over the seat and gracelessly squatted backwards into the clunker. The young couple searched each other's eyes in silent doubt, then turned for one final glimpse of their house before Dale pulled away.

A few minutes later, Dale was reviewing his plans with Brooke in front of a local ma and paw grocerette. "Okay now!" he plainly explained, "I'm gonna go in 'n act like I'm shopping, go up to the counter and ask for the money."

Brooke immediately began her unconstructive criticism of the plan, "Ask for it?! You're jus' gon' walk right up and ask for his money!" The two stared at each other briefly before she pleaded with Dale, "Baby, don't do this! Let's figure out ... "

"I also got this for a little motivation!" he interjected and lifted his shirt to pull out a .38 revolver.

"Are you crazy? Where'd you get that?" she exclaimed loudly, "Why do you need a gun?! Don't you think ... "

Dale raised his index finger and placed it over Brooke's lips. Once her raving was silenced, he articulated simply, "I'll ask for the money and flash the gun, that's all! It's just for show. He'll give me the money and we'll be outta here!" He closed the ill-planned plot with an additional lure, "Then we can start our new life!"

"I don't know, baby. I'm scared!" she confessed once again. "What if something happens?"

"Nothing is gonna happen!" Dale contested angrily. "Geez! Will you please just give me a little freakin' credit and have some faith? Huh!?" He abruptly opened the door and climbed out. Before slamming the door, he reached into the back seat, grabbed Brooke's magazine and threw it at her, "Read your book!" He leaned over and glared through the driver's side window before turning to walk away. Brooke didn't smile.

"Okay! Here we go!" Tommy began. The children quickly sat up to take note of Tommy's instructions. "If you had one wish … one wish. … and could be a super hero … what would your special power be?"

Tommy tried to shrug his shoulders high enough to muffle his ears as the spastic boys screamed simultaneously, "Invisible! Strong! Fast! Smell good! Smart! Bullet proof! Be an animal! X-ray vision!"

"Oneatatime!" Tommy barked, "One at a time! One … at … a … time!" "Bobby!" he said with authority, "You're a super hero right now! What can you do?"

"I'd be super strong!" Bobby stated with much vigor.

Tommy pried for more information, "So you could … "

"So I could beat up anybody that did something wrong," he reasoned.

"Ah, I get it! You'd be the guy to put the hurt on 'em, huh?" Tommy helped to confirm Bobby's idea. "The strong, long arm of the law! Jr. G man!"

"Yeah man! Put the hurt on 'em!" Bobby bounced on the seat and gloated with pride at having gone first to make a wish.

"All right, that's good. We gotta have strong heroes like that."

"Daryl!" Tommy beckoned as he searched the rear view mirror, "You're up, son! Super power! What'd you do?"

"I'd be invisible!" Daryl said confidently with an almost evil squint in his eyes, as if he had planned this all along. The four boys sat still and completely mesmerized as Daryl described in great detail exactly how he would use this special power, "Man, no one would see me … and they'd just be talking normal and stuff about robbing a bank … but I'd really be there and listen to everything and tell the police."

Tommy leaned his head to the side and looked at Danny with a face that seemed to say, "Hey! That ain't bad!"

"And the police could arrest 'em," he continued, "and they'd be in jail sayin' 'How'd they know we were gonna do that?'" Daryl paused a moment to let the idea to sink in, then finished strongly with, "Cause I'd of been there and would have known what they all look like, and I could trip 'em or hit 'em wit sump'n'!" Once finished, Daryl smiled broadly, bobbing his head in triumph.

"Invisible, huh? Pretty good." Tommy complimented.

Dale timidly pushed open the glass door to the old neighborhood grocery store and inadvertently struck a bell on a string. As he entered, he spied Larry Pilgrim, the store owner, sitting behind the counter, reading his newspaper. Dale looked down and away while turning down the first of four aisles.

"Good morning!" Larry greeted pleasantly, folding his paper. "Beautiful day, isn't it?" Dale didn't answer as he stalled for time and picked up a loaf of bread and a gallon of milk. "You findin' everything ya need?" Larry volunteered. After not receiving a response from his second question, Larry stood and commented, "Ain' seen you in this neighborhood 'fore? You moving in?" As he approached the checkout stand with his groceries, Dale breathed long and deep a few times to prepare himself. He quietly placed the items on the counter in front of Larry. "All right now." Larry mumbled and turned the groceries toward him. He muttered the prices to himself, punched the buttons on the old manual cash register and, after ringing up the total, told Dale, "That'll be two thirty-eight please." Dale remained transfixed on the gallon of milk. "Son? That'll be two thirty-eight, please." Larry repeated.

"I heard you the first time!" Dale shouted and pulled the gun out of his pants. He shakily pointed the gun directly at Larry's face and nervously demanded, "Put the money on the counter, now!" His voice cracked slightly with the rush of both fear and adrenaline as he ordered, "All of it! C'mon! Move!'

"Billy! You're up! Super powers! Wha'da'ya got?" Tommy's voice rang out. The four others turned to Billy in anticipation at what his secret wish might be. "I'd be able to run fast, be fast and grow really tall," Billy announced.

"What do you mean tall?" Tommy asked, confused.

"Well, when you're tall," he rationalized, "people look at you 'n are afraid of you 'n … cuz they don't get afraid that way of you when you're short." The car remained quiet.

"Okay … " Tommy answered, hesitantly. "I can buy that."

"C'mon! I don't got all day!" Dale yelled impatiently. "Get the money out of the drawer and on the counter!"

"I don't have the money in the drawer," Larry explained, gently lowering his arms. "It's down here … in my cigar box." He pointed to the back side of the counter and slowly squatted down.

"You think I'm stupid?" Dale questioned, waving the pistol "Keep your hands where I can see 'em! And whatever you're thinkin' about doin'? Don't!"

Larry began to panic and tried to explain, "I'm getting you the money, son. Just … take it easy, now. I keep it in a cigar box away from the register." He again started to bend down and lower his left arm towards the backside of the register.

Dale cocked the gun, "I don't wanna shoot ya … so keep your hands up and quit moving!"

"I'm just getting the money! Please! Just … hold on!" Larry pleaded as tears streamed down his cheeks.

"Are ya listening to me? What are ya stupid, you old man?" Dale jabbed the gun in the air and accidentally squeezed off a round, hitting Larry in the chest. At almost point blank range, the .38 caliber bullet violently ripped through his ribcage and lung before exiting through the shoulder blade and finally lodging itself in the wall. Brooke jumped in her seat at the sound of gunfire as Larry fell against the wall then slid down to the concrete floor.

"Jimmy! Your turn!" Tommy cheered. "I'd have all the cool stuff, like Batman!" Jimmy hypothesized, "Poisonous dart guns, radar-controlled boomerangs, cars you can drive from your wrist, walkie-talkies in your wallet. Man, I'd be cool!"

"So, you'd rather be more of an engineer or inventor rather than have special powers?" Tommy asked.

Jimmy, not really thinking about the question replied, "Nah! I just wanna make cool stuff that catches bad people and drive a cool car!"

Larry's wife, Caroline, rushed from the back room upon hearing the shot. Dale stood in shock with his gun still held out in front of him when Caroline rounded the corner of the counter. Brooke turned to look through the rear window from the passenger seat. She drew her knees into the seat and placed her hands on the head rest, resting her lips on her knuckles.

"Augh! No! No!" Caroline screamed at the sight of her husband, lying in an ever-enlarging pool of blood. "Larry? Larry? Augh! No! No!" she wailed uncontrollably as she knelt down to her husband and tried to pull up his torso to embrace him one last time.

"I didn't mean to!" Dale explained. "He was ... reaching for his gun! I just wanted the money. I didn't mean to. It just kinda went off!"

Caroline looked at Dale in questionable amazement, "What gun? We don't have any guns!" she scorned then hid her face in her hands. "You killed him!" she screamed mournfully, "He's dead for money?" She crawled on her hands and knees to the other end of the counter to where Larry stood just moments before, leaving a trail of bloodied hand prints on the floor. Her weeping grew louder and louder until finally she screamed, "There!" and threw a King Edward's cigar box over the counter at Dale. "That's what you wanted, isn't it? There's your money!" Heart stricken, Caroline crawled back to Larry's lifeless body and laid on top of him, embracing him.

Dale gazed upon the rubber band wrapped box lying at his feet, stained with blood. His eyes were then distracted by Caroline rising up off of Larry. Trying to keep her balance, she leaned against the wall for support as she struggled to stand. Sobbing uncontrollably, almost convulsively, she hobbled toward the phone.

"Hey!" Dale quipped, shaking his gun, "What are you doin'?" Caroline reached out to the old wall mounted rotary phone. "Get away from the phone!" he commanded, looking out the glass front door for any customers.

"You killed him!" she screamed as she picked up the receiver, "Augh! You killed my love!"

"Get away from the phone! Now!" Dale warned, "Don't!" The two stared at each other as Crystal Gale's "You've Been Talking in Your Sleep" played on the overhead speakers.

Caroline broke the silent standoff by calmly asking, "Are you gonna shoot a woman?"

"Put ... the phone ... down!" Dale explicitly instructed then shouted, "Look at your husband! You wanna be next? Put the phone down!"

She dared not take her eyes off Dale as she fumbled with the phone. Her fingers found the zero and clumsily dialed the operator. After one ring, Dale heard the line connect. Grief stricken, Caroline could barely speak as she turned away from Dale, "Yes ... I'd like ... I'd like to report ... my husband." Dale fired once more, shooting Caroline in the back. With the phone still in her hand, Caroline fell to the side with a thud, landing a few inches from that of her dead husband. Brooke jumped once more as the sound of gunfire again resonated in her ears. Shaking and near the point of hyperventilation, tears ran down her cheeks. Unable to see inside, Brooke squeaked a long, high-pitched sob like that of a tea kettle slowly reaching its boiling point. Dale stood alone.

"Okay, Danny, you're next," Tommy said, looking over to his son. "Super powers!" The backseat foursome pulled themselves up to the back of the front seat to listen to Danny's wish.

"I'd like to, um, I'd think I'd like to ... " Danny pondered.

"Kiss Jessica Holder!" Daryl hollered.

"Shut up, Daryl!" Danny yelled angrily with a jump and turn onto his knees to face Daryl.

The boys immediately began singing in unison, "Jessica and

Danny … sitting in a tree. … k-i-s-s-i-n-g!" Danny turned back to face the front, embarrassed, folding his arms in front of him.

Tommy stepped in to control the situation with a chuckle, "All right settle down, settle down." He leaned over to Danny and gently inquired, "You don't wanna kiss ol' Jessica Holder, do ya?"

Danny turned away to look out the window, trying in vain to hide his smile from his father. With a sudden surge of confidence, he then whirled around to confront Daryl, "I've already kissed her!"

Tommy and the boys reacted to the prideful boast with a mighty, "Whoa!"

Dale reached down and clumsily picked up the cigar box covered with Larry's blood. He then tucked the gun into his pants and stepped to the glass door. From the doorway, he thought to himself, no one would be able to see the bodies of the couple unless they walked over to edge of the counter and leaned over. Dale took a few cleansings breaths then casually walked out the door with a jingling from the bells.

As he exited, Dale spotted Brooke walking toward the store, crying loudly. "What are ya doing?" he screamed and grabbed Brooke by the arm. He turned her around with a sudden and vicious yank, "Get in the car! C'mon!"

"You never came out!" she explained nervously as Dale forcibly escorted her to the car. "You said you'd be right back! Are ya hurt?" she asked, stopping to examine Dale. "What were you doing in there? What happened? Are you okay, baby?"

"Would you shut up?" Dale complained, slapping her hands down, "I'm out! Look, I'm okay! All right? I'm okay! Let's go!" He gruffly stuffed Brooke into her side of the car and slammed the door in frustration. As he hurriedly walked to his side, Brooke's eyes followed him all the way around the car, watching his every movement like a cat. Dale threw the cigar box in the floor board as he entered the car and placed the gun in the seat next to him.

"What were you doing in there?" Brooke asked as Dale stepped on the gas, squealing the tires.

"Nothing!" he declared. "Here! Open it up!" he instructed and with a toss of the bloody cigar box on her lap. "What'd we get?" Brooke wearily slid the rubber band off the box. Dale accelerated, blindly and carelessly running the stop signs in the local neighborhood.

Brooke counted out loud as she separated the bills "Twenty, forty, forty-five, fifty, fifty-five, sixty … eighty."

"Eighty?" Dale cried with a whip of his head, his eyes filled with pandemonium. "Eighty bucks? Eighty stupid bucks?" he exclaimed, his voice getting louder. He grabbed the cigar box and slammed it repeatedly against the dashboard, "I don't believe this!"

"Baby?" Brooke cooed softly, trying to understand, "What happened in there? I heard gun shots?"

The green Cadillac neared the downtown area as Tommy urged Danny to declare his super powers. Danny, however, was reluctant to speak after receiving the taunting from his friends. "Okay, guys, that's enough." Tommy coaxed the pod of hecklers, "C'mon tiger. What would you do?"

"I'd do something nobody's ever thought of," Danny stated. "Nobody would know me or who my family is. I could blend in and go unnoticed. I'd help people 'fore they got in trouble."

Dale raced recklessly down the tiny residential streets. "Why are you driving so fast?" Brooke asked.

"Would ya shut up and let me think!" Dale bossed. "The quicker we get outta town, the harder it'll be for the police to find us … Anyway, there's nothing we can do for them now!"

"Them?" Brooke asked, open mouthed and wide-eyed, "Who is 'them'? Oh my God! Did you shoot someone? Baby? Did you shoot someone?" Dale's eyes remained focused on the road ahead as Brooke interrogated him, his face transfixed in a scowl. Brooke sat back in shock and disbelief, holding her hand to her mouth. Seconds passed before she passionately rationalized to Dale, "We can't just leave them there! Oh my God, baby, we gotta go back!"

"Go back? Are you outta your freakin' mind?" he badgered. "We go back 'n you know what happens? Huh?" Brooke cowered against the door with a shake of her head, "They get me! They get me, then they get you as an accessory for after the fact and guess what?" Brooke sat motionless, frightened and vulnerable, like a child receiving a harsh scolding from her parents. Dale finished his belligerent onslaught, "If they get you then our baby's gonna be born in jail! Is that what you want? For our kid to be born in a jail? Huh?"

All of a sudden, in a fit of rage, Dale picked up his gun and backhanded Brooke. "I only wanted to be with you!" Brooke explained, sobbing, holding her bleeding left cheek. "I just want my baby to be happy!"

"Shut up!" Dale shouted, hitting her again with the barrel of the gun. "Just shut up! I'm tired of you always telling me what to do! Shut up!" Brooke struggled in vain to block Dale's blows, but he was too strong. Blind with rage, he struck her over and over. The barrel and butt of the gun made repeated contact with her skull, cheek, eyebrow and lips.

"Stop it! No!" Brooke cried out, trying desperately to protect her belly as Dale struck, swerving madly out of control. "Momma!" she wailed. "Let me out! Let me out! Augh! Momma!" With an unexpected burst of courage and energy, Brooke turned the tables and lunged out at Dale, trying to scratch his face. "I hate you! I hate you!" she shrieked.

Tommy cruised slowly through the historic brick buildings of the old downtown area. "What do you mean?" Tommy asked, "How'd you do that? Daryl already said he'd be invisible."

"I know," Danny admitted. "I wouldn't be invisible."

"Well, how'd you do it then?" Tommy again asked.

"Read minds? Telepathy? Tell us!" the boys demanded.

Ron and Casey lounged in the living room while John, Jason and the women parked themselves outside on the wraparound porch, sipping coffee and talking. Ron and Casey took their fair share of turns getting out of the recliners, walking over to the large wood encased Curtis Mathis television and flipping through the television stations. Casey turned to one of the local stations and just so happened to come across anchorman Glen Armstrong, broadcasting from a live remote in the downtown area. "We're live outside the Radio Active Comics store," Glen reported, "Waiting patiently, or should I say impatiently for the arrival of Superman." The camera zoomed across the street to the long lines of high spirited children. "And as you can see, Superman has a lot of fans, waiting to ask some questions and maybe get his autograph or picture. Some are just arriving and some have been here since late last night, like this father and son that drove in late last night, all the way from Grapeland … "

"Hey ya'll!" Ron bellowed to the others on the porch. "Ya'll c'min here! Tommy and the boy's gon' be on TV." The patio tables cleared with a flash as the remaining parents crowded into the living room. They watched intensely as the camera panned from one side of the downtown intersection, down the sidewalk, into the parking lot and back up to the other side of the next building. "I don't think we're gonna make it to Texoma 'til late tonight!" Jason sorrowfully admitted.

Butch had a corner flat on the second floor of a three-story apartment building. From his bedroom windows, if you looked straight down, you could see the entire alley, more over, you could also see the busy intersection of the main drag and a few shops, including the brightly painted windows of the Radio Active comic store. Butch's apartment building bumped right up against the Greyhound bus terminal. It was noisy at times, even more so it seemed during the summer months, particularly in the early mornings and late afternoons. Butch exited through the back side of the apartment building into the alley, crossed the street and made a short jaunt to go do some shopping at the local men's store, French's. He was in need of some new trousers and dress shirts for his first day on the job, that coming Monday.

Brooke, bloodied about the face and head, tried desperately to open her door to jump out as Dale continued his barrage. "Get in the car!" he yelled, "What are ya trying to do? Get yourself killed?" Brooke leaned against the door, raised her left leg and gave a mighty thrust into Dale's right side. She struggled to climb over the seat, crying and kicking, as Dale gasped to regain his breath. She collapsed into the floorboard, screaming violently. Her shirt and skirt were ripped and blood dripped from her head and face. Fear and tears filled her swollen red eyes. With the gun still in his hand, Dale stretched his right arm over the seat.

"Get away from me!" she shrieked, as she climbed from the floorboard to the seat, leaning back as far as she could. "Augh! Take me home! I wan' go home! Momma!" She managed to slightly open the door just as Dale lunged out with his right hand, momentarily taking his eyes off the road.

"C'mere, you little … " he commanded and accidentally squeezed off a round that struck Brooke in the left side of her chest. Dale stared at her chest in disbelief as bright red blood began to seep out of the entrance wound. Brooke, with her eyes opened wide, looked down and brought her right hand up to touch her chest. She slightly pressed her fingers on the blood soaked wound and raised her head. One single tear trickled down her cheek as she mumbled, "Baby?" She leaned her head to the right against the unlocked and slightly open door.

Butch was in the process of paying for his new shirts and pants in French's when he took notice of the long line gathered across the street at the comic store. "There a parade or sump'n goin' on today?" he asked the clerk.

"Oh, the comic store." The clerk answered, handing Butch his sack, "They have book signings every once in a while. I think I heard Superman was coming today?" "Superman, huh?" Butch grunted. "Maybe I can pick up some good reading material. Thanks." Butch smiled, exited the store and headed back to his apartment, observing the long line of people as he walked.

As Tommy's Cadillac approached the intersection where the comic store was located, he could already see the crowd of people through the busy, early Saturday morning traffic. "I'd see what was gonna happen a few seconds before it happened," Danny stated. His friends and father were mesmerized at the brilliance and simplicity of the idea. "And all I'd have to do is one little thing like … buy something at the store and stop a crook or … talk to someone on the street for a few seconds to keep 'em from walking down an alley so they won't get mugged … anything for just for like … two or three seconds, just enough time for something to not happen."

Dale barreled down the street toward a crowded and busy intersection. "Let's talk to some of these dedicated ... Whoa!" Glen Armstrong stated as Dale's car whisked by, missing he and his cameraman by mere inches. Butch watched the near mishap from the sidewalk and lumbered out into the street, hoping to watch the speeding car as it headed toward the busy intersection. Ron and the other couples watched the car race by the newsman on the TV. "Whoa! What was that!" Casey hollered as he sat up. "Guy almost got it!" Jason commented. The cameraman caught a glimpse of Butch as he leaned out into the street. "Hey, there's Butch!" said John, "What's he doin' there?"

The cameraman ignored Glen and followed the car as it sped toward the intersection.

As Tommy waited at the intersection for his turn signal, Danny finished his wish for his super power looking at Tommy as he spoke. "That's what I'd do, Dad!" Danny declared. "I'd see the future."

Tommy smiled and looked past Danny to see Dale's oncoming car. No time.

Suddenly realizing he was not watching where he was going, Dale turned to face the front and tensed up at the sight of a car stopped directly and perpendicularly in front of him. He slammed the brakes and turned the steering wheel to his left, thereby making the right rear end swing out. The centrifugal force of the skidding vehicle flung Brooke halfway out the rear passenger door. Barely alive, she could see the oncoming car and closed her eyes. Dale's car careened into the rear passenger side corner of Tommy's. Brooke was instantly decapitated as the door crushed and pinched her neck. Dale's head struck the seam where the windshield meets the roof as his body hurled against the steering column. Little Billy Williams body was launched through the rear driver side passenger window and into oncoming traffic. Knocked unconscious, he landed on the asphalt in front of a truck as it was passing through the intersection.

The driver, incapable of reacting in time, rolled over his frail, tiny body, killing him instantly. Bobby, Jimmy and Daryl were tossed about like rag dolls from the force of the impact. Their heads and bodies struck against each other as they flew to the left side of the backseat.

Tommy and Danny both hit their heads on the frame separating the back and front doors. The left rear end of Tommy's car swung out into the path of an oncoming bus, headed to the terminal on the next street. Tommy sat squarely in the way of the bus and watched as the driver, unable to stop, delivered the monolith to its target. Although slightly disoriented from the first crash, he still had enough sense to lean as far away from the door as possible before the collision. Tommy's shoulder was immediately dislocated; his collar bone shattered and tiny shards of glass riddled his neck. The door buckled directly at his side, breaking three ribs with one of them piercing his lung. The door cave-in punched his knee down and backwards, tearing away at the ligaments.

Once more the boys were brutally thrown about the large backseat. Daryl shot through the rear passenger side window and landed almost completely upright, but was crushed between Tommy's and Dale's cars when the rear of Tommy's car swung back to the right.

The cameraman captured the entire wreck on tape, live and on the air. Sarah and the parents at home sat quietly for a moment, stunned at the sudden turn of events. The cameraman zoomed in past the front of the bus to Tommy's car. Sarah screamed, "Tommy!? Tommy!" and rushed to the television, crouching on her knees. The camera then focused on the crowd of people and the few that hurriedly crossed the street to help. "Tommy!?" Sarah whimpered as both Joey and Monica drew in close, kneeled beside her and joined hands. Terri gave a mighty scream as the camera again turned and focused on the mangled green Cadillac. Ron instinctively jumped up and dialed the local DPS station. Busy signal.

Butch, with his bags in his hands, ran to the scene as well as Glen Armstrong and his cameraman. Dale groggily raised his head from the steering wheel and felt the blood running down his face. With his wits not yet about him, he leaned over to the floorboard and clumsily grabbed at the cigar box and gun. Rapping at the window and loud, muffled voices called out to him as he gradually regained his senses. Dale shoved open his door as helpful onlookers gathered around him, eager to help.

Unbalanced, he staggered slightly and waved his gun wildly as he roared at the gathering crowd. "Get away! Get away!" He turned towards the car, looked into the backseat and saw the crumpled, blood splattered door and Brooke's headless body lying in the seat. With his heart and head filing quickly with fear, sorrow and rage, Dale let loose with a mournful scream as he barged his way through the multitude. As he approached the wreck, Butch heard a woman scream. He rushed to the side of an elderly woman who had found Brooke's head, lying in the curb gutter. He thanked and politely directed the woman away then removed one of his new shirts from his bag, unfolded it and laid it over the head.

Glen and the cameraman were fast approaching the intersection when Butch intercepted them. "Get these people away!" he instructed.

"What?!" yelled Glen.

"I am assuming control and currently have jurisdiction of this scene until local law enforcements arrive. I need your help! I need you to get on that camera and call for any and all emergency personnel that can get here and get here now!" Glen looked at Butch then at the wreck. "Now!" Butch demanded with a shout. Glen jumped and told his cameraman to start broadcasting.

Ron finally got through to Sgt. Huddleston at the DPS headquarters as Sarah and the other couples ran out to the driveway. Panic stricken, they hastily detached the boats and recklessly unloaded the two off-road vehicles to drive the nine of them into the city.

Dale darted down the sidewalk then ducked into a hunter's supply and outdoors showroom. He dashed through to the back door and tore down the alley to the rear entrance of the bus terminal near Butch's apartment. Butch neared the wreckage and noticed Daryl's corpse pinched between the rear tire well of Dale's car and crumpled door of the Cadillac. Tommy, in terrible condition, but semi-conscious, groaned lowly and painfully as Butch rushed to his side.

Tommy turned his head in excruciating pain to look at his son. "Danny?" he whispered, trying to touch his boy. "Danny?" he again called with a gentle nudge of his son's left shoulder. He began to shake as tears rolled down his cheeks. "Jimmy? Billy?" he cried out. Butch looked in the backseat and threw up violently at the sight of Jimmy and Bobby's bloodied and mangled bodies. Like Tommy, Butch's tears flowed down his face. He removed his shirt, leaned through the shattered window into the backseat and covered their tiny crushed skulls.

Even as some witnesses started to give their accounts of what happened, Butch gently pushed the people back when he again heard Tommy, "Bobby? Daryl?" Tommy reached up with his right hand to turn the rear view mirror. The sight of the blood covered backseat, along with Bobby and Jimmy's bodies twisted about each other, was more than his heart could take. He clenched his eyes tight and let loose with a heart wrenching scream of agony and helplessness.

Dale ran past a homeless man sleeping in the alley, but not before slowing down to steal his hat and throw the blood tainted cigar box in a dumpster. He glided through one of the doors leading into the bus terminal and quickly wound his way through the mass of travelers to the men's room. Rushing to the last sink and mirror at the end of the counter, he took a peak under the hat and found a large, gaping cut on his head. He frantically grabbed at a role of paper towels and dunked a large clump under some hot water to rub off the drying blood. Once done with picking the glass from his scalp and cleaning his face, he cautiously exited the men's room and proceeded to the long line at the ticket counter. He watched several police cars go racing by the terminal with their lights flashing and sirens blaring, alerting all to their presence.

Sarah and the four sets of parents sped down the highway. The men in both vehicles used their CBs to ascertain as to which hospital Tommy and their sons were being taken. The lifelong girlfriends wept uncontrollably as they clung to one another, struggling in vain to stay calm.

Eventually, police, fire and emergency personnel arrived at the scene and assumed control. Tommy was being extracted from his car when he passionately shouted, "Danny! Danny!" and watched the EMT's pull Danny's limp body out of the window. "Danny! Son!" he pleaded, but Danny showed no sign of response.

Butch, irritated by the flood of news cameras and reporters, hurriedly, but politely, answered all the questions he could before jumping into the ambulance with Tommy for the ride to the hospital.

Dale removed the bloodied eighty dollars from his pocket to purchase a bus ticket. The bus wasn't scheduled to leave for another fifteen minutes, but had already begun loading passengers. Dale briskly walked through the terminal, out to the parking lot and climbed aboard his bus. Suddenly, two police cars pulled into the terminal. He intensely watched the officers through the windows of the bus as they jumped out of their squad car and rushed inside. Dale scurried to the end of his bus and opened the bathroom door. Jumping inside, he crammed himself behind the door into the space above the sink, leaving the light on and the door open. In the stillness of the moment, he could feel and hear his heart racing. Minutes passed, and soon the sound of heavy footsteps resonated on the hard plastic floor. One of the policemen had come on board to inspect the seats. From several feet away the officer looked down the aisle and into the open bathroom. He cautiously crept towards the bathroom, withdrew his gun and gently nudged the door completely open with his foot. The officer observed nothing unusual or out of the ordinary, holstered his fire arm and walked out, closing the door to the bus behind him. Dale sat on the bathroom vanity breathing heavily.

The Jeep and Jimmy came to a screeching halt in the covered circular drive of the hospital. News crews were already on the scene, just waiting for the nine friends to show up. As they climbed out of their vehicles, a gaggle of flash bulbs and flood lights blinded their eyes while microphones and cameras were shoved in their faces. Sarah was first to reach the ER registration desk. "My names is ... " she blurted, trying to catch her breath as Holly approached and took her hand. "My name is Sarah Albright ... and I believe my husband and son were brought here?"

"Mrs. Albright! Yes!" the nurse's attendant agreed. "Just a moment please?" The attendant picked up the phone and tried to quietly say, "They're here ... right now." After a moment she finished with an anxious, "All of them." The attendant turned back to Sarah when Holly started to speak, "I'm Holly Hall and my ... "

"The doctor will be right with you," The nurse interrupted quasi-politely but free of emotion. "We have a room over there you all can wait in," she pointed nonchalantly as she resumed her paperwork.

Sarah and the others forced their way to the waiting room, still bombarded by the reporters. John and Casey, the shortest tempered of the five men, approached the brood, showed their badges and loudly shouted, "This is official DPS business! Leave these families alone!"

The bulbs kept flashing until John, almost face to face with one particular reporter, yelled a very convincing "Move! Now!" With that, the crowd gradually fell back, leaving the nine to themselves.

Dale snuck to his seat from the bathroom once the bus was moving. From high in his seat, he peered through the window while the coach passed the scene of carnage. A knot tightened in the pit of his stomach at the sight of the blood on the asphalt and the spraying of blood on the inside of Brooke's and Tommy's cars. The bus eventually made its way down the street, passing by the downtown shops and businesses, the suburban schools and finally the feed lots and factories on the edge of town, delivering all to where they wanted to be: anywhere and out.

Sarah and the other couples sat impatiently in the waiting room. "What's taking so long!" Jason complained, loud enough for the nurse to hear and jump on the phone once more. Ron leaned his head back against the wall while Holly rested in his lap, her head laying on his shoulder.

"Remember the day we brought him home from the hospital?" Holly wearily asked.

"Sure do!" Ron said, trying to grin. "He was so small."

The conversation was being repeated on the other side of the room between Casey and Terri. "I looked down at his face," she reminded Casey as he stroked her hair. "Just moments before he was in me … a part of me … then all of a sudden … he's looking at me … with these big … beautiful … blue … " then stopped to break down into tears once more.

Suddenly, the double doors to the emergency room opened. Dr. Lee Rankin and Dr. Patrick Artle stood in front of the doors, looked into the waiting room and called out, "Sarah Albright?" Sarah stood up quickly and walked over to greet the doctors. Joey also stood and escorted her. "My name is Dr. Rankin and this is Dr. Artle," Lee said as the two men extended their hands to Sarah and Joey. "I'm Sarah and this is my friend Joey." "Joey, nice to meet you," Lee complimented. "Sarah, I need to talk with you for just a moment, if you'll follow me please?" Lee opened the doors to the ER and motioned for Sarah to follow him. Sarah and Joey hugged and kissed each other, wiped their eyes, then Sarah disappeared into the hallway.

Sarah had been gone but all of ten seconds when Butch emerged from the ER corridor. His clothes were splattered with blood from helping to cover and move bodies, including Brooke's head. The four sets of despairing parents watched the reporters swarm around him as he entered the foyer. Dr. Artle appeared again in front of the double doors leading to the ER and motioned for the octet to come over to the other side of the waiting room, away from prying eyes. As Butch was answering questions, he turned slightly and overheard Dr. Artle as he delivered the dreadful news that all of their sons were dead.

Horrible screams of anguish filled the room. Monica shut her eyes clenched her fists to her eyes and wailed with pain. Jason wrapped his arms around his wife and began to weep with her as she shook and stamped her feet in disbelief. Joey sniffed for a moment then lightly breathed, "Hon?" before fainting and collapsing in John's arms. Holly and Terri embraced each other as they fell to the floor in a lump.

Ron walked about the room, building up steam. He shook his head in prideful denial with his hands on his hips repeating, "No! No!" Casey followed, he himself upset, but still trying to soothe his friend. "My boy's not dead! He's not dead! You here me?!" Ron picked up one of the large cushioned arm chairs and hurled it across the room through the window. "He's not dead! Where's my boy?" Casey struggled to restrain Ron as he kicked over a table. Upon hearing the commotion, Butch hurried from across the room to help. The threesome fell hard to the floor in a pile with Ron on the bottom, still refusing to accept the truth. "He's not dead! Bring me my boy! Augh! Bobby! Where's my boy! Augh!"

Dr. Rankin led Sarah out of the X-ray lab to the CCU. As they walked, he showed her the proofs by holding them up to the lights and explained the injuries Tommy sustained during the wreck. "Is he going to live?" Sarah asked before coming to a stop in front of Tommy's curtain enclosed bed. Dr. Rankin pulled back the partition, revealing her banged up husband. Tommy lay with tubes running in and out of him. His arm and shoulder were already bandaged up and his leg was being put in a cast. His torso had been wrapped tight and on his face were tiny, slightly bloody pock marks from the shattering glass.

Sarah rushed to his right side, weeping, took his hand and kissed it. Tommy opened his eyes with a flutter. "Hey!" he mumbled. "What's this I hear?" Sarah leaned over and kissed her husband. "Should I call in Monday?" he tried to joke with a painful cough. Sarah sniffed as her chin began to quiver. "How's my boy?" he asked. Sarah tried to be strong and control her emotions and breathing, but was incapable of answering at the moment. "Sarah?" Tommy asked, raising her head.

"He's … in a coma!" Sarah blurted. "He has a concussion and severe whiplash." Tommy closed his eyes tightly to hold his tears back. "They … they don't know if he'll wake up!" she added.

After a brief moment Tommy opened his eyes and gurgled, "The boys?" Sarah couldn't answer. Instead, she turned away from her husband, pressing her hand over her mouth and slightly shook her head.

The women were moved to a private room after they were informed of their son's deaths. One of the ER staff members snuck out earlier and brought back a fifth of Wild Turkey and gave it to Joey. As the women shared drinks and confronted reality, Dr. Artle, in the meanwhile, had taken the four fathers downstairs to identify their sons' bodies. Once all of the release papers were signed, the men returned upstairs to their wives. Later, Joey, Holley, Monica and Terri, weary from the day, were rolled out of the ER in wheelchairs with their husbands pushing them. John, Joey, Jason, and Monica climbed into one vehicle with Terri, Holly, Ron, and Casey piling in the other. The cars gingerly pulled out of the hospital parking lot for a long, quiet trip home.

Requiem

The news spread like a prairie wildfire. Local and national radio and television stations were interrupting their broadcasts to inform the public of the great tragedy; how four children and a pregnant seventeen-year-old girl all lost their lives in a horrible downtown car crash.

Sarah tried to get comfortable in the uncomfortable square chairs in Danny and Tommy's hospital rooms. She would stay a little bit with Tommy, then go down the hall and stay awhile with Danny. Prayer was never a stronger ally for Sarah. The thoughts of potentially losing either one of her boys conflicted with her brightest and fondest memories of each.

Sarah had called Tommy's father, Johnny Lee, from the ER room's courtesy phone with the disheartening news. Before heading into the city to meet Sarah, Johnny, who happened to be the town mayor, called and spoke directly with then Texas governor, Dolph Briscoe, in Austin. Soon Governor Briscoe, Johnny Lee, local and county officials and members of state had set up an emergency collection fund for the befallen families in banks across the land. The Office of General Counsel to the Texas Department of Public Safety sent out bulletins to all six DPS district headquarters to notify their troopers of the terrible accident. By Monday, July 25th, total collections were in excess of $118,000 dollars.

The money, as determined by Tommy, Sarah, and their friends, went toward securing a large tract of plots in the town cemetery. The plot, measuring almost an acre in size, was more than enough to allow all the boys, as well as other family members in the future, to be buried together. After an exhaustive discussion, it was agreed upon that the family's plots would be formed in five triangles. When joined at their bases, the five elongated isosceles triangles would form the shape of a Texas star with one of the boys buried at the base of each arm. The rest of the space in the arm would be for future use when members of that family would pass. Even though there wasn't enough time for the plots to be landscaped, eventually, the design elements would come together for a beautiful memorial.

Casey thought there needed to be something in the middle of the star. Something symbolic maybe to remind themselves and the local townsfolk of the history of these friends, their families, the love they all had for their boys and of the boys love for each other. Casey and Terri contacted Brad Butler, a friend of theirs living in Slaton, who did contract specialty work for cemeteries and designed memorials. Brad came up with the idea of making a tall, pentagonal monolith and to place it in a round, shallow pool in the middle of the star with the flat sides facing the base of each arm of the star. He went further to suggest using "Sunset Red" granite from Marble Falls, the same granite that was used in the making of the Texas State Capitol.

Pastor Brock, Pastor Cregan and Deacon Farley went to the high school to talk to Holly. They all agreed that the church was too small to support a public mass funeral. After much deliberation between the parents, church, and civic offices, it was decided that the services would be held at the school gymnasium, with private graveside services to be held at the cemetery.

It was a beautiful morning for such a sad day of closure. Not a cloud was to be seen in any direction. The wide Texas sky was a deep blue and only the slightest of cool, early morning breezes played in the trees. Sindecki's Limo Service, forty-five miles away in the city, sent out twelve white stretch limousines, three each to the families of the boys, free of charge. The four sets of parents opted to meet at the parking lot of The Longhorn Ranch House restaurant, the local hotspot, prior to heading over to the school.

At around nine a.m., Wednesday, July twenty-seventh, Monica and

Jason were first to step out of their limo. There was an eerie stillness about. The schools, civic offices, and banks were all closed in respect to the families. Main Street was practically abandoned. From one end of the lane to the other, not a car was to be seen. One by one the remaining eleven limousines pulled into the parking lot. The parents and immediate members of the four families climbed out of the long, snow white cars to greet and hug one another. Minutes later John came to Jason and tapped his watch. Time to go.

The whole town must have been there, John thought. City, county and state law enforcement vehicles lined the streets; their red, blue, and yellow lights flashed brilliantly, but made not a sound. Cars, busses, trucks, and vans spilled over from the school parking lot onto the baseball field. Local and state news crews were gathered under the awning of the high school main entrance, just waiting for a glimpse of the stoic families.

The caravan of twelve limousines arrived at the school just before 10 a.m. They pulled into the rear parking lot by the emergency double exit doors leading into the back of the gymnasium. John and Joey's limo was first to arrive at the makeshift church. Joey wearily approached the double doors and squeezed John's hand tightly. Through the closed doors she could hear an organ softly playing, "How Great Thou Art."

The low hum of talking stopped completely when the doors opened and Joey shakily and meekly entered. The entire multitude of respectful mourners rose and stood in motionless, silent reverence. Texas Governor Dolph Brisco, members of his cabinet and representatives of every law enforcement agency in the state, lined the first two rows of gym risers. The sorrowful populace remained standing until all four sets of parents and their families were seated. The coffins of the four boys were lying side by side, spaced evenly out in front of the podium with their lids closed.

Just before the ceremony began, the gymnasium doors opened once more. Tommy was wheeled through the doors and placed beside Jason at the end of the front row. His left shirt sleeve and left pant leg had been cut away to allow his casts to pass through. He wore his hat with pride and his right boot has been buffed to a bright shine. Jason took his lifelong friend's hand in his. Pastor Brock stepped up to the podium, looked over the crowd and silently motioned for them all to be seated.

Sarah sat next to her unconscious son, lying in bed. Tubes ran into his arms while sticky patches connected wire leads to his head and chest. The heart monitor spoke up every few seconds to let her know his heart was working fine. The ink capsules on the brain activity monitor barely moved as the graph paper scrolled by. Sarah wept silently, convulsing, as she watched the television broadcast of the funeral ceremony from Danny's room. She felt her heart being torn in two: half of her was a loving, caring mother that knew she needed to stay with her son, yet the other half yearned to be with her friends in their desperate time of need, loss, and pain.

After an emotionally and spiritually grueling hour had passed, the services were finally over. The four sets of parents remained seated as the long train of Texas diplomats and kind townspeople passed by. Although well intended, the smiles and handshakes were futile in lightening the load of all those who suffered from the tremendous loss.

The exiting line of cars stretched all the way down Main Street. The hearses and limousines were already unloading a mile and a half away, while back at the school, cars were still waiting just to exit the baseball field and parking lot. The news crews had left early in the hopes of getting a good spot to film the motorcade as it entered and left the small town cemetery. Even though closed to the public, the cameras moved about the fence and kept rolling during the funerals.

Pastor Cregan and Pastor Brock had a difficult time in presiding over the graveside rituals. The ceremonies, even though genuinely heartfelt and delivered sincerely, felt like a conveyor line. The children's graves were more than fifty feet away from each other and, to make matters worse, the mid-morning sun was starting to beat down as the cool breezes subsided.

All were gathered at Daryl's grave for the first service, after which the Arterberry family stayed behind while the shrinking crowd walked over to the white tent for little Billy Williams service. Casey stood at the end of the grave as Terri read a letter out loud to her son. They, along with Casey's parents, stayed with Billy's casket while the small band sluggishly walked over to the awning for Bobby's service.

Ron tried to stay strong through Bobby's eulogy, but Holly, sensing her husband's tension, wrapped her arm around his shoulder. He lowered his head and unleashed a distressing wail for his lost son. Jimmy's services were performed last. Jason and Monica, although outwardly appreciative to all who attended, seemed not mentally present. Rather, they were far, far away in their hearts with their son.

Lynnly Ives and Sybil Pittman stood in the middle of the four small tents, and, at the right time, played and sang, "Softly and Tenderly."

Tommy sat alongside Johnny Lee next to Lynnly and Sybil as they played. Listening to the words of the song, Tommy whispered a prayer of thanks to God for sacrificing his son Jesus Christ, for sparing the life of his own son and for Him to please be with and comfort the souls of his eight friends. Upon hearing the words "Come home, come home, ye who are weary come home." Tommy loosened the reins of his emotions as he watched the four small caskets being lowered into the ground.

Dark clouds appeared on the western horizon. Sarah stroked her son's hair.

Suddenly, the speaker in Danny's brain monitor pinged loudly several times. The arms holding the ink capsules sprang to life and swung in broad and brightly colored arcs from side to side …

October

After the wreck, Tommy underwent surgery for his pierced lung, followed by arthroscopic surgeries for his knee, shoulder, and arm. Rehab was slow, seeing as how it was almost completely one side of him that needed the work. Dealing with her baby boy in the hospital and a full grown baby of a husband at the house had been anything but easy for Sarah.

For the remainder of July and the month of August, once she was finished with work, Sarah would drive to the city and stay with Tommy and Danny for the night. She'd sleep in the extra bed next to Tommy, then go back the next morning and start all over again. Once Tommy was able to start light work in mid September, he and Sarah took turns staying with Danny.

Tommy and Sarah were told that when the paramedics arrived at the scene of the wreck, Danny was unconscious and more than likely the recipient of blunt force trauma, whiplash, and a concussion. The car moved sideways from the force of the impact, thereby causing Danny's head to hit the door frame, then his body slumped over in the seat. His comatose state was due to hypoxia, meaning his brain was receiving oxygen, but at greatly reduced levels. The worrisome couple were dealt more bad news when they were later told that children twelve and under have the highest risk of not surviving closed cranial trauma followed by a coma.

Every once in while though, Danny's electro cerebral activity would jump off the chart and his eyes would move wildly under the lids. His heart beat would accelerate and his blood pressure would increase. For a few brief seconds his lips would part and his lungs would expand and contract with great intakes of air. Unfortunately the promising signs of life would diminish just as quickly as they appeared.

Friday afternoon, October 16, 1978. After completing physical therapy, Tommy was temporarily reassigned to assist with administrative office duties. "Tommy?" said April, one of two receptionists, "You got a phone call on two."

"Albright!" Tommy stated bluntly as he picked up the phone, distracted with his work. "Yeah. Hello, how are ya? No, no, you're fine. How can I help ya? He what? When?" Tommy asked. Unknowingly, he brought the entire staff to a standstill when he pulled out his chair and inadvertently knocked over a large stack of files. "Is he okay? When did this happen? Can he talk?" Jason and Casey approached the side of the desk to listen in on their friend's call. Judging from his facial expression and tone, the news was not good. "I'm on my way; give me ... gimme forty-five minutes ... Thank you."

Tommy began to cry as he hung up the phone and covered his face with his hands. Casey leaned over to pat his friend and inquired, "Tommy? You okay?" He didn't answer as Casey continued, "Is it Johnny Lee? Is he okay?" Jason and Casey looked at each other and shrugged in question. Other eyes made contact around the room as if to ask, "what now?"

Tommy leaned back, removed his hands from his face and let loose with a laugh as he declared, "He woke up! Danny woke up!" Clapping, cheering, hugs and tears filled the room as he further explained, "He's all right! He knows who he is! He knows who Sarah is!" Ron and John walked into the celebration and joined the three men at Tommy's desk as he elaborated, "He wants to eat! He can move! I gotta get outta here!" he suddenly realized, grabbing his keys and hat "I'm standing here and my son's waiting!"

Traffic in both directions yielded to the shoulder as Tommy and his buddies flew down the highway with sirens blaring and all lights flashing. Sarah called and broke the good news to her girlfriends who immediately dropped everything to head into town, but not without first stopping for balloons and flowers. Before long, the three speeding patrol vehicles caught up to the two slower moving cars of their wives and interspersed themselves in between. The five vehicles of nine friends, happy and smiling, sped to the long awaited awakening and reunion.

Sarah stood near the bed as the neurologist and nurses continued to check Danny's vital signs. As she monitored the care being given to her son, she faintly heard the high pitched wailing of emergency sirens. She turned to the window and saw the motorcade coming down the street to the hospital. The cars came to a screeching halt in front of the emergency room doors. From high above on the fifth floor, Sarah watched her husband and eight friends spill out of their cars with balloons, flowers, and stuffed animals. "Well?" she sighed with a shrug and a smile, "Your father's never been one to make a small entrance!"

All activity in the ER waiting room halted as the five DPS Troopers quickly entered. Tommy was first to reach the elevators and pushed the up button over and over, as if the repeated action of pressing the button would make the car get there any faster. "C'mon!" he stammered, looking at the floor numbers. "I don't believe this! I can drive a hundred miles an hour, run red lights for a thousand miles, but I can't get to my son 'cuz of a stupid elevator." The nine parents impatiently watched the floor numbers illuminate, ever so slowly. "I can't wait!" Tommy admitted and turned to go up the stairs.

"It'll be here any second!" Ron yelled as Tommy entered the stairwell. Sure enough, just as Ron said they would, the doors to the elevator opened.

Tommy attempted to run up the stairs, but after the first floor, the aching in his knee made it difficult to walk. He pushed himself through the pain and hopped primarily on his right leg up the remaining four flights. As he climbed, shedding tears of joy, he hollered out, "Danny! I'm here, son! I'm a comin'! Hoooo!" laughing to himself as he continued celebrating. "Here I come, Superman!"

He finally reached the fifth floor, breathless and sweating from his workout, then hobbled down the hall. Just as he entered Danny's semi-private room, he heard the soft bell of the elevator behind him.

He passed an older black woman, Emilie Parks, who now shared the room with Danny. Emilie arrived last week with problems related to her diabetes. She waved to Tommy as he crept by slowly, careful not to make any sounds.

As he was coming in, a nurse was exiting and, with a gentle squeeze on his arm, informed him, "He's in and out, but he's doing good!" Tommy stepped out from behind the curtain separating Danny and Emilie. He was asleep for the moment with Sarah sitting at his side. Tommy approached the bed, hugged his wife and stared in disbelief at his son. He couldn't recall a time when his boy was more beautiful. He silently pulled the chair closer to the bed and delicately lowered the rails. Sarah's heart raced as Tommy took his son's hand. Danny's eyes fluttered open, allowing the two to smile at each other.

"How's my Superman?" he asked tenderly.

"Hey, Daddy," Danny squeaked.

"I've missed you!" Tommy admitted, leaning over to kiss his son's head. Danny wrapped his arms around his father's neck. Tommy embraced his son and held him in his arms. "Ah!" he exclaimed, struggling to stand up straight, "My big man! Boy howdy, it feels good to hold you!" Sarah embraced both her husband and son, patting and scratching their backs. She glanced at the curtain and noticed a forest of legs on the other side.

"Hey, cowboy … " she said, "You got some company."

Ron and Holly, John and Joey, Casey and Terri and Jason and Monica gleefully disrupted the reunion.

"Boy, we thought that you were likin' to never wake up!" Casey exclaimed.

"You wouldn't believe the chores you gotta catch up on!" John bellowed.

"And all the horse crap you've gotta scoop!" Jason added. The group had a good laugh as Danny was passed around like a sack of potatoes, receiving more than his fair share of kisses and hugs for the next ten years.

"Boy are we gonna have a party!" Tommy announced as he again hoisted his son in his arms. "Wit' everybody from the church and ball team. We are gonna celebrate!"

"Where are Billy and Daryl?" Danny asked innocently. "Are Bobby and Jimmy here?" he inquired, leaning to the side to look past the curtain. The room grew still and silent as the smiles disappeared and heads turned away. Ron moved towards the window to look outside as Terri bit her lip. Jason excused himself past John and Joey.

"We're glad you're doin' good, hon!" Holly forced out, struggling to smile. "Glad to see you all healthy. Ronnie?" Ron came to Danny, kissed his head and patted his back. Tommy looked at Ron with sorrowful eyes. The two men leaned into each other before Ron escorted Holly out of the room.

"We got to run, hon. We got a lot of stuff to do … " Joey explained. "And these boys got to get back to work. Don't ya, John?" John stood and stared at Tommy and Danny, but in his heart could see only himself and his son.

"Yeah. We gotta go, Danny." John lamented.

"We been prayin' you and your daddy would be all right," Joey finished. Joey took Sarah's hand, squeezed it tightly, then turned abruptly to leave.

"We love you, Danny," Terri choked, "We love all of you. Baby?" Casey winked tearfully to Danny and tapped Tommy on the elbow before putting his arm around Terri's shoulder.

"We'll call ya'll later. Maybe come by in a day or two," Monica suggested as she hugged Sarah. "Y'know, let ya'll get settled and sorted out."

"I'm so sorry!" Sarah whispered in Monica's ear.

"I know!" Monica hissed. "Oh, dear God! You know I'm happy for you! You know that! I just miss my baby!" Monica hurriedly broke her friends embrace and turned to leave. She crossed the hall to the stairwell to find Jason already there. The two slumped down on the steps together and wept.

"What happened, Daddy?" Danny asked as Tommy laid him back down. "Why were they crying?"

Tommy scooted the chair back to the side of the bed and asked, "Danny, remember how I was wantin' to talk to you soon? About the man you're becoming?"

Danny nodded with his eyes now open wide and said, "Yeah, but that was last week?" Sarah knew what was coming and left the room. She entered the nurse's linen closet across the hall, closed the door and bawled into the stack of towels.

"Danny, what's the most recent thing you remember?" Tommy probed.

"Well … ?" Danny recalled, "You and me and the guys were talking on the way to the comic store."

"That right, good! You're right," he encouraged, "We were driving to go see who? Do you remember?"

"We were gonna go see Superman," Danny stated.

"Superman! Right! You're doin' good. Do you remember talkin' 'bout anything special?"

"Yeah. I was gonna see the future and Billy just wanted to be tall."

" Yeah, yeah he did." Tommy chuckled as he thought back to the wish of the happy runt. "Billy wanted to be tall. Son?" Tommy paused, scooting closer to the bed. "I want you to pay close attention to what I'm gonna tell you." he said and reached for Danny's hand. "This might be difficult for you to understand … " Danny looked at his father, confused. "Son … we were in a bad car wreck … just about the time you were talking … and I'm sorry, but … " Danny waited for Tommy to finish, "that was four months ago." Danny's chin began to quiver. "You and I were hurt in a real bad way," Tommy continued. "And we were brought here to the emergency room. They took care of me 'n they've been taking care of you … while you been asleep."

"What about Jimmy and Billy?" Danny asked shakily with tears welling up in his eyes. "Where'd they take Bobby and Daryl?"

"Son, we were hit really hard and … " Tommy stopped. Danny turned beet red as he tried to hold back his tears, then pulled the blanket over his face. Sarah re-entered the room and stood at the other side of the bed. Emilie commenced to pray out loud for Danny.

Tommy pulled down the sheet to reveal his boys face. "Are … are they dead?" Danny spurted. It broke Tommy's heart to tell his son the truth, but he knew it had to be done and it would be for the best. He looked his hurting son squarely in the eyes and sorrowfully answered, "Yes."

The blanket came back over Danny's eyes as Sarah consoled her boy, "Danny? I know this hurts, and it's gonna take a while to work through it. But there is a good way to look upon this. Your friends … well, they knew you loved 'em, darlin,' and they loved you." Her words flowed smoothly and patiently. "And son? That love will never die and never fade!" She pulled the blanket down and wiped away his tears. "And their spirits are in this room with you right now!" she claimed, holding her arms out. Danny looked about the room curiously as she testified. "They just watchin' o'er you. Jesus and your friends will always, always be with you. We love you dearly," she added, stroking his head. "And are so, so sorry that this has happened."

"But why them?!" Danny asked angrily. "Why'd God take my friends?"

"Son?" Tommy perked up. "God has His plans. And it's hard to understand God's ways sometimes … like why He lets some things, bad things, happen the way He does. And why do people, good people, people we love, get hurt? There's a lot of things I don't understand myself. But, one thing I do know, is He had a purpose in allowing His children to go home. He sent them here to be your friends, to love you, support you, to help you grow … "

Sarah interrupted, "And they learned a lot from watching and listening to you … "

"That's right," Tommy agreed. "And God has a lesson to teach us … something for us to learn right now while their gone. Not that we did wrong or are being punished for something, but more like a lesson to learn for when we get older, for knowing how to be strong in Him for everything, for all our lives."

Danny clinched his eyes tight and extended his arms to his father. Tommy leaned forward and scooped his son in his strong arms, completely and securely enveloping him. Sarah walked to the other side of the bed, leaned over and embraced her two boys, sandwiching Danny. The three gently rocked back and forth with Sarah's head resting on Danny's shoulder. She could hear his heart pounding.

From behind the curtain, Emilie faintly hummed "Amazing Grace"; a soft smile rested on her lips.

The Fold

"He's okay, but he's not okay." Tommy said just above a whisper, peering through the thin crack between the door and the frame. "His eyes, his face, his behavior, they're all different now." He walked about his study as he described Danny's condition to Dr. Rankin. "The other day we were playin' ball after church and Pastor Mike hit a grounder to him, and he just stood there ... stood right there and watched it go by. Didn't try ... didn't move ... then walked to the dugout." He once again looked out his study at Danny doing his homework at the kitchen table.

"Uh-uh. What's he like during the day? Is he interacting with everyone?" asked Dr. Rankin.

"Well," Tommy started, "he won't participate in church, will hardly eat, and doesn't ride his horse. It's like a little ... zombie ... moping through my house. He's a great kid and I know he's been through a lot, but we don't know what to do!" Dr. Rankin remained silent. "And there's more." he reluctantly admitted.

"More what?" Dr. Rankin probed.

"He ... " Tommy hesitated, "he says he's having these dreams where ... he sees ... the wreck happen. That he's above the car and watches it happen! I know what happened and it's weird that he knows these things in such detail."

"How often does he have these dreams?" the doctor inquired.

"It's more like when doesn't he. Each time he has this dream he comes into our room, stands at the side of the bed and he'll be starin' at me 'n Sarah with his eyes wide-open, sound asleep. And … I'll feel him there. I know somehow he's there and wake up … then … he starts reciting what happened. And each time there's a little more than what he said previously."

"Does he try to go anywhere? Get out of the house? Hide?"

"Nah. He'll say what he's got to say and I'll tell him to go back to bed. He says okay and I'll follow him. Doesn't even know he's doin' it!" Tommy sat down with a hard slump, "Do these kinda things happen a lot?"

"Well, normally, no," Dr. Rankin explained. "Most people who are … "

"He says he saw the driver of that car shoot a woman!" Tommy interrupted. "Now how do you explain that?"

"Well … " Dr. Rankin began, but was again cut off.

"That's just weird! My son's telling me what happened twenty minutes before a wreck that he didn't witness after he's been in a coma for four months!?"

Dr. Rankin finally had an opportunity to speak, "Danny is more than likely going through what is called post traumatic stress syndrome. Now, some can identify their own problem, or problems, and work themselves out of whatever it is that's happened: the death of a parent or sibling, people who have gone to war, whatever. They can work themselves out of it and go on with their lives."

"But?" Tommy pushed.

"Well, some can't, or won't, and block out everything else," he stated frankly. "They get emotionally and psychologically trapped in the 'if only' and the 'why me' of the situation." Tommy wrote out the doctor's hypothesis as he dictated.

"Some go so deep into depression that who we once knew ceases to exist. Some withdraw from society, some drink, some do drugs, some commit suicide."

"Do you think Danny's that bad off?"

"I'm not saying that," Dr. Rankin stated. "What I am saying is it's too early in the game to tell. Danny's been out of the hospital now for less than four weeks. His greatest strength right now is you and Sarah just being there for him; letting him know that you love him, hearing your voice, seeing your faces, constant positive interaction. Danny's world disappeared without him knowing it and these wounds, these are deep … and they're gonna take a long time to heal. He's going to need your patience."

Tommy watched Sarah as she helped Danny with his homework. Dr. Rankin offered a suggestion, "Now, for his dreams I don't know what I can do. But there's a counselor I want you to see. Her name is Tracy. She deals primarily with children with communication problems that stem from just such a loss. She's excellent for providing an outside voice to keep things kind of fresh and light. I think you'll like her. I'll call and see about setting up an appointment maybe next week for late Friday. Is that Okay?"

The roads were wet that Friday afternoon; an early winter cold front had blown in. It wasn't cold enough to freeze, but cold enough nonetheless. Tommy was driving the family home from the city after having finished their first meeting with Tracy, the counselor Dr. Rankin recommended. "Well, that wasn't so bad!" he stated jovially, looking at Danny in the rear view mirror. "I kinda liked it. Didn't you, Sarah?" he nudged with a wink.

"Yeah!" she declared, turning herself sideways in the seat. "She seemed nice. Real attentive, too. I think it'll be good for all of us!" Tommy and Sarah smiled to each other, then to the backseat. "What do you think, Danny?" Sarah asked. Danny sat quietly, staring out the back passenger window.

Once Sarah turned forward, Danny finally answered, lowly, "She was all right."

Tommy looked in the mirror, then boasted to Sarah as he took her hand in his, "Good! See? Making progress already!"

"Baby, can we get something to eat?" Sarah suggested. "I'm hungry. And I mean hooon-greee! Danny, son, you hungry? Can ya eat?" Again, no answer. "I bet I could eat two longhorn burgers," she proclaimed.

"Dano? Ya hungry?" Tommy asked with a slight turn of his head to the back seat.

Again, after a long pause, Danny stated bluntly, "Yeah, I can eat."

"Well, let's go celebrate!" Tommy declared, bouncing slightly in the seat. "Let's go to the Longhorn! That sound all right with ya'll? Cuz I'm in the moooood for eatin' a steak!" He bellowed like a cow. "Get it? Moooood? Longhorn? Steakhouse? Get it?" Tommy over exaggerated his laughter to make his wife and son smile. He stretched his long arm over the bench seat back in search of his son. Danny squirmed to get away but to no avail; his father's large and muscular hand found his knee and began to pinch. After weeks of relative silence, Danny broke the quiet routine with beautiful childish laughter; music to their hearts.

Tommy pulled into the parking lot of The Longhorn Ranch House and all three scrambled to get in out of the frigid driving rain. Upon entering, a majority of the patrons stopped to stare at the family. Tommy led the way across the dining room to their usual table, whereupon some conversations resumed. Danny hesitated, though, as he panned the room, uncomfortable with the many faces watching him.

"What'chu all lookin' at?" Ernestine, the waitress, quipped with a wave of her towel in the air. "Danny, you go right on in, hon. Me or Lorien will be right with ya." With that, she gently swatted the young cowboy on his behind to set him on his way. As he passed the tables, the faces gradually made the transition from stares to smiles as pats, hugs, and winks helped to build up his self-esteem.

As he walked through the diner greeting the locals, Danny spied Jessica and her family on the far side of the restaurant, sitting near the corner. He took off his coat and hung it on the back of the chair, all the while transfixed on Jessica. "I'll be right back." Danny stated confidently.

"Well, whadya want to drink?" Tommy asked. As Danny turned to answer his father, both men stated "DP."

"Go get her, Superman!" Tommy encouraged with a nod of his head.

Mr. Holder looked up to see Danny approaching their table. "Mr. and Mrs. Holder?" Danny asked softly, hesitant to interrupt dinner. Jessica whipped around in her chair at the sound of Danny's voice.

Mrs. Holder dropped her fork to happily greet him, "Well, hello Danny! How are you? C'mere and give me a hug!" He leaned into Mrs. Holder as she squeezed him. "Oh! It is so good to see you!" She folded Danny's arms down and pushed him back a little to get a good up and down look.

"Put 'er there partner!" Mr. Holder leaned back around his wife and extended his hand. "Good to see you. Ya sure picked a cold night to be out! How ya feelin'?" Danny pulled his arm back, but did not answer right away.

Jessica spoke up before he could answer, "Hi, Danny Lee."

"Hey, Jess." he answered. The two gazed at each other briefly before Jessica's signature blush emerged, then turned away.

"I'm all right, I guess," Danny finally answered Mr. Holder. "We just went to a doctor to talk for a while."

"Oh! You and your parents go to a counselor?" Mrs. Holder inquired, hungry for gossip. Mr. Holder slightly pinched her elbow, embarrassed. "Yes, ma'am. We went so we could kinda … kinda say what we're all thinking." "Well, that's good, Danny, real good!" Mr. Holder stated, then finished the conversation with, "You tell your mom and dad we wish 'em the best!"

"Yes, sir. Ya'll have a good night." Mr. and Mrs. Holder smiled and nodded politely to Danny as he turned to walk away.

Jessica spun around to look at Danny once more and softly called, "See ya, Danny Lee."

Two hours later, Danny strode into the kitchen dressed in his long thermal pajamas and thick socks, ready for bed. "G'nite, Momma." he said as Sarah loaded the dishwasher.

"Goodnight? You're usually the last to turn in on a Friday!" she said, surprised. "You feeling all right? Anything wrong?"

"No," he said, "I think I just ate too much and my brain is tired."

"Oh! The ol' splodin'-full-belly-tired-brain syndrome, huh?" Sarah diagnosed, tickling her son, "That's the worstest and most serioustest of all the dromes. Well, okay. We'll see you in the morning. I love you." She bent over, hugged and kissed her son, then spat him on the behind, "Snickle britches!"

"'Nite, Mom." he mumbled, heading toward his father's study.

Danny peeked through a crack in the door and watched his father make a fire then light his pipe.

Tommy looked up from his desk as Danny pushed the door open slightly, "Hey, tiger!" You cold? It ain' that bad. Thanksgiving's just a week away." Danny sat on his knees in one of the arm chairs and leaned over his father's desk.

"Daddy?" He asked, timidly.

"What? You okay? You … you wanna talk or something?" He pushed back his chair and approached his son. Danny quickly stood in the arm chair and embraced his father.

"I love you." he said.

"I love you, son!" Tommy replied, swaying with his boy.

Late that night, Tommy and Sarah woke up to the sounds of Danny screaming. After rushing down the hall, they threw open the door to Danny's bedroom. Danny sat upright in his bed, yelling "He shot her! Dad! He shot her!" "Whoa, whoa! Sshhh," Tommy and Sarah comforted. "You're all right! Nobody shot anyone. It's just a dream. You're okay."

"Tommy, he's shaking!" said Sarah, hugging her son.

"Get him some water, will ya, hon?" Tommy asked. "Danny, look at me! You're okay, it was just a dream."

"Dad!?" Danny explained, "I saw him! I saw him shoot her and she fell out of the … "

"Okay, okay. Slow down!" Tommy interrupted. "Tell me now exactly what you saw!"

"He … well, he … " Danny began, then stopped to rub his eyes.

"What's wrong? Your eyes bothering you?"

"I can't see … it's … red!" he answered, opening his eyes wide then squinting.

"Red?" Tommy asked concernedly. "What's red? What do you mean?"

Danny rubbed his eyes once more, pointed to over Tommy's right shoulder and explained, "That light … it's red!"

"Son … what light? Where do you see it?"

"Right here." Danny answered, slowly reaching up. Unbeknownst and invisible to Tommy, just above his right shoulder, was a thin strip of brilliant red light. Shaped like an oversized toothpick, the light glowed with a slight pulse.

Danny waved his finger into the red light. His body flung backwards onto the bed with animalistic moans emanating from his open mouth. "Sarah! Call an ambulance!" Tommy screamed, thinking Danny was experiencing what could be more readily identified as a diabetic seizure.

Danny's body lurched, contorted and twisted as his mind was overrun with the entire history of Tommy's life in pictures. Like going to a large drive in movie theatre, Danny saw a big screen of memories and events from Tommy's life with hundreds of tiny television sets surrounding it, showing the smaller, less significant snapshots of his life. His seizure lasted the entire ambulance ride from the house to the hospital. While being wheeled to the ER, the tiny televisions in Danny's mind abruptly stopped. The big screen took over and rolled by what looked more like a movie preview than a memory. Although slightly blurred, he could see the distinct images of two figures moving about. He also heard the sound of a single, muffled voice and heavily pouring rain. In his mind, he saw one of the figures lift its arm and aim a gun ...

'Tis the Season

A few hours later, Dr. Rankin reviewed the X-ray results with Tommy and Sarah. "From the pictures we took the day of the wreck," he explained, pointing to the older set of proofs, "we weren't able to see any hemorrhaging or major damages to the spine … the cervical disks were all right … no compaction or pinching of the spinal chord. He did, however, suffer some whiplash, but for being in a coma and lying still for so long, he kind of underwent his own therapy without the need for drugs or a neck brace and so forth."

"Now," he said, holding up the newest set of prints, "we can almost lay tonight's X-rays directly on top of the old ones … "

"Could there be brain damage we can't see? Something inside?" Tommy asked, looking closely at the negatives.

"Well, sure." Dr. Rankin agreed. "He could have something like axonal diffuse syndrome and we not know about it until later. We can only see so much with an X-ray. This won't show every minuscule nerve or any deep internal damage to the white matter, but it does give us a good look at the big picture of what's going on."

"Well that doesn't really tell us anything then does it?" Sarah snapped as she lit a cigarette. "Why was he floppin' 'round like that? His eyes rolled into his head then nuthin'! Nuthin'!"

"What she's sayin' is … " Tommy apologized, taking the cigarette out of her hand, "if you're not showing anything to be wrong with him … then what's wrong with him?"

"I can understand your frustration."

"Frustration?" Sarah blasted, "My son was rollin' 'round in his bed lookin' like, like … for twenty minutes! Frustrated?"

Irritated with Sarah's interruptions, Dr. Rankin slammed a file on his desk and sternly said, "Look! Danny had a closed wound head injury, whiplash, and a severe concussion. He was comatose shy of four months and woke up just six weeks ago. His friends are dead; he's missing four months of his life and you just this evening completed the first of many counseling sessions! From what I can see, I can't explain right now why he went into a seizure. But, what I can do … is pray with you; keep him overnight, run some tests and hopefully, find what caused this and stop it from happening again!" He looked at the couple for a moment, giving them time to absorb the chastising.

"Can I see my baby?" Sarah meekly asked.

Danny lay fast asleep as a nurse monitored and recorded his readings. She noticed Tommy and Sarah as they entered the room and greeted them, smiling "All his vitals are stable. I hope you don't mind me saying, but, for what this boy's been through tonight and these past few months? He's got a lot of angels watching over him." With that the nurse shook their hands and exited quietly.

"He looks so peaceful … " Sarah commented.

"Probl'y worn plum out … " Tommy added. Danny stirred briefly then fluttered open his eyes.

"Hey! How ya doin,' Superman?! How's my boy?" they asked. "Dad!" he said, surprised, "You're okay?" Danny sat up in his bed and hugged his father tightly. "What happened? I saw you … " he began, but stopped in mid-sentence and looked about the room.

"What? Saw what? What'd you see?" Tommy and Sarah asked.

"You got shot! I saw you, by the car … " Danny exclaimed.

"No, no, Daddy's okay. I'm not shot. I'm right here. Daddy's not hurt," The two loving parents reassured.

"But I saw it!" Danny insisted with a quivering chin, "Just like before the wreck at the grocery store! You were … "

"Hey, c'mon now. This was just a bad dream," Tommy insisted. "That's all there is to it. I know sometimes how bad dreams can seem real! But, listen to me: I'm not shot now, haven't been shot and ain't gonna be shot."

"Sshhhh, ssshhhh," Sarah added, placing her finger over her son's lips.

Saturday, three weeks later. Tommy and Danny stood in the front door entryway preparing to go into the city for some Christmas shopping. "Now ya'll be careful!" Sarah warned as she entered the vestibule with Danny's gloves. "The wind is supposed to be on the leading side of this storm and if it hits late enough, you'll be sure to hit some black ice on the way home! So be careful! But hurry!" Tommy opened the door and an icy gust slashed through the foyer. "I love you," she said to Tommy with a kiss then knelt down to Danny for a quick embrace. "And I sure do love you!" Father and son ran down the steps to the squad car and hopped in. As they pulled out of the driveway, Sarah waved goodbye, then walked the length of the wrap around porch to the other side of the house. Dark, ominous clouds hung low on the horizon.

Just as Sarah predicted, the winter storm hit hard and earlier than originally predicted. The storm also brought with it a rare and incredible show of green and purple strikes of lightning. Due to the tall, downtown buildings and intensity of the lightning, Tommy was unable to tune into a radio station. "Man alive!" he declared, "I ain't never seen so much lightning. You ever see lightning like this, Dano?"

Danny shook his head as he gazed out the front windshield, "Nah … not like this."

"Augh! Stupid radios!" Tommy slapped at the dial. "More trouble than what they're worth! Awww! Now what?" he moaned as the traffic slowed to a complete standstill.

"Why don't you turn on your sirens and go see what's ahead?" Danny suggested, sitting up to get a better view.

"Well, son?" Tommy enlightened, "the bozos, I mean the locals, are on it, hopefully, and … I have no jurisdiction over city operations.

Plus, we're packed in too! I'm afraid we're stuck for a few. Plus with this bad weather, I think that … " Tommy's words seemed to drift and fade as Danny noticed Dale sitting in a car, going in the opposite direction on the far side of the two-lane street. The traffic loosened up and both directions slowly resumed their movement.

"Dad! There he goes! It's him!" Danny hollered, slapping Tommy on the right arm. "Him?" asked Tommy "What are ya talking about? Him who?"

"The guy who hit us and shot his girlfriend!"

Tommy looked his son squarely in the eye, "Say that again!"

"It's the guy who hit us!" he cried. "The guy who shot his girlfriend and the couple at the store! It's him!"

"Son, who told you that?" Tommy questioned, attempting to play down the situation.

"Nobody told me nothing! I saw it!" Danny testified.

"Come on now, stop it!" Tommy ordered, pulling his son back down on the seat, "That's enough!" "Son," he explained gruffly, "you weren't looking, you were watching me … and you … "

"Just go look! Please!" he implored. Tommy looked in his side mirror as Danny continued his begging. "You can at least go see? If it's not him, then it's not him, but you just gotta go! Dad?"

"If you're wrong we don't talk about this anymore! Okay?" Danny bounced in his seat with delight. "You get me? No more! But if you're right, then, um, then, okay you were right! But just this once!"

"All right!" Danny shouted excitedly as he slapped at the dashboard.

"Turn on my radio … " Tommy said, then called out on his CB, "four twenty-seven to base, four twenty-seven to base." The lightning was causing too much static to get reception. Danny turned around in his seat to watch the mystery car.

"He's getting ready to turn, Dad! He's gonna turn!" he announced as Dale's car stopped at the corner.

"Four twenty-seven to base!" Tommy called once more but still received no response. He turned on his emergency lights and made with a couple of yelps from the siren as he made a U-turn.

"Woo Hoo! Jus' like Gene Autry!" Danny cheered, snapping his seat belt. "Go git 'im, Dad!" Tommy again called on the CB, "Four twenty-seven to base." Dale heard the siren and saw the flashing red and blue lights in his rearview mirror. As soon as Tommy's squad car completed the U-turn, Dale hopped the curb, riding half way up onto the sidewalk then rounded the corner with a squeal of his tires.

Tommy, too, rode up onto the edge of the sidewalk to make it past the slow moving traffic. He accelerated so as to not lose sight of the fleeing vehicle as the rain beat down hard on the windshield. After traveling a couple of blocks, Tommy thought that he might have lost the mystery car. "Well … Dano?" he addressed his son, still panning the side streets, "Looks like we … "

"Dad! There it is! There it is!" Danny shouted triumphantly, looking back over Tommy's shoulder.

"Where? Where is it?"

"Back there in the alley!" Danny answered. "Hurry!" Tommy fishtailed in the middle of the street, doubled back and turned slowly into the remnants of an older warehouse district.

He pulled up behind the parked and abandoned car. The engine was still running and both the driver and passenger doors stood wide open. "Four twenty-seven to base," Tommy called on his radio. "Officer needs assistance at the intersection of Patterson and Cunico. I repeat, officer needs assistance at the intersection of Patterson and Cunico." Not wanting to wait for a response, Tommy firmly instructed Danny, "Son, I need you to get on down in the floorboard!"

Danny unbuckled his seat belt and started to climb over the bench seat. He paused to tell his father, "Thanks for believing me, Dad!"

"Well, whoever he is," Tommy continued "whether your right or wrong, he sure took off. Got a guilty conscience over sump'n.' Question is, what?" They held each other in their gaze and shared a quiet moment before Tommy lovingly spanked Danny's behind, "Go on! Git!"

Tommy exited the car into the pouring rain and opened the back driver side door. He pulled the seat back down, exposing the trunk, and yanked out a blanket, "You stay down, ya hear? I'll be right back. Right back! Okay?" He leaned in to give Danny a reassuring hug and kissed him on the head. Tommy closed the door and took stock of the situation. The weather, coupled with the lack of radio response and inhospitable surroundings, wedged an uneasy feeling in his gut. Danny watched his father until condensation covered the windows. Once Tommy departed, Danny laid himself down and pulled the blanket over his head.

With his gun drawn, Tommy drew close to a corrugated metal covered warehouse. He poked his head around the corner and on the next building, noticed a large bay door drawn halfway open. "The Lord is my shepherd, I shall not want;" Danny whispered, "He maketh me to lie down in green pastures … " Tommy approached the warehouse and cautiously made his way inside. The only light in the building emanated from a few busted out painted windows bordering the catwalk above. The sound of the rain on the metal roof was not only deafening, but disorienting and confusing. Because he could not clearly distinguish what sounds came from where, Tommy was constantly turning in circles as he crossed the warehouse floor. Near the end of the warehouse he spied a stairwell going down to a lower level. As he neared the stairs, he could see a metal fire door at the bottom, opened just slightly with no light. He looked above and all around, trying to muster the courage to walk down the dark concrete staircase. One by one, he crept down the musty steps. He braced himself against the wall and prepared to enter the basement, pulling his gun up close to his shoulder. Just as he placed his boot at the base of the door to give a kick, a gunshot rang out.

Under their breaths, father and son called out to one another in quiet panic:

"Dad!"

"Danny!"

Danny prayed fervently, "He leadeth me beside the still waters; He restoreth my soul; He leadeth me in the paths of righteousness … " Tommy raced up the concrete stairs, through the warehouse and into the rain, all the while repeating, "Danny! Danny!" He ran to the corner of the warehouse and snuck a quick glance around. The squad car and mystery car were just as he left them. He looked above and all around before making his way out into the open, then darted to the back of the squad car, careful to stay crouched down. He raised his head to see his son still hunkered down under the blanket.

"Danny!" Tommy whispered coarsely. "Danny, it's okay … it's me. C'mon, it's all right, you can come out now." Danny heard the mumbling and hesitated to rise, unable to discern who was speaking. Tommy then knocked on the window loudly and raised his voice "Danny! C'mon, son! It's all right!"

All the while, behind Tommy and hidden by a stack of wooden pallets, Dale had been lying in wait. He stepped out from behind the stack of pallets and walked up to Tommy. Danny sat upon his haunches and completely lowered the blanket from his head. His heart skipped a beat as he suddenly found himself remembering the scene from the movie in his head. He watched, helplessly, as Dale placed his .38 revolver to Tommy's right temple and squeezed the trigger. Blood and tissue splattered the window as the bullet breached his skull.

Danny braced himself against the door, speechless and shocked at what he just witnessed. Dale then dashed to his car and drove away, leaving Danny in the backseat to himself, his prayers, and his dead father on the ground. Tommy's body lay on the cold concrete in a spreading pool of blood. The rain was turning to ice.

Fold #2

November, 1986. Danny maneuvered listlessly through the melee of teenagers as they rushed to beat the tardy bell for their next class. He, however, was in no hurry at all to reach Mr. Townsend's biology class, a subject he had been performing poorly in all semester. Danny, now seventeen and a senior, was accustomed to a majority of his fellow students turning their back to him as he walked the halls. His heart had grown calloused from years of rumors, speculation, horrible lies and ridicule. He couldn't help or hide his past, but that didn't stop the cruel gossip and slander from spreading.

Just as he was nearing the doorway of his classroom, coming from the opposite direction was Jamie Shipman, the starting varsity quarterback with his brood of jock henchmen in tow. They were the popular ones that either everybody hated or dreamed of being just like. Jamie spied Danny and ran straight at him, broadcasting loudly, "He has only seconds to go! Can he make it?" He then lowered his right shoulder and bulldozed into Danny's left side, launching him violently against the wall. Jamie's friends laughed and applauded as he smiled down at Danny and his books, sprawled out on the floor. He thrust his fists into the air victoriously, turned to his friends and arrogantly declared, "He scores!

The Mustangs win!" High fives and derogatory sneers filled Danny's ears as the other players shuffled by.

Sore and embarrassed, Danny picked himself up and entered the room. Keeping his head down, he attempted to pass Jamie unnoticed and take his seat in the last row of desks. "Watch this!" Jamie whispered to one of his teammates as he brought his fingers to his temples. He closed his eyes and started humming. "Hmmmm." Danny stopped to listen, but did not turn to face him. "Ooo, I see a retarded freak not passing his biology test!" Jamie predicted while his friends laughed pitilessly.

From out of nowhere, Mr. Townsend appeared in the doorway just as the tardy bell rang. "Clear your desks please!" he instructed firmly from the hall while kicking up the doorstop. "Cutting it pretty close, aren't we, Miss Holder?" he commented before shutting the door. "Sorry, Mr. Townsend," Jessica said as she passed through the doorway, winded "I had to talk to Mr. Arp about rehearsals for the musical."

"Well, we have a test to take today, so if you don't mind … " he hinted, holding his hand out for her to sit down. Jessica passed Jamie without so much as a glance and took a seat directly next to Danny on the last row.

"How nice of you to join us this morning!" Danny whispered as she situated her belongings. "Can I get you anything? Drink? Something to eat? A cheat sheet maybe?" Jessica put her head down on her desk, shaking from side to side.

"Don't tell me you didn't study!" she said in disbelief. "Danny! You know you can't afford to flunk another test!"

"Ah, I don't care none!" he boasted, slouching in the chair. "What am I gonna do with knowing what a trapezius dorci is?"

"All right, all right!" Mr. Townsend announced, "Your desks should be clear with the exception of a pen or pencil." Danny mocked him as he handed out the tests, desk by desk. Jessica attempted to stifle her giggling as Mr. Townsend dryly commented, "I hope you all studied. This test will count for more than twenty-five percent of your semester grade!"

Jamie slapped the arm of his friend sitting next to him and nodded in Danny and Jessica's direction. Again holding his fingers to his temples and closing his eyes, Jamie boldly predicted, "Hmmmm! Now I see two freaks from weirdoland that aren't gonna pass the test!" Once more, the brainless and heartless band of rude jocks laughed cruelly.

Irritated, Jessica stood in her chair and revealed her own prediction, "Hmmmm! I see … I see … Oh, how exciting! Oh, hmm, wait … a little fuzzy right there!" Jamie's friends looked at Jessica then back to Jamie, amazed at her audacity. "Oh! There it is!" she stated happily. "We're gonna lose another homecoming tonight 'cuz you can't throw!" She opened her eyes and briefly glared at Jamie before stepping out of her desk seat. The other students laughed at Jamie as he panned over their faces, helpless and angered at having the tables turned. "Why don't ya'll just shut up!" he demanded.

He turned around and glowered at Jessica with a snarled lip. Acting as if without a care in the world, she leaned her head and smiled tenderly, batting her eyelashes. To add more insult to injury, she suddenly stretched across the aisle, pulled Danny to her and kissed him on the lips before the entire class. Danny waved smugly to Jamie.

"All right, you two!" Mr. Townsend softly reprimanded with a wink as he placed the tests on their desks, "No teasing the animals!" Jessica turned to Danny and mouthed the words, "I love you."

After the test, Jessica and Danny walked down the hall and out onto the lawn for their lunch hour. From out of nowhere, Jamie jumped in between them and broke their handholding. "Oh, excuse me! I'm so sorry!" he apologized sarcastically with a bow. The rest of the football players slowly passed between the split couple. Before walking away, Jamie taunted Danny, "Look out for that bus, Dad! Bam!"

"You know you're a real jerk, Jamie!" Jessica yelled.

"Don't worry about him!" Danny commented. She threw her books down and started after Jamie. "Don't worry about him!" He again instructed, pulling her back. "I don't care."

"Well, I do!" she grunted, "Ugh! I can't believe people sometimes!" Danny smiled proudly, drawing his lifelong love close to him.

"So … what do ya wanna do for lunch?" he asked before kissing her softly.

"Oh, baby!" she lamented, looking at her watch, "I gotta go to Mr. Arps' class for lunch! You know, the musical."

"Okay … then what time do you want me to pick you up tonight?"

She pondered as he squatted and gathered up her spilled books, "Mmmm ... how 'bout six. That way we can go eat 'fore the game. Okay?"

"Sure. Love you!" he stated, sealing the date with another kiss.

"Love you!" she blurted, returned his kiss and darted across the courtyard. "See you tonight!" she yelled happily, spinning in a circle as she scurried to her rehearsal.

The frigid rain came down in sheets. Puddles of water riddled the football field. Deep ruts of mud and upturned grass scarred the turf from lack of movement of the line of scrimmage. The spectators cowered under their slickers, umbrellas, and tarps on the cold aluminum benches. Danny and Jessica hunkered under a blanket on the uppermost level of the bleachers. With under two and a half minutes left in the fourth quarter, it appeared the fighting Mustangs, led by senior quarterback Jamie Shipman, could win their homecoming by at least three points.

"You wanna Dr. Pepper?" Jessica asked.

"Sure." Danny answered. "You want me to get it?"

"Nah." she replied with a quick smooch, "I'll be right back."

Jamie stepped backwards out of the huddle to get the signals from the sideline for the next play. Just above the coaches heads he spied Jessica walking down the bleachers. The two momentarily made eye contact. She placed one of her fingers to her temples, stuck out her tongue, contorted her face and imitated an awkward throw. He quickly grew irritated as he watched her charade, then stomped back into the huddle. The players exited the huddle and took their positions. Jamie took his place behind the center, received the snap and put the play into motion. Surprisingly, he threw a short pass completion, giving the Mustangs another first down as they drew closer to the end zone. Jamie strutted back to the huddle and held out his hands to Jessica as if to say, "How'd ya like that?"

Jessica returned from the concession stand with the large DP and crawled under the blanket with Danny. With only seconds left on the play clock and a few more remaining in the game, Jamie took a short huddle with his teammates. The young men quickly took their positions, anxious to bury the hatchet. Jamie looked to his right and left, called the play and took the snap. He faded back, looked down the field then to his right. He was momentarily distracted by Danny and Jessica standing at the top of the risers, mocking a pass. The two clowns jumped up and down, missing each others' high fives, all the while shouting to each other "Duuuuhhhh! Gimme de bawl!" With his attention focused on the circus in the stands, Jamie got blindsided by four defensive linemen. One of them hit Jamie's arm with his helmet and forced a fumble. Lying on his back with seven hundred pounds of seniors on top of him, he watched the ball get scooped up and ran back for a touchdown. The Fighting Mustangs were now down by three. Jamie wearily stood himself upright and looked into the rapidly emptying stands. The coach screamed at him as he approached the sideline, grabbing him by the facemask. There was no win and no applause.

Later, parked on the shoulder of a lonely farm road, Danny and Jessica were in the back seat, working themselves into a hot lather. Still in their wet clothes, she straddled his lap and kissed him deeply and passionately. "Whoo! Hold on!" He exclaimed, pushing her back. "Man! What's gotten into you tonight?!"

"What? You don't like it?" she inquired seductively, "Well, I'll just … " and began to climb off.

"Hey! Who said anything about not liking it?" he asked, pulling her back on top of him. "That's the problem. I like it too much!" he admitted. The two love birds smiled at each other. "Hey, I got something." he said excitedly as he reached down under the front passenger seat. "You ever had this?" he asked and exposed a half full bottle of Wild Turkey bourbon.

"Danny Lee Albright!?" she snapped with a devilish grin as she grabbed the bottle "Wild Turkey, huh?! You plan on being a wild turkey tonight?" she questioned, mounted Danny's lap and rotated her hips on his thighs. He watched in amazement as Jessica held the bottle to her lips and took a large swig, allowing a bit of bourbon to run down her chin.

"Hey! Not so much!" Danny advised, yanking the bottle out of her hand. "You gonna get sick! This ain't your daddy's Schlitz!"

She reached down and held his hands, then kissed his fingers as she looked him in the eye. Placing both of his hands on her breasts, Jessica closed her eyes and drew a deep breath, relishing the feelings in her heart and the tingle in her body. She opened her eyes, leaned back against the seats and started to unbutton her blouse. Danny stopped smiling, removed his hands from her chest and pulled her shirt back together. "We don't have to do this, you know?" he informed her as purple flashes of lightning illuminated their faces and rumbles of distant thunder shook the car. "We can wait." he suggested.

Jessica leaned against Danny with her right elbow on the back seat headrest. "I knew ... deep in my heart," she began, lightly running the fingers of her left hand across his face, "since the first day I saw you ... that you're the one I'm gonna spend eternity with ... and you're the one I wanna experience everything with." He sat quietly, mesmerized by Jessica's words. "I love you more than I can ever say." They unabashedly lunged into one another, kissing heavily again with whale-like moans. He started to untuck Jessica's shirt as she kissed his neck.

He leaned back and announced with a chuckle, "I shoulda been giving ya Wild Turkey years ago!" Jessica sat up straight and giggled as she again started to unbutton her blouse. Danny was horrified to see a thin, bright strip of red glowing light suddenly appear above her right shoulder. "Whoa!" he hollered in shock, then turned away with his eyes closed.

"Well, don't let this frighten you," she stated. "I'm not saying we're gonna get married right now ... " He opened his eyes and looked again at the fold of bright light. Images of his father lying on the ground in the frozen rain with a bullet in his head flashed through his mind. "Oh my God! Oh my God!" he repeated anxiously as he wriggled his way from under Jessica.

"I don't think that marriage is the kind of thing some one needs to get so upset over!" she commented sarcastically as Danny climbed over the seat. He sat with his hands over his face, gasping for air. "Baby, are you all right?" she asked tenderly, wrapping her arms around him from the back seat. He lowered his hands and looked in the rearview mirror to see the sliver of red light still above her shoulder.

As Jessica started to pull herself over the seat back, Danny panicked. "Oh, my God! No! No!" He started the car and tore down the road, throwing Jessica backwards.

"Gotta' git you outta here!" he mumbled, sitting close to the steering wheel and slapping at the dashboard. "No! No! No!" Jessica regained her balance and climbed over the seat to join Danny.

"Will you slow down, please? Geez, what is wrong with you?" she asked buttoning the rest of her blouse. "You're acting like ... like ... " she started to say, but stopped and leaned her head against the window.

"Like what?" he asked defensively, "What am I acting like!?"

"You're acting crazy again!" Jessica accused. "What's wrong with you?! We're talking and having fun, then next thing you're driving like there's no tomorrow!"

"Well, if you had seen what I just saw then you'd understand why I feel this way!" he explained.

"Oh ... my ... gosh, Danny! Again?" she complained. Danny listened but kept his eyes on the road. "You don't say anything for seven years and just when I decide to really open up my feelings for you, you pull out this old crap! Geez! My dad was right!" she exclaimed shaking her head in disgust.

"Whoa! Hold on!" he replied with a squint, "What do ya mean your dad was right?"

"Nothing, Danny. Just forget about it!"

"No, no! C'mon!" he persisted, "Let's hear it! What was 'Mr. Perfect-been-around-your-whole-life-daddy' so right about? Huh?" She paused then turned to face him.

After contemplating her words, she admitted "He said that I was wasting my time with you!" The words pierced Danny's heart. "And that you were crazy, you would always be crazy and would never recover from what happened with Bobby, Jimmy, and the others and your dad ... and you would always find some way of not committing to anything!" She turned away with tears running down her face then finished with a quiet and painful realization. "Mainly, he said, you would never commit to me." He didn't answer or look at Jessica, but concentrated instead on driving, keeping his eyes glued to the wet and muddy road.

After a good while of silence Jessica asked, "Where are we going?" and raised her head away from the window.

"I gotta get you outta here ... somewhere safe." Danny answered confidently.

"Oh, Danny, no!" she pleaded and clutched at his right arm. "Just pull over and we can talk this out." Silence. She scooted close to his side and whispered "Danny? Don't you love me?" He glanced down to his left, away from Jessica. "Don't you wanna be with me?" she asked as she touched his face.

"Yes, I do." he admitted lowly, "That's why for right now I need to take you somewhere away from me." and gently pushed her hand away. Feeling jilted, she leaned against the door, curled her knees up and wept.

Danny pulled up in front of a local diner-gas station and parked next to a utility pole with an illuminated spinning sign. He stepped out in the pouring rain and sloshed through several deep puddles to a pay phone to call Jessica's father.

Jessica called out from the car and slapped at the window. "Danny! Please!" she begged, "I'm sorry! Just talk to me!? I love you!" Danny finished his phone call, turned to face Jessica, then sat at the base of the phone pole. As they held each other in their gaze, one prayed to be to be loved, the other prayed for life.

Mr. Holder arrived minutes later. He came to a screeching halt directly in front of Danny's car, climbed out and walked toward the front passenger side. He yelled at Danny as he stood under the telephone light. "What did you do to her!?" He didn't respond to Mr. Holder as he opened the door to help Jessica out of the car. "You're not gonna ruin my daughter's life, too! You stay away! Ya hear me, boy? You stay away from her, you freak!" Jessica nearly fell headlong into the culvert ditch from the force of her father yanking her out of the car.

"Danny? Talk to me!" Jessica pleaded as she tried to break the grip of Mr. Holder. "Danny! Please? I love you!" Danny watched as Mr. Holder aggressively placed Jessica in the front seat of his car.

"Stay away, Danny!" he yelled once more. Danny could see Jessica in the front seat, rocking back and forth, wailing uncontrollably.

He watched the car pull away into the driving rain and felt his heart breaking. He was confused about what he had seen and done and how he hurt Jessica, but convinced himself that sending her away was probably the only thing he could do to save her life.

"It's okay! It's okay … we're going home." Mr. Holder consoled his angel, handing her a towel. "Here, wrap this around you. You're shivering." Jessica grabbed the towel out of her father's hand. "He's gone now, you're all right!"

"I don't want to go home!" she blasted, throwing the towel against the dashboard. "I wanted to stay with Danny! I didn't need for you to come get me!"

"Jess, I know how you feel!" Mr. Holder persisted, "You're just confused right now and … "

"You have no idea how I feel!" she interjected defiantly. "You don't know what he's been through and what he's said to me! You know nothing about … Dad! Look out!" she shouted, startling her father. He had momentarily taken his eyes off the road and inadvertently wandered into the other lane. Mr. Holder overcorrected while heading into a curve and fishtailed into the path of an oncoming truck and trailer. Danny watched the incident from only a few hundred yards away. Mr. Holder's car narrowly escaped a collision with the truck, but went up and over the shoulder, down the culvert ditch and slammed into a utility pole. The truck jackknifed for a few yards, but the driver managed to regain control and steered the vehicle to the shoulder.

Jessica was ejected through the windshield and landed several yards away, face down in a shallow puddle of water. Mr. Holder was knocked unconscious as his head and chest struck the windshield and steering column. The utility pole then crashed down over Mr. Holder's driver's side door, crumpling the frame and door together. Live electrical lines began to dance wildly around the car, causing brilliant flashes of orange, purple and green as they came in contact with the vehicle. Danny hopped in this car and drove to the scene.

Besides the driver of the truck and trailer, Danny was first to arrive at the crash site. He ran through the rain and down the embankment to the wrecked vehicle. He looked in the passenger window to find Jessica not in her seat. "Jess!" he called out in panic, looking all about. "Jess!"

"Hey … hey." Mr. Holder mumbled as he slowly regained consciousness. He looked at the seat next to him, but Jessica wasn't there. Still disoriented, he tried opening his door and hollered "Hey! Somebody get me outta' here!" Flashes of light from the downed lines popped in front of his face. "Jessica! Help me!" he called out anxiously.

"Jess!" Danny cried, spying her body yards away across the water-filled depression. He waded into the knee-deep water calling her name "Jess! Jess!" Jessica, barely alive, suffered from a broken back, cracked skull, a punctured lung and was spitting up blood. He knelt down and gingerly laid her head in his lap. "It's okay. I'm here, baby!" he comforted his love, wiping the hair, grass and blood away from her face. "I'm right here!" he repeated, trying to remain calm. He switched hands to support her neck and saw his fingers covered in blood. "Oh! Oh my God! Oh, baby! Okay, we're gonna git you outta here! You're gonna be great!" he said and attempted to lift Jessica.

"Ow! Ow! Danny!" she screamed. "Don't! Don't move me!" He looked down at her and began to weep. Even when trying to protect her, he couldn't help.

Mr. Holder began yelling, "Somebody! Get me out! Help!" with fear and panic consuming him. The truck driver went down to the vehicle to offer his assistance but could get nowhere near it due to the downed electrical lines.

"Oh, Jess! Jess!" Danny tearfully confessed, "I'm sorry! I'm sorry!"

"Hey, baby. It's okay." she said, trying to smile. "Go on and help Daddy." Danny shook his head sternly. "I'm not going anywhere … I'll be okay. Go and help Daddy." "No! No!" he again refused. "I don't want to leave you! I have to … "

"Shhhh … now. Baby, please, for me," she lightly insisted. "Go help Daddy?"

"Jessica!" Mr. Holder again shouted.

"Okay, but I'll be right back!" he reluctantly promised. "I love you!" he chocked, then embraced Jessica. "I love you Jess! I love you!"

Jessica grinned slightly and blinked her eyes slowly. She looked up at Danny and whispered, "You know I've always … " Danny waited for her to finish her statement as he stared at her open eyes and frozen expression "Jess? Jess!" Shaking her shoulders, he whimpered "No! No! Jess! Oh, God! Oh, God! Jess!" He pulled the love of his life close to him for the last time, rocking her dead body in his arms.

"Jessica! Jessica help me!" Mr. Holder screamed, "Get me out! I smell gas!" Danny gently removed Jessica's head from his lap and laid her down easily in the wet grass. He stood, took one final look at her body, then dashed to the crippled vehicle with Mr. Holder still trapped inside. Like the truck driver, Danny couldn't get close to the car without running the risk of being struck by one of the electrical lines. He could see the flashing lights of the oncoming emergency crews in the distance.

"Hold on, Mr. Holder! They're coming right now!" he yelled.

"Jess! Jess!" Mr. Holder screamed, "Help me, Jess!" One of the power lines came into contact with the roof of the car, sending a cascade of bright orange sparks down the rear window and trunk. The sparks ignited a small pool of gasoline from the cracked fuel line and immediately engulfed the car in flames. Danny and the truck driver listened to Mr. Holder's horrific screams as they watched the fire consume the vehicle. A fire truck arrived first and barreled down the embankment, followed by an ambulance and two county sheriff's vehicles.

While the firemen were busy dowsing the flames, Danny and the truck driver were questioned by the sheriff and his deputy. After telling them all he could about the crash, Danny, with Jessica's blood still on his face and clothes walked to his car, climbed in and drove away into the cold, rainy night.

At around three in the morning, Danny's car ran out of gas and sputtered to the side of the road into a muddy bar ditch. He stayed in the cold car for the next three days and nights, drinking from the bottle of Wild Turkey. He repeatedly fell in and out of consciousness, throwing delusional fits of rage and moaning with ultimate sorrow.

On the third night, he vowed to never go home again. He sincerely believed Tommy Lee and Jessica lost their lives because of him. Now, he reasoned, if he went home, surely his mom would be next to die. Before lying down to sleep, he spoke out loud, "God? Why did you do this to me?" He peered up through the back passenger side window; the sky was clear and there was no moon, but the stars shone brightly. He was cold and alone. Tonight there would be no prayers.

And so It Begins

Tuesday morning. After three days and nights of little sleep, drunkenness, and emotional unrest, Danny finally exited his car to take stock of his immediate surroundings and assess his situation. The rain stopped two days ago, but with the temperature being as low as it was, coupled with the low cloud cover, the road was still wet and the ditches full of water.

He extended his arms high over his head and drew in a deep cleansing breath as he twisted and stretched. He looked up the hill in the direction from which he came on Friday night, then to the rise in the opposite direction. His mind flashed back to the sight of Jessica in his arms and Tommy lying on the ground. The love for his mother and the want to be with her were strong, but not enough to overcome the desire to keep her safe and alive. Thrusting his hands into his pockets, Danny started walking the long and lonely road of a self-imposed exile.

Several hours had passed when he came to a rise in the road that overlooked a cozy little town. Later, he was approaching the city limits sign when he noticed a gas station just beyond by a few hundred yards. He pulled out his wallet to find only seven dollars. Since he had little money, no place to stay and was nearly starving, he had better find a way to get some cash and quick.

A weathered and rusting sheet metal sign read "Charlie Doyle's" above the awning covering the gas pumps. Leaned up against the inside of the office window was a "Help Wanted" sign. One of two bay doors was open and bent over the tire well of a car was Charlie himself.

"C'mon! You stupid … " Charlie blasted at the downed vehicle. Danny cautiously approached, taking in the dirty and unkempt garage.

"'Scuse me." he timidly interrupted.

A muffled "Yeah?" resonated from under the hood.

"Um … I saw the sign that you're looking for help … what kinda help?"

"Any and all I can take and then some." came the reply. "Charlie Doyle," he said, rising up to greet Danny. Danny was shocked to observe a purple-green sliver of light above Charlie's right shoulder. He stood frozen, unable to speak, his mouth agape. "Said the name's Charlie Doyle!" he stated again gruffly and extended his hand.

"Danny, sir … Danny Lee." It took all of his concentration just to answer the old man. "Well, Danny Lee. What can ya help me with?" Charlie asked as he returned to his work.

Danny stared for a moment more at the green beacon of light, then listed his talents. "I can fix starters. Change out your fluids, replace belts … I can do just about anything you want…I helped my daddy rebuild an old car. You know … body work, paint."

"Who's your daddy?" Charlie inquired, "I ain't ever seen you 'round here!"

Danny hesitated then stated, "Oh, you wouldn't know him. I ain't from here."

"Well, where ya from?"

Danny walked around the blocked car as he invented his past, "Back east … near Jersey … a small town you wouldn't a heard of."

Charlie stood up, tossed his wrench in the open toolbox drawer and placed his hands on his hips, "Well, you gotta fill out an application; I gotta get your social sec … "

"Do ya have to?" Danny interrupted, "I mean, I took off a few days ago … and my, uh, my car is broken down several miles back … and I don't wanna go back. I can't go back!" He felt his emotions rise as he explained his situation. "And if you do that, they'll … "

"Am I gonna get in trouble?" Charlie interrupted bluntly, feeling uncomfortable with Danny's appearance and questionable past. "Did ya do something? Huh!? You runnin' boy?" he sternly interrogated. "Don't you lie to me now!"

"No, sir!" Danny stated firmly. "There was some trouble but … I didn't do anything wrong. The point is, sir … I can never go back." Charlie gave Danny's dirty and bloodstained clothes another glance over. After seeing the strain of emotion on his face, he asked concernedly, "You okay?"

"No … no, sir … not really."

"Tell you what I'm gonna do … " Charlie bartered, "I'll start you at six dollars an hour for a week. One week!" He held up his greasy index finger and nodded before continuing. "We'll see how you're doing at the end of the week … and if … *if* you do good … then … I might keep ya 'round, maybe give you a raise." Danny's eyes beamed with joy. "Deal?" he asked with a smile.

"Deal!" he answered zestfully as he shook Charlie's bear-sized hand. He smiled nervously and tried not to shift his eyes to the green and purple light still above Charlie's shoulder. "But you got one week!" he restated. "And I don't want any trouble. None! You savvy!?" "Yes, sir! One week! One week!" Danny concurred, "Thank you, sir! Thank you!"

Charlie tossed a set of keys to Danny from on top of his tool chest. "What are these for?" he asked.

"This establishment has opened at six a.m. every morning for the past twenty-six years," Charlie stated proudly. "Those are the keys to the pumps, doors, and the office. You'll be here no later than five-thirty a.m. and spruce the place up 'fore we open." Charlie continued his instructions as Danny looked at the untidy floor, "I have an extra set of keys in the office. I'll lock up tonight and you be here tomorrow at five-thirty."

Danny agreed to Charlie's instructions and terms energetically, "Five-thirty a.m. Yes, sir! Thank you, sir! I won't be late!" and shook his hand once more. "You won't be sorry!" he guaranteed, pulling out his wallet. "I ran out of gas several miles back … um, do you have an extra gas can?" Charlie pointed to a stack of plastic five-gallon jugs.

As Danny picked out a tank and funnel, Charlie added, "Oh and uh … I'll pay you cash for a while … just so those Jersey folks don't come a lookin for ya."

Danny looked back and replied with a smile, "Yes, sir!"

Danny waddled under the weight of the five-gallon gas jug for nearly eleven miles. Exhausted, he finally reached his car after dark, poured in the gas and drove back to town. It was half past twelve when he opened the back door to the gas station to use the restroom. Examining himself in the bathroom mirror, he was surprised to find clumps of dried blood still in his hair and faint streaks of blood on his forehead and cheek. Thinking himself un-presentable for work the next morning, he filled the sink with hot water, stripped down and washed his clothes. He snuck through the garage, cold and naked, looking for the portable heater he saw earlier in the day. He carried it to the restroom, tied some twine across the stall door and hung his clothes to dry. After hanging the clothes, he submerged several shop rags in the hot water and proceeded to give himself a much-needed sponge bath. Once he was clean and dry, he darted buck-naked across the rear parking lot and jumped into the backseat of his car.

At around four a.m., after only a few hours of restless sleep, Danny opened his eyes and sat up. He wrapped himself up in his blanket, stepped into his tennis shoes and climbed out into the cold darkness to urinate. Standing under a large oak tree in the back parking lot, he shivered in the early morning air, "Whoa! Jeez! It's freakin' cold!" He tried to hurry and drain his bladder with a repeat of his proclamation, "Jeez! It's freakin' cold!" Once finished, he grabbed the keys from the backseat and made a mad dash to the restroom for his warm, dry clothes. Semi-clean laundry never felt so good.

Tommy and Sarah raised Danny right by stressing the importance of doing a good job and doing it right the first time. He swept and mopped the front office, cleaned the windows and started a pot of coffee. Charlie arrived at the four way stop sign a block away and noticed a bright light coming from the direction of his station. He pulled into his parking lot and, to his surprise and delight, discovered the overhead doors already open, the garage floor swept and the concrete still wet from a good rinsing. Sneaking into the office, he noticed a light coming from the bathrooms. He opened the door quietly and found Danny in one of the stalls, mopping the floor with his back turned to the sink. "Boy!" he shouted with a slap on the counter. Startled, Danny jumped, slipped in the mop water and fell down in the stall. "What time did I tell you to get here?"

"Five-thirty, sir." Danny replied, gasping, "You said five-thirty."

"Huh!" Charlie grunted before walking away. "Boy was 'ere 'fore I was. Ain't never been open this early."

One week later, a loud and sudden banging on the passenger window rattled Danny from his backseat slumber. "C'mon! I want to show you something." Charlie commanded, looking down through the glass. Minutes later he was driving Danny through town in the pre-dawn hour. He hung a left at the First Baptist Church and went a few blocks before slowing down.

"Well, there it is." Charlie declared, coming to a stop under a streetlight. Danny leaned forward to look past Charlie at a run-down, two-story house sitting back off the street. "She been living here for as long as I can recall … at least since I first moved to town … that was a long, long time ago. Poor thing!" he lamented.

"Why's that?" Danny asked. "Husband died in fifty-nine and never remarried … stayed widowed … twenty-seven years she been alone." he informed. Danny looked over the dreary home and dilapidated two-story garage apartment in back as Charlie continued "Don't go out of the house none … pretty much let life get the best of her! I'd be willin' to bet, that if you just help her with the house she'd let you stay in that garage for a song."

Later that afternoon, Danny walked past the Baptist church while making his way to the widower's house. When approaching the south fence he heard the sound of children's laughter and then a man's voice say, "Whitney! Whitney, can you pass these out to the kids please?"

A strong, "Good evening!" greeted Danny as he passed a row of cedar trees and came into view of Pastor Tyson Pate. Pastor Pate was on the lawn with a group of very young children and one girl, around eleven years old, with long, dark, curly hair. Danny kept on walking, trying to ignore the smiling pastor as he waved. Suddenly, from above the pastor's right shoulder, a bright strip of purplish-green light appeared. He stopped and stared in amazement. Pastor Pate, thinking Danny wanted to talk, started to walk towards him. Danny, frightened by the sight of another new color of light, abruptly turned away and broke into a run, looking back over his shoulder to the man at the fence.

Thinking that the church was far enough out of sight, Danny slowed himself down to catch his breath. As the old widower's house came into view, he took a mental picture and started mumbling a "to-do list" to himself: the white wooden fence, with its half-unhinged gate was in need of repair and paint; the grass, long and yellow in spots with weeds interspersed, needed cutting and wild rose vines had engulfed the paneling, latticework and guttering.

Danny climbed the squeaky, wooden steps of the porch and knocked on the screen door. The arched windowpanes in the front door were clouded with dust. He faintly heard the sound of footsteps approaching the foyer, but saw no motion through the window. The door then opened with a long, low groan. From the lightless entryway a frail, quivering voice called out, "Yes? Who's there?"

"M … my name is Danny," he said.

"Who?" asked the voice in the darkness.

"Danny!" he repeated loudly. "My name is Danny! Danny Albright!"

"I don't know any Lenny Ballright," the confused woman commented.

"No, ma'am … my … name … is … Danny … Albright!"

"Oh!" she peeped. The bowed out screen door opened slowly and the smiling, five-foot widower exposed herself to the light. With a continuous slight twitching of her head, she gleefully received her unexpected visitor, "Okay, Danny. How can I help you?" He was preparing to answer, but upon seeing a glowing, white sliver of light suddenly appear above her right shoulder, he instead stood silent and transfixed. "You'll have to speak up, hon! These ears don' work like they used to!" Miss Magness admitted.

The garage apartment door swung open and the smell of moldy, wet carpet engulfed Danny. He entered the dark, musty room and felt for a light switch on the wall. He flicked it once or twice, but the bulbs were burnt out. Reaching a little further past the light switch, he gave a mighty yank on the heavy, pine green velour drapes, flooding the lonely apartment with late afternoon sunshine. Ms. Magness hadn't stopped talking since Danny knocked on her door more than half an hour ago. "I'll take it!" he yelled.

"What? 'Scuse me?" she replied, confused.

"I said I'll take it!" he again shouted to his new landlord.

"Oh! Good! Good!" she clapped lightly, pleased to finally have some company. After closing the door, he offered his arm to assist Ms. Magness down the stairs. "Now!" she stated, "First thing I want to talk to you about is the paint ..."

Danny would leave his apartment at five a.m. and return around three-thirty in the afternoon. Ms. Magness would now sit and wait patiently in her front parlor with the drapes open. She followed Danny wherever he went, expectorating an unending barrage of family history, tales of growing up on the plains of Texas and events of the past twenty-seven years without Mr. Magness. The only words Danny need mutter were "You don't say!" "Well, then!" "Amen!" "Uh, huh!" "Well I'll be!" and "Good Honk!" These exclamations served only to fuel her preaching and story telling.

December twenty-third, 1986. All day long Danny watched the low hanging clouds speed by, driven on by fierce and bitter winter winds. It wasn't until after he left the garage that the swift winds died down and a light snow began to fall.

Later that evening, he decided to go for a walk. A thick dusting of white covered the streets, roofs, and cars. Christmas lights glowed through the falling flakes. All was peaceful as he neared the fence of the Baptist church. Just as he reached the row of cedar trees, a car slowly rounded the corner, turned off its headlights and coasted to the curb near the side entry of the enclosed churchyard. For some strange reason, he quickly ducked below the brick and wrought-iron fence. He poked his head above the wall and saw a young girl, maybe in her late teens, exit the car, carrying a basket. She quietly lifted the gate latch and tip-toed to the door leading to Pastor Pate's room and the day care center. Danny watched curiously as she knelt down, rustled with the basket for a moment, covered it with a blanket and dashed back to the waiting car. She entered on the passenger side and rode past a few houses with her door open. Once the vehicle was down the street a ways, it accelerated and she slammed her door.

Danny looked around; no cars, no one walking by, and all porches were free of movement. He stealthily approached the gate, keeping his eye on the basket. As he pushed open the gate, he saw a shadow of movement inside the church sanctuary. A tiny whimper and subtle movement of the basket peaked his curiosity. Thinking himself quite clever, he briskly crossed the sidewalk, keeping in mind to step only in the tracks left by the young girl. He crouched down to investigate and delicately peeled back the blanket. Inside he found a baby boy, not more than a few months old, dressed in a light blue one-piece sleeper with teddy bears and sheep printed in yellow and white.

Danny picked up the tiny child and wrapped him gently in the blanket. The boy was obviously physically retarded and was born with a cleft lip. The mother, not yet willing or ready to accept her responsibilities, just up and decided to disappear into the night, content with abandoning a piece of her life. The baby let loose with another whimper. Danny made a small attempt to provide some kind of fatherly protection. "Ssshhh! I'm right here," he smiled, gingerly bouncing the boy in his arms. "It's okay now. You know where you are? Hmm? You're in a safe place." He pointed to the side of the church, illuminated with the silhouette of a cross. "He's here with you now!" With baby in hand, Danny stood up and prepared to knock at the door. Something, however, stopped him from knocking.

He knelt down and placed the infant back in his basket, then walked to the fence and unlatched the gate. Taking his stance to "ding-and-dash," Danny looked over his escape route and prepared to run. He banged on the door and rushed toward the gate. The sidewalk was slick from the snow, causing him to slip and slide out into the street. While struggling to get to his feet, he saw the shadow of Pastor Pate approaching the doorway. He finally secured his footing and tore around the corner of the wrought-iron fence. Pastor Pate opened the door, reached down, gently removed the baby from the basket and stepped out onto the sidewalk. He saw Danny running down the street and yelled out, "Thank You! God bless you! Merry Christmas!"

As he ran, the memories of Christmases past with his family consumed his mind. The pictures in his head were interlaced with the disturbing visions of Tommy's and Jessica's deaths. Tears streamed down his face as he raced to his apartment. In his mind he could still hear Pastor Pate yelling "Merry Christmas" as he took the stairs two and three steps at a time.

He burst into his small, dingy room breathless and angry. There was no tree, no gifts, no lights, no family, and most importantly; no love. He paced about anxiously, then yelled mournfully, "I hate you, God!" He flung himself on his couch and shook his fists as his torn soul cried out "Augh! Why me, God? Why?"

1988

Butch forged his way through the dense and twisted mix of mesquite and cedar trees, tall Buffalo grass, Indian paintbrushes and bluebonnets. He and three officers from the Ellis County Sheriff's Department were near the northernmost tip of Lake Sawyer, a couple of miles southwest of Alma. Just a few hours earlier, a hitchhiker stumbled upon the body of a young girl while looking for a shady spot to escape the mid-August heat.

"She ain't been moved since we called … we were waiting for the coroner to get here." Deputy Leon Radakowski stated as he, the other officers and Butch steered themselves through the trees.

"Anybody touch her? Move her?" Butch asked.

"Nope. Scared the hitcher plumb to death, though!" Leon chuckled, desensitized to the thought and sight of a dead body. "He ran back up to I-forty-five and thumbed down a truck … almost got himself runned over." Butch and Leon were first to breach the small clearing where the girl's body lay in deep, thick grass. Butch stood directly over the head of the young girl, removed his sunglasses and tipped his hat back a bit.

"Anybody been walkin' 'round 'ere?" Butch called out as the other two deputies emerged from the thicket.

"Nah," Leon answered, "This is the only path we walked on. So as far as we can tell … we think we still got a clean scene … we think."

As he listened to the deputy, Butch closely examined the deceased youth. She was lying face up with her open and lifeless eyes staring out into space. She would have stood near five-foot-three and had dark, curly hair with eyes of brownish green. He estimated her to be twenty-two to twenty-four years of age. Her skin was tanned and she had beautiful, broad, full lips that barely covered her straight and snow white teeth. Her hands and wrists bore no evidence of a struggle and there was no bruising about the neck or throat. None of her fingernails were broken and all of her jewelry was intact. She was completely clothed, her shoelaces were tied and there appeared no visible signs of rape or molestation. The only telltale sign of her actually being dead and not asleep, other than her eyes being open, was the single, clean gunshot wound to the left side of her chest.

"This guys's pretty good, ain't he?" Leon commented with a smirk as Butch continued his preliminary investigation, circling the body.

Butch squatted down and inquired, "Why do you say that, deputy?"

"Well," Leon began with a quick glance to his cohorts for support, "He really didn't leave us any evidence."

"Good!" Butch patronized as he wrote in his notebook. "But what makes you think it's a he that did this? Why are there no signs of any environmental disturbance, Deputy Radakowski? Or better yet, answer me this, why is there no supporting evidence of the homicide taking place here? How do you know this was even a homicide? Could of been a double suicide attempt and the second party didn't go through with it!?"

Radakowski stumbled as he tried to support his comment "He, uh … well most of those who, uh, commit homicides are, um … male … and, uh … more than likely … uh."

"Because this is not the true crime scene, Deputy Radakowski!" Butch interrupted bluntly. "This is merely the dump site … the geographical location chosen specifically for the disposal of evidence and for marking the end of a single, intentional transaction … a very well-thought out transaction at that if I may add."

"Yes, he is good." Butch agreed as he scrutinized the leaves on the trees and kicked through the deep grass. "Statistically speaking, Mr. Radakowski … the perpetrators of homicides are predominantly single, white, males between the ages of twenty-three and thirty-seven.

They have a history of having suffered through and endured a variety of substance, sexual, psychological and physical abuses or combinations thereof. So in turn, they commit their crimes of passion to show off their skills, their supposed intellectual superiority, power, authority and control … they use all of these as a cover for what really comes down to as an extreme act of rebellion, regret, or vengeance!" Radakowski and his fellow deputies remained silent during the lecture.

"Know why I think we're gonna have our work cut out for us on this one?" Butch motioned for the deputy to bend down with him beside the body. The others leaned in close to listen and broaden their horizons. Butch reached over the girl's chest, grabbed her shoulder and rolled her onto her side, revealing the exit wound and slightly pressed, clean, green grass.

"Where's her blood?" he whispered.

1993

It was a dry and windless July day. The blazing sun bore down hard as Butch and the Henderson County sheriff, B. W. Saggaser, trudged through the rows of freshly turned topsoil at Norwin Kirby's peanut and watermelon farm. Norwin's farm was southeast of Athens off highway 175 and just a few miles west of Lake Athens.

"I found her when I was about to start on the northeast corner," Norwin explained as they walked. "I don't usually get out and look around while I'm drivin,' but I thought I saw a large animal or something near the well head. When I came up close enough, that's when I realized this ain't no animal!" Sure enough, just as Norwin described, there lay the body of a girl in her mid-twenties, face up and dead in the dry, red dirt. She had long brown hair that was slightly curly on the ends, was wearing jean cut off shorts and a Hondo's restaurant t-shirt with one single gunshot wound to the left side of her chest. Her skin was clean with no visible bruising, nor were there any open wounds about the face, neck, throat, or abdomen. There were no foreign materials such as skin tissue, fabric or hair fragments, under her finger nails or blood splatters on her or the ground around her; she was also completely drained of her blood.

Minus the fresh shoe prints of Butch, Norwin and B. W., there were no other tracks about the girl. Butch had seen this before.

1999

Luther Carmichael and his son, Brett, woke up early and drove southwest of Emory to the Sabine River for a long day of fishing. The humidity was high and although there was a steady breeze blowing, they enjoyed little to no cloud cover. While walking through some high weeds and grasses, Luther spied the body of a young girl lying in the shallows on the other side of the river, barely visible through some low hanging branches of a willow. He held his arm out to the side and stopped his son, saying, "Stay here! Do not move!" Brett took his father's tackle and watched him slowly ramble across the river.

Luther waded to the opposite shore and cautiously approached the corpse, bending slightly to investigate. "What's wrong?" Brett yelled anxiously from the riverbank. Luther turned to respond when all of a sudden, a possum quickly darted from the dark and wet recesses of the willow. Startled, he let loose with a high-pitched squeal and slipped on the rocks in his rubber waders, falling backwards on his rear into the river.

"Call 911!" he yelled as he tried to regain his footing.

"What?!" Brett hollered back. The wind, water and distance distorted his father's voice, proving it difficult to understand what he was saying.

"Call the police!" he again shouted.

Brett dropped the poles and tackle to find his cell phone. He finally located it in his vest pocket and raised it triumphantly to his father. Luther stared at the girl's feet and hesitated to approach again as he was unsure about the condition of the torso or if another animal was lurking about, just waiting to pounce. Out of the corner of his eye, he could see Brett rustling about on the shore. Brett held up the phone and shrugged his shoulders. "Keep trying!" he urged.

"Nine-one-one" a voice finally answered.

"I got 'em! I got 'em!" Brett shouted jubilantly.

"What's your emer … Hello? … Is there?" The line was full of static, making it almost impossible for him to hear the operator, then he lost the signal and the line went dead. Frustrated, he waved for his father to come help. Luther crossed the river, took the phone with him up the hill and tried calling again, this time getting stronger reception. His call was answered quickly and immediately redirected to Butch's office, who had now been with the Texas Rangers for five years. Butch answered the phone and, like a dam bursting, Luther hurriedly unleashed an incoherent torrent of information as he explained what had happened.

After giving Butch the directions to where he could find the girl's body, he tried his best to describe her condition, albeit he saw very little.

"Well, thanks for calling, Mr. Carmichael. We'll have somebody there, shortly."

"No problem. I just wanted to make sure someone knew about her before the pigs and coyotes got a hold of her." Luther offered.

"Right." Butch agreed. "Say, are you near the body, right now?"

"Uh, yeah, well, not too close, but I'd say I'm about twenty, thirty yards away."

"I wondered if you could do me a small favor and tell me if you see anything particular?"

"Uh, anything like what?"

After a pause Butch replied, "A gunshot wound to the left side of the chest?"

Just One of Many

As of summer 2005, Danny was still living in the tiny, one bedroom garage apartment, even though Mrs. Magness passed away in December of 1988. Mrs. Magness' only daughter, Charlotte, inherited the house and tried to sell it after she and her husband, Gary, cleaned it up a bit. But after having it listed for just over a year, the house hadn't sold. So, Charlotte took it off the market and Danny agreed to pay half his normal rental rate in exchange for monitoring and taking care of the house in his off hours and weekends.

As he was walking to work early one Saturday morning, he passed by the church playground and observed Pastor Pate sitting at a small picnic table, drinking his coffee and reading the Dallas morning paper.

Upon hearing his footsteps, Pastor Pate raised his head to greet Danny as he passed, "Looks like it's gonna be another beautiful day, eh, Danny?" But as usual, like he'd done for years, Danny simply ignored the sincere solicitation and kept his pace, acting as if he hadn't heard. Not to be deterred, Pastor Pate leaned over slightly and raised his voice as Danny turned the corner, "Have a great day!"

Just after lunch, a new, black Acura DMX pulled up to the gas pumps at Charlie Doyle's garage. Danny casually sauntered out of the office and greeted the driver as he exited the vehicle, "Fill it up for ya?"

"Sure! Please!" the man replied. Danny looked him over as he began fueling his car, spying a splinter of white light above the man's right shoulder. The driver, in his mid-fifties, walked around the shiny SUV, gloating as he admired his new purchase.

"Where ya headed to?" Danny asked, as the man stretched his legs, raising them higher and higher with each step.

"Phoenix!" he proudly replied. "Gonna' go meet the missus. She flew out two weeks ago to get the new place settled while I've been tying up the loose ends here." "Mmm, Phoenix!" Danny purred. "Heard it's nice. Pretty hot though, ain't it?"

"Yeah, but it's a dry heat." he commented as Danny tightened the gas cap and replaced the nozzle. "Just heat. Very little or no humidity, or at least not like home." Danny walked behind the man to his right and waved his left hand through the white light. His mind was immediately, but briefly, consumed by a scene of beauty and tragedy; he envisioned a man standing on the green of a beautiful golf course preparing to take a swing then suddenly fall over dead. "Forty-two fifty, please." He stated softly as the two walked to the office. "Where's home?" Danny asked, standing at the register behind the counter.

"Leesville!" the man declared while handing Danny three twenties. "Just outta Fort Polk. Sold our old house on the Whisky River."

"Wow! That's gonna to be quite an adjustment." Danny stated. As he handed back the change and closed the drawer, he followed up with, "Ya think yer up to it?"

"Sure! Heck, I'm only fifty-three!" the man admitted with a smile and pat of his belly.

"Well, thanks for stopping by and, uh, good luck to ya'll in Phoenix." Danny offered as he and the man exited the office. The driver turned around and proclaimed, "Thanks. Looking forward to nothing but sun 'n golf!"

Danny darted back into the office and reappeared at the door holding a Polaroid instant camera. "Hey!" he hollered to the driver as he neared the end of the car, "Smile!" Without really stopping to think about it, the man struck an impromptu pose by raising his foot and resting it on the back bumper. He flashed an insincere smile and leaned over with his elbow on his knee. The synthetic smile quickly disappeared once Danny took the picture. The man then squatted down to look at where he had just placed his foot. He licked his finger and wiped off the slight smear of dirt, smiling arrogantly to himself.

Danny pulled the film out of the Polaroid, flapping it in the air as he approached the man and explained, "I take pictures of all our new customers. You know, vacationers, visitors. Not that many people moving into town."

"Right … " the man affirmed unsteadily. He climbed into his car, started it up and tore his way out of the shaded carport onto the highway.

Danny looked at the slowly developing picture, waving it every few seconds. He went back to the office, walked around the counter and picked up the handset on an old, black rotary style phone. He dialed the number "0" and spoke with an operator, "Phoenix, Arizona. The Phoenix Sun? Thanks. Subscriptions please." While waiting to be connected, he pulled out a large spiral notebook and began entering numbers and dates onto a clean page. He then stapled the picture of the man to the paper and noted the time when the picture was taken. "Yeah, I need to order a paper please. Thanks, but no, not a whole subscription, just one or two days. Yes, please." Danny read over the new entries in his journal as he answered the telemarketer's questions, "Um, let's see, Monday, August twenty-third through Wednesday, August twenty-fifth." He paused momentarily, then asked, "Say, instead of getting the whole paper and all, is there any possible way ya'll can just send me the obituaries for those days?"

The Catalyst

Later that same afternoon, Danny closed the garage and walked two blocks past the Snazzy Pig restaurant to Jigger's, the local liquor store. Beth, who usually worked the late shift and weekends, looked through the wrought iron bars covering the window and saw Danny approaching. She immediately reached for her canister of pepper spray under the register and stepped back as far away from the counter as she could.

Danny entered the liquor store and walked directly to the bourbon aisle for a bottle of Wild Turkey 101. Beth remained leaning against the shelf behind the register when Danny, still dirty from his day at work, slammed the bottle on the counter, startling her. He didn't try to hide his cruel chuckle as he rifled through the pockets of his cut-off camouflage pants. "Thirty-two twenty-five." she bluntly stated. He pulled out a wad of crumpled and filthy one-dollar bills and change, a few nuts and bolts and a lighter. He counted the money into three stacks of one-dollar bills, plus two singles and a quarter. "Hey, you have a great night, Beth!" he patronized as he picked up his bottle and opened the door. The bells on the door handle jingled with a bright but false ring of merriment as Beth stood her ground, waiting for Danny to disappear from sight. It wasn't until he was clear across the street that she finally relaxed and collected the money from the counter.

Danny drank from his bottle and reviewed the notes in his journal as he aimlessly wandered the streets. He loudly preached his victims names and dates of death and waved his arms wildly about as he relived vision after vision. All passers by would either step out of the way or go so far as to cross the street and stare at him.

It was almost eleven when he climbed the stairs to his small and clammy garage apartment. He opened the door and flicked the light switch. One dull and yellowed bulb hanging from the middle of the living room ceiling sputtered on, barely illuminating the old, putty colored walls. Pizza boxes, hamburger wrappers and burrito tissues were strewn across the kitchen floor. Ashtrays overflowing with extinguished cigarette butts littered the room. Oil and grease stained shirts, shorts, jeans, socks and underwear lay on the backs of the couch and chairs and across the kitchen counter. Dishes, pots and pans, sticky with food and mold filled the sink. Trash heaped as high as the refrigerator handle spilled out onto the plaid, cracked and curling solarium floor.

He tossed his notebook on the grimy kitchen table and hobbled to the stereo with the bottle of Wild Turkey still in his clutches. He turned on his favorite Dream Theatre CD, *Awake*, to prepare him for making another entry on his wall. The walls were littered with Polaroids, ripped pages of scribbled notes and obituaries. Like a time line that a child creates in elementary school, the walls bore witness to Danny's history of pain and years of suffering. From floor to ceiling, starting with the first vision he recorded in 1986, Danny hung his pictures and hand written notations in chronological order. His collection of ghastly predictions completely covered three of the living room walls with the fourth wall more than half way concealed.

The notes and obituaries had red X's and green circles scattered about them. The first few of his recorded visions were marked predominantly with red X's whereas the most recent entries consisted primarily of green circles and checks. He tested himself constantly by staying in his visions for as short a time as possible, yet see how much he could remember. He circled those parts of the premonitions that coincided with those found in the obituaries: dates of death, cause, where, even down to the point of what time of death and who would be the one to find them. Red wrong, green right. As he sat at the table and wrote in his journal, James Labrie sang his favorite song, "Voices;"

> Voices were calling me
> "Feeling threatened?
> We reflect your hopes and fears."
> Voices discussing me
> "Don't expect your own Messiah
> This netherworld which you desire
> is only in your mind"

At three a.m., in an emotional, drunken fit of rage, Danny exited his apartment. With his whiskey bottle in hand, he stumbled down the stairs and staggered out into the street. With all the candor of a town crier, he spewed forth the names and dates of those who had already met their demise. He also recited the names of those whose had not yet come to pass, including the conditions under which they were to die. Curtains, shutters and doors parted open a bit to see from where, or from whom, the disturbance was coming.

As he approached the end of his street, he noticed that the stained glass foyer of the First Baptist Church was dimly illuminated and could see movement inside. He unsteadily climbed the narrow red brick staircase and cracked open one of the large, white, solid wood double doors. Like a restless child peeking down a hallway for a glimpse of Santa Clause at Christmas, Danny poked his head in and softly called out, "Hello!? God? You in there?" Upon receiving no response, he laughingly pulled the door open to let himself in. The foyer was empty, but the candles were lit. Through the bottom of the sanctuary doors, he again noticed a shadow of movement. With his curiosity peaked, he decided to enter the sanctuary. It was the first time for him to be in a church since his father's death in 1976. Taking a few steps down the aisle between the sections of pews, he looked about for who, or what, created the shadows.

"Oh there you are!" he exclaimed sarcastically to the cross above the podium. "Well," he proclaimed, "Here I am, Lord! What? No response? Hmm?" Danny's anger and bitterness quickly surfaced as he confronted God, "You know, I was told to praise you, to love you, obey you … trust in you. I did everything asked of me and you do this to me in return?" He took another large mouthful of bourbon from the almost empty bottle before throwing it at the cross. "*I trusted you!*" he screamed as the bottle shattered on the wall. "You took everything I had! I loved you and you took them from me! Why?" he cried as he fell to his knees, unable to support himself or control his emotions. Images of Tommy and Jessica flooded his memory, adding fuel to his fire. He leaned over and grabbed a hymnal and Bible from the pew back cradle and ranted belligerently as he threw them at the cross, "I hate you! You hear me? I hate you!"

Franklin Pate, the baby boy Danny saved years ago on Christmas Eve, approached stealthily from behind and offered his testimony. "He has a plan." he stated softly, interrupting Danny's rampage.

Danny stopped throwing the books to turn and stare in disbelief at who was speaking to him, then asked, "He what?"

"He has a plan for you. He has a plan for all of us." Franklin repeated.

"Oh, that's just great!" Danny responded condescendingly. "He planned for my friends to die then, right … for my father to die and have his head blown off in front of me? Hmm?" he patronized. "Jess? Her too?! The only one I ever loved to die in my arms? He planned that?"

"He plans for all of His children to be with Him." Franklin replied simply.

"Then what's His brilliant plan for me? Huh?" he demanded, "Why leave me here alone?"

"You're not alone! You … "

"Oh don't start the whole 'Footprints in the Sand' crap!" Danny interrupted as he took a few steps towards Franklin, "Why don't you … "

"Hey!" Pastor Pate hollered from across the sanctuary. "Let's all just calm down now." he sternly suggested as he walked between the rows of pews.

Danny, drunk and barely able to stand, grasped the armrest at the end of the pew for balance. Instead of reacting with a harsh chastisement, Pastor Pate soothingly inquired, "How you doing tonight, Danny?"

"I'm sorry for all of the yelling," he muttered. "I just, um, I don't feel so good. I think … I think I'm gonna … " Danny collapsed onto his hands and knees and threw up violently on the carpet.

"Franklin? Can you go start some coffee and bring some towels, please?" Pastor Pate asked, holding on to Danny as he continued retching.

"Oh no! Let me go!" Danny declared upon hearing the pastor's request to Franklin, "I ain' stayin' here!"

"Hey now. Stay for a while and rest a bit. Hmmm?"

"No! Let me go!" he demanded as he stood.

"Look, you're drunk, you're upset and … "

"I said let me go!"

"Danny! Come on now, stop fighting! Just calm down!" Pastor Pate pleaded gingerly. He overpowered Danny and wrapped his arms around him as he flailed.

"Let go! Please, just let me go! Let me go!" Danny spewed with tears streaming down his cheeks. He desperately clutched at the pastor's robe, trying to his ignore his pain and deny his hunger for the touch and love of another human, any human. This was the first time for him to be comforted by a man since Johnny Lee held him at Tommy's funeral in 1978. Memories of Tommy and his love flooded Danny's brain. He and the pastor collapsed as Danny sobbed and wailed uncontrollably, unleashing nearly eighteen years of penned up grief, anger and confusion.

Franklin squatted at Pastor Pate's side, equipped with a couple of warm, wet towels. "Hush now. You're gonna be fine. Everything's gonna be just fine," the good pastor stated. Danny wept so intensely that his body started to convulse and shake, "Hey now, keep still. C'mon now. Breathe. Breathe for me now, Danny, c'mon, slow down." With his hands still clenched on the pastor's robe, Danny passed out, going limp in Pastor Pate's arms. Franklin helped to lay Danny on the carpet. "You did fine, son, just fine!" he complemented Franklin with a twinkle in his eye, "Why don't you say a prayer for him while I get a room ready … okay?"

Pastor Pate left the young retarded boy gingerly rubbing Danny's face with the warm towel. As he opened the sanctuary door to enter the corridor of classrooms, he could hear Franklin softly recite, "The Lord is my shepherd; I shall not want … "

Secrets Revealed

Pastor Pate called Charlie Doyle early Monday morning to let him know that Danny was okay and not to be worried as he never showed up to open the garage. They talked for a few minutes about what had happened late Saturday night, what Franklin said and how upset and sick Danny had gotten from drinking. He also mentioned that when he peeked in to check on Danny that it appeared as if he hadn't stirred one bit. Here it was Monday morning and he was still asleep after having been placed in one of the spare guest rooms at four a.m. Sunday morning.

From down the street he could hear Charlie's '62 International tow truck, rumbling its way toward the church. Charlie pulled to the curb in front of the wrought-iron gate with a small wave to Franklin as he played on the swing set. "Morning, Franklin!" he called out, not quite sure if the boy would be willing to talk again. Franklin jumped out of the swing set with a not-so-perfect landing and fell forward to his hands and knees. But like a jackrabbit, he was quickly back on his feet and raced across the lawn. He gripped the metal fence and pressed his face tightly against the staves.

"Did you see me, Charlie? Huh? Did you see me jump?" the boy asked, smiling broadly.

"I sure did! You keep on practicing and soon you'll be on the roof!"

"Really?"

"Sure ya can! Ain' nuthin' holdin' ya back 'cept you!" Charlie confided.

"Did you hear that, Daddy?!" Franklin asked excitedly. Pastor Pate lovingly scruffed his son's head as he approached the gate and simultaneously answered Franklin and greeted Charlie.

"Good morning, Charlie. No I didn't, son, what did he say?"

"Charlie said if I keep swinging hard I can swing onto the roof!"

"He said that to you?"

"Yeah!" he quipped, "I'm gonna practice some more!"

"Okay, well you be careful … I'll be back in just a while," he said with a kiss on the head. He unlocked the gate, closed and locked it behind him and smiled at his son who had now been made anew. After climbing in the passenger door of the truck he called out to Franklin, "If Danny wakes up before I return, just tell him I'll be back in a few minutes. Okay?"

"All right!" Franklin hollered as he turned and ran away to the swing set.

As Charlie pulled up to the old two-story house, Pastor Pate commented, "I'll go on upstairs and get him some clean clothes."

"Okay … I'll check his car for insurance or a drivers license." Charlie replied. Pastor Pate climbed the stairs, opened the unlocked door and hesitated briefly before entering the musty, dirty room. Danny had gone so far as to cover the windows with his newspaper clippings and journal entries, allowing for very little light to enter the room. Meanwhile, Charlie raised the garage door to reveal Danny's '75 Impala, covered in dust and filled with cobwebs. He opened the passenger door and plopped himself down on the dirty seat to take a look in the glove compartment. In the vehicles owner's manual was a letter of insurance dated to 1985 and the certificate of registration with Danny's full name on it. He took both the letter and certificate, closed the car door and dropped the overhead door behind him as he exited.

"You won't believe what I found!" Pastor Pate declared loudly upon hearing Charlie coming up the stairs.

Later that afternoon, in the quiet of his study, Pastor Pate called the Texas Department of Public Safety.

"Department of Public Safety, how may I direct your call?" a polite woman's voice answered.

"Yes, can I please speak to a Mrs. Tommy Albright?"

"Hold please." the voice requested. He waited patiently while listening to the phone courtesy music play Patsy Cline's "Back in Baby's Arms."

"Sarah, you have a phone call holding on three." a voice called out as Sarah made her way past the operator's console.

"I don't have time right now! You'll have to take a message or let them know I'll … "

"You really need to take this call!" the operator politely interrupted and exited her cubicle to follow Sarah to her office.

"Uhhhh!" she grunted in frustration with the operator in tow, "I need to get this months schedule done for Huddleston and Farley. I don't have time to lollygag!" After unloading her armful of paperwork on the desk, she pulled out her chair as she greeted the holding line.

"Albright!" she answered shortly and took her seat. "Yes, this is Sarah Albright. Good morning to you, sir. How can I help you? "What?" she asked, looking up to her co-worker with tears in her eyes, "Are you sure?"

A Personal Resurrection

Tuesday. Danny fluttered his eyes open to see the cream colored ceiling of the guest room. *What time is it?* and, *How long have I been asleep?* were two of the many questions swirling through his mind, along with *How did my clothes get changed?* Things seemed very out of place.

The windows, with their almost sheer lace drapes, bathed the entire room with white brilliance. He raised his head and chest to take a look about, propping himself with his elbows at his sides. It was a simple room with one double bed and a small closet with two sliding doors. A double-bowl hurricane lamp with hand-painted bluebonnets rested on a small nightstand next to the bed. There was also a dresser, a padded arm chair with a dark floral print and one extra door leading to the back courtyard. He looked around for his glasses, but didn't notice them on either the dresser or nightstand.

He stood and stretched then slowly ambled to the door leading to the hallway of classrooms. "Hello?" he bashfully called. After getting no response, he closed the door, sat in the armchair and slipped on his boots. While lacing his boots, a bright red image flashed by the window followed seconds later by a horde of laughing children. He exited the spare room to the courtyard where the day care children were playing.

The late morning sun was so intense that he had to raise his hand above his eyes and turn his head down to the side. He also couldn't help but notice how bright and magnificent the colors now seemed to be. Roses in bloom that usually appeared dark and crimson, now glowed a brilliant red like a stoplight. Yellows, greens, lavenders; all things glimmered in fresh and radiant hues. He walked a few steps to the corner of the building and spied Pastor Pate sitting under one of the oak trees. Just at that moment, Franklin and a swarm of children darted past him. Franklin, now nineteen years old, blended right in with the other children, running and laughing as if he didn't know he was different. But then again, Pastor Pate never treated Franklin differently from the other children.

"Good morning!" Pastor Pate called out jovially.

"Good morning, Danny!" Franklin echoed and rushed to Danny's side. He lunged into him and lovingly surrendered a tight, short squeeze before running away again with the other children.

"Hey now!" Danny huffed and raised his arms in the air, not quite sure as how to take the greeting. "Good morning!" he retorted confusedly, but only after Franklin had already rounded the corner.

Danny took deliberate, slow strides to the small concrete picnic table to sit with the good pastor. "Morning." he offered lowly. Franklin raced to the table with the other children and lunged this time into Pastor Pates left shoulder.

"There's my boy!" he boasted, hugging his son. "Franklin, will you please get Rip van Winkle here some coffee?"

"You want that black?"

"Sure, black is fine." Danny replied to Franklin and, like a bolt of lightning, off he charged. "Man! I feel good!" Danny commented as he stretched once more before sitting down, then pointed behind him, "That's a great bed! I ain't slept that hard in years!"

"Glad to hear it." the pastor replied as he picked up his newspaper, "Three days and nights of sleep can do wonders for the soul."

"Three?" Danny repeated, confused.

"It's Tuesday. You've been asleep for three days." he replied nonchalantly. "! Three days? Shut up!"

"Three days! You know what else happened in three days?"

"Uh … no."

"Christ arose from His tomb three days after His crucifixion. God rolled away the stone sealing the cave that Christ's body was laid in. Later He appeared before His disciples in the flesh." He let the statement sink in for a moment before offering more facts. "Jonah was delivered safely to Nineveh with a message from the Lord after being in the belly of a whale for three days."

"Then there's me." Danny interjected smartly. "I was asleep for three days. So what? I ain't no Messiah and I ain't in no whale." "No," the pastor agreed, "But this is twice now that your being here has changed the life of someone." From out of nowhere Franklin appeared at Danny's side with a fresh cup of coffee. As he gingerly set the cup and saucer on the table, Pastor Pate looked over Franklins shoulder and noticed Whitney entering the back of the courtyard. "Franklin? Why don't you go see if Whitney needs help with anything inside?" he asked.

Franklin turned abruptly and ran to the courtyard, calling loudly "Whitney! Whitney!"

"I can understand maybe the first time when he was out on the porch at Christmas, but sleeping for three days? What does that have to do with anything?" Danny asked, with a sip of his coffee. "Your three days of sleep didn't help anyone but you, but … you came here." Danny sat silently and watched the children play as the pastor continued, "You know … Franklin has been here ever since you left him. You had nothing to do with him being put here, but, had it not been for you delivering him to me, he would have frozen to death. And that's no coincidence, bizarre twist of fate or mistake. God planned for you to be here at that time, that place, that night to make a choice to protect him. And since that night, even though I'm the only father he's ever known, until Saturday night he had yet to speak a word to me or anyone else."

Danny quickly turned to face the pastor. "Okay, I don't understand this … he just spoke again a few minutes ago and hugged me earlier."

"The first words to ever come out of his mouth were not meant for me, but for you from Him! Franklin said to you, 'He has a plan.' Do you remember that?"

"Yeah, I think so." Danny struggled to remember, "Something that God has a plan for His kids or wants all of His children to be with Him?"

"Right." he replied, "His first words were not of his love for me, the only parent he's ever had, but for you … from God … that He loves you. He brought you here, that you might know He loves you and for Franklin to be the witness to that. Don't you see?"

"He's never spoken to you?" Danny confirmed with a slight glance at Franklin.

The pastor answered with a slow shake of his head.

"I need to be honest with you, Danny." Pastor Pate offered, somewhat reluctantly, "While you were asleep I went to your apartment to get some clean clothes for you. I also talked to Charlie about your being here." Danny felt a surge of panic and insecurity rush through his heart. He rose from the picnic table and began pacing back and forth nervously as the pastor continued his confession, "I also know who you are and where you're from."

Danny glared for a moment at the pastor before turning to walk away. "Danny!" he called and stood, "You've spent the past nineteen years alone and look at you! What did it get you? Where did it get you?" Danny stopped in his tracks. "I can help you … I will help you! I know you have hurt in your heart, but, this gift you have … "

"Gift?" Danny exclaimed, whirling around.

"Gift, foresight, ability … whatever you want to call it. You can't blame God." Danny remained silent. "I'm not saying you're not seeing what you think you're seeing, or that it's not real, but do you actually believe God would punish anyone with something like this? Punish someone with this heavy a burden? Hmm?" Danny mumbled lowly and inaudibly. "I'm sorry, I can't hear you?" the pastor leaned in sarcastically, turning his head to the side.

"I said I don't know!"

"Oh … well, if you don't know … then why blame Him? You can only blame yourself for your choices and actions. And to choose to turn away from God because you're sad or upset, that doesn't help." The pastor then changed the flow of Danny's private sermon and inquired, "Have you thought that maybe you should embrace God and do something useful with this instead of hiding and drinking and blaming Him?"

"Use it? Use it for what?"

"Well," he pondered, walking back to the table. "What do you see? How do you see it? When do you see it"

Danny was momentarily dumbfounded by the direct questioning and tried to walk through one of his visions, "Well, I don't really know how … but I see everybody with it … and I hate it. I see it on kids, old people, everybody, you. Red, purplish green, white, everyone I see has one!

"Okay, good." he coaxed, taking his seat at the picnic table. "So, you see something on someone. Then what happens?"

"Well," he explained uncomfortably, joining the pastor, "that depends on the color of the fold. If it's white … "

"Wait, wait, wait," he interrupted. "What do you mean the fold? A fold of what? What is that? Explain fold to me"

"Well, I guess you could pretty much call it anything you like, but I call it a fold, of like, I think time."

The pastor sat with a blank expression on his face, not yet grasping the concept, but probed for more pertinent information. "Okay, these colors you see on people … what do they mean?

" Well, for as long as I've been able to do this, I've found that everyone has one 'til they die. Now if it's white, the uh, the fold … " Danny paused and chuckled to himself.

"What? What's so funny? Why are ya laughing?"

"You know I never thought about explaining this?" he admitted. "Huh! Well, if the light I see on whoever is white, then that tells me that person is gonna die just because it's their time. They're old, heart failure or heart attack. You know, something natural. Some go to bed and just don't wake up."

"Good … who else gets these?"

"I see a purple-blue, kinda greenish light mostly on kids and teens like Franklin, young adults … you. I been seeing ya'lls' for a long time." Pastor Pate looked around him as Danny continued, "So, bluish-purple green to me says that this person is safe and has a long way to go before they die."

"Does anyone know that they have these?"

" No one but me!"

"Okay … anything else you can tell me?"

"Well," Danny hesitated, "there's one more fold color. It's red."

"Red?"

"Red."

"Why red? Red for what?" he asked, his curiosity sparked.

"Not a whole lotta reds. But every once in a while one will come through town."

"Red is bad?"

"Yeah!" Danny answered, excited at the prospect of now having someone to confide in who will actually listen to him. "Suicide, homicide, a stabbing, shooting, hanging, a drowning. Usually the bad stuff and it'll be happening soon; like within the next couple of days, maybe tomorrow."

"What do you see? I don't mean the color, but exactly, what do you see?"

Danny thought about it for a moment then asked, "Did ya ever watch Johnny Carson?"

"Oh, I'd catch a few minutes here and there, at least 'til he went of the air in the nineties."

"Well, you know the spot lights would be on that huge curtain, goin everywhere before the show starts. The drums start goin' and Ed McMahon would say 'Heeeeeeeere's Johnny.' You remember?" The pastor nodded with his recollection of the scene. "Then all of a sudden the curtain would open just a crack and out steps Johnny Carson. He comes out … then all the guests come out … then it's over. I see that with everyone. I open this fold and I see their last living moment. Don't know how I do, but … they're living now, right here in front of me and then in my head … they're dead. The last seconds of their lives flash before me. Me! Like I'm somebody who's supposed to be in there! Now how is that supposed to be good?"

Pastor Pate concentrated on what to say in response, "The other night you were yelling that God cursed you … that He took all the people you loved. Do you remember?"

"I remember yelling but not anything in particular." Danny confessed.

"How familiar are you with the Bible?"

"Oh, man! It's been years since I read any of the Bible!" he jokingly declared.

"Well, in Deuteronomy we're told, 'No one shall be found among you who makes a son or daughter pass through fire or who practices divination, is a soothsayer, an augur, a sorcerer, or one who casts spells, consults with ghosts or spirits or who seeks oracles from the dead. In Leviticus 28, 'a man or a woman who is a medium or wizard shall be put to death; they shall be stoned to death.'" Danny concentrated on the two verses. "So!" he concluded, "If God doesn't want us to deal with fortune tellers, tarot cards, Ouija boards and séances, then why do you think He would curse you with what He doesn't want you to know? We read in Genesis that Joseph's brothers were jealous of him; jealous because their father, Jacob, loved him the most. So, Jacob gave Joseph a special coat to show his love and preference for him. Then, in retaliation and revenge, Joseph's brothers plotted to kill him and tell their father that he was devoured by a wild animal." Danny sat like a young child with his knees curled up to his chest as he listened intently. "But instead of killing him, the brothers threw him into a big pit with no food and water. He was then found, brought out of the pit and sold into slavery. His own brothers sold him into slavery to the Ishmaelites."

"I'd hate to go to their family reunion!" Danny jokingly commented.

"Years later, however," Pastor Pate continued, "Joseph would come to be owned by the Pharaoh of Egypt … and he liked Joseph. In fact, he grew to like and trust Joseph to such a point that he put him in charge of everything in Egypt. *Everything*."

A moment passed and all Danny could muster was a short and dry, "So?"

"Well, years later, during a famine, Joseph's brothers came to ask him for forgiveness for what they did to him years ago. The pit, slavery and all, and Joseph said to them 'Even though you intended me harm, God intended it for good!'"

The pastor rose to his feet and joined Danny on the opposite bench. He placed his hand on Danny's shoulder and firmly advised, "Whatever you have, you need to take it to God. Right now. Don't try to stifle it or hide it and run away from Him. You can find a way use this in a manner that will bring glory to His name." Danny managed to crack a small smile at the kind words of Pastor Pate. "Then and only then can you be released from this … 'cuz you know, He can do anything … anything at all … if you just give Him the chance."

Danny closed his eyes for a moment and tried to remember the last time he felt this peaceful, relaxed and confident. Yet as he opened his eyes, deep inside his heart he knew that some doubt still lingered, "I don't know … "

"Go home!" Pastor Pate encouraged with a smile and a slight pat on the back. "Go home to God; home to your life; home to your mother. They're all expecting you."

A Not So Joyous Reunion

With one strong jerk, the heavy, wooden overhead door stubbornly gave way, moaning of rusty springs and greaseless bearings. Danny entered the dark, musty garage below his apartment where his white '75 Chevy Impala lie entombed since his arrival in 1986. Due to the lack of light, along with the accumulation of dust, dirt, and spider webs of the past nineteen years, the white paint and vinyl roof resembled the color of old, spoiled milk.

He pushed his jalopy out into the driveway and waited for Charlie to arrive with his truck to tow it down to the station. There he checked the tires, changed all the fluids, replaced the filters and filled it up with a new tank of gas. With bittersweet happiness, Charlie watched Danny as he meticulously washed and vacuumed his car in preparation for his journey home. Once he was done, Danny shook Charlie's hand and embraced him, stifling his tears, "Thanks." He hopped in the car and pulled out of the driveway onto Main Street. A short "goodbye" cruise through town left him with an uplifting feeling of optimism and hope.

He arrived at his apartment and briskly climbed the stairs. With a slight nudge against the peeling wood door, he entered his self-imposed asylum and grabbed a few articles of clothing. After halting briefly for a quick glance about the room, he locked the door behind him and scurried down the stairs to his running car. With a click of the radio knob, as if planned by God for years, Robert Earl Keene started singing "Feeling Good Again." He could hardly hold back the tears as he listened to the simple words and melody. He looked in the rear view mirror and watched as the only home he'd come to know for all these years, slowly disappeared from sight.

As he drove through the picturesque Texas hill country, with it's tall oaks, deep grasses, small creeks and ranches, Danny could feel his excitement and nervousness building. But as he neared his parents' farm, his heart sank when he found only remnants of what used to be. He pulled off to the right alongside the culvert ditch and stopped the car. His parents' house looked nothing like he remembered or how he expected it to be. Tall and yellowed grasses and weeds littered the unimproved fields; the once dazzling white barn and garage were now faded, peeling and stressed. From the outside it appeared that since he left, or maybe even as far back as Tommy's death, that more in this world had deteriorated than just his own life. A strange and unsettling silence suddenly overcame him.

He walked across the tinhorn to the gravel driveway, looking all about him. The fleeting memories of his childhood were slowly returning to him when he realized something was missing, something he hadn't yet seen or heard: the animals. He strode across the weak and thin lawn to the barn and slid the door open only to find empty stalls and pens. The sheep, cattle, pigs, horses, everything … were all gone. He next went to the garage and pulled back the large, sliding door to find his father's two International Harvester and three John Deere tractors slowly dying, sitting in the darkness with flat tires and fluids collecting in puddles underneath.

He closed the door and headed toward the house as the echo of metal hitting metal resonated. He timidly stepped onto the wooden wrap-around porch and stood at the front door. The small diamond shaped glass window was dusty from within and dirty from without. The wounded screen door hung slightly off its hinge while a section of the screen was torn away at the bottom of the frame.

Danny waited for what seemed an eternity before drawing in a deep, cleansing breath and rapped lightly at the door. From behind the door came the muffled sound of boots on a wooden floor. The dull brass doorknob jiggled and twisted. The door groaned slightly as it swung back into the darkness of the foyer. From the shadows a faint voice called out:

"Danny?"

"Momma?" he choked in return. Sarah entered the light and pushed open the screen. Time had not been good to Sarah; her once long and flowing strawberry blond hair was now brittle and streaked with grey and white. Years of despair and grief left deep trenches in her forehead, leaving her skin loose and wrinkled.

"My baby!" she blurted out, wrapping her arms around her lost son.

"I'm sorry! I'm sorry!" he cried into her shoulder. The two swayed gently in each other's arms as the sun exited the sky.

That night Sarah prepared a homecoming feast for her son: chicken fried steak, whole-wheat biscuits, mashed potatoes with cream gravy and cornmeal battered and fried okra with squash. She also made some homemade banana pudding to top it all off. After dinner and dessert, Sarah brought out a bottle of Wild Turkey. They spent the next few hours smoking, drinking and talking about what all had happened in their lives since their separation.

"So, while she was in a neck brace," Danny explained, trying to contain his laughter, "Charlie had me put two tires on one side that were smaller than the two on the other side, so when she was leaning her head, the road looked level."

After a brief lull in the laughter, Sarah poured herself another glass of bourbon and stated, "So!" smiling thinly at Danny.

"So." he replied.

She stood and picked up the dirty dinner plates, turned to the sink and bluntly asked, "So, why'd you leave … or runaway, whatever you want to call it … after Jess's wreck?" Danny leaned back in his chair and began to honestly explain his reasons for his actions, "Well, after all I had seen with Daddy, when I saw the same thing on Jess … I just freaked! I didn't know if I would see this again and if I did on who! I knew sum'pn was about to happen, but not sure just … "

"Geez, Danny!" she interrupted angrily, slamming the plates in the sink, "Would you please give it a rest and drop the pity line! What happened to your daddy was almost twenty-seven years ago! Quit crutching it!" She continued her chastisement after sucking in a deep drag of her cigarette. "Do you know what it's like to walk through town and have your friends turn their back on you 'cuz they say your kid's crazy!? Huh?" she asked, waving her arms as she continued belittling her son. "All those counseling sessions, medications, doctors, and therapists! For what? Little delusions? Some nightmares? You see this, you saw that!" She brutally patronized him all the more as she drew in close, raising the pitch of her voice, "He shot her, Daddy! He smashed the car, Daddy!' 'I see lights and Daddy's gon' die!' Stop it! Just stop it! I'm tired of you saying … "

Danny interrupted gruffly, "Wait a minute, I never asked … "

"No! You wait a minute!" she interjected, shoving her finger in his face "If you hadn't of been making up one of your stupid fantasies, your father'd prob'ly still be alive."

"I can't help it for what I saw! I didn't shoot him!" he proclaimed in self-defense, raising his voice.

"No, no you didn't … but you sure did deliver him to his execution, didn't you!"

"You're my mother!" he screamed, jumping out of his chair. Tears rolled down his cheeks. "I'm your only son! Why didn't you believe in me? You're supposed to love me unconditionally! You're more concerned about your stupid, precious reputation than what I was going through!"

Danny towered over Sarah, backing her against kitchen table. "You didn't see pieces of Dad's head on the window! You didn't hold Jess in your arms with her skull cracked open! Do you know what it feels like to not have your own mother trust you? Huh? Do you know how it feels knowing someone is ignoring everything that you say? Huh? D'you know that feeling? You stupid drunk!" In bitter retaliation, Sarah reared back and slapped Danny's face. Blind with rage, he backhanded Sarah, knocking her sideways across the corner of the dinner table.

Sarah screamed as she and the dirty dinner dishes crashed to the floor. Danny stood above her, crying and confused, pressing his clenched fists to his eyes. His head was swimming with images of his father and Jessica. Sarah wailed loudly, lying face down on the floor in the food and bourbon. "I miss him too, you know!" he declared defiantly.

Danny stormed out of the kitchen, leaving Sarah to herself. He stomped heavily as he climbed the stairs to go to his old bedroom. He angrily gave the knob a twist; the door was locked. Sarah heard him jiggling the handle then pacing in the hallway. She exited the kitchen and hollered to Danny from downstairs, still sobbing, "I wanted to leave it exactly how you left it. When you didn't come back I … "

He didn't want to wait for her explanation and decided to kick in his own bedroom door. As he entered the room, his heart and mind were simultaneously set afire with memories, wishes and regrets. The posters, lamp, sheets, furniture, clothes … all were exactly how he left them that fateful night in 1986. Even more so, all had remained the same since his father's death in 1978. It was as if time had skipped over his room.

Danny kicked off his boots, stretched out on his bed, and stared at the ceiling. Above his bed were the sun bleached and faded posters of Gene Autry, John Wayne, Superman, and the Dallas Cowboy Cheerleaders. He heard Sarah trying to quietly climb the squeaky stairs and raised up just in time to see her shadow stop in front of his door. She raised her hand and leaned forward in preparation to knock, but instead turned away and went to her bedroom.

Danny lay restless and awake in bed, late into the evening. He then remembered something his father said to him years before when he was little. Tommy once said, "You know, if you can't sleep, you can count your blessings to sleep. Works for me!" With that he began to go through all the things he was thankful for. He was soon fast asleep, but like his grandfather, mother and daddy, Danny snored something fierce.

Something stirred him from his sleep. He woke up completely alert and sat upright in his bed. His bedroom door was closed and nothing appeared disturbed, but sensing something was amiss, he quietly tiptoed to the door. He pulled it open with a slight creak, back just enough to peek through, but there was nothing to be seen. He climbed back in bed, laying on his right side, turned away from the door. As he closed his eyes, he heard the faint but distinct sound of boots walking across the downstairs wood floor. He opened his eyes when he then heard the stairs squeaking, then the sound of his door opening. He tried to lie still, but fear, nervousness and curiosity got the best of him.

He quickly sat up to find his door now open and Tommy standing at the end of his bed. He rubbed his eyes in disbelief for a moment to make sure he wasn't dreaming, but Tommy didn't move. His father's hands were clasped in front of him and he was dressed in his best black suit. His full, curly blond hair was slightly swept back and his skin had a healthy bronze sheen, as if he had been working outside for a while. He looked as handsome and healthy as the day he died. With a loving smile Tommy spoke softly, "Danny, why are you so angry? Why do you cry for me?" Danny paused for a moment and looked about the room, searching for the right words to answer to his dead father.

"I still love you!" he proclaimed. "I miss you so much! And you're not here anymore to help me!" Danny lowered his head to his hands and wept heavily after having finally admitted his fear and loneliness. Seconds passed before he raised his head to find that his father was gone.

"Daddy?" he called, yearningly. Looking to see that the door was once again closed, he fell back onto the bed and cried deeply, silently and breathlessly. While rolling onto his right side, he drew a deep breath to refill his expired lungs. He wrapped his arms around the extra pillow and felt the warm sensation of his father's hand lightly sweep across his forehead.

Sleep came peacefully, almost immediately. He was home.

The Morning After

It was late in the morning when Butch arrived at the DPS offices. He made it a point to visit each of his three precincts at least once a month and spend a couple of days with the district's Sergeant. While making his rounds of greeting the officers and staff, he noticed that Sarah had yet to arrive. Thinking he may have just simply missed her somewhere along the way, he went back to the break room, poured himself a cup of coffee and headed to the operators console.

"Has anyone heard from Sarah this morning?" he asked the dispatch operators, glancing at his watch. His only reply was that of shrugging shoulders and shaking heads. He had recently received several formal letters of complaint from members of the administrative staff expressing concern over Sarah's noticeable dependence on alcohol. The complaints ranged from "not showing up on time" and "falling asleep at her desk" to "erratic behavior and emotional instability" and "appears incapable of focusing on or completing assigned duties." He had counseled her many times over the past few years and recommended she check herself into a detox center, as well as attend AA classes. Unfortunately, reaching out for help was not one of Sarah's strong points.

Butch entered his temporary office and walked behind the desk, sipping on his coffee. As he opened his leather satchel to unload his computer and paperwork, Sarah tried to briskly walk past his open office door without being noticed. "Sarah!" he bellowed, without skipping a beat. She stopped dead in her tracks, tilted her head back and released a deep sigh. "Sarah? Would you come here please?" She slowly wrapped herself around the doorframe into the brightly lit office.

"Good morning!" he proclaimed zestfully. "Good to have you here with the rest of the family!" he stated with a slight slap of his palms on the desk. "Can I get you anything?" he asked politely as he stood then walked toward Sarah and the two arm chairs in front of his desk. "Have a seat! C'mon, let's you and I just talk for a minute." She sat down somewhat clumsily without saying a word, making sure to keep her sunglasses on and her head tilted down to the left away from Butch. "Sarah," he began quietly, but sternly, "you have got to get this under control! You can't allow yourself to continue down this road. I won't allow this behavior to persist, and Huddleston surely wouldn't put up with this if he knew. You need to … "

"Can you close the door please?" she requested sheepishly, interrupting Butch.

"Sure. Yeah. I'll close the door." he agreed.

"Something happened last night. Something that I hadn't expected … " she explained as Butch took his seat to her right.

"Hm mm." he murmured as she removed her sunglasses and turned to face him.

"Wow! Are you okay?" he asked, surprised to see the large swollen and discolored area on her left cheek and eyebrow.

"Yeah," she laughed nonchalantly, "as okay as can be expected, I guess."

"What happened?" he asked, pulling her chin up and to her right to get a better look in the light. As he examined her bruise, tears began to roll down her cheek.

"You're not gonna believe this!" she stated, trying to reign in her emotions. "My baby came home last night."

He removed his hand from her chin and hesitated before responding, slightly taken aback from the statement. "You sure? You weren't uh … you weren't just drinking and imagining this? I mean, 'cuz, I know you been waiting a long time for some kind of news."

"My baby came home!" she stated proudly, taking a Kleenex from her purse, "He came home yesterday afternoon. He walked up on to the porch lookin' like he had come back from goin' to go to the store or sumpn.' He just walked on up to the house."

Still a little skeptical of the validity of the story, Butch offered a flat response "Well, good. I mean … that's great! How long has he been gone? Thirteen … fourteen years?"

"Nineteen." she answered, "Almost nineteen years."

"Well, good for him. I mean good for you. Good for both of you! I guess we need to celebrate."

The Homecoming

A few weeks later, Sarah hosted a cookout in celebration of Danny's return. It was a late Saturday afternoon and most of the DPS staff was in attendance, including Sgt. Huddleston. John, Jason, Ron, and Casey were also there, however, their wives didn't come as there had been a gradual falling out of the five girlfriends. Joey, Monica, Holly, and Terri remained as close as ever, but Sarah's continued downward spiral into isolationism, alcohol and depression, coupled with her withdrawal from church, placed a hefty strain on the quintet's relationship.

After a few rounds of hand shaking and civil, yet insincere greetings, Danny retired to the safety of the kitchen for some quiet time and a beer. Moments later, he peered through the kitchen window and watched as Butch pulled in, exited his car and walked up the gravel drive with a platter of deviled eggs in hand. He sipped on his Shiner Bock, watching Butch greet each and every officer before approaching Sarah. . After a word or two Sarah turned and pointed to the house. Butch handed her the platter of deviled eggs and followed her motion with a nod and smile.

One could always tell where another person was in the Albright house by way of the wood floors and how the house communicated through sound. Danny could hear Butch and the high pitched, hollow knocking as he and his boots strode across the wood planked front porch. Next was the sandpaper shuffle as he stopped in front of the door, followed by the tightening sproing of the screen door spring and ultimate slam against the frame. Finally, a pair of Tony Lama's made low, dense thuds on the hardwood floor, letting Danny know that Butch was nearing the kitchen. He stood there, quietly staring out the window, just waiting for Butch to enter. "What's a guy gotta do t' get a beer 'round here?" Butch asked jovially as he pushed open the two-way swinging door.

"Bottom of fridge." Danny mumbled, pointing to his right.

"Thanks!" he belted out, pulling back the handle on the old Frost Point refrigerator. "Ah," he cooed as he reached in, grabbed a beer and twisted off the cap, "Good ol' Shiner!" He stood a moment in awkward silence, smiling, waiting for a response. "Here's to you, Danny!" he kindly offered, extending his bottle. Danny turned his head ever so slightly to the right and raised his bottle with a slight roll of his eyes. "Welcome home!" he congratulated as the two men toasted each other, clinking their bottlenecks. "Great party!" Butch commented politely, "Ribs, slaw, burgers, beer … it's a beautiful day!"

"If you say so … ?" Danny grunted, then turned and walked out of the kitchen.

"Well, it's probably good to see all these people after such a long time. Ain't it?" he inquired, following Danny through the swinging door to the living room. Danny behaved as if he hadn't heard a word and slumped heavily into his father's leather armchair.

"Do you know who I am?" Butch asked, taking a seat on the couch directly across from Danny. "I haven't seen ya in a long time. When I did see you, it wasn't exactly the most … "

"You're Cleo Farley." Danny bluntly interrupted, taking a swig of his beer. "You're the one who helped pull me and Daddy out of the car. You didn't throw up when you found the girl's head by the curb of the sidewalk but you did when you saw Billy out in the intersection."

Butch sat upright, placed his beer on the coffee table, clasped his hands together and concentrated on his words, "I know this is hard for you."

"You know nuthin' about what's hard for me!" Danny exclaimed rudely.

"I'm just sayin' I know what it's like to not have a dad or mom around." he restated and explained. "You're a kid who's forced to grow up too fast. I know. You 'n I are a lot alike." he confided with a smile and a nod of his bottle.

"Oh, really!" Danny smirked, "And how's that?"

"Well, for one we both lost our dads. You were what … nine? Ten?"

"Ten."

"I was just turning ten when I decided to lose my dad." Butch stated, momentarily revisiting his past.

"Decided?" Danny quipped.

"Yeah. Mom ran off when I was seven. My dad was a professional drunk!" he smiled slightly as he thought back to his early childhood. "He used to hit on her something fierce. Happy, sad, great day, bad day … daddy would drink to escape and mom 'n me would wish to do the same. One mornin' Mom went to work, n' never came home. That's when Daddy turned his attention to me."

"Bad?" Danny asked with a grin and sip of his beer.

"Bad enough." Butch admitted with a chuckle. "But when I got older I'd go to ol' man Cierly's garage and he'd give me two dollars to sweep, clean, pick up, dump, mop, shovel, fill 'er up. Two dollars!" Danny recounted similar scenes of his past nineteen years at Charlie Doyle's as he listened to Butch's tale. "I'd stay as late as I could just to not go home. Stop by the store on my way home, get some bologna and bread, make me some sandwiches, maybe leave one for him. I'd take a bath, get some clothes, then do my homework. Daddy would always wake up loud from a big night of drinking. I mean he was *loud!* If he was up, then everybody was up. I'd hear him coming outta the living room and man, I'm tellin' you … I'd jump up and outta that bed and hide between the wall and mattress!" he briefly chortled to himself as he reminisced. Only now could he look back and try to laugh through the pain. "I did that for years 'til I got outta high school. Went to college, graduated with a double major and honors. Now … here I am, having a cold one with you."

"So, how does that make you and me a lot alike?" Danny asked, not seeing the similarities.

"Bad things happen." Butch stated plainly. "That's life and you can't get away from it. You can't let the events in your life take the life out of you! You and I, and maybe that boy who caused your wreck, we're alike in a lot of ways. We were all trying to run away."

After pondering the statement, Danny rose from his chair saying, "Maybe so … " and walked past Butch. "But then again … " he added, pausing at the door, "you and I didn't shoot the ones we loved." The spring on the doorframe recoiled and slammed the screen shut. Butch sat alone on the sofa, slowly sipping his beer.

Prove It to Me

Early that following Monday, just two days after the cookout, Butch heard the beeping of the motion detector for the foyer doors of the DPS offices. He rose from his chair, walked to the door and poked his head into the hallway to see who, or what, set off the alarm. He was pleasantly surprised to find Sarah not only arriving early for work, but smiling and humming to herself.

"Sarah?" he called, and motioned for her to come to his office. He paced in a small circle until she appeared at the door. "Sarah! Hey, good morning!" he greeted enthusiastically, shaking her hand, "I just wanted to say thanks for having us out to the party on Saturday. Great time!"

"Oh yeah! Sure!" she smiled broadly, "You did have a good time, right?"

"Yeah, oh yeah! A ball. Got fat as a tick," he admitted, patting his belly.

"Say, I went in to go get me a beer and Danny was in the kitchen … "

"Yeah, he said he had a talk with you," she interrupted, "Did you get along with him okay?"

"Yeah, yeah … got along fine … " He held out his hand for Sarah to join him at the armchairs in front of the desk. "I was wondering, and

I hate to ask this, but ... did Tommy ever talk about case specifics or impending investigations with Danny?"

"No, not directly." she answered, trying to recollect anything out of the ordinary, "But I imagine every once in a while we would talk about something he needed me to do with some filings or assembly of reports that had to do with a case, but with Danny? Never. Why do you ask?"

"Well," he began with a clear of his throat, "he said something about a particular event with some very specific details that have never actually been released as public information."

"You know ... Danny was always a great kid ... that is he was a great kid 'til the day of his wreck." she stated, but with a slight shake of her head and sorrowful look. "After he came out of his coma, he started saying he could see who was driving the car that caused the wreck ... what happened ... then what was gonna happen. Very unnerving! Then one day he said Tommy was gonna be shot ... then he get shot." The two sat and silently read each other's face. "But you and I know that's just coincidence!" she dismissed with a wave of her hands and a slight, nervous chuckle.

"Right ... " he agreed, but not at all convinced.

"I'm gonna pick him up for lunch later, you want me to ask him anything for you? 'Cuz I ... "

"No, no," he interrupted as they both stood, "I'll just talk to him next time I see him."

"Well, he's comin' back with me from lunch so we can do some shopping later. He needs some new clothes. Badly!"

"Well, why don't you let me go pick him up?" Butch suggested, "That way he and I could talk a while. We'll pick up your lunch and maybe, uh ... I'll let ya leave early to go shopping." Taken slightly aback at the sudden act of generosity, Sarah stood quietly, skeptical of the arrangement. "That sound all right?"

"You sure about this?" she asked, uncertain if she should be suspicious or grateful.

"Sure I'm sure!" he confirmed.

"Well ... yeah! Yeah. Thanks, that'd be great!" She shook his hand and turned to leave his office. Although she outwardly smiled and said "yes," deep down inside she hid a frown and her mind told her "uh-oh."

At around eleven a.m., a dense, loud knock at the front door surprised Danny as he ate a bowl of Corn Pops at the kitchen table. He jumped to his feet and briskly walked to the entryway. Upon opening the door, he was shocked to find Butch standing on the porch. After a brief pause, with his arms spread out wide, Danny smartly greeted Butch, "Ah! Officer Biggus Brainus Goodus Gradus! You grace me with your presence once again." He opened the door wide, bowing as he spoke, as if addressing and making way for royalty, "Entrée, entrée." Butch glanced over Danny's wardrobe of bleached and tattered shorts, oil stained t-shirt, mismatched socks and unshaved face. "Where's Mom?" he asked, closing the door behind Butch, "We were supposed to have lunch then go shopping."

"I volunteered to come 'n get ya." Butch admitted with a friendly smile. Danny turned and entered the kitchen without so much as saying a word while Butch further explained, "Yeah, I, uh … wanted to get out for a while 'n get a bite anyhow."

Danny emerged with his Doc Martens in hand and welder's glasses on. "You ever not wear those glasses?" Butch inquired.

Danny plopped himself in the armchair and grunted, "Sensitive eyes." After lacing his boots, he rose to his feet and stood in front of Butch as if to signify he was ready to leave.

After one more look over Danny's clothes, Butch commented, "You sure didn't get paid much at the garage, did ya?"

Danny inspected the immaculately clean interior of Butch's Crown Victoria as they began their long drive back to the city. "So?" Butch opened, nonchalantly.

"So!" Danny volleyed, watching the rows of corn race the car. "You, uh … you really surprised me the other day." he stated.

"Really? You … the professor? Surprised?"

"Yeah, 'cuz, uh … I never told anyone that I got sick that day."

"Well, you can rest assured that your little puke secret is safe with me." He assured Butch with a smile. "Not much point value now in telling someone you threw up."

"Not now, no ... thank you," he agreed, then prodded cautiously, "But, how did you know that? That it was me that was there? The head?"

"I just do!" Danny answered shortly, returning to watch the pastures go by. "I wished for it, and now I can."

"You see when stuff is gonna happen or after the fact?"

"Look!" Danny huffed, turning to face Butch, "I know Mom has probably warned you about my parlor tricks, but, what and how I see things, I don't know! I see it everywhere on everyone! Period! So I would appreciate it if we could just skip the interrogation." He glared at Butch from behind the black lenses of his homemade glasses.

"Is that, uh, why the whole glasses thing?" he inquired.

Danny decided to change gears and engage in Butch's conversation "Yeah, some ... well, no ... not really." Butch glanced back and forth from the road to Danny, waiting for an interpretation of the answer.

"Back in town I would see into a few people a day. 'N after that I would see 'em around town and ... I just got used to it. Then we'd get busy on weekends and holidays and I started seeing way more than I care to. So, I took a lens out of a welders mask and put it in these frames." He felt vulnerable and exposed, lowering his guard to describe to Butch what he saw.

"So, that's why you stayed there for so long?" Butch concluded, "Small town, same people ... wouldn't have to see strangers everyday? Right?" Danny turned to face Butch, amazed at his perception. "Was it, or maybe I should ask, is it ... confusing? I mean how do you know what's reality and not some fantasy?"

Feeling frustrated and that he's not being taken seriously, Danny suddenly barked out, "Look! I don't expect someone like you to understand! You couldn't and probably won't ever understand what this is."

"Hey, I'm sorry! I didn't mean to ... "

"Yes, yes you did!" Danny finished rudely, turning to face his interrogator. "Just drive the car and wake me when we get there!" he demanded, leaning back against the headrest. Butch continued the drive in silence, feeling a sense of remorse for having pushed Danny so hard.

Just over an hour later, Butch lightly nudged his snoring passenger, "Danny? Danny, wake up, son. We'll be there in a sec." Danny began to stir and stretch in the reclined seat. "Man, when you go to sleep you go to sleep!" he complimented with a smile. "You're like my cousin, Casey! He's a pro at sleeping. I take too long to wind down when I go to bed."

"If I've had a few all-nighters I can sleep for a day." Danny admitted, taking off his glasses and rubbing his eyes. "Where are we?"

"I'm takin' you to one of my favorite restaurants. Think you might like it!" he asserted, then complained as he came to an abrupt stop. "Aw man! I hate this intersection! On a Monday at lunch, too!" Danny listened to Butch's rant as he raised his seat back, "Look at that! Against green lights, against traffic, people still walkin'! Geez! I'm surprised we don't have more hit and runs on this street." Danny finished rubbing his eyes and was shocked to see hundreds of people walking in front of and beside the car. Danny's mind flashed with pulses of light and past images of funerals, car wrecks, suicides, and horrific scenes of death. The parade of passersby continued, all of whom were completely oblivious of the mark they carried and the destiny that awaited them. Gripping the door handle tightly, Danny requested anxiously, "Get me outta here!"

"What? What did you say?"

"Get me outta here! Now! Now!" he demanded, raising his voice.

"All right, hold on … we gotta red light and need to wait for these people to … "

"Didn't you hear me?" he yelled, slamming his left foot on top of Butch's right foot on the gas. Danny grabbed the steering wheel with his left hand and shouted, "Get me outta here! Go! Go! Go!"

The Crown Victoria lurched forward with squealing tires, almost hitting several pedestrians. "Danny! Danny! Stop it!" Butch pleaded as he tried to regain control of the vehicle, "Danny, let go! You're gonna kill us!"

"Move!" Danny screamed at the pedestrians and cars, "Get outta the way! C'mon!" Butch elbowed Danny in his left side, knocking the breath of him. He regained control of the vehicle and swerved to the right, narrowly missing a mother and her baby as they crossed the street. Butch turned onto a side street and brought the car to a screeching stop. "Are ya just trying to kill us?" he shouted with his eyes wide open, breathless and sweating.

"Man! I told you I didn't like being 'round a lotta people!" Danny restated angrily, also breathless.

"I'm sorry! Okay?" Butch snapped. After taking an opportunity to catch his breath and calm down, he tried to make light of the situation "I'm sorry ... I didn't know you couldn't sit at stop lights like that!"

Danny squinted his eyes with a double take at Butch, unsure of what he just heard, "What? I don't have a problem sitting at stupid stop lights!"

"No! Really!" Butch promised, trying to not smile. "For now on, no stop lights or intersections for you!"

"I can sit at stop lights all day!" Danny quipped, irritated, "I've actually driven myself to a stop light once or twice in my life. We even had a couple of intersections with stop lights back in town!" Butch couldn't contain his laughter at Danny, who, after listening to himself, began to laugh as well.

The two men exited the car and headed towards the alley off the side street "Where are we?" Danny asked, pausing to look around.

Butch walked ahead of him and pulled back the glass door to the restaurant, declaring triumphantly, "This is the home of the best onion burger in Texas!"

"We drove over an hour for this?" he lamented, looking at the junked and dirty alley, "We're eating in there?"

"What's wrong? C'mon! Oh! I get it." Butch supposed, releasing the door, "you're afraid you might see one of your little lights, huh?" He stood in front of Danny with his hands on his hips, biting the inside of his lip.

"You don't believe me, do ya?" he accused Butch. "Whether I do or don't believe you is irrelevant! The point is, whatever it is you think you got, if ya really got it, you're the one who's gonna live with it." Danny turned away, trying to ignore Butch's impromptu sermon. "Don't turn away from me when I'm talking to you!" he ordered, grabbing Danny by the arm, "We're just ... talking." Only after he turned him around did Butch relax his grip on Danny. "If you get cancer, just because you stay in your house doesn't mean the cancer's gonna get better or go away! At home you got it, work you got it, at school, with your wife, wherever, you got cancer. So, deal with it and do what you can! Make the best of this cuz' your momma's not, I'm not, and no one else is gonna be here to hold your hand, blow your nose, and wipe your butt!" With that being said, he did an about-face, walked back to the restaurant and ended the conversation, "And I want an onion burger!" Danny reluctantly and sluggishly inched his way to the open door.

They entered the small downtown diner, packed with the local lunch crowd, and forced their way to the last open table; a booth on the end of the row in the corner. Butch liked to sit with his back to the wall so he could see all who entered and left the building. Danny slumped into the other side of the booth with his back to the door. A kindly, older waitress with dyed platinum blond hair and a fake red, silk corsage on her blouse was delivering lunch to the table next to Butch and Danny. She placed the plates in front of the patrons and leaned over to ask, "Can I get 'cha somethin' t' drink, hun?"

"Ice tea for me. Danny?"

"DP." Danny grumbled, "Man! Why'd we have to come here?"

"The atmosphere is good." Butch answered.

A period of silence passed before he again spoke out, "So, do I got one?"

"One what?"

"One of your little colors. What do call 'em?"

"A fold."

"A what?"

"A fold! I call it a fold, okay?" Danny snapped.

"What do I gotta do to get one? Does it just pop up?"

"You still don't get it, do ya?! I can't control this! They just appear."

"You know ... I went to school for years. Studied hard to get ahead; did research papers, case profiles, went to institutions, professional seminars, met with doctors, specialists and scientists, you name it, I did it ... to figure out the whys, the how's, where's the body, what's their identity ... and you just see it?"

Danny sat with his arms folded in front of him.

"Dr. Pepper and an iced tea." The waitress repeated the drink order as she placed the glasses down on the worn, Formica tabletop. "You boys ready to order?" she asked. Before Danny even had a chance to look at the menu, Butch recited, "Two onion burgers. Heavy on the onions and two fries."

"Two onions and two spuds. Give me a few, darling.'" She repeated with a wink.

"Tell you what ... I'm gonna help you! Starting today, right here, right now." Butch proclaimed.

"Your gonna help me."

"Yep!"

"You!"

"Yes, sir!"

"Uh-huh … yeah."

"I'm gonna help you first by introducing you to the best onion burger you'll ever have … " he announced, adding lemon juice to his tea.

"Then?" asked Danny.

"Then you're gonna learn to use this for somethin' good."

"This? What do you mean 'this'?"

"You know," Butch motioned to his head and eyes, "that whole … thing."

"Oh! Okay, whatever." he agreed, mockingly, and turned away.

"No! Don't do that to yourself!" Butch snapped, grabbing Danny's attention. "C'mon, say it with me! 'I'm gonna learn to use this for somethin' good.'" Danny stared at Butch intensely from behind the dark lenses of his glasses. "I didn't hear you!" Butch smiled and extended his hand across the table "Say it like you was Anthony Robbins or Zig Ziglar!" Danny looked down at Butch's open hand, not really knowing what to do. "Go on … take my hand. Take off the glasses, son, and quit hidin' … c'mon, let's see those eyes.'" he persisted. "It's okay. We're jus' friends talking and havin' a burger." Danny slowly reached up and removed his glasses, but bowed his head and cast his eyes downward. "All right." Butch congratulated tenderly, smiling, "Now … 'I'm gonna learn to use this for somethin' good!'" Danny meekly extended his right hand as he spoke. Butch suddenly lashed out and firmly grasped Danny's hand, pulling him to the edge of the table "Good! Now, c'mon, say it with me 'I'm gonna learn to use this for somethin' good.'" Danny softly repeated the words, but did not raise his eyes to meet those of his new friend.

"Again!" Butch demanded encouragingly, squeezing Danny's hand.

Danny squeezed back, smiling slightly as both men repeated the statement with more vigor, "I'm gonna learn to use this for somethin' good." The two men sat hand in hand, locked eye to eye as the smile on Danny's face began to widen.

"All right!" Butch affirmed, releasing his grip, "That wasn't so bad, was it?"

"Purple."

"'Scuse me?"

"I said purple. Your fold is purple." Danny explained before taking a straw full of his Dr. Pepper.

"It is? Huh! Purple. Never really been a purple fan."

"No?" Danny asked, "Well, hey man, it looks good on you!"

"Really! You sure?" Butch asked, looking at his shoulders.

"Sure I'm sure!" he restated, "Good lookin' guy like you? You go and get yourself a dark purple button up like a Versace or sumpn'… like what Tim McGraw and Kenney Chesney wear? Hoo! You'd hafta beat 'em off ya!"

After taking a moment to contemplate the possibilities, Butch explained, "I've always seen myself as more of a conservative dresser, like white or pastels or light blue shirts with khaki trousers. You know, can't be too flashy with what I do."

"Oh I can definitely see that!" Danny agreed without hesitation.

"What about them? What do you see with them?" he asked with a nudge of his head toward the guests. Danny turned to look over the unknowing diners and their signs of life. After surveying the room, he turned to Butch and coldly asked, "Which ones?"

"What do you mean which ones? Them over there." he pointed, "Or do they all have 'em?"

"Yep! Right down to the grill cook."

Butch looked around the room, to Danny, back to the guests and once more to Danny. Knowing that Butch was still a skeptic of his morbid talent, Danny energetically stated, "Say! I got an idea. Since you're so interested and want so bad to be helpful, Mr. College Professor Detective, why don't you pick any three and I'll tell you how it'll happen?" Butch leaned back in the booth, unsure as to how he should address the challenge laid before him.

"How what'll happen?"

"How they'll die!"

After contemplating the outcome, Butch low-balled Danny's challenge, laughing nervously "You almost had me there for a second! Man, oh man! You're good!"

"No! Don't do that to me!" Danny demanded with a pound of his fist.

"C'mon, you're supposed to be helpin' me! 'Member?" he reminded his counselor. "Or do you just say that to make yourself feel better?"

"No, I said I'll help you and I'm gonna help you." Butch answered, nervously, timidly.

"Let me help you now!" he offered boldly and stood up beside the table. "I'll pick out the three that are gonna be happening soon! And I mean real soon!" he announced.

Butch tried his best to diffuse the situation as several of the diners turned to watch the spectacle, "No, that's not necessary. Look, you don't have to … "

"Oh, yes I do!" Danny interjected, speaking loudly as he slowly backed away from Butch, "'Cuz I think that *you* think I'm a nut job whacko and that this is just some kinda hoax. Right?" Danny held his arms out wide waiting for an answer. Butch sat silently, helplessly, embarrassed at not knowing how to address Danny's behavior or accusations. He could feel the eyes of the customers focus on him as Danny continued, "'Cuz it makes sense to you that it would be stupid for me to think that I would know that … " He quickly turned and waved his hand through a bright white fold on an elderly woman's right shoulder. Images of the woman's last living moments flashed through Danny's brain as he over exaggerated the experience and flung himself on top of their table, screaming, "Oh! Oh my God! It's horrible! Friday, Mabel, Friday! Your … hear t's … gonna … stop! Ooohhh!" Mabel's lunch flew from the table and landed on the floor with a mighty crash.

Danny rolled on to his side and grabbed Mabel's son, Red, by his shirt collar. "Red!" He yelled to the middle-aged, pear-shaped son as their drinks spilled to the floor, "Sunday! You're gonna find her Sunday when you go to pick her up for church!"

"Danny!" Butch yelled over the panic stricken crowd as they rose to their feet. "Danny, stop it, that's enough!" He apologized profusely as he fought his way through the mesmerized mass, "I'm awful sorry folks, he … Danny!" Butch tried in vain to calm everyone down and take control of the situation, "It's okay, folks! I'm a police officer! Everything's all right! Ya'll go on back to your lunches!" But the patrons ignored him and crowded around Mabel's table.

Danny spied an older black woman sitting by herself with a red fold above her right shoulder and dismounted the tabletop. She remained frozen in her chair as the madman approached and waved his hand by her neck. "Sally! Sally! Don't drive your car! It's too dangerous!" he pleaded.

The frightened patrons streamed out of the restaurant and down the alley to safety. Butch pushed upstream against the fleeing throng and grabbed Danny from behind, wrestling him to the ground.

Sally's mood quickly changed from fear to one of anger and resentment as she gathered her purse and dismissed Danny's ominous request, "No one gon' tell me not drive my car! My car my own business! Ain't no problem wit my car!" As he and Butch tousled about, Danny started to laugh, almost madly, insanely. He peered into the kitchen and noticed the grill cook, Bob, watching the action. Danny elbowed Butch in the stomach, knocking the wind out of him, scrambled to his feet and dashed into the kitchen.

The waitress, Joyce, tried to calm her customers down through the melee, but they continued to leave the restaurant in droves, "Sally, I'm sorry, hon!" she apologized, then nudged Butch in the rear as he struggled to regain his breath. "Why don't ya get him outta here 'stead a scarin' all our cusmers away?"

"Good afternoon!" Danny yelled to the short and portly cook. "Get away from me, you freak!" Bob squealed, darting to the opposite side of the stainless steel prep table. "I just want to talk to you! C'm'ere, big boy!" Danny called and began chasing Bob in a circle around the table.

"Danny! That's enough! Danny!" Butch shouted from outside the kitchen across the order counter. After completing a couple of laps in the kitchen, Danny tackled Bob on top of several large bags of sweet onions.

"Someone get 'im away from me!" he shrieked.

"Bob, Bob, Bob … sshhh!" Danny brought his volume under control as he sat on top of the short, plump man. Joyce, Butch, and the remainder of the customers suddenly found themselves silencing their voices as well. He gently waved his hand through a bright red fold above Bob's right shoulder and stated concernedly, "I just wanted to tell you to be careful when you drain that fryer at night!" Danny smiled and raised himself up off of Bob, picked up his tissue hat and assisted the rotund chef to his feet. "Now!" he continued, handing him his large spatula, "Why don'tcha fix me up with one o' those onion burgers I been hearin' 'bout?" Like a mannequin, Danny placed Bob in front of the grill, motionless and shocked.

Danny calmly exited the kitchen, passed Butch and Joyce and made his way back to the rear booth. He lightly sat himself down, reached for his Dr. Pepper and exclaimed, "Man! Am I hungry!" Joyce handed Butch all the remaining order tickets hanging on the kitchen wheel and politely remarked, "Thanks for coming in, but we can't serve you today. And, thanks for not ever coming back!" Butch, with a handful of tickets stared at Danny in disgust. From across the still and silent restaurant, Danny's innocent defense rang out: "What?!"

Once they had paid their tab and were out in the alley, Danny described the scene he just created. "Man, were you *white*!" he declared, laughing. "You were the whitest black man I ever seen!"

"Thought that was all pretty funny, huh?"

"'I'm a cop!" Danny imitated, "It's all right! Everything is under control!" making himself laugh all the more.

Butch failed to see the humor in what had just transpired, "Pretty big joke, huh?"

"A joke?" Danny repeated as they climbed into the car, "You think that was all just a joke?"

"Well, what else do you want me to call it?" Butch snapped with a squeal of the tires as he pulled away from the curb, "The big show? The parade? The circus? Huh? You know when you go and do those kinda things … you embarrass your mother, me, and yourself! So, yeah, it looks like a joke and it makes it just a tad difficult to believe in you!"

"So, you still don't believe me, do ya?"

"Sure I do! Of course I do! Why not? From that little bit of insight into your delicate, little precious world back there? Yessiree, I believe you!" he patronized with a slap on the steering wheel and a thumbs-up. "Especially after you chase a grill cook around a table and throw 'im on top a bag of onions. Now that's a convincer!"

"Okay, so maybe I went a little overboard."

"A little?"

"I was serious though … anyhow, you got nineteen days."

"What? I got what?" Butch asked.

"Nineteen days … in nineteen days each of those will have happened exactly as I said they will." he stated bluntly.

"To who? Those people back there? Oh this'll be great!"

Danny opened the glove compartment and began rooting around, dropping napkins and straws.

The Folds | 177

"What're you doin'?" Butch asked, irritated at the mess Danny was creating "What're you lookin' for?" Danny closed the compartment without answering, lifted the center console lid and removed a small sticky note pad.

"First one," he announced and grabbed the pen out of Butch's breast pocket, scribbling as he spoke. "Four days from now, on Friday … Mabel will have a stroke and die in her recliner … her son, Red, will find her two days later on Sunday just before six p.m. when he goes to pick her up for evening services. That's one … " Danny removed the sticky note and slapped it on Butch's forehead just to spur him on.

"What am I supposed to do … "

"Two!" Danny interrupted loudly as Butch removed the paper from his head. "Eight days from now, on Tuesday, Sally, with her great impatience, poor hearing, vision, and incredible stubbornness, will attempt to get her social security check cashed by driving herself to the bank. Her car will stall out on the railroad tracks. She won't hear the train, she won't see the train and when she finally does … well … "

"What do you expect me to … ?"

"Three!" he interrupted for the last time and placed sticky note number two over Butch's mouth, "In nineteen days, good ol' onion burger Bob, in a hurry to meet his buddies, will incorrectly drain the fryer, melt the sole of his shoes, slip and fall, break his neck, and burn his body in a pool of 450 degree grease. And be alive for the whole thing." Danny placed the third sticky note on the rear view mirror just as Butch was pulling into the DPS parking lot. Sarah was already waiting outside, sitting under a tree on a bench by the steps of the station. "You'll hear from me in twenty days." Danny simply stated as he opened the door and waved to his mother. "Oh, and by the way," he added with a buddy punch to Butch's right shoulder, "thanks for the great lunch!"

A Prophecy Fulfilled

Monday morning. One week had come to pass since Danny and Butch's disastrous lunch. Butch had been completing paper work since six a.m. and decided he could use a break. Standing up to stretch, he took a few lunging paces around his office, lifting his elbows high as he twisted from side to side. He left his office to go to the snack room for a mid-morning bite to eat.

As he neared the intersection of the two hallways joining the administration offices to the training and dressing rooms, he heard laughter and multiple voices coming from the break room. The casual conversation and jocularity came to an abrupt halt upon his entry. The relaxed and laughing employees immediately resumed their crime-fighting, law enforcement personas, complete with good posture. "Morning all!" Butch smiled as he greeted the staff with handshakes and pats on the shoulders.

He pulled a handful of coins from his pocket as he contemplated his choices from the vending machine, "Rice Crispy Treat," he mumbled to himself softly, "or Bugles?"

"So I said, 'Okay sir, sir, calm down please.'" he overheard two of the dispatchers talking.

"Bugles." he decided.

"'Sir, please calm down and tell me where you're calling from.' And he was just rambling! I could barely get his address he was freaking out so bad!"

"Oh, poor thing!" the second dispatcher sympathized. "I can't imagine what I'd do if that happened to me."

"If what happened?" Butch inquired, joining in on the conversation. He opened his bag of Bugle chips and stood over the two women, waiting for an answer.

"Well, last night, the son of an elderly woman went to pick her up for church services and when he got to her house she was dead … "

"Who was he? How'd she die?" he politely interrogated. The two dispatchers glanced to each other, nervous to answer. Butch hardly, if ever at all, asked any questions of dispatch calls unless there was a problem.

"I don't know." she answered, "But the son did say that she'd had a history of heart problems. She may have had a stroke or a heart attack."

"A name?" he asked impatiently. "Did you get a name?"

"I remember his first name was Red, but don't recall his last … " Without so much as a word, Butch turned and walked briskly out of the break room.

Digging Up the Past

Danny turned his '75 Impala onto Andi Boulevard, looking on both sides of the street for any sign of an address. "Seven Eleven Andi." he muttered as he slowly cruised by dilapidated shacks and abandoned shanties. Judging from the condition of the asphalt, one would have thought they were driving down " Pot Hole Lane;" from curb to curb, the entire street was a web of tar-injected crevices with potholes littering its length. He spied a yellow "Dead End" sign mounted on a corrugated aluminum cross bar at the end of the street after passing the remnants of a burnt house on his left. As neared the end of the block, he noticed a single, rusted mailbox with the barely legible letters "F-A-R" on its side. The lid on the leaning postbox was dangling from one rivet and the red flag was bent permanently into place. On the corners of the split and crumbling concrete driveway were the weathered ghosts of spray-painted "711." He had successfully located the home of Chester Farley, Butch's estranged father.

   He pulled into the driveway and sat in his car for a moment to take note of how discouraging the house appeared. Not looking anything at all like the home in which he was raised, Butch's childhood home reflected the image as never having had any love contained within. The house, with its chain link fenced yard of barren and unleveled red dirt, bumped up against a Shamrock Oil Distribution Center. The smell of oil, petroleum, and gasoline filled Danny's lungs. There were no trees or shrubs on the property, with the exception of one tall, gray stump of a dead willow in front of the first bedroom window. Judging from its size, one could assume that at one time, when hope still lingered in the air, that maybe the tree felt loved. The reddish orange bricks framing in the small staircase to the front door were stacked irregularly with barely any mortar between them. One black shutter clung to the house near the window frame of the master bedroom.

As he continued his visual examination of the run down house, Chester exited the screen door. The door closed behind him with a flat slam; the glass was busted from the top frame and the screen ripped halfway out of the bottom. Chester, only in his mid-sixties, hobbled as if he were in his eighties. He lived the younger part of his life fast and hard, but after he married and had Cleo (Butch), he tried to live faster. The good times disappeared all too quickly for Chester, mostly through the bottle. Now it would appear that the only friend he had was hard times.

Danny watched Chester as he crept down the stairs, carrying a blue plastic watering can. He's was clad in a yellowed, ribbed under shirt, brown trousers with elastic suspenders and mismatched winged-tip shoes. Chester ambled to the faucet, filled the watering can and lumbered awkwardly under its weight as he crossed the yard to where there sat a single, potted purple tulip. Danny could hear Chester mumbling to himself as he bathed the flower. How odd, sad and out-of-place Danny thought to himself: for all that Chester had done in his life, the one thing he now had to show for himself, was that flower.

Danny quietly exited his car and walked to the waist high gate and fence, waiting for Chester to finish his watering. As Chester turned back to the house, Danny politely spoke out, "Scuse me! Mr. Farely? Chester Farley!"

Chester glanced up, answering as he scooted along, "Depends on who want'n to know!"

"My name's Danny Albright, sir."

"Don't know no Andy Fallright!" Chester replied, approaching Danny.

"That's Danny Albright, sir."

"Danny, huh?" Chester asked, now standing merely feet away inside the fenced yard. "Well, Danny, you'll hat'ta f'give me. These ol' ears and bones ain' doin' so well."

"No need to apologize." Danny insisted, smiling. "But I was jus' wonderin' if I could talk to you for a minute of two?" he asked, shielding his eyes from the bright red setting sun.

"Talk to me? Why?" Chester inquired suspiciously, backing away from the fence, "What'd I do?"

"You didn't do anything, sir. I just wanted … "

"I ain' 'n trub, am I? 'Cuz I tol' 'em to stay off my prop'ty, and it was my gun … "

"No, no, no! You're not in any trouble," Danny persisted with a slight chuckle, "I just wanted to know if I can talk to you about this?" Chester approached the fence cautiously then snatched a folded newspaper from Danny's extended hand.

After squinting and adjusting the paper, Chester sluggishly spewed out, "'New Generation of Law Enforcement.' Wha' this got' do wit me?" he asked, confused.

"Well, if you read further on," Danny suggested, opening the gate to let himself in "it's about your son, Cleo."

Chester slapped the paper against Danny's stomach and sternly declared, "I don't have a son!"

He turned away to climb the porch steps, but Danny energetically persisted, jumping in front of him, "Sure you do! You just ain' seen him for a while. If you could just … "

"Look!" Chester interrupted angrily. "My son been dead for years! You need to get off my prop'ty for I lose my temper!" Danny could see the tears beginning to well up in his eyes.

"He's a detective now!" Danny boasted of Butch. He unfolded the paper and read aloud a couple of lines from the article as Chester began climbing the stairs. . "Graduated valedictorian of his high school class … First black valedictorian as a matter of fact." He too, then climbed the steps to the porch as he continued reading, "Graduated with a double major and honors from UT."

Chester again choked out, "I ain't got no son!"

"Mr. Farley, I didn't come here to upset you." Danny explained. He reached around Chester and held the paper in front of him with Butch's picture and article. "I just wanted you to know it's okay now. Whatever happened … it's done. It's in the past and it's okay now." Chester stood quietly with his head hung low. Danny watched his thin shoulders rise and fall with each sorrowful and regretful breath. "You should go see him." he suggested.

"What if he won't see me?"

"He'll see ya, I'm sure of it. I think he's been meaning to, but … maybe he's been wonderin' the same 'bout you." Chester turned to face Danny with tears slowly trickling down his face, but had a thin smile curling the edge of his lips.

"He doin' all right?" Chester inquired hopefully.

"Doin' great!"

He once again gazed upon the picture of his son before inquiring, "He big now? Like me?"

"He's huge!" Danny answered, stretching his arms to the side, leaning back.

"I ain' seen 'im since he was ten." Chester lamented and struggled to read, "Vadel … vale … "

"Valedictorian." Danny pronounced, "It means he was the smartest in his class." Chester couldn't hide his smile or overcome his crying. With a gentle pat of encouragement on the old man's shoulder, Danny tenderly coaxed Chester, "Go see him."

An Unwelcome Visitor

The next day, Tuesday, Butch was on the road, making his way back from Austin. He overheard a transmission on his radio as he entered the outskirts of town: "All units, officer needs traffic assistance and crowd control at junction of Yarbrough and La Plata."

Butch picked up the microphone and responded, " Ranger two two nine nine, what is current situation?"

"Single car collision with freight train and fire."

He slumped the handle in his lap, shaking his head. Reluctantly he replied, " Ranger two two nine nine in transit."

Upon arrival at the scene, he found Jason at the intersection between the railroad tracks and highway. Yarbrough was backed for miles as rubberneckers slowed down to view the fatality. Butch waved to Jason as he directed traffic, letting him know he was there.

He stopped and parked just in front of the engine, spying the engineers and rail hands clustered together. Thick, dark smoke billowed into the sky as flames from burning flesh, rubber, fabric and oil danced brightly through the pillows of black. As he neared the front of the engine, he could see the rear end of the burning car had yet to be incinerated. He jotted down the license plate number then turned to address the engineers. "What happened here, boys?" he asked, just as friendly as if entering a coffee shop and seeing his closest friends.

"She just stopped!" Patrick replied, holding his arm toward the wreckage.

"Just stopped." Butch repeated.

"Yeah!" Patrick answered again, this time yelling as the siren of the hook and ladder truck arriving on the scene drowned out his voice. "It's like there was an invisible chain. The car made its way up onto the crest of the tracks, then just stopped cold." Butch listened closely as Patrick described the gory details. "I think she was still alive," he added, "But by the time we stopped, backed away and got down here, the fire had already started and we couldn't get close to her." Patrick's friends rubbed his shoulder as the burly man broke down, sorry for what had happened, sorry for what he couldn't control.

"Thanks for your time." Butch politely stated, nodding to the quartet of men before turning to his car.

As he passed the hook and ladder truck, he watched as two more local law enforcement vehicles pulled up to assist, along with an ambulance and two more fire engines. Butch removed the small spiral notepad from his breast pocket and flipped it open to the page he wrote the license plate number on. He didn't notice it at first, but when he reached in through the open window of his car for the radio, he saw "That's Two" written on his windshield in white shoe polish. "Ranger Two two nine nine." he called into his handset as he looked around, but found no sign of Danny anywhere.

"Go ahead two two nine nine."

"I need a license plate ID, please?"

Butch gave the dispatcher the license plate number from the burning car and took another long look at the crowd of spectators for any signs of Danny or his car. She repeated the number and asked Butch to wait a moment.

"Two two nine nine?" the dispatcher called.

"Two two nine nine." Butch answered.

"Yes, the car is registered to a Sally Carmichael of Killeen, Texas in Bell County." Butch tossed the handset on the seat and placed his hands over his head, laughing in disgust and dismay.

"Copy, two two nine nine?"

"Copy, two two nine nine?"

He leaned in through the open window and grabbed the handset, "Two two nine nine, yes … copy that."

Later that same day, Butch was standing behind his desk, reading from a stack papers in his hand when a familiar voice echoed in his ears. "Man alive! They got you all setup!" Chester declared proudly as he entered Butch's office, admiring the plaques, pictures, certificates and fine furnishings. "You doin' good, boy!" Butch remained focused on his paperwork as his estranged father kept the compliments rolling, feeling the leather winged chair. "Big chairs and couch! Man!"

"What're you doin' here, Daddy?" Butch asked bluntly, flopping the paperwork on the credenza behind him. Unmoved by his presence, he crossed his arms and stared at his father with deep, unforgiving brown eyes.

"What'm I doin' here?" Chester asked nervously with a small chuckle. "Wh' kinda way is that to talk to your daddy? Do I gotta have a reason t' see my boy?"

"Yes, yes you do!" he answered coldly. "All these years and you just up and decide to come to my office?" The two men looked each over.

"Well, I was jus' out drivin' 'round and thought I'd stop by."

"Drivin' around, huh?" the Doubting Thomas commented.

"Hey, what's with 'Butch' on the door?" Chester inquired, thumbing over his shoulder. "We named you Cleo."

"I like Butch!" he replied anxiously, then immediately tried to calm himself before continuing, tilting his head back. "I go by Butch now, all right? Cleo is in my past."

Chester began to cheerfully explain, "You know, we named you Cleo 'cuz you was just like … "

"Look! I'm busy! I don't got time to stop and play your father-son catch up thing."

"All right. I, uh … I guess I be goin' then." Chester painfully acknowledged. Before passing through the doorframe of the office, he commented, "I'm guessin' you got more important things to do." He turned the corner into the hall and was gone.

Butch reached for his stack of reports and resumed his reading. Not more than two minutes had passed before he slammed the paperwork on the credenza and shouted, "Dad!"

He bolted out of the office, hopped down the front stairs and looked for signs of his father. He spied Chester halfway down the block and sprinted to catch up to him. He finally caught up, grabbed him by the arm and turned him around. From across the street, under the shade of a large oak tree, Danny proudly watched as father and son smiled and shook hands.

The Third Time's a Charmer

Butch passed a large crowd of people on Friday morning as he turned on to LBJ Avenue. They were gathered near the alleyway, just outside the diner he and Danny visited nearly three weeks before. He slowed down to take a look, then suddenly, from somewhere in the crowd, Danny emerged holding three fingers in the air, smiling broadly. Laughing to himself with a shake of his head, Butch immediately pulled over and parked the car across the street from the scene with the emergency lights flashing.

"Shame to hear about good 'ol onion burger Bob, huh?" Danny called out to Butch as he exited his car. They met in the middle of the street, shook hands, then headed towards the gathering crowd.

"Oh, let me guess what this is!" Butch patronized as the duo casually walked side-by-side, "Hmmmm. Could it be that he may have slipped on some mayo?"

"Uh … " Danny began with the same play in his voice, trying hard not to laugh. "No … no, sir! No dairy products involved whatsoever." The two smiled at each other as they approached the restaurant.

At that moment, an ambulance pulled up behind them and made with a quick blast of its siren. The two men jogged a few paces out of the way before Butch continued with his exaggerated hypothesis, "Or maybe they were being robbed and he got shot?"

"Oh … " Danny winced with clenched fists, "Sooo close! But ahhhh … No!"

Two EMT's with a gurney rushed past them and then another one darted by carrying a large medical toolbox. "Hey, Butch, ain'tcha goin' in?" the technician hollered, turning to walk backwards.

"Don't need to!" Butch hollered back, glancing to Danny with a smile and nod. "The guy slipped on spilt fryer grease."

"Yeah!" Danny finished with the full, morbid description, "Slipped and broke his neck. Burned up his whole face!" The EMT briefly stared at Butch and Danny with a puzzled look on his face before turning back to race to the restaurant. Butch and Danny slowly strolled past the mayhem to the town square and it's early morning shoppers.

"A man of many talents you are, Mr. Albright." Butch complimented as the two looked into one of the storefronts, taking their time to pause, talk and window shop.

"Heavy on the 'mister' please." Danny insisted.

"*Mister* Albright, excuse me." Butch retorted.

"That's better! Talented you say? Explain 'talented.'"

"Talented, gifted, blessed?"

"In what way would you imply that I be talented, gifted and or blessed, sir?"

"First of all, that's Sir Farley to you," Butch demanded politely.

" A thousand apologies, Sir Farley." Danny corrected himself, bowing deeply.

"Thank you! Thank you!" Butch answered, returning the bow. "Talented in the sense that not only can you determine the exact ending point of someone's life … but you're also good at bringing 'em back from the dead!"

"Well, I do have to admit, *Sir*, that I have *no* earthly idea of what you're talking about!"

"You know darn well what I'm talking about … " Butch stopped walking to look squarely at Danny.

"Well," Danny tried to justify, "I just thought, you know, you 'n

I … we ain' had our daddies since we were ten. And now I'm back with Mom. I … " He hesitated, feeling his emotions beginning to surface, "I never knew how much I loved and missed her 'til I came back. So … " he finished with a shrug and both men resumed walking.

"Feel strange being back?" Butch asked.

"Yeah … but, after a few days it was like I had never left. We just picked up where we left off. You know you can, too." he suggested with a smile of encouragement.

Oil and Water

Danny rolled back the heavy metal door, bathing all in the barn with bright, early morning summer sunlight. He stood there, momentarily, and hearkened back to the days of long ago when he and his friends had their sleepovers in the upstairs loft. But now the paint, life and glory of the two-story barn had faded from years of neglect. Spider webs, nests, animal droppings, dust, and dirt encapsulated the contents of the barn, as if frozen in time. He approached his father's workbench, pulled back the shutters on the wall and flicked on the overhead work light. The tubes flickered briefly and made a low hum as they illuminated the paint and oil-stained tabletop. Above the bench was Tommy's old stereo, still covered with a plastic trash bag. He blew off the dust before taking off the sack, exposing the hi-fidelity 8-track player. Under the sack he also found a box of old tapes: Elvis, *Live from Hawaii*; Neil Diamond, *Gold*; Roy Orbison's *Greatest Hits*, Waylon Jennings' *Greatest*, and Frank Sinatra's *Songs for Swinging Lovers*. He removed the Neil Diamond 8-track from the dusty box, gave it a good wipe down and turned on the stereo. The stereo came to life with bright, miniature orange bulbs illuminating the knobs. He gently pushed the tape in. After a moment or two, the speakers began pumping out, "Cherri, Cherri."

Sarah heard the music blaring from her upstairs bedroom. She got up out of bed, leaned her head out the window and watched as large plumes of dirt and dust billowed from the barn. After a few vain attempts of yelling at Danny to turn down the music, she donned her robe and made her way downstairs. Danny, who was completely oblivious to Sarah's presence, joined Neil's backup singers and belted out, "She got the way to move me, Cherri," shaking his rear as he danced and swept. Noticing Sarah's shadow by the open door, he turned to see her holding her hand over her mouth, trying to suppress her laugh. He strutted toward her, wiggling his hips in rhythm to the music and took her hand. He gave his mother's arm a mighty tug and yanked her towards him. She lunged slightly off balance into her son's arms with a small squeal and began to jitterbug. A broad smile gradually crossed her lips as she gaily danced and sang. After a couple of spins, Danny turned his mother loose and watched as the greenish-purple fold above her right shoulder suddenly faded to white. His heart sank with despair as waves of nervousness and nausea rippled through the backs of his knees and stomach. He stopped dancing and solemnly walked the few paces to the workbench to turn down the music.

"Whoo!" Sarah yelped, breathing extremely heavy, "I haven't danced like that in years!" Danny offered no response as he stared out the window. "Danny? Hon, what's wrong?" she asked and began walking towards him.

"Ah, nuthin," he shucked with a wipe of his eyes, "It's just all this dust in here." He turned away from her, picked up his broom and quickly changed the subject as he resumed his sweeping, "Did ya hear Chester came to see Butch at his office?"

"Chester?" she asked, leaning against the bench as Danny swept, "Who's Chester?"

"That's his father!"

"His father? I thought his father died?"

"Well, evidently he got better."

"Wait a minute," she inquired, "How'd you know that?"

"When I came by to see you the other day. You were somewhere, so I talked to Butch for a sec."

"I was somewhere, huh! When was I somewhere?"

"I don't remember exactly," he falsely admitted, then again changed the subject, "Hey! I got an idea. Why don' you 'n I take Butch and his dad to The Longhorn for dinner? You know a kinda dual reunion thing?"

"Oh, I dunno!" she contemplated, puckering her lips and biting her inner cheek as she thought aloud, "When other people get involved with separated families, those old feeling that haven't been laid to rest? It can get pretty intense!"

"Not Butch!" Danny scoffed, "You and I will be there to kinda act as a buffer if things gets outta hand. I think it'd be good for us all."

"Well, let me think about it a while. Now don't you go sayin' anything to him. Ya hear?" she finished, turning with a pointed finger.

"Oh, yes, ma'am!"

A few days later, Sarah was covering a lunch shift for two dispatch operators when a call came in. She connected the line, answering calmly and professionally: "Department of Public Safety, what is your emergency?"

"I need help! Quick!" came a panic stricken voice over the speaker. "You gotta send someone out here! Oh my God! Oh my God!" The two other dispatchers, upon returning from their lunch break, leaned over to listen to the exclamations.

Sarah tried to calm down the unidentified caller, "Okay, sir. I need you to settle down and tell me what's wrong?" Heavy breathing and suppressed weeping masked the words, "It's horrible! Oh, it's so horrible!"

Sarah tried again to ascertain the information from the caller, "Sir … sir, please calm down. What's horrible? What's wrong?"

"It's … it's my gravy!" the weeping voice lamented. Sarah looked to the other operators for confirmation of what she just heard.

"I'm sorry, sir, your what? Did you say gravy?"

"Oh my God, it's too clumpy!" the caller cried out. "It's crushing my biscuits!"

"Danny Lee Albright!" Sarah yelled into the headset as she turned off the recorder, "You idiot!" She leaned back in her chair, obviously irritated, but laughing in disbelief at the joke played on her. Glancing over to her chuckling coworkers, she ran her hands through her hair and took a deep breath before lambasting her son, "Don't ever do that to me again! This line is for emergencies!"

"Well, it is clumpy. How do you thin it out?" he asked as he stirred the skillet over the fire. Spilt milk and flour covered the stovetop and kitchen counter.

"You don't have enough milk and your fire's too high!" she pointed out then inquired "Did you use the bacon fat to the right of the stove in the coffee can?" "Uh … okay and no." he replied as he turned down the gas under the cast iron skillet, opened the can and scooped out a spatula full of fat.

"Hey, I was just calling to ask if you'd like to meet me for dinner at The Longhorn?"

"Uh, sure, I guess. What's the occasion?" she asked as she sorted through her paperwork.

"Well … why not? We ain't been out since I came home. Besides, this gravy is beyond saving, You could patch drywall with this stuff. C'mon, please?!" "Um, okay." she finally agreed. "You want me to meet ya when I get off?"

"Yeah, just give me a holler when you're leaving."

"Okay, that'll be in 'bout three hours. I love you!"

"I love you, too!" he replied, then quickly hung up. He immediately picked up the phone again and dialed a number written on a sticky note on the refrigerator. Once the line was connected he requested, "Detective Farley, please."

Several hours later, Sarah entered The Longhorn Restaurant, the town's best and only diner. The early evening setting sun bathed the west side of the dining room in brilliant orange light. The walls of the restaurant were covered with the mounted heads of game the local hunters had downed and donated over the years. Joining the ranks of deer, bobcat, javelina and mountain lion, stuffed and mounted largemouth bass and catfish also hung on the walls. The prized catches came from places as close as Lake Texoma, south to the rivers near the Gulf Coast and as far away as Lake Allan Henry, just outside Justiceburg. Collections of barbed wire, branding irons, lassos, and metal tractor signs were also scattered throughout. Old coffee pots, hand cranked cherry pitters, cowboy hats, and worn out boots dangled from the rafters. Pictures and posters of John Wayne, Mac Davis, Waylon Jennings, Buddy Holly, Gene Autry and Willie Nelson hung in hand crafted wood frames.

For dessert, the Longhorn boasted a menu of eleven kinds of pie, all made by hand and available pretty much everyday. They made chocolate, coconut, coconut crème and lemon meringue pies with meringue thick enough to sit on, but melted in your mouth like air; fresh fruit pies, pumpkin pie and their signature, deep-dish pecan pie. When the Thanksgiving, Christmas, and Easter holidays rolled around, you couldn't even get a piece of pecan pie unless you ordered a whole one at least a month in advance. Or, by some act of God, an order was canceled or not picked up.

Sarah could hardly see the customers in the dining room from the glare of the sun. On the far side of the restaurant, however, she spied the silhouette of Danny, waving his hands in the air. She crossed the room and greeted several of the patrons, treating each and every one she encountered like a lifelong friend.

"I tried calling earlier," she proclaimed as Danny pulled out her chair to sit. "Where've you been?"

"Oh, I had errands to run and came straight over." he answered before giving her a large hug and kiss. He finished with, "Had a good day?" as she sat and he pushed in her chair.

"Stellar!" she answered flatly, already suspicious of his overboard behavior. "What're you doin,' chicken fox?"

"Doing?" he replied, chuckling in denial and confusion, looking above her head as he responded, "What do ya mean what am I doin'?"

As she opened her mouth to speak, Sarah was suddenly interrupted by a deep and scratchy, "Scuse me?"

Before she could turn to respond and get a full visual of the man standing next to her, Danny stood and cried out excitedly, "Hey! Wow! Chester Farley!" "What're … what're you doin' way out here you ol' rascal?" he queried and extended his hand. He shook Chester's hand aggressively and smiled at his mother, but was met instead with a puckered lip with a raised eyebrow. "You wanna join us? Here, give yourself a rest." he suggested, pulling out one of the chairs.

"Oh, thank ya! Don' mind if I do." Chester accepted gladly. He was dressed in faded and worn brown, pinstriped trousers with the hem of the legs frayed at the bottom. His shirt was rose colored, embroidered with a small floral print and faded at the cuff and collar. His long hair, even though unwashed, was slightly kept and his scraggly nest of a beard had flecks of white and gray. His finger nails and teeth also appeared to have been neglected for the longest of time.

"Hello, Mr. Farley, I'm Danny's mom, Sarah," she greeted confidently with a handshake. "You're Butch's father, right?"

"Yes ma'am, and may I say Miss Albright, it is a divine pleasure!" he replied seductively with a sly smile and a small pat of his free hand on top of hers. "Whoo! What a handshake!" he exclaimed.

"Watch'er, Chester!" Danny butted in, nudging him on the shoulder. "That's her shootin' hand!"

At that moment Danny noticed Butch entering the foyer of the restaurant and began waving wildly. Sarah glared intensely at her son, shaking her head with a not-so-amused look on her face. Danny rose slightly out of his seat, looked at his mother and whimpered a guilty sounding, "What?" He continued with, "Come on over ya workaholic!" hollering playfully, as the other patrons took notice of Butch standing at the door. Chester stood next to Danny and motioned for Butch to join them. Butch moved not a muscle. Sarah shrugged and pointed at Danny as if to say, "It was all his idea!" Butch forced his concrete encased feet across the old plank wood floor, feeling his stomach tighten as he drew closer to the table.

Sarah was first to greet him, albeit semi-enthusiastically, "Hey, Butch." "Sarah, Danny," he solemnly addressed and paused before acknowledging his father, "Daddy." "How you doin,' boy? Good to see you!" Chester sugar coated his greeting as he patted his son's back, "You lookin' good! Don' he look good?" "Daddy!" Butch snapped politely with a shake of his head, making it known that his bloated compliments were not appreciated.

"Hey, Sarah!" April hailed as she walked up to the table. "What'll ya'll have to drink?"

"How you doin,' April," she replied, "I think I'll have a sweet tea, please."

"Make that two." Danny interrupted before Sarah could make her introductions.

"April, this is my boss, Butch, and his father, Chester."

"It's really Cleo! I named him!" Chester interjected.

"Cleo Farley, ma'am," Butch clarified, then turned to his father as he continued, "But you can call me Butch."

"Well, Mr. Boss Cleo Butch Farley, what can I git' ya'll to drink?"

"I feel like celebrating!" Chester piped up. "I'll have a bourbon!"

"Whoa!" April belted out quickly. "Sorry, but you're in a dry, dry, dry county. Closest place you'c'n'go an' git a drink is clean clear all the way to Henderson County." Chester contemplated his choices as he looked around the restaurant. "Well, I think I'll just have me … uh, maybe a … "

Butch leaned over and sternly, but discreetly, advised his father, "Daddy, please. Just have the tea. You don't need anything, you can't get anything." Without breaking eye contact with Chester, he instructed April, "Make that four sweet teas."

"Whew! Tall order here!" April chuckled, sensing the tension, "Don't know if I can remember all that! What're ya'll havin' to eat?"

Danny tossed his menu to the middle of the table and recited, "Chicken fry, double mash, extra gravy, extra biscuits 'n okra."

"Shoulda known better!" April commented without bothering to write his order down, "Some things never change!"

"Hey man! What ain't broken don't fix it!" he stated proudly.

"Make it two." Sarah added, leaning hers and Danny's menu to the side. April looked to Butch and Chester as they perused their menus, waiting for a response.

" Just make that four." Danny instructed impatiently and snatched the menus out of their hands.

"All right! Four chicken frieds, double mash'n'gravy 'n okra." April tallied and briskly walked away.

Chester and Butch looked at Danny questioningly, "Jus' think of it as the best onion burger you've never had!" he commented sarcastically with a smile.

"I love onion burgers!" Chester admitted, "Best place to go get an onion burger is on … "

"Twenty-third and Dorothanell." Butch and Danny answered simultaneously.

"Yeah!" Chester agreed, nodding his head, "I can remember goin' there when I was a boy! The owner was this big ol' white boy an' he an' his wife wu' jus' cook onion burgers and fries all day long."

"His grandson owns it now, Daddy," Butch informed Chester. "Danny met him the other day. You remember, Danny. What was his name?"

"Uh, lessee … " Danny forced himself to remember. "His name was Bob!"

"Was Bob?" Chester asked. "Whachu mean 'was'?"

"He died a couple days ago." Butch answered.

"Really?"

"Yeah!" Danny confirmed.

April returned to the table with a tray full of large glasses, alerting all to her presence, "Four iced sweet teas!"

"So, Mom … " Danny began as April divvied out the beverages and placed a small bowl of lemons on the corner next to Sarah and Butch, "I was thinkin' of goin' to church on Sunday. You wanna go?"

"Oh, I don't know!" she winced, looking for an excuse to not go, "I got too many things to do this weekend at the house."

Danny reached across the table, groping for the bowl of lemons. Sarah slapped his hand with a quick, "Manners!" and handed him the bowl.

"C'mon!" he urged, grabbing four lemon wedges before offering any to the others, "You can't postpone a little bit a work for an hour and a half? I ain't been to church in nineteen years! How 'bout you, Chester?"

" I love goin' to church!" he quickly confessed and scooted his chair closer to Sarah.

"Really?" Danny asked, surprised.

"Well, that nice." Sarah stated.

"No, you don't!" Butch corrected his father before attempting to convince the others. "He really doesn't!"

"Sure I do!" Chester insisted.

"You go much?" Danny inquired.

"I'm a Baptist!" he declared, scooting again ever closer to Sarah.

"No! He doesn't!" Butch contradicted.

"I jus' ain' been in a while, that's all."

"Which church do you go to?" Sarah probed.

"Oh, I been lookin' 'roun' to find one I feel comfortable with."

Butch put his foot down to end the charade by asking, "When was the last time you went to church?"

"What does that matter?" he replied, then resumed his flirting with Sarah. "I got me a real nice burgundy dubl'brest'd coat that I like t' wear."

"Really?" she smiled, "Well, Chester you must be the belle o' the ball!" Butch laughed out loud in disbelief, "You're still wearin' that thing?"

"Still?" Danny asked, "How long you been wearin' it?"

"Since I was a boy and even then it was worn out!" Butch interjected.

"It ain' wore out!" Chester declared defiantly, then leaned in towards Sarah for a seductive finish, "It's just now getting comfortable … startin' t' show some maturity of character!"

"So, Daddy," Butch chimed in as he reached for a couple of lemons. "Once more, please, tell us when was the last time you went to church?"

Chester leaned far back, struggling to remember, "Oh … uh … les-see naw!" As his father mumbled to himself, Butch slowly stirred his tea, shaking his head.

"1962!" he stated. Butch immediately doubled over and guffawed out loud. "Whachu laughin' at?" Chester asked, as all three enjoyed a good chuckle at his expense. "I been wait'n to see which one I wanna go 'n dedicate myself to."

"So Chester, how about. … ?" Danny started out, but was distracted by Butch as he silently and intensely mouthed "No" over and over. Danny paid no heed to the sign language and asked anyway, "How about you 'n Butch go to church with us on Sunday?" Chester proudly slapped his son's leg with a big smile and nod of his head. Butch rubbed his face in irritation and disgust.

April approached the table with her arms loaded down, "All right now! Four chicken frieds!"

All Old Things are Made New

On Saturday morning, Butch pulled into a parking space in front of French's, one of the local men's fine clothing stores. He exited quickly and stepped onto the sidewalk where he impatiently waited for Chester just to get out of the car. His father's body, now worn, stiff and lanky, wearily pushed against the weight of door on the Crown Victoria. He slowly crept to the sidewalk and joined his son. Chester stood back a bit as Butch opened the first set of double doors to enter the foyer.

As the first one closed behind him, Butch gripped the handle of the second set of doors. He paused, turned back to his father and firmly stated, "All right now, this is how it's gonna be. We're here for a jacket only. Hear me? One jacket, nothing else." Butch and Chester looked each other square in the eye and nodded in agreement before entering the store.

"But I told you already, son, you ain't gotta be goin' to git me no jacket!" Chester lamented.

"Look, we've been invited as guests to a new church," Butch stated breathily as a sales assistant approached them, "and you're not gonna wear that Fred G. Sanford jacket."

"Good morning, gentlemen," the clerk greeted them with early morning enthusiasm, "What are we in need of today? Blazer? Trousers? Ties? Shoes?"

"All the above." Chester blurted out jokingly.

"A jacket, please. Just a jacket," Butch dryly corrected, then leaned back and inquired, "What're you wearin' these days, Daddy?"

"Why don't we go over to the fitting room and I'll measure you, just to be sure." the assistant suggested, motioning for the two to follow. Butch politely held out his arm to let his father pass. "Whoowee!" Chester crooned as he passed a few rows of new fall suits, "Boy, ain' them sharp!"

"Well, if you was workin' 'stead of drinkin,' you might a been able to come 'n get you one!" Butch stated bluntly as he followed close behind.

Once in the dressing room, Butch slumped heavily into an arm chair, as if he was tired from shopping all day. Chester stood on the platform in front of three mirrors with his arms stretched out wide as the sales assistant measured his chest, waist, and arms. The clerk mumbled to himself and exited the dressing room, leaving the two men alone. Butch quietly looked his father up and down, taking in the sight of his old clothes, poor posture and frail presence. Chester, uncomfortable with being up in front of the mirrors, tried his best to make himself more presentable.

The clerk jubilantly entered the room with three different coats, announcing, "Here we go, sir! Try the navy double breast with two on three buttons." He held the coat open and helped pull it up onto Chester's shoulders, "Goes great with almost any color of pant. There … how's that feel?" The clerk stepped back, placed his hands on his hips and waited for some kind of positive response as Chester examined his reflection in the mirror. He was overwhelmed at the sight of himself in a new coat and felt his emotions beginning to rise.

Butch and the sales clerk traded looks with each other before asking, "How's it feel, Daddy?" Chester rubbed the sleeves and pivoted sideways to admire himself. "Daddy? How does it feel?" Butch repeated, raising his voice a bit.

"Feels good! Real good!" Chester admitted proudly. "But don' they got this in red or sump'n?"

"Excuse me for just a moment, won't you?" the clerk asked with a smile as he backed out of the dressing room.

"Blue is more practical!" Butch advised and pulled himself out of his chair. "Besides, I'm the one buying it." he reminded. "Looks good on ya." he complimented softly, looking at his father in the mirror. "Daddy?" he timidly asked, feeling the fabric of the new coat, "Why didn't you ever take me to church ... after Momma left?" Chester's confident smile slowly dissolved into a frown of embarrassment and shame.

He turned away from his reflection and drew a deep breath before shakily answering, "Because I ... I didn't think that after all what I had done was ... " Chester stopped in mid-sentence, then raised his head to face Butch in the mirror before finishing, "I felt like I wasn't forgivable." Butch wiped a tear rolling down his cheek and turned away from the mirror.

The sales clerk again entered the dressing room and, upon seeing the facial expressions on the two men, realized he'd interrupted something. Trying to keep the feel of the moment light, he inquired, "What were you planning on wearing with the jacket? Did you have a favorite shirt?"

"Well, this one of course." Chester informed him. The clerk could easily see the worn cuffs and collars and mismatching buttons. Trying not to embarrass Chester, he innocently informed Butch, "Sir, we do have some smart looking dress shirts on sale if you wouldn't mind looking?" Chester flashed a devilish grin to his son.

Butch made it an all-out day with Chester. After purchasing the jacket, they crossed the town square and headed over to Brett's to match up a shirt, tie, socks, suspenders and trousers. The bosom buddies then went shopping for shoes and a new hat at Shipman's and ended the day by swinging through Eddie's Barber Shop to get a hair cut, a pedicure and manicure. Over the course of the day, the two talked about the old times and when things were good. They shared a tear or two as they informed one other as to what had been happening in their lives over the past twenty-plus years. After a long day and a relaxing dinner at Furr's cafeteria, Butch drove his father home.

He didn't turn off the car after he pulled into the cracked and crumbling driveway. Chester exited quietly, opened the back passenger door to collect his bags of clothes, then returned to his still open front passenger door. After a moment of contemplation, he sheepishly inquired, "You ... wanna come in for a spell?" and motioned to the house.

"Uh ... nah ... " Butch answered, looking at the dimly lit and dilapidated home. "Not tonight, but thanks anyways. Maybe another night." he smiled as he continued his polite bow out. "I need to get back to the house. I wanna be ready for tomorrow ... we got a big day ahead of us."

"Yes, sir!" Chester agreed, smiling back, then closed the door. Butch watched his father climb the porch steps and open the front door. Chester turned and raised the bags with a smile and nod as Butch backed out of the driveway and waved goodbye.

As she lit up a cigarette, Sarah confessed nervously, "I don't know about this, son!" She took in a deep drag and exhaled a long plume of smoke. "I haven't been here in so long ... I don't feel comfortable." She and Danny sat in his car in the parking lot of the First Baptist Church, waiting for Chester and Butch to arrive. She fidgeted like a nervous cat, looking all around her, almost incapable it seemed of sitting still.

"Mom," Danny consoled, lighting up a cigarette as well "It's church ... our church. Big deal if you haven't been in years. Neither have I."

"People are gonna' be lookin' at us n' whisperin' 'n. ... "

"Well, go on and let 'em whisper! Let 'em talk out loud for all I care!" he ranted with a wave of his cigarette. "I'm nervous—we're both nervous! So, we'll be nervous together!" he confided, reaching for his mother's hand.

"You think they'll show up?" she asked, looking at her watch, "It's already ten after ten."

A few more cars of latecomers trickled into the almost full parking lot. " Butch said they were gonna go shopping yesterday to get Chester sump'n to wear," he informed as he looked around the church grounds, then focused his attention on the baseball field. "Man! I used to love comin' here," he lamented longingly.

"Me too!" Sarah agreed.

"I remember Daddy and Pastor Cregan ... man, they musta' spent hours teaching me ball in that field!" he reminisced with a warm smile, "I loved playing ball."

From out of the corner of his eye, Danny caught sight of Butch's white Crown Vic as it entered the opposite end of the parking lot then pulled up and parked next to he and Sarah. All four exited their cars, nervous with anticipation at not knowing what the morning will bring. As Sarah rounded the front passenger side of her car, she greeted Chester with a high pitched squeal, "Whooweee! Say Butch! Ain't ya gonna introduce me to this handsome young friend of yours!" She was greatly surprised at the appearance of Chester with his hair cut and new clothes, looking like a fine southern gentleman.

"Well, what do we have here!" Chester proclaimed as Sarah spun around in her pastel yellow dress, flipping the back of her hair. "Am I to be blessed with the company of this fine young lady?" Butch and Danny remained expressionless as they watched the two senior teenagers light up in the sight of each other. With his prideful chivalry placed in overdrive, Chester extended his arm to walk Sarah to the church. The two sons looked to each other with a roll of their eyes.

"Man, what took ya'll?" Danny inquired with a slight slap to Butch's shoulder, "We probably already missed the Lord's Supper!"

"Mornin'!" Butch replied, flatly.

"Man! You need to relax!"

"What? I'm okay! I'm completely relaxed!"

"Okay." Danny agreed and turned to walk to the church. After a few steps, he looked back to see that Butch hadn't moved from his spot next to his car. "Let's go! C'mon!" he beckoned, snapping his fingers and slapping his lap as to call a dog, "You okay?" Butch remained firmly planted, anxiously playing with his keys in his pocket. "What's wrong?" he asked.

"I don't know what to do."

"What do you mean 'what to do'?" Danny laughed.

"I have no idea what I'm doin' here," he admitted ashamedly, "What goes on, what to say, how to act?"

"You ain' gotta do nuthin'!" Danny instructed with a thin smile and hand on Butch's shoulder, "Just go on in, sit down with us, maybe sing a song and listen. That's it."

"Sit and listen?"

"Sit and listen." he repeated with a twist of his head toward the church, "C'mon, I'll even let you sit by me!"

"Oh, goody!" Butch retorted smartly, "I suppose now you're gonna want me to write you a note during class!"

Sarah and Chester waited for Danny and Butch in the foyer. The heavy, white wooden doors to the sanctuary swung open, bathing the back rows in brilliant early morning light. The stream of sunshine perfectly illuminated the center aisle from the back row all the way to the stage and podium where Pastor Ray Brock was just getting into the opening lines of his sermon. Pastor Brock paused for a moment to see who had entered. Several others in the congregation turned to look as well, including Monica and Jason, John and Joey, Ron and Holly, and Terry and Casey. Sarah and Danny were immobilized with fear, but tried their best to put on a pleasant face. With a broad smile of pure joy, Pastor Brock motioned for them to take the only seats available, down on the front row. Pastor Mike Cregan leaned to the side to get a visual of who entered the services so late. Danny took a deep breath, extended his elbow to Sarah and slowly and quietly escorted his mother to their seats. Butch played his best poker face as he followed closely behind Danny and Sarah. Chester, on the other hand, unmoved by the blatant stares, smiled and winked to the members as he respectfully tipped his hat.

As Danny approached the front row, both he and Brother Mike locked eyes. Mike immediately clasped his hands to his chest and prayed silently to God, thanking Him for finally delivering Danny and Sarah back home.

Pastor Brock finished reading the scripture he had begun prior to the quartets entry, "Therefore let all bitterness and wrath, and anger, and clamor, and evil speaking be put away from you, with all malice: And be ye kind one to another, tenderhearted, forgiving one another, even as God, for Christ's sake hath forgiven you." He removed his glasses and momentarily rubbed his eyes as the foursome took their place on the bench and settled in, "You know, I had this big sermon planned for today ... but, now I think I'd rather tell you a story instead." He paused to collect his thoughts and paced in a small circle.

"There was a father who had two sons," he began, "He had several servants and livestock and land to work ... a pretty well-to-do guy ... then one day the youngest son asked for his inheritance and left his father and brother with his fortune to seek out his own desires." Pastor Brock strode slowly from one side of the stage to the other, making direct eye contact with his flock. "This son spent his money quickly and lived wildly!" he continued, "He didn't stay in touch with his father or brother ... and then all of a sudden ... the money ran out. There was a famine at the time, so the son went to work for a man who would only let him live and eat with his pigs." He crossed the stage and stopped directly in front of Danny and Sarah.

Chester turned to Butch, smiled softly and placed his hand on his son's knee, patting him tenderly a few times. "Then one day," Pastor Brock continued, "the son said to himself 'Maybe I should go home! I don't feel so good about my decisions!' 'I think was better off when I was in my father's house!' His father's house. So he goes home. He goes home. His father sees his son coming down the road and runs to him, embracing him, kissing him, then yells out to his servants: 'Get my son the best robe and put it on him! Get him some shoes! Get him a ring for his hand! Kill the fatted calf! Let us eat and be merry! My son who was once dead is alive again!'"

Danny felt his chest begin to tighten. His throat was drying out, his head pounded and his heart raced. Pastor Brock pointed to the heavens and closed the story with a triumphant declaration, "He was once lost! And now is found!" Tears of pain and joy flowed down Sarah's and Danny's faces. He tried to suppress his tiny, wispy yelps of emotion, struggling with all of his might to not have a complete breakdown in front of the congregation. Butch sensed a great beating in his heart, a longing pressure he hadn't felt, or at least allowed himself to feel, in years. A feeling that comforted him and told him everything was going to be okay, that all was forgiven and he could have faith once more if he tried.

Pastor Brock stood directly in front of Danny and tenderly confessed, "We all get lost sometimes, and it's okay. It's okay because our Father never loses sight of us." Sarah pulled a handkerchief from her purse to dab around her eyes as she attempted to regain her composure. "Let us pray." he instructed.

After church services, Danny, Sarah, Butch and Chester approached pastors Brock and Cregan near the podium. "Man! It is so good to hear your voice again!" Danny exclaimed as he energetically embraced Pastor Brock, "I didn't know I missed being here so much!"

"Well, I just thank God you're safe, you're all right and more importantly that you're here!" Pastor Brock beamed as he grasped Danny's shoulders, giving him a good looking over. "How're ya doin,' guy?"

"Great! Doin' great!" he replied jubilantly as he reached back for Butch and his father. "Brother Ray ? These are friends of mine, Butch Farley and his dad, Chester. An' you know Mom!" Sarah reached out with both arms and embraced Pastor Brock, clinging to him tightly as she wept tears of happiness.

"What a great morning!" he announced while hugging Sarah, "This is such a blessing!"

"Now don't you get me all riled up again!" she requested with a wipe of her eyes, "You already done it once today!"

"And it's a blessing to see some new faces in the crowd. Butch? Chester? Y'all from out of town?"

"Butch works with mom." Danny blurted, "He's her boss."

"Well, he's not really my boss," she politely contradicted, "But I do work directly with him quite a bit."

"Thanks for the good speech." Butch began timidly and extended his hand to the pastors. "Chester Farley, sir, and how lovely to meet you!" his father stealthily interrupted with a flash of his signature grin, ready to make his great first impression.

"Very uplifting message this morning, sir," he spewed, "Very touching, moving, uh, inspiring … " In not finding any other impressive words to describe the sermon, Chester stood awkwardly with Pastor Brock, still shaking his hand vigorously.

"Thank you, thank you." he replied, breaking Chester's handshake, "So, what finally brings ya'll out this mornin'?" Pastor Cregan piped in.

"Danny invited us to come out today for a little change of scenery." Chester explained before anyone could get a word in. Butch stared at his father in disbelief as he continued with his performance. "And I am sure glad we did! This is beautiful." he stated as he looked about the sanctuary.

"So what church do ya'll regularly attend?" Brother Mike asked. The quartet of friends looked to one another, waiting for someone to come up with an acceptable explanation.

"They've been to several around the north lately, haven't you?" Danny remarked with a wink to Butch to join in the charade. "I think ya'll said Northridge First Assembly, right?" Pastors Brock and Cregan looked at each other confusedly, being not at all familiar with the name.

"They're out looking for a place to call a second home. Isn't that what you said the other day over tea, Chester?" Sarah added.

"Oh … yes … yes, sir!" Chester agreed with a chuckle as he caught on, "Second home, that's right! We been waiting to see where we feel welcome and comfortable … to devote our extra time so we can get to know the congregation."

"We'd love to have you here!" Pastor Brock suggested, "We sure got great people … people that'll make ya feel more 'n welcome!"

"We're not too big, but not too small, just about the right size to know enough but not everything and still feel secure!" Pastor Cregan chimed in for the closing pitch as he picked up hymnals from the seats.

"Great! Sounds good." Butch and Chester admitted, nodding their heads in agreement.

"Now, Chester," Pastor Brock began advising as he motioned for them to walk toward the foyer, "you'll probably want you to start with the seniors group. I think you'll fit in well with them. And Sarah," he suggested firmly with a low glance over his glasses, "You might wanna get back into the women's home group again?"

"Danny?" he continued, raising his voice back over his shoulder. "You and Butch can start in the adult group!"

"Oh, I've been gone so long," Sarah stated, wincing with a lack of confidence. "I don't think the girls would like it if I were to … "

"I think," Pastor Brock interrupted, stopped and turned to Sarah, "if you would give them a chance, they'd prob'ly like to give you a second chance!" He opened the door of the sanctuary that led to the foyer. As Sarah entered the foyer, her heart took flight when she spied her best friends waiting for her. Monica, Holly, Terry, and Joey, along with their husbands, all stood to welcome home their sorely missed life-long friend. She raised her hands to cover her face, unable to contain her emotions. The four women, now with tears streaming down their cheeks, walked over to Sarah and encircled her, wrapping their arms around her.

"I'm so sorry!" she gushed, so full of pain and happiness at the same time. "Sssshhh, it's all right! It's okay now. We know it's been hard." the quartet sympathized. "I love you all so much. I've been so stupid and selfish. I'm sorry!" she confessed.

"It's okay, hon. You don't need to apologize." The girls offered up their support while holding Sarah's hands, stroking her hair and rubbing her back.

Pastors Brock and Cregan, along with Butch, Chester, Danny and the four husbands, formed a ring around the group of embracing friends, placing their hands on their shoulders.

The nine men then bowed their heads as Pastor Brock prayed aloud, "We thank You and praise You, our most kind and gracious heavenly Father … "

Another Door Closes

It was in late August of the following year; Butch was in his office at the Texas Rangers station. His desk was cluttered to the point of complete obscurity by the stacks of files and notebooks. The walls, covered with photos, maps, dry erase boards and flow charts, masked the numerous awards, plaques and certificates he garnered over his many years of dedicated and consistent service. Danny brazenly entered the office, unannounced, to pick him up for lunch. As he watched Butch search for a specific file in his stacks of paperwork, Danny plopped himself down hard on the couch, waiting to be acknowledged. He couldn't help but notice the level of irritation and volume in Butch's voice as he finished a phone conversation.

"So what did ballistics say?" he asked, aggravated, with his free hand on his hip. "Well, there has to be! Look! You can't fire a gun four times and have four different groove patterns. It just doesn't happen," he blasted, waving his arm in the air before continuing, "Well, run it again! I'm not coming down there to do your job! That's what I want to confirm: if the grooves match all four times, then we got the same gun. Run it again!" he ordered with a slam of the phone.

Butch stared at his desk and the volumes of congested information. "Troubles with the democrats again?" Danny asked smartly, lying nonchalantly on the couch with his leg dangling over the arm.

"Oh!" Butch stammered, tossing his pen and glasses on top of the desk. "A hitch hiker reported a body just outside of Grapeland in Houston County." He turned to face a large detailed map of the entire state of Texas behind his desk, pointing out the area as Danny rose to his feet and joined him. "Says that he had a single self-inflicted gunshot wound," Butch volunteered as he placed a red push pin in the map, "We found the bullet is very similar … "

"Man, am I hungry! Let's go!" Danny interrupted, slumping in the arm chair next to the desk, lifting his legs to prop his feet.

"*Very similar* … " Butch repeated with much vigor, slapping Danny's legs off the desk, "to that of three girls that have died over the past nineteen years. Their bodies have been found anywhere from fifteen to eighty miles of the metro area with the same … "

Butch was again interrupted by a female officer who poked her head in, "'Scuse me, Butch," she quickly blurted, "There's an emergency phone call for you on two." She finished with a slap on the doorframe before disappearing. Butch picked up the receiver and was ready to press the flashing red light when he noticed Danny watching him with hurt in his eyes.

"What?" he asked.

Danny spied Butch standing at the end of the hallway speaking with Chester's doctor. The two men were silhouetted against the large window overlooking the side lawn of the hospital. Although he didn't know specifically what was being said, he could tell by the shaking of the doctor's head and Butch's folded arms that it wasn't good news. As he sat outside Chester's room, Danny watched the doctor reach up and pat Butch's shoulder, then turn to enter the stairwell. Butch faced the window, bowed his head and leaned onto the windowsill. Moments passed before he straightened himself and began walking slowly toward Danny.

"How's he doin'?" Danny asked softly as he rose to meet his dear friend. He could see the pain in his eyes.

"Pancreatic cancer," he stated with a crack of his voice, "Advanced stage. Got five, maybe six weeks. Doc thinks that he probly knew he was sick and was trying to hide it. Didn't want anyone to know or … maybe didn't have the money to do anything about it."

He turned away from Danny and wiped his eyes, sniffing deeply as he exclaimed, "This is all my fault!"

"Your fault?" Danny asked, confused. "How's this your fault?"

"If I hadn't o' left … I coulda been there to get him help! I woulda known."

"Don't do that to yourself!" Danny instructed sympathetically. "How can you blame yourself? This isn't your fault. People die. Your daddy, like my daddy, will die. And I'm sorry … so sorry for this … but it's not your fault." Butch nodded patronizingly in agreement, but was still not convinced.

"Did, uh … did you know this?" he solemnly asked, pausing a bit. "How? When? Is that why you went and found him?"

"Yes."

"Why didn't you tell me?" Butch growled, throwing his hands in the air in disbelief, "Why didn't you say something?"

"Well," Danny explained, "at the time you thought I was full of crap and if I had it wouldn't have changed his being sick." The two men briefly stared at each other before he continued, "If I had told you, told you right then what was going to happen, you would of probably treated him just as a responsibility … a 'have to.' All of a sudden, 'Here I am, outta nowhere' and 'take care of me'!" Danny let his words sink in for a spell before closing his defense, "He wouldn't of been your friend. He would of been just an old, sick guy who you were gonna stay angry at and to be tolerated for a while. I don't' know, maybe you woulda just found some way of putting him in a home or assisted care, euthanizing him."

"You think I'd have my own daddy put to sleep?" Butch questioned angrily, cocking his head to the side.

"Well, it really didn't seem to matter much to you a year ago whether he was alive or not!" he jabbed smartly, "Not a whole lot of reaching out on your part!"

Butch rubbed his face and irritatingly asked, "What's that?" pointing to a book in Danny's hand.

"What? This?" he confirmed, with a light and informative tone, "This is the book my daddy used to read to me. Thought you might be able to use it now … it's called *The Men Who Wore the Star*." Butch took the book from Danny and opened the old and faded hard cover to look at the table of contents. "It's stories about the Texas Rangers 'n I figured: we're in Texas, you're a Texas Ranger, so … just a little sump'n to pass the time." Danny placed his hand on Butch's shoulder and gently offered, "If ya need me, you call me."

The two men hugged tightly as Butch painfully whispered, "I'm losing him again!"

"Hey, c'mon now! You can't let him see you like this? That'll just get him down." Butch broke the embrace, wiped his eyes and drew a deep breath. "Give him our best." Danny instructed and turned to walk away. "Call me later!" he hollered from down the hall, walking backwards.

Butch straightened his shirt and rolled his shoulders in preparation for what lay on the other side of the wall. He gingerly pushed open the heavy and wide wooden door. The beige full length blinds were drawn shut, making the room seem not at all friendly and lacking hope. He approached the side of the bed and drew up an arm chair from the wall. Reaching out to tenderly stroke his father's hand, he felt his thin, soft and wrinkled skin. Chester's eyes fluttered open. He laid motionless, looking at the ceiling before turning his head.

"You're a site to wake up to!" he smiled with his voice cracking, "How long you been here?"

"Few seconds … How ya doin'?"

"Oh, you know me. I'm a fighter," Chester bragged with a smirk, "Just knocked down a bit, that's all. I'll be up and outta here in a couple days."

"Yeah, well, we'll see how you're doin,' Ali."

"Whatchya got there?" Chester asked, glancing down at the book clutched in Butch's hand. Like Danny earlier, Butch also changed the inflection in his voice, "This is the book that Tommy Albright used to read to Danny when he was a little boy, and Danny thought we both might like it."

"That's nice of him! What's it about?" he inquired, tilting his head to see the title, "Ah! Cowboys and Indians!"

"Ya interested?"

"Sure, sure!" he answered, raising himself to lean against the headboard. Butch pulled the drawstring on the blinds to let in more light. The late afternoon sun flooded the room, lightening the mood.

"Well, lessee now, *The Men Who Wore the Star*," Butch stated, donning his glasses.

"You remember me readin' to ya?" Chester asked.

"No … no. I don' think I do." Butch admitted after trying to recollect just such a time.

"You were jus' a little thin'! Yeah! You'z four or five. Be time for bed an' you'd be playin' sick and you'd tell one o' us you had a headache." Butch laughed at the idea of himself, which made Chester laugh. "I'd ask you where it wuz that you hurt an' you'd rub your belly an' holler, 'Oh! My haidache! My haidache!'" Butch placed his hands on his face, shaking his head as he envisioned the scene "'N you'd stick out your lip a little and say, 'I think I'd feel better if you'd read to me.' Ha! You knew how to work it even back then!" Chester complimented with another full belly of a laugh.

"I was pretty clever, huh!"

The laughs subsided as Chester lamented, looking up at the ceiling, "Yeah! That was probl'y 'bout one o' the last times I ever got to pick you up n' hold you." Butch looked away in silent contemplation then removed his glasses and lowered the rails on the bed. He gently climbed onto the bed and laid his head on his father's chest. Chester closed his eyes in peaceful bliss as he wrapped his arm around his son, curling a hand up to rub his head. Butch felt his own heart racing as he listened to the slow and faint beat of his father's, looking at the picture of Jesus Christ hanging on the wall at the end of the bed.

After a brief moment of serene silence, Butch's voice broke as he squeaked out, "Daddy, I'm sorry. I'm sorry. I … "

"Sssshhhh! Hush now!" Chester advised softly, slightly rocking his boy side to side, "Ain' nuthin' to be sorry for!" "You know?" he asked, looking to the widow and the sun shining through the blinds, "I used to feel alone n' afraid. I was ashamed … n' I was scared of dyin.' But you know what now? I'm happy!" Butch's eyes welled up with tears as his father spoke the words he had so longed to hear, "I'm at peace when I'm with you, son! I love you, 'n I'm proud o' you!"

A couple of weeks passed and on one particular Sunday, Butch drove Chester to church for what would prove to be the last time. The effects of the cancer made themselves ever present as the two men inched their way down the aisle to sit with their clan of friends. Danny, Jason, Ron,

John, and Casey all did their best to assist Butch in getting Chester seated and making things as comfortable as possible. From the moment he helped Chester out of the car and into church, Butch dared not let go of his father's weakened hand.

An hour and a half later, Pastor Cregan led the congregation in a closing prayer. The sermon ended and members of the church almost immediately, formed a small line at the end of the pew to greet Chester and shake his hand. Although thin and feeling a great loss of strength, he didn't let his pain show as he smiled and chatted with the members of his Men's Bible Study Group, the choir and others from his senior class.

While Chester and Butch were preoccupied with their socializing, Danny stealthily left the group and pulled Pastor Cregan to the side.

"'Scuse me, Mike, but Butch needs to talk to you and Pastor Brock for a second. He's kinda wantin' to get some advice."

"Is he all right?" Mike inquired, concerned.

"Oh, yeah, fine … he's fine." Danny confided, glancing back, "I think he actually just wants a little 'encouragement' or opinion on something."

Several minutes had passed by when Pastors Brock and Cregan finally the group, still talking and laughing. "Butch? You okay?" Brother Ray spoke up, "Danny said you needed to talk?" The huddle of friends quickly hushed themselves and turned their attention to Butch. He rose from his seat and attempted to diffuse the situation by discounting the comment.

"No, I mean yeah, well, I don't really need to, uh, well?" he stammered, looking to Danny for some support. Danny tossed his head to the side, nudging him to talk to Pastor Brock. "Well, I was wonderin,' I mean I was thinkin' 'bout maybe, if ya'll do this kinda thing here for someone like me, that uh, maybe, we could talk about uh … " Butch cleared his throat with a nervous chuckle and rubbed his hands together.

"Baptized!" Danny proclaimed with a smile, jumping in to finish the statement, "He wants to be baptized, right?"

"Really?" Pastor Brock confirmed with a pat on the shoulder, "That's great! You think you're ready? I mean, do you know why you want to be baptized and what it means?"

"Yes, sir, I do." Butch replied confidently as the other men congratulated him and shook his hand.

"That's my boy!" Chester added.

"Thanks, Daddy!"

"Oh, Butch!" Sarah cooed as she kissed his cheek, "That's great! God bless you!"

"Good. Good." Pastor Brock nodded before continuing, "Well, when are ya thinkin' 'bout wantin' doin' this?"

"Today!" Danny blurted, "Like, now."

"We can go up and get started if you like?" Brother Mike suggested enthusiastically. "I do have one request, however, if you don't mind?" Butch asked, moving to Chester's side, "that my father be baptized too, if he's ready and willing." Chester raised his eyes to meet those of his son.

All remained quiet as Chester shakily, but proudly answered, "I'll do it with you!"

Pastor Brock, beaming with pride and joy announced, "Okay then, let's go."

The two pastors, along with Sarah, lead the way, followed by Butch and Danny as they helped Chester along. Monica and the girls, along with Jason and the rest of the husbands, remained seated downstairs in their pew.

Chester was sandwiched in the stairwell with Danny behind him and Butch facing him, walking backwards up the stairs as he held his hands for support. As he neared the top of the stairs leading to the baptism pool, Chester looked past Butch and noticed the two pastors taking off their coats in preparation. Sarah was already seated in an extra side chair at the top of the landing near the baptism pool. Butch turned loose of Chester on one side and placed his father's hand on the rail leading down to the water. Butch, unknowingly, merely kicked off his shoes and stepped down into the cool water, still dressed in coat, tie and all. Sarah, Chester and Danny laughed at the sight of Butch standing fully dressed in the cold and more than waist deep water. Pastor Brock exited the dressing room and came back to see what the laughter was for and saw Butch already standing in the water. The scene unfolded like a play for the four couples sitting below and innocently joined in on the laughter. Not to embarrass Butch any more by what he'd done, Pastor Brock decided to forego the rubber trousers and waded in by his side.

"Mike?" Pastor Brock called out, "Mike?"

"I can't untie my laces!" Mike whispered back as loud as he could.

"C'mon, now!" Pastor Brock urged. Not wanting to wait any longer, he loudly asked, "Cleo Farley … do you come unto the Lord filled with love in your heart for His Son Jesus Christ?" Mike appeared at the edge of the stairs leading to the baptism pool and tried once more to balance himself and untie his shoes. He inadvertently lost his balance and fell headlong into the shallow pool, completely dressed, creating a wave that spilled out over the wall onto the choir's chairs and dripped down the wall. Pastor Brock allowed the peanut gallery below a few moments to get the laughter out of their system before returning his attention to the matter at hand.

Butch regained his composure as well, swallowed dryly and lowly answered, "Yes."

"Do you accept Jesus Christ as your one and only Savior?"

"Yes." he again replied.

"Then Cleo Farley … " Pastor Brock began.

"Hold on!" Butch interrupted. He turned to his left, extended his hand and called out, "Daddy?"

Danny and Sarah helped Chester remove his coat and shoes then down the stairs to edge of the water. Mike took his arm and lead him through the pool to Butch's right side, then joined father and son by their hands. Butch turned to his father for reassurance, smiled, then faced forward as Pastor Brock triumphantly declared, "Cleo Farley, I welcome you as a brother into the Kingdom of God in the name of the Father, the Son and the Holy Spirit. Signifying the birth, death and resurrection … "

Pastor Brock and Chester, along with the help of Mike, leaned Butch back into the water. As his head dipped below the surface of the water, the pastor's words were replaced with faint whispering and beautiful, calming humming sounds that resonated in his head. Suddenly the water felt rather warm, like he was moved somewhere else or in some sort of enclosed vessel. Sensations rippled throughout his entire body, like that of fingers of newborn babies touching their mommy for the first time. Time ceased to exist as he lay under the water; peaceful and content, yet feeling compelled to open his eyes. The Holy Spirit flowed through him as he looked in amazement through the water at the illuminated images surrounding Danny, Chester, Sarah, and the pastors.

" … Of Jesus Christ," Pastor Brock finished the baptism, pulling Butch out of the water. Butch lunged into his father and embraced him tightly, weeping with excitement at what he just experienced. His heart pounded fiercely as he drew bigger and deeper breaths of air, clutching his father. Chester and Butch clung to one another in the baptism pool as the spectators watched from below. Danny, Sarah, Pastor Brock, and Pastor Cregan recited silent prayers while the two men embraced each other. Butch was so overcome with the burden of guilt from sin being lifted from his shoulders, he couldn't control his weeping.

Pastor Brock politely interrupted to move things along, "Chester?" Chester switched places with his son and took hold of Pastor Brock's outstretched arm while still clutching Butch's hand. Pastor Brock smiled, looked him squarely in the eyes and asked, "Chester Farley, do you come before God, filled with love for His Son, Jesus Christ?"

"I do, sir." he, too, answered, slightly gasping.

"And do you proclaim that His holy Son, Jesus Christ, is your one and only Savior?" Chester nodded and squeezed Butch's hand. "Then Chester," Pastor Brock offered, "I welcome you as a brother into the Kingdom of God in the name of the Father the Son and the Holy Spirit!" He and Butch slowly lowered Chester back into the water.

Almost effortlessly, it seemed, they pulled Chester up out of the pool. The water trickled down his face as he breathed smoothly and deeply. He opened his eyes and looked about him, smiling; how brilliantly everything now glowed, as if washed clean and made anew. Danny and Sarah then entered the water, both fully clothed, to embrace their friends.

On Tuesday, Butch went to Sgt. Huddleston's office to discuss the case specifics of the suicide victim found earlier last month. "Well, to keep it simple stupid," he blared, tossing a file on the desk in front of Butch, "ballistics said that your theory was right: All three rounds found in the female victims, and this fourth victim in Henderson County, were indeed fired from the same gun, and that the gun found on our dearly departed John Doe was the weapon used on the others." As he finished, he leaned back in his chair, placed his hands behind his head and sarcastically asked, "So … ?"

"Sir?" Butch replied, looking up from the file.

"So, what happened? Our boy gets a conscience all of a sudden and thinks 'Oh my! Look what I've done'! No explanation? No note? Just kills himself? This make sense to you?"

"Well, sir ... " Butch began, clearing his throat to explain, "Serial killers are sometime known to ... " Before he could get a chance to give his interpretation, the two men were interrupted by a tiny knock on the doorframe.

Sarah stood at the door with red and swollen eyes, clutching a tissue. Her voice cracked a bit when she called out, "Butch?"

It was a good ending. You couldn't have asked for a more beautiful day to have graveside services. The sky was a clear, deep blue with only the slightest of breezes. The air was filled with the scent of grass that had just been cut and, on the far side of the cemetery, water sprinklers danced in large, white arcs across the great lawns, tossing their fine mist into the wind. Lilac trees, along with the different varietals of roses, were in full bloom. The bright lavenders, reds, yellows, and whites contrasted against the deep blue-green of the grass, spruce, and cedars, stood as delicate and beautiful reminders that this place of rest was but only one of the many steps in God's plan, and not necessarily the last.

If it weren't for Butch, Danny, Sarah, the members of the church and officers from the DPS coming to pay their respects, the attendance level for Chester's services would have been nil. Butch sat in front of his father's casket, alone. He had no sisters or brothers to share this burden with because, like his father, Butch was an only child. There were no large arrangements sent from family members from far away to show their respects, wishing to be there. But now, gathered around to offer their support, were the newest members of Butch and Chester's family.

Danny stood directly behind his grieving friend, gently rubbing his shoulders as Pastor Brock delivered Chester's eulogy. After a short, but eloquent summation, Lynnly Ives rose from her seat and sang, "How Great Thou Art," her voice ringing angelically across the finely manicured cemetery. From the corner of his eye, Butch caught a glimpse of movement between a few of the headstones. He turned his head to see what it was that caught his attention and spied his mother in a bright red, formfitting dress, leaned up against a car with her arms folded. Although she tried to obscure her face by a pair of large framed, black sunglasses and a wide-brimmed hat, he knew it was his mother. He offered her only a brief and emotionless stare from the makeshift church as Lynnly sang.

His mind was suddenly awash with the repeating childhood memory of standing in the doorway of their home and her leaving to go to the grocery store, those words forever resonating in his heart: "I'll be right back." She wasn't interested enough to come over and pay her respects or to approach Butch. As the hymn ended, and without so much as a polite wave of her hand, Butch's estranged mother opened the door of her car and stepped inside.

He stood, removed his boutonniere and gingerly placed it on his father's casket. Butch briefly gazed upon the closed coffin and the single flower with bright red petals, blooming with life, lying on the cold metal surface. Lynnly then began singing, "Softly and Tenderly," one of Chester's favorite hymns. As the music played, he received and shook the hands of Pastor Cregan and Pastor Brock, then those of friends, coworkers and church members. Slowly the line dwindled down to Danny and Sarah. The three stood silently as they viewed the flower encrusted casket, sitting on the straps, ready to be lowered. Across the great lawn, some stragglers crisscrossed the grounds, seeking out the headstones of deceased family members. Sarah squeezed Butch's hand, kissed his cheek, then turned to walk away.

Butch and Danny looked about the cemetery. Without speaking they turned away from the casket and exited the shade of the canopy. The two men squinted tightly from the late morning sun, then donned their sunglasses. Once a few paces away from the tent, Butch broke the silence, "Thanks for bringing back my daddy." Danny silently gave his friend a consoling pat on the shoulder. The flowers were in bloom.

It's Okay to Let Go

The early morning sunlight streamed through the east bedroom windows, reflected off the hutch mirror on the west wall and hit Sarah's eyes at around eight thirty. She was further rousted from her sleep by the sounds of a power air blower, the echoing bangs of a broom head on corrugated metal and a booming Jimi Hendrix asking, "Are You Experienced?" She wiped the sleep from her eyes as she clumsily lumbered her way to the window to see what, or who, was causing the commotion.

As she lifted the window, she watched churning clouds of brown dust billow from the large, metal double barn doors. "Hey!" she yelled, but received no reply. After donning her robe, Sarah groggily trudged her way downstairs and out to the barn while Mr. Hendrix belted out "All Along the Watchtower." Danny was once again tackling his summer cleaning.

As he blew the dirt and ages away from the tractors and farm implements, Danny's mind was set adrift, reflecting upon his time at the gas station and the years he spent working for Charlie Doyle. He couldn't help remembering Charlie without thinking of his dead father and how Tommy never had the chance to see him as a grown man. With broom in hand and his back to the doors, he unknowingly gave an impromptu performance for his mother who now stood in the doorway, chuckling to herself.

"Hey!" she hollered, "What ya doin' out here all alone?"

"Momma!" he bellowed with a startled jump and rushed to turn down the radio. "Gosh, you scared me!" he laughed breathily as he gave her the traditional 'good morning' hug.

Sarah remained locked in the embrace a few seconds longer than usual. As he pulled away, Danny sensed something was amiss and innocently asked, "You feeling okay?" He resisted the temptation of looking inside the bright white fold hovering above her shoulder and instead commented, "You lookin' kinda worn."

"Uh, nah!" she brushed off with a smile, "Just a little old age settin' in. Some get old when they're still a kid you know?" She turned away and creakingly ambled to the John Deere riding lawn mower. He watched as she strained to swing her leg over the back of the seat.

"You all right?" he inquired, "Want to talk about anything?"

Sarah gazed at her son, then with a slap on her leg she exclaimed confidently, "Yes, yes there is!" Danny raised his head at the sound of her voice. "You come 'ere young man!" she commanded with a slight smirk, pointing down to the ground in front of the lawn mower.

He smiled and timidly approached his mother, for fear of having done something wrong, "Yes, ma'am?"

"Did you know how much I love you?" she questioned, taking his hands in hers, her eyes beaming, "And how happy I've been these two years and how thankful to God I am for you?"

"Aww, Momma!" Danny blushed, turning his head away, still clutching her hands.

"Don't awww me!" she demanded. "You are such a good boy! 'Scuse me, you are such a great man! And I know deep in my heart that God has something, and someone, special planned, for Mr. Danny … Lee … Albright! I love you, my son!" Sarah rose from her seat and, using Danny for balance, gingerly stepped off the mower. Danny walked back to his broom but turned to watch his mother slowly walk away, grabbing the edge of the metal doors for support as she exited.

A few days later, in the early evening, Danny pulled his father's old International tractor up next to the barn from disking the southwest sections. The soil, having not been worked since he left in 1986, was overrun with weeds and an irregular patchwork of remnants from the last cotton harvest. He shut down the tractor and headed straight for the water faucet at the end of the barn. Pulling the valve handle all the way up, he stuck his head under the torrent of fresh, cold well water, scrubbing his hair. He removed his faded and ripped Threadgill's t-shirt and soaked it in the water to scrub his face, arms, neck, and chest. With one more rinse of his hair and a final swishing of his mouth, he stood up straight and shook his head like a wet dog. Glancing toward the house and looking over the top rail of the porch fence, he noticed that the screen was not completely closed and the front door was partially open. "Mom?" he shouted, and darted around the fenced yard to the side steps of the porch. Once parallel with the front deck, he could see Sarah's legs sticking out the door.

Butch exited the elevator into the CCU and walked briskly down the hall; his eyes open wide with anxious concern. He got the call from Danny just as he was leaving the office and reassured his friend that he wouldn't be alone during this time. As he turned the corner near the nurse's station, he looked down the length of the hall and saw Monica, Holly, and Terri standing next to the vending machines and Danny, still in his work clothes, was further down the hall talking with Sarah's doctor.

Butch paced from one side to the other as Sarah's physician, Dr. Schropture, consoled Danny with a pat on his shoulder and shook his hand before entering another room.

He turned to face Butch, his face clad in loving sympathy and walked wearily towards him. The two men grasped each other in a strong embrace. "How's she doin'?" Butch whispered in his ear. They broke their hug as Danny choked on his words.

"She has breast cancer. Both breasts." He felt his head go light and his knees trembled as the words left his mouth, "It's spread to her liver, lungs, and lymph nodes. She's in a coma … " Danny's body suddenly convulsed as he covered his face, bent over and wept. Butch softly rubbed his friend's back, his own mind and heart set awhirl as he related Danny's pain to his upon the passing of Chester. Danny quickly straightened up to finish the explanation of the diagnosis, "Dr. Schropture thinks there's a possibility for her to wake up, but after that, she maybe has only two to three weeks."

"I'm sorry!" Butch offered, "If you want anything, anything, you let me know. You say it and it's done. Okay?"

"Thanks." Danny squeaked, wiping his nose on his arm and hands.

"You gonna stay the night? Want me to stay?" Butch looked behind him and motioned for Sarah's friends to come see their ailing friend. "I can ask Terri or Monica to stay; I can go 'n get … "

"Nah!" Danny interrupted graciously, "I'm gonna stay. I'll sleep in the chair or sump'n. Thanks though."

"Well you at least gotta get cleaned up," Butch stated with a smirk and nudge as he insulted Danny, "You stink! You want me to go back 'n git ya some clean clothes?"

"No," Danny answered, reaching back to grab his wallet. "Jus' go to, uh, the uh … what's around here?" he inquired, still sniffing, grabbing a handful of cash.

"I don't want your money!" Butch jokingly exclaimed, pushing Danny's money-filled hand away from him, "I'll find you something."

"What ya got there?" Danny asked as he reluctantly tucked away his wallet in his back pocket.

"What! This?" Butch answered sarcastically, reaching under his arm to expose Danny's childhood book. "Oh this belongs to a very dear friend of mine. He gave it to me to hold for a while." Danny, slightly amused, smiled as more tears filled his eyes at the thought of his father and his voice. "His daddy … " Butch continued explaining, thumbing through the pages, "used to read it to him when he was a boy an' he gave it to me to read to my daddy." He closed the book and extended his arm, "And I was thinkin' that maybe you could use it right now." Danny was so overcome with regret and pain that he lunged into Butch, clutching him tightly. "Is this the end?" he questioned softly in Danny's ear, "Do you know this?" Danny clenched his eyes shut, but offered no answer.

Trying to be strong and not to show his pain, Butch broke away to wipe his eyes and nose. Danny looked down the hall and noticed that Joey had now joined Sarah's three waiting friends. Butch grabbed his friend by the back of the neck and offered him a tight-lipped smile and small nod before departing into the stairwell.

With the exception of using the restroom or the walk-in shower, Danny remained at his mother's side for the next five days, constantly talking and reading to her Monica and Holly went by the Albright house, as well as their own homes, and brought picture albums for Danny to describe to her. Each night the CCU head nurse made sure that he had fresh sheets and a pillow for the extra bed in the room.

All day long and late into the evening he read to her; her eyes remaining closed and lying perfectly still as he spoke. The only interruption to Danny's narrations was the hourly checking of Sarah's vitals by the CCU staff who quickly recorded their findings and departed as quietly as possible. As he read the stories of his beloved Texas Rangers, the soft beep of Sarah's heart monitor continually reminded him of his mother's imminent demise.

On the sixth day, Danny finished the last story. He sat in the arm chair next to the semi-upright hospital bed, closed the book and looked at his mother. He then stood and took a few steps to the window and pulled the chord to spread the vertical blinds wide open. The room was immediately awash with the fuchsia and burnt orange rays of the setting sun. "Momma?" he called out, still watching the sky, "I wanted to tell you a few things."

Standing in front of the window, he turned to his dying mother and began his farewell. "I want you to know that you and I are okay with each other, and I'm sorry I left you." The heat monitor continued with its beeping. "I left because I felt like you didn't have any faith in me," he continued, "And that's okay. I know it was hard. It was hard for both of us. But, if you can hear me, I'm sorry." As he confessed his apology, pictures of his father lying in his casket flashed through his mind, making it all the more difficult for him to speak. "And I hope that you can forgive me," he squeaked, trying to retain some composure, "And that I love you!" Sarah's right index finger twitched slightly as he continued, "I have been so happy with you. Can you hear me?"

He lowered the bed rail and pulled his chair up close to hold Sarah's hand. "You 'n daddy were such a tremendous blessing in my life ... and I know your heart's been hurtin' since he's been gone." Wiping away his tears, he choked as he stated, "I know you're hurtin' inside, and you're sick of being sick. So ... " he covered his mouth and tried to suppress his whimpering, breathing through his nose, "I want you to know that if you're ready to go, it's okay. I'm all right and everything between you and me is all right." He held her hand to his cheek and confided, "You don't need to be afraid or afraid for me, or be in pain anymore. You 'n Daddy are gonna be with each other. So, if you want to, you can let go now."

He gazed lovingly upon his mother. Sarah's heart monitor almost immediately showed a strong surge in her beats per minute. The needles recording her brain activity began to flail from side to side and her fingers tenderly flexed and brushed his cheek. She slightly bent her knee as the beeping of the heart monitor increased. Her eyes suddenly fluttered open and her lips parted. She wearily turned her head toward Danny, blinked slowly and softly whispered.

"Hey, Superman!"

"Hey, Momma!" he grunted, trying to smile through his pain. Sarah's smile broadened as she once again closed her eyes. The beeps of her heart monitor then started to slow themselves down as the wide strikes of the colored wands on the brain monitor diminished. All but in vain, Danny tried to hold back a torrent of emotions and began to wail loudly, clutching his mother's hand. The beeps of the heart monitor, like that of the tolling of the bells, grew further and further apart until finally, only one long hum resonated.

He buried his head into the mattress next to his mother's side and screamed with grief. As he mourned, Dr. Schropture and the nurses rushed in to assist with the resuscitation. With his head still down, Danny raised his arm and held out his hand, motioning for them to stop. Respectfully, Dr. Schropture stepped quietly to the heart monitor, turned both it and the brain scanner off, then marked the official time of Sarah's passing at eleven minutes after seven p.m. He and the nurses exited the room and left Danny alone with his mother. The sun disappeared below the horizon.

History Repeats Itself

Butch found himself growing ever more concerned with Danny's behavior, or lack thereof, and overall well-being. Danny had yet to return any of his phone calls since Sarah's services four weeks earlier and, upon each unannounced visit to the Albright farm, the house would always be dark with the doors and windows locked.

Butch pulled up to the Albright home to find his luck had finally turned around as Danny was sitting on the porch in his jeans but wearing no shirt. He appeared dirty, as if he'd been working outside. Shiner beer bottles were strewn across the length of the porch fence rail. "'Scuse me? I'm in need of some help." he stated professionally as he exited the car. Danny remained silent with a bottle in his hand and his feet propped up on a cooler. "Could you direct me to the residence of one Danny Lee Albright?" he asked sarcastically and pulled a tiny spiral notepad out of his pocket as if ascertaining valuable information from a witness. Danny didn't see the humor in Butch's patronizing and offered no response. "He supposedly lives around here," Butch commented as he moseyed up the porch steps and reached for a beer, forcing Danny's legs off the cooler, "You know him?" He raised his left thigh to rest on the rail then continued, "Sometimes refers to himself as uh … " he stammered, looking back at his notes, "'Superman'?" Danny surrendered a slight smirk and a slow nod of his head. "Well, I'll be but if you don't look like 'is spittin' image!" Butch admitted strongly. "Been calling," he stated quasi-gruffly, taking a swallow of beer, "Why ain't ya returning my calls?"

"Busy!" Danny replied flatly.

"Ah, busy." he repeated, "So, are they gone yet?"

"Who?"

"Your memories," Butch answered almost jovially, finishing with, "Fears, anger, sadness, regrets. They all gone?"

"Not hardly!"

"I'm sorry," Butch nodded, "Sorry my daddy's gone, sorry your daddy's gone, your girlfriend's gone … I'm sorry your mother's gone. I know she was good to ya. But, none of this is your fault and you can't bring her back."

"So what do you want me to do?" he timidly asked.

"Keep living!" Butch demanded proudly, "I remember a time when you acted this very same way. I told you then and I'll tell you now: 'Whatever you got, you got it.' It doesn't appear to be leaving and you can't keep running away." Again, Butch was answered with silence. In a display of support and encouragement, he stood up, clenched his fists and loudly commanded, "Get up off your butt and go do something about it! Come on, now! I'm still here to help."

"Okay, Mr. Psychoanalyst," Danny retorted, "How do you propose to help?"

"Well," he said, leaning back on the rail, "First and foremost, I think it'd be good for the both of us if you came to live with me in town for a while." Danny smiled in silent disbelief before confirming the idea.

"You want me to be your roommate?"

"Yeah!" he exclaimed and stepped over the cooler to take the chair next to Danny. "I mean, you and me been through quite a bit this past year, right?" Danny nodded in agreement, sipping slowly from his beer as Butch continued with his proposal. "We both lost one of our parents, I'd like the company, you're all alone, you don't go and visit anyone. I ain' never had a son, you ain't had a daddy for a long time, and … you're my friend!" Danny's smile broadened as he toasted his friend. "Top notch! Huh!?" Butch exclaimed proudly of his spiel, taking a deep swallow of his beer.

"So … when did you want to have this slumber party?"

It was the same apartment he'd lived in since his placement with the Texas DPS in 1978. Danny followed Butch through the loud oral impromptu tour from room to room. "All right, all right, all right!" he announced, much like a circus ring leader. "Your new home!" He clasped his hands together loudly and briskly rubbed his palms together. "We got your satellite TV! Anything you need is right around these few blocks," he announced and pointed out the windows as he ranted, "We got groceries, theater, auto parts … "

As he listened, and with his belongings in one duffle bag still slung on his shoulder, Danny walked about the den area looking at Butch's life history in photos, newspaper articles, diplomas, awards, and certificates. "The mall is about seven blocks down," Butch continued, "The post office is on the street behind me." He stopped abruptly and darted into the kitchen. He quickly returned with two opened Shiner Bocks and handed one off to Danny, exclaiming, "Here we go! Here we go!" The two men were standing in the middle of the den when Butch offered up a toast, "To our new lives!"

"New lives!" Danny repeated with a clink of the bottle necks.

Butch acted like a teenage school girl, all giddy with anticipation, "Ya hungry? I feel like celebrating!" then turned to go back to the kitchen.

"I can eat!" Danny hollered. His eyes were drawn to Butch's desk and the opened files and pictures strewn about. "There's a place down the street that's got great wings and onion rings," Butch shouted with his head still inside the fridge.

"Sure. Always got room for wings. Can't go wrong with wings!" Danny volleyed. He looked over the stack of black and white photos while Butch continued describing the restaurants amenities, "They got shuffle board, too … Ziegenbock on tap." Danny pulled one thick file from the stack with several different colors of highlight tape sticking out.

He tilted the file tab sideways and hollered back over his shoulder, "Hey, this, uh, 'foursome' file … what's this?"

Butch began answering as he approached Danny and the desk, "That's the hitch hiker. You know … the gunshot wound to the head?"

"Oh, yeah!" Danny remembered, "Okay … okay."

"Is this all you got?" Butch asked, slightly tugging on the duffle bag shoulder strap. "No furniture, clothes, kitchen stuff?"

"This is just what I brought back with me. The rest of my junk is back at the apartment. I was gonna get it later but never got around to it." He opened the file to look at the pictures. "Besides, I didn't know if I was gon' stay or not, so Gary and Charlotte said I could keep it there, seein' as how they still haven't sold the house."

"Well, I'm off the day after tomorrow. We can go and get it." Butch suggested, watching Danny as he concentrated on each individual picture.

"Yeah, sure," he distantly confirmed, "day after tomorrow."

"Can you see anything when they're dead? Like touch 'em or see a picture? You know some psychics … "

"I'm not a psychic. I don't know the winning lottery numbers. There are no aliens coming and I don't know where Elvis is!" Danny ranted sarcastically, tilting his head back, "And no … I can't see anything from a picture or someone who's already dead."

"So it's just when someone's alive, right?"

"Yup! Let's celebrate. I'm hungry!" he stated factually, closing the file. A small black and white photo accidentally dropped out of the "foursome" file as he tossed it on the desk. While bending down to pick it up, Danny glanced at the girl in the picture and inquired, "Hey! Who's this?"

"That's one of the girls that was murdered." Butch answered, taking the photo from his hand.

"Really!" Danny asked, yanking it out of his hand and closely examining her face.

"I'm in the process of finishing some reports right now so I can finally close the case."

"Man! She's cute!" Danny admitted then handed the picture back to Butch, "She almost looks like Brooke!"

"Uh huh." Butch agreed unsteadily, still looking at the photo. He started sorting through the hundreds of pictures stored in his mind until he finally arrived at the memory of Brooke's decapitated body in the back seat of a car. He could still see her head lying on the asphalt, a mere block from his apartment. "Hey, before we go," he spoke out, "I wanna pick sump'n up at the station to look at later tonight. Ya mind?"

Behind the Eight Ball

Butch unlocked and pulled open the heavy steel sliding door to the evidence archives at the DPS station. Row after row of metal shelves were stacked with file and evidence boxes, marked alpha-numerically by year, dating as far back as the 1930s. Danny struggled to follow Butch with an awkwardly rolling metal staircase. He moved about the warehouse quickly, pulling out boxes and briskly thumbing through the files.

Not ten minutes into the scavenger hunt, Butch instructed, "You can leave the stairs here."

"That's it?" Danny asked, panting from his workout.

"That's it." he confirmed as he took the stack of files from Danny. The two men exited the evidence room with a deep, hollow slam of the metal door.

Twenty minutes later, the duo were playing pool and, as usual, drinking cold Shiner Bock. Danny put almost ten dollars in the CD juke box, playing almost every song in the Doors and Jimi Hendrix library. The waitress soon delivered a platter of sixty hot, crispy chicken wings with all the trimmings. In no time at all, the table transformed into a literal pigsty of napkins, ranch dressing cups and chicken bones. An hour later, more than ten empty bottles were lined up where the table meets the partition wall.

As Butch prepared to sink his fifteen ball, Jim Morrison crooned, "Riders On The Storm," while Danny thumbed through the remaining "foursome" files.

"So, did that guy murder all these girls?" he asked amazedly. With a grunt of disgust, Butch watched as his fifteen ball bounced off the corner of the side pocket bumper.

"Agh! Yer up. Solids." he stated, then took a sip of his beer, "Great life, huh? Just go 'round shootin' people whenever you want?" Danny walked to the other end of the table and squatted down to look over the balls on the table.

"Shot 'em all?" he asked, knocking down the three ball.

"Yep, one shot to the left side of the chest."

Danny paused, lowered his cue then leaned over the table and drew a bead on the four ball. "Not to change the subject, but … " he stated as he deftly cut the four ball to the corner pocket, "did ya'll ever find that guy, oh what was his name … the guy who ran into my daddy's car?"

"Sorry to say, but no." Danny's shot on the yellow one ball, like Butch's fifteen ball, bounced off the corner of the side pocket bumper. "They closed the case." Butch lined up and delicately sank the fourteen ball as he explained, "Huddleston said to close it as a cold case with a kidnapping, grand theft auto, a triple homicide, armed robbery and four charges of vehicular manslaughter." He then missed an easy bank shot on the thirteen while finishing his recitative, "So I closed the investigation. We know what happened, who done it, where and to who, but never found the who done it."

"Kidnapping?" Danny asked, confused. "Who got kidnapped?"

"The girl!" Butch answered gruffly.

"Brooke? Backseat Brooke?"

"Brooke."

"Headless Brooke?"

"Yes! Headless Brooke! Backseat Brooke. The only Brooke in the whole thing!"

Danny stepped up to the table and dropped his six ball with a crack as he bluntly gave his interpretation of the scenario. "She wasn't kidnapped."

"She most certainly was!" Butch countered.

"Okay! What idiot kidnaps someone, takes their car, and then takes them with him to rob a store?" As Butch prepared to speak, Danny raised his finger and smartly added, "Mind you now, not tied up, gagged or put into the trunk, but left sitting alone … waiting … in a running car … out in front of the store?"

"Now see right there! How do you know that?" Butch asked, frustrated. Danny smiled and squatted for his next shot then pointed to his head, giving his skull a tap. While Danny prepared to drop the four ball, Butch suggested, "They think that he probl'y shot her before he went into the store."

"Okay, then," Danny rephrased, "what idiot kidnaps someone, takes their car, shoots them and decides to take their dead body with him to rob a store?" Danny tried not to laugh as irritation washed over Butch's face. "Look, I'm sorry. We didn't have anyone else to go to!" Butch explained, "I was doin' what I was told! This was my first investigation and it was a monster."

"Did ya'll ever find who shot my daddy?" Danny quipped with a piercing stare. Butch was speechless. "Woah, woah, woah … let's get this straight!" he snapped, "Three girls get shot and out of the blue, a dead guy shows up out in the country somewhere and lo and behold, this new dead guy just so happens to be the murderer of the three girls over the past fifteen years! Yet after twenty-seven years, you can't find the man who murdered my friends and my daddy?" Danny tossed the pool cue onto the table. He shook his head, stifling his anger as he walked back to the table to finish his beer.

Delicately, Butch tried to console him, "Look, I know how you feel. I … "

"You have no idea how I feel!" he hissed through clenched cheeks. After a brief and intent glare, he looked past Butch and hollered, "Yo!" hoisting his bottle in the air, motioning for the waitress to bring another round. Danny drew in a deep breath, calmly stepped over to the pool table and picked up his pool cue. Stretching out his arm to aim at his five ball, he inquired, "Just outta curiosity, when did this last girl die?" Butch turned back to the table and looked through the file as Danny finished his shot. Once the ball sank, the waitress appeared with another round of beer.

"Uh, she was, uh, lessee … July twenty-third." Butch answered. Danny dropped his beer at the mention of the date. The sound of crashing glass on the concrete floor drew everyone's attention to the two men. The waitress quickly reappeared with another beer and extra bar towels then squatted to help Butch pickup the broken glass. Danny took his seat and gazed at the picture of the last murder victim.

Once the beer and broken glass were swept up, Butch joined Danny at the table. "What was that?"

Danny looked pale when he asked, "What about the others?"

"Huh?"

"The others! The others! When were they killed?"

Butch began thumbing through the files and recited the dates, "July twenty-third 1991. And … July twenty-third 1989. So?" "So … ?" he repeated, waiting for Danny's response. "So he murdered them all on the same day! So what?" he asked, rising from his seat, taking his pool cue with him. "Serial killers maintain special behavioral patterns that they establish for themselves." Danny listened to Butch's seminar while flashes of Brooke and Dale's faces intertwined with those of his father and four friends. "It could be something like the process of picking someone out by a physical characteristic, a career fixation on the victim; they all did this one particular thing," Butch elaborated, "It could be a color, a location, a way of committing the crime … sometimes keeping a particular amputated piece of a body as a souvenir."

"Could it be date related?" Danny piped up.

"Could be a date," he said, shrugging. "Wouldn't surprise me. So what's the big deal? We got the guy! Actually, he got himself for us!"

"Do you know what happened on July twenty-third 1978?"

"Yeah," Butch immediately recalled, "That's the day a kidnapping, an armed robbery, a triple homicide, grand theft auto and the vehicular manslaughter of four children occurred." Butch sank his eleven ball while describing the events of the day, "I know! We went through this already and that case is closed. I'm sorry, but … "

"Well, it needs to be reopened!" Danny demanded. "Doesn't it seem strange?" he added, "A bit odd that these occurred on the same day?"

"I told you what the habits of serial killers are. So, they have a common date? Big deal!"

"You're making these out as two separate cases and they're not!" Danny pointed out, rising from his seat.

"They're completely separate!" Butch refuted, "One is a car crash and so on, on one day. The other is three murders spread over fifteen years with one … "

"How did all your girls die?" Danny interjected, "All were from one gun shot wound to the left chest. Right?"

"Uh huh," Butch nodded in agreement.

"And how did 'Backseat Brooke' die?"

"Decapitation." Butch answered, turning to look at the table.

"But she was shot first!" Danny corrected with a smile.

"Then she was decapitated!"

"She was shot first and fell out a door! And what kind of gunshot was it?" Danny asked, holding his hand up to his ear. Butch walked around the table in an attempt to get away from Danny as he pressed for an answer, "Where? How? Excuse me? Where was Brooke shot?"

"A single shot to the left chest! Okay? There, I said it! A single gunshot wound to the left side of the chest"

"Exactly!" Danny agreed, then closed with the recap, "Four girls, all shot, shot on the same day and all look alike! One person did this!"

"You're pretty proud of yourself right now, aren't you?" Butch asked with a smile and a nod of his head.

"Man, I am good!" Danny boasted, raising a fist in the air.

"All right, I'll bite," Butch offered, leaning against the table, crossing his arms, "So what happens now, Inspector Clouseau?"

"Well, I don't rightly know. Hey! You got a pic of John Doe?"

"Yeah!" He walked back to the table, looked through the file and handed the black and white to Danny, "Here we go. That's him."

Danny took a quick glance at the face of the dead man and confidently stated, "This ain't your boy!" He tossed the picture on the table then walked to the pool table for his next shot. "What do ya mean this ain't our boy?" Butch countered, looking at the picture under the light. "Of course it's our boy! The ballistics from the girls all matched the one found in his head! Not our boy! You either need another beer or you don't need another beer! How do you know that ain't him?" Danny again smiled and pointed to his head. "Oh, would ya quit with the whole head thing! This is serious!" Butch demanded.

Danny leaned on the pool table, blasting back, "You think I'm not serious? My whole life has been nothin' but serious! You tell me to use this for something good and then you shoot me down! What's with you?"

"Nothin'!" Butch mumbled, rubbing his eyes, "What are you getting at?"

"Reopen the cases! Both of 'em!" Danny suggested.

"Hah!" Butch bellowed, covering his eyes in disbelief.

"Is there something funny? Something I'm missing?" "Oh no! Nothing at all!" Butch patronized, "I'll get right on that first thing in the morning. Are you freakin' crazy?"

"Yes! No! Well, yes but really no … "

"Aw, come on! Listen to you!" Butch complained, "This is all circumstantial!"

"I would almost be willing to bet you," Danny challenged with a smile, shaking a pointed finger, "That the ballistics analysis of the round from Brooke's report would match those found on all three of your girls and your John Doe. And … if you were to check the same report for my daddy, it would match too!"

"All right. Here's the run down as I see it! Now correct me if I'm off base here." Danny leaned against the table top, slowly nursing his beer in preparation for Butch's lecture. "You want me to go to Huddleston and say, 'Sir, I want to re-open both of these cases because there was a kid who was in a car wreck in 1978. Remember the ten year old kid, the one who started seeing things after his daddy got shot? The boy who went to all kinds of counselors and psychiatrists, given all kinds of medications? The one that ran away from home when his girlfriend died? That kid? Remember?'"

"Know him well!" Danny interjected.

"Well," Butch resumed, "He, that kid, has come back home after being a drunk run away for nineteen years, and now says he had a vision! He thinks that these cases are related to each other by the very slim chance to none that the shooter is the same person in both. And, and … the John Doe, the hitcher, isn't the shooter at all. He's just a guy, a decoy. The shooter, the real shooter now, mind you, is actually still alive somewhere and is responsible for the seventy-eight triple homicide, the grocery store robbery, the vehicular manslaughter of four children of four Texas DPS troopers, the seventy-eight homicide of a Texas DPS Trooper and three, no make it four, four more homicides over the past seventeen years!" Danny nodded, smiling at Butch's summation. "Is that it?" Butch asked, frustrated, "Is that what you want me to say to Huddleston?"

With a poke of his finger on Butch's arm, Danny exclaimed, "Exactly!"

Testing the Hypothesis

"You want me to what?" Sgt. Huddleston shouted. Danny heard it clear down the hallway as he sat and waited for Butch to finish his meeting. "Are you outta your mind?" also echoed from behind the closed door.

"Sir, I know that what I'm suggesting sounds a little unorthodox … " Butch confessed. "You bet it does!" Sgt. Huddleston blasted, leaning across his desk. "Farley, this request of yours is teetering on the brink of stupidity! Where in the name of lunacy did you get this idea?"

"Well, sir," he began with a crack in his voice, "I was talking to Danny Albright the day before yesterday and … "

"Danny Albright!" Huddleston repeated, astounded, "There's your problem! No disrespect to his mother and father, God rest their souls, but you been spending too much time with Señor Whacko!" He smiled sarcastically and tapped his finger on the glass topped desk, "I strongly recommend you rethink your proposal, identify who your real friends are, remember what your job is and what you were hired to do, and get your head out of the clouds or whatever orifice you've got it shoved into."

Butch momentarily closed his eyes, trying to remain calm, "Sir, if you can just … "

"If I can just nothing, Farley!" he interrupted angrily, "Quit tryin' to rewrite the past. I can't believe what I'm hearing!" Sgt. Huddleston began pacing back and forth behind his desk, waving his arms as he continued, "You honestly expect me to reopen two closed investigations because an unstable Jesus freak has a nightmare or two? Huh?"

Rising out of his seat to address the verbal attack, Butch stated clearly, but firmly, "Sir, with all due respect, I think this is the right thing to do. And you don't need to reassign this to anybody else. I can do this. I want to do this and all that I'm really going to need is … "

"You don't get it do ya, Farley?" Sgt. Huddleston interrupted again, "I been tryin' to talk some sense into ya but you just ain't taking the hint! So! Here's what I'm gonna do for you! I'm giving you the rest of the day off!"

"A day off? For what, sir, if you don't mind me asking?"

"So you can get up off your brain and get it back where it belongs!" Huddleston replied, speaking slowly and politely as he took his seat.

"Sir! That is not necessary and if you would … "

"Don't you interrupt me when I'm talking!" he barked, glaring up to Butch. "That's two days!"

"Please just allow me the opportunity to collect more information … "

"Make it three!"

"I think there is more than justifiable cause to reopen both investigations … "

"Now it's a week, Farley! Keep it up!" the sergeant shouted, standing once again.

Butch raised his voice level to that of Huddleston and pointed his finger, "Due to acts of gross negligence committed by you, me, and this entire department with regards to evidence gathering procedures, incomplete and inconsistent evidence reporting, tampered and adulterated crime scenes … "

"That's two weeks, Farley!" Huddleston bellowed.

"And all likelihood there is an unstable predator still out in the public sector!"

"Two weeks and no pay!" he roared in Butch's face. The room fell silent.

"He's my friend." Butch stated softly, "I have faith in him and I trust him. I've gotten more outta life this past year and a half because of that guy. I've learned more about life in the past eighteen months than what this job has taught me in over twenty five years." He walked to the door, prepared to leave, but instead turned to Huddleston and asked, "Tell me something, who and what are you living for?"

Butch exited the office and slowly strode towards Danny as Sgt. Huddleston yelled out, "Hey! You get back here and close that door!"

"So!" Danny quipped, clasping his hands together in sarcastic joy, "Everything's okay, huh? When do we start?" Butch turned around to see Sergeant Huddleston exiting his office. Danny continued his sarcastic jocularity with a slight punch to Butch's arm and stated, "I smell another promotion!"

"I don't think that's what you smell." Butch commented.

"Farley!" Huddleston blasted as he approached the two men, "You hard a hearin'? I said for you to close that door!"

Danny jumped in between Butch and Sgt. Huddleston, holding his hands up as he jokingly explained, "I'm sorry, sir, but my client here, Mr. Farley, is currently unemployed and is not to be subjected to cruel and unusual verbal punishment! So if you would please refrain … "

"Shut up, Albright!" the sergeant ordered, pushing Danny to the side, "Get him outta my hallway, Farley!" Danny regained his balance, turned to face Sergeant Huddleston and placed his fingers to temples. He glared at him and made a low humming sound.

"Oh, great! Now ya done it!" Butch lamented, shaking his head.

"Done it? What do you mean "done it"? Done what?" he asked, backing away from Danny.

"Now he's gonna find out how it happens!" Butch replied.

"How what happens? Find out what?" he asked, uneasy with Danny's behavior. Danny moved to stand directly beside Sgt. Huddleston, leaning into his face, humming all the while.

"Stop that, you idiot! Why's he doin' that? Stop him!" he complained, cowering slightly backward.

"Well, that's how he does it." Butch answered with a sinister smile, crossing his arms.

"Does what?"

"Sees when and how someone's gon' die." Butch whispered, "And now you'll know how you die!"

Danny abruptly stopped humming, closed his eyes and let loose with an, "Ohhh! Wow!" and a foreboding, "Uuuuhhh oh!" then stood perfectly still. For a brief moment, the hallway was quiet and void of any movement. Sgt. Huddleston waited for Danny's next move as small beads of sweat appeared on his forehead. Danny lightly chuckled to himself as he slightly peeped open his right eye, amused at the look on the staunch sergeants face.

"You!" Huddleston shouted, waving his finger at Danny, "I don't want to see your sorry lookin' face again! Is that clear?" "And you!" he added, turning his attention to Butch as he and Danny started walking away, "That's two unpaid weeks! Ya here me, Farley? Two weeks!" Danny stopped, did an about face and took slow, concentrated strides back to Sgt. Huddleston.

"Hey!" he whispered, standing face-to-face with Sergeant Huddleston, "A little word of advice: don't use the bathroom in your guest bedroom and make sure you never park under the tree in your front yard! Oh, and check the expiration date on your milk!"

The next day, the duo were driving back to town to get the rest of Danny's personal belongings. Minus a few wisps of bright white, finger-like clouds, the wide Texas sky was a clear, bright blue. They joined Pat Green as he sang "Wave Upon Wave," holding their hands out the windows. They arrived at Danny's garage apartment and before too long, had sorted through his belongings and decided what to keep and what to throw or give away. By four o'clock, when the last box was loaded, both men were pleased to find that all of Danny's earthly possessions fit perfectly into one load. As the two climbed into the cab of the truck, Danny smiled to himself, confident about the new change in his life.

Pulling away from the apartment, Danny instructed Butch, "Hey, take a right here on Doris … I wanna see if Pastor Pate and Whitney are at the church." Butch turned the wheel and headed toward the church just as Danny requested. Nearly two years had come to pass since he left town and the idea of seeing Pastor Pate again now excited him. He scanned the side courtyard and playground in anticipation. Butch's truck was turning the corner when Danny saw Whitney, the long-time child care assistant, holding the door open and an army of children rushing out past her. Danny quickly leaned to his left and watched Whitney in the side mirror. His eyes grew wide with horror then screamed, "Stop! Stop the truck!"

Butch, surprised by the shout, screamed himself with a short, "Augh!" while jumping in his seat. He stiffened his arms and slammed on the brakes, coming to a screeching halt in the middle of the street. Danny's ironing board flew over the cab and landed on the hood, making a long, white scratch in the black paint before falling to the ground in front of the truck.

"What was that?" Butch asked angrily, "Geez! We probl'y broke half the stuff." Danny remained transfixed on the mirror and Whitney's reflection. "Hey. You okay?" Butch inquired, calming down a bit, "I'm sorry I snapped at you … "

"Whitney," Danny stated bluntly, interrupting, "that's Whitney Taylor." Butch tried to look over his right shoulder to see. "She's been Pastor Pate's assistant since I came here in eighty-six." he explained. "Cute," Butch complimented as he watched the reflection of the young woman tossing a child in her arms, "You talk to her?"

"No," Danny sighed, "But I saw her almost everyday on my way home from Charlie's. 'Cept I never really saw her like this though."

"Like what?"

"Well, look at her, man!" Danny snapped, "She's a Betty! I guess I've always thought of her as just a kid."

"So what's wrong?" Butch asked, taking another look.

Danny slumped back in his seat, closed his eyes and stated, "She has a fold."

"She does? What color is it?" Danny spoke not a word. "Red?" he asked with a lift in his voice. Again, Danny spoke not a word.

"So what do we do?" he asked anxiously, his eyes fixed on Whitney, "What do we do about this?" Danny shrugged his shoulders, staring at the roof of the truck. "What I guess I should be asking is … what are you gonna do about this?" he rephrased, leadingly. "Whatever it is you got, you got it. So let's learn how to fix it."

Butch quickly threw the truck in reverse and began backing up to the church fence. "What're ya doin'?" Danny hollered, springing to life, "Hey! C'mon!"

"I'm helpin' you help her!" he answered with a smile. He stopped in front of the brick and wrought-iron fence, turned off the ignition and grinned at Danny.

"Don't you dare get outta this truck!" he warned as Butch unfastened his seatbelt, opened the door and climbed out. "Butch! Butch!' he heard Danny hiss at him as he passed in front of the truck, finishing off with, "Cleo!" Butch stopped, frowned and made the "shame-shame" finger gesture then stepped onto the sidewalk near the gate.

"'Scuse me! Miss?" he called out to Whitney, waving his badge, "Miss, can I have a word with you?" Whitney, along with Franklin and several other children, started walking toward the fence. "Good afternoon, ma'am," he addressed her politely, "I'm detective Butch Farley and this is my friend … Danny Lee Albright." He pointed to the truck cab behind him. Danny, failing to see the humor in the situation, put on his dark glasses and looked straight ahead.

"You two know each other?" Butch asked innocently, placing his badge in his rear pocket.

"Well, I wouldn't say we know each other," Whitney explained, looking at Danny through the iron fence braces, "but we certainly know of each other."

"What's he done?" she asked with a smirk, "I always knew that someday I'd see him in police custody."

"Oh, he hasn't really done anything worth being arrested for," Butch explained with a small chuckle, "or at least none that I'm aware of, but uh … "

"Why do ya got your glasses on?" Whitney asked loudly, interrupting Butch.

"Sorry?" Danny replied, not really hearing what she said over the sound of the children playing.

"Did you know in all the time I been here I ain't never seen him without those weird lookin' glasses?" she discreetly informed Butch. "Do you ever take 'em off?" she again hollered to Danny.

"I don't always wear 'em!" Danny protested from the safety of his seat. "Yeah!" Butch agreed with Whitney, nodding his head, "You're always wearing those glasses! Why don't you take 'em off a while?" He smiled coaxingly, motioning for Danny to join him, "C'mon!"

Danny reluctantly exited the truck cab and slowly stepped up to the fence. "Please?" Whitney asked seductively, "I bet you got pretty eyes!" Butch and Whitney waited for Danny, who, after much deliberation, finally succumbed to the pressure.

"All right," he agreed sheepishly, "But I don't always wear 'em!" He lowered his head slightly and removed the glasses.

"There!" Butch commended patronizingly with a pat on Danny's shoulder and wink to Whitney, "Now that wasn't so hard was it?"

"No, it wasn't hard! Cleo!" Danny elbowed his friend before raising his head. Whitney bit her lower lip as she and Danny locked eyes. He tried to hold back the warm smile he felt spreading across his lips.

"See … I told you you had nice eyes!" she professed, blushing.

"Miss Taylor," Butch interrupted, "would it be possible to have a word with you for a moment?" Whitney didn't hear a thing. "Miss Taylor!" he repeated, raising his voice.

"Oh! Sure!" she answered happily, breaking the staring contest. She lightly hopped away as if skipping on air.

Danny playfully slapped and punched Butch while waiting for Whitney The two boxers stopped their horseplay just as Whitney, with Franklin in tow, rounded the fence corner. She walked straight up to Danny and gazed deeply. He leaned back slightly, uncomfortable with her direct attention, "What're you doing?"

"I was just wantin' to see your pretty eyes up close." she answered enticingly, just above a whisper. Franklin leaned out from behind her, pointed at Danny and began teasing, "Pretty eyes! Pretty eyes!" "Franklin, would you mind watchin' the kids for a while?" she requested with a laugh, turning him away with a pat on the shoulder.

Franklin turned around, pointed and again taunted, "Pretty eyed Danny! Pretty eyed Danny." Danny lunged toward Franklin with a growl and clenched his fists, sending him off squealing with childish delight.

"Miss Taylor," Butch politely stated as he extended his hand, "nice to meet you. Thanks for speaking to us. I have just a few routine questions."

"Oh, sure! I don't mind talking.' But uh … " she paused and did a quick double take at Danny, "I don't understand what this has to do with him?"

"Well … " he started out, but hesitated to finish his answer. He shifted his eyes to Danny, shrugged and held his hands up. "There's a sensitive and unusual situation in which we are involved." he informed her. He gently grasped Whitney by her right arm and began walking with Danny following silently behind them. As Butch elaborated on the circumstances of their visit, Danny reached out and swiped his hand through the bright red fold hovering above Whitney's right shoulder.

Danny's knees immediately buckled. His eyes rolled back in his head as he fell to the ground; his body curled up, crippled by the violent seizure. Images of Whitney, Brooke and the three murdered girls bombarded his mind. Wild explosions of light, flesh and blood coursed though his brain as adrenaline, fear, and pain raced though his heart. Panic stricken and unsure of how to help, Whitney stood on her tip toes, screaming.

"Danny! Danny, come on! It's me! Get out of it!" Butch calmly coached as he tried to restrain his flailing arms, "Danny! Get out of it!" Whitney screamed again. The children on the church playground, having been alerted to the situation, rushed the fence.

"What's wrong with him?" she fearfully asked. The corralled and shocked children remained quiet as they watched. Danny's body gradually slowed down its series of tensions. He suddenly opened his eyes and looked wildly about.

"That's it! That's it!" Butch smiled, comforting his friend, "Here we are … it's okay … you're all right"

With tears welling up in his eyes, Danny grunted, "It's her! She's next."

"What?" Whitney asked, still reeling from witnessing Danny's seizure.

"Who does she look like?" Danny asked between shallow breaths, trying to regain his composure. Butch stared at Whitney in disbelief.

"Oh, my God!" he mumbled.

"Who do I look like?" she cried, horribly frightened, "The next what?"

Butch helped Danny to his feet. "What was that?" Whitney asked near hysterics, "What happened?"

"I need to talk to you." he said softly as he stepped towards her.

"What is this?" she asked, looking to Butch for help or an answer. "No!" she growled as Danny delicately placed his hands on her biceps. "Stop it! Get away you freak!" she loudly demanded and twisted free.

"I didn't mean to frighten you," he explained, taking a step backward, "I'm sorry. I'm scared right now and I've been scared for a long time about a lot things." Whitney looked over at Butch for some reassurance then back to Danny as he continued, "But if you give me just a few minutes of your time, listen, and have a little faith in me, then you'll understand!"

Whitney looked deeply again into his eyes; a tiny smile crossed her lips. He smiled in return, placed his hands behind his back and silently tilted his head twice toward the sidewalk. Whitney remained unmoved with her arms crossed. Butch winked at her and also nodded his head forward.

Danny and Whitney took their first few steps together with Butch following close behind. "I came here in 1986," he stated, looking around as he began narrating his life story, "I ran away from home."

"What happened? Did ya do somethin'?" Whitney curiously interrupted.

"Well, yes and no," he replied, "Somethin' did happen, and I thought I was responsible. I felt like I did something wrong. And I never faced the truth or consequences of my actions." He thought about the night of the wreck and Jessica lying in his lap, her cracked skull and blood running down onto his jeans. Whitney watched as he stopped and closed his eyes, clenched his fists and began breathing quickly through his nose. She turned back to Butch who motioned for her to move toward Danny.

"Hey … it's okay," she softly whispered while ever so lightly placing her fingers on his arm, "Talk to me." Just the touch of her hand sent a jolt of energy through his body, erasing Jessica's bloodied face from his mind. He opened his eyes as Whitney gingerly curled her arm in his. Danny resumed telling his story, "This all started back in nineteen seventy-eight … " Butch smiled to himself as he chaperoned the young couple from a safe distance.

It was almost dark. The sun had set, but broad arcs of dark orange, red and cinnamon separated the silhouetted horizon from the oncoming evening sky. The threesome decided to stop off at Pokey's Diner and take in an early supper. The forty-something-year-old restaurant was empty, sans the trio. They sat in the last booth against the back wall directly across from the long service counter. They indulged themselves on oversized platters of hand breaded chicken fried steak, black eyed peas, fried okra, and jalapeno cornbread. Various shades of yellow and white incandescent ceiling lights washed the dining hall in a dull, creamy hue. The waist-high walls were covered with black and pastel colored tiles with bright, glossy red tiles interspersed.

Danny was giving his interpretation of the conversation with Butch at the pool hall two days prior, "I told 'im that I think whoever this jacked up guy is, he's still out there and he's like, 'You're the one who's jacked up!'" Whitney laughed a bit as Danny continued, "So, that was the day before yesterday. Then, uh, yesterday this guy went to Sgt. Huddleston. A guy who's hair hasn't moved in thirty years and says, he says, uh … what did you say? I just heard a lot of yelling."

Butch exited the booth and solemnly explained, "I just stood up, looked him in the eye and told him, 'He's my friend, I trust him … we're in love, we're running away together and I'm pregnant with his love child." Whitney and Danny laughed out loud for a moment with a lingering, flirtatious stare.

"So, were you two like separated at birth?" she asked, jokingly, "I mean ya'll act like ya'll are brothers or something.'"

With a chuckle, Danny and Butch gave each other a quick look over and compared skin tones. The table grew quiet as Whitney's tender smile disappeared and she peered out the window, "Do you really think what you say you saw will actually happen?"

"I don't know," Danny offered with a shrug, "'Cuz, uh, to tell you the truth … I've never interfered with whatever I've seen and … "

"What do you mean you never 'interfered'?" she blasted, "You knew when these people were gonna' die and you never said anything to anyone?"

"What do you expect me to do?" Danny fired back, raising his voice, "I hadn't told you a thing and you already called me a freak!"

Butch interrupted to calm the situation and placed his hand on Danny's arm, "We don't know if he can change or alter the outcome of his premonitions … whether they be on you or anyone else. So, I'm sorry to say that you're the test case for this idea. We're both here to try and prevent anything from happening. Furthermore, I don't think I've ever seen him smile as much as he has today." Whitney brightened up as Danny elbowed Butch in the rib. "And if something did happen … " he continued.

"All right! All right!" Whitney interrupted, irritated, "I'm tired of hearing how I'm gonna be shot at the Piggly Wiggly by some idiot!" With a curled lip and nod of her head she boasted, "If I'm gonna go I wanna at least go without feeling any pain! I want a beer! You boys wanna beer?"

Both men simultaneously turned to the cashier, raised their hands and bellowed, "Check please!"

Scars in the Heart

Whitney, Butch, and Danny sat at a small round cocktail table on the edge of the dance floor at Rinkydinks, the area's version of a honky-tonk. Neon signs for Bud Light and George Straight illuminated the local watering hole while the patrons danced, played pool, darts, shuffle board, and tossed indoor horseshoes.

"So, who do you think this is?' Whitney hollered as she grabbed a handful of peanuts from the bucket in the middle of the table, "You been talking 'bout serial killers but I ain't heard anything about any serial killers in Texas for a long time."

"Well, this guy is obviously attracted to brunettes," Butch elaborated, trying to talk over the noise. "You're about the height and proportion and age as the first victim. All the victims were found with one bullet wound to the left side of their chest." he informed her as he too grabbed some of the peanuts. Danny sat silently, drinking his beer, letting Butch do his job. As he listened to their conversation and looked about at the bar guests, he was pleasantly surprised to see mostly green and purple folds. "There've been no signs of struggle, rape, bondage, or strangulation." Butch added as he and Whitney continued de-shelling their peanuts. "They weren't drugged or chemically subdued. So, more than likely, they knew him intimately, or had knowledge of who he was, and were also with or around him of their own free will."

Leaning his chair back on two legs, Danny spoke up, "Is he from around here?" His eyes were glued to a couple of young wannabe cowgirls dancing together. They held their beer bottles high as they hooped and hollered in front of the band members.

"Oh, yeah!" Butch confidently confirmed, "I'd say he lives no more than a hundred miles outta the metro. Travels a lot, too. A vendor or salesman or something. Maybe makes deliveries to the outlaying towns with a courier service." Whitney looked at Danny then turned around to see what had captured his attention. She watched the girls dancing together. A tiny sting of jealousy pierced her heart as she noticed a devilish grin cross Danny's lips. With an obvious sigh loud enough to hear, she turned back to Butch with a toss of her long hair. "He has to be going somewhere that's easily accessible with the greatest variety possible," Butch continued to theorize, "He's got to find the one who has the look, the right look, like the first girl, Brooke."

"That was her name?" she asked.

"Yep!" Danny interjected, turning his attention back to the conversation and lowering his chair, "She was his girlfriend."

"He killed his own girlfriend? What a sicko jerk! Don't men know that we women need to be treated tenderly? We're not jus' a tub of … of … sausage?" Butch and Danny looked at one another as they listened to Whitney, noticing she was exhibiting signs of intoxication.

"So! Misser Lanny Dee Rallbight!" she stated as she tucked her hair behind her right ear, "What do you do to your girlfriends?"

"Don't have 'girlfriend-zah,'" he smartly replied, "'cuz I don't have ah girlfriend. So, pretty much don't do anything!"

"No girlfriend?" she repeated as she peeled the label from her bottle. "You ain't married, are ya?" she quickly flared up, "'Cuz if ya are … "

"I'm not nor have I ever been married," Danny stated, smiling, "In fact, I haven't had a girlfriend since Jessica." Whitney and Butch locked eyes, shocked at what they just learned.

"Wait a minute!" Butch leaned in and winked at Whitney, intrigued, "The entire time you were here you never dated? Messed around with anyone?"

"Nope! Not a one."

"So, Jessica was it? Right?" he furthered probed, "I mean, she's the only one you ever had, uh, 'experiences' with, right?"

"Yes!" Danny answered, growing aggravated and embarrassed.

"No drunken one-nighters?"

"Nope!"

"No other woman ever?" Whitney asked. Danny shook his head.

"So, did you and Jessica ever … ?" she paused and looked down, smiling in anticipation, "You know 'homerun?'"

"Did we what?"

"Plow the field?" Butch jumped back in.

"Did ya'll ever shuck some corn?" Whitney volleyed.

"Put the pig in the pen?"

"Reap the harvest'?" Whitney laughed out loud.

"No! No we didn't plow! No we didn't reap! No, no, no!" Danny roared angrily, slamming his bottle on the table, "We didn't get around to it! Okay?" Whitney and Butch leaned back in their seats and lowered their heads, trying not to laugh out loud again.

"Hey, I'm sorry. Okay? I'm sorry," Butch confessed with a pat to Danny's right arm. "There's a lot of white boys out there that can't!" he insulted with a laugh. Danny shot up out of his chair, knocking it backwards, "You know what, you can just … " Whitney jumped out of her seat and grabbed Danny by the arm.

"C'mon, I wan' dance!" she said as she yanked Danny away from the table then forced her way onto the crowded dance floor.

As they neared the middle of the floor, the band started playing Chris Isaak's "Wicked Game." He nervously stood in front of Whitney with his hands in his pockets. Like a little boy being dressed for school, Whitney had to pull Danny's hands out of his pockets and wrap his arms around her waist. She leaned heavily into his body and slowly encircled his neck with her fingers.

"Were you serious back there?" she asked, genuinely concerned, "I don't wanna pry, but, you never have?" He looked into her big brown eyes and shook his head.

The cocktail waitress came back around to Butch; she said nothing but pointed at the table and made a circular motion, playing a quick charade for "ya'll wanna beer?" Butch answered her by holding up his bottle and making a slice to the throat gesture, as if to say "I'm cut off." She smiled, nodded and walked away. He noticed her stop and stare at a customer sitting at the front of the bar then shake her head. She mouthed a few words then waved her hand as to shoo away a fly. Butch kept his eye on the waitress who, after not getting the results she desired, approached the edge of the dance floor. She stood on her tip toes, looked over the crowd then pushed her way through the slow dancing throng.

He glanced at the customers in the bar area for any irregular or sudden movement. After disappearing for a brief moment, the waitress reemerged in the middle of the dance floor next to Whitney and Danny. He watched as the two women leaned in to each other, trying to talk over the noise level. Whitney quickly reared back, clenched her fists and thrust her forearms down in anger. The waitress again leaned in to speak while pointing to the front of the bar, shrugging her shoulders. Butch looked in the direction the waitress was pointing to catch a glimpse of who had caused such a reaction, but with the exception of the door opening for someone to enter the bar, no one or nothing appeared out of the ordinary.

In an aggravated huff, Whitney led Danny around the edge of the dance floor to stand directly in front of the cocktail tables. She aggressively pulled him in to her, pressing her full body against him. Danny, confused at her sudden change in behavior, lowered his head and inquired, "What's wrong?" "Nothing!" she snapped, anxiously looking around her, "Just some guy that won't leave me alone … kiss me!"

"What? Who? Where is he?" he asked, scouring the bar area. She grabbed him by the neck, pulled his mouth down to hers and passionately kissed him. He kissed her back, deeply, as his physical desire quickly took control. Whitney pulled away; her heart was racing and her eyes were opened wide like a doe standing in the headlights of oncoming traffic. Danny couldn't contain his feelings of arousal as he looked at her eyes, lips and body. Whitney looked to the front window and spied the man still watching her. She leaned in to Danny and laid her head on his chest.

Butch observed the man, but was unable to clearly see his face. He watched the front doors swing open again and the stranger dart across the street. Trying not to alert Whitney of any possible danger, Butch decided to take the drunk decoy route. He stepped onto the dance floor and loudly called out to Whitney and Danny, "All right you two, I'm leaving." "And you, Missy!" he blurted, wrapping his arm around her shoulder, "You are in custody of this perpetrator and I recommend immediate house arrest!" Danny laughed out loud while Butch whispered in Whitney's ear, "Can you bring him to the hotel later?"

"No problem," she whispered back, then loudly asked, "Are you okay?"

"Yeah man! You ah-ight?" Danny inquired, grabbing his friend by the shoulder. "Sure!" Butch played on, "I just wanna get to the hotel 'fore this really kicks in." "Well, okay," Danny agreed, looking to Whitney, "I don't want you to get into trouble."

"You kids have a great time and you get him home safely!" he offered the young couple.

"Thanks!" Whitney replied with a kiss on the cheek, "He'll be fine. I promise." Butch turned to leave with a clumsy pat on Danny's head. Only when Butch was a few paces away did Danny ask, "What'd you say to him?"

"I told him I'd have you back, safe and sound … " Whitney playfully confessed with a pause and a kiss, "First thing in the morning."

Once outside, Butch straightened up so as to not draw attention to himself. He looked all around for any sign of movement, but only heard the sound of a heavy duty truck starting up. He briskly walked to the end of the building; the warm hum of the music masked the sound of his footsteps. He cautiously poked his head around the corner to watch a Penguin Ice delivery truck speed away.

One would have thought that God himself pulled the moon closer to Earth, judging from its size and luminosity. It was well after one a.m. and Whitney and Danny hadn't made that strong of an effort to keep their mouths off each other since they left Rinkydinks. They kissed on the dance floor, they kissed outside the bar, they kissed in her '76 Chevy Luv pickup and now, in Whitney's backyard, under the bright Texas moonlight, they kissed in her porch swing. She felt so familiar to him, as if he had been holding her all of his life. He was now so strangely attractive to her, even though she had always thought of him as dangerous and forbidden. As they kissed under the light of the full moon, they felt their bodies calling out with desire.

Whitney managed to break free of Danny's embrace, climbed off the swing and said, "I'll be right back." She leaned down and kissed him once more, departing with, "Make yourself comfortable!"

Danny clung to her arms as she pulled away until just her fingertips were in reach. With a chuckling gasp he fell back into the porch swing and watched her skip away through the opened sliding glass door and billowing white drapes. She popped her head out the door and threw a sly wink in his direction before vanishing. He laid back in the corner of the swing, letting his right leg dangle down to rock himself. While looking up at the moon, his smile turned into a frown as his mind was suddenly cast back to that fateful, rainy homecoming night in nineteen eighty-six. He remembered how good it felt to hold, touch and kiss Jessica. He could still see her face, covered with grass and blood. He sat up, uneasy, jittery. *Where is she?* he asked himself, *She should have been back by now.* Feeling his breath coming on in short, shallow bursts, he stood up and began pacing, talking out loud, "Jess! What am I doin'? You should be here!" He turned to the patio doors and pulled back the drapes.

As he entered the living room, he noticed a soft glow emanating from the hallway. He cautiously called out, "Whitney?" but there was no reply. He started walking towards the hallway and again called out, "Whitney?" with the light growing brighter and brighter. He walked down the hall until he came to the doorway leading to her bedroom. Votive candles were scattered across the nightstand, dresser, armoire, and bed chest. The fresh and light, enticing scents of cinnamon and mulberry lingered in the air. Whitney emerged from the bathroom with her hair swept to one side and wearing a white, oversized men's button-up shirt. He shook his head and quickly blinked a few times.

She approached him, took him by the hand and walked backwards to the edge of the bed. The two gazed wantingly into each others eyes as she brushed her fingers across his lips, then tenderly kissed him. Without taking her eyes off of his, she unfastened the first button on her shirt. When she moved her fingers down to the next button, Danny pulled her hands away and said, "Wait … wait!" He pushed her softly onto the bed and backed up a few steps. With a dry throat and quivering knees, he untucked his t-shirt then pulled it over his head. Whitney leaned onto her right elbow and raised her legs onto the bed, enjoying the show. She felt herself growing more and more excited as her eyes roamed over his perfect body; the firmness of his pectorals, the swollen veins in his biceps and the tightness of his abdominals. He unbuckled his belt, unzipped his jeans, then slowly lowered them to the floor, showing his dark, tanned skin against his white, cotton boxer shorts.

Whitney smiled and made a gentle pat on the mattress, but Danny moved not a muscle. She extended her hand and pulled him down next to her. He pushed Whitney onto her back and climbed on top of her, looking directly and intensely into her eyes. As he lowered himself and opened his mouth to kiss her, Jessica's face once again flashed before his eyes. He stopped, rolled off of her and turned his head away, all a tremble.

"Danny … " she said, reaching up to feel his biceps and shoulders, "Danny, baby, you're shaking." She then noticed a tear running down his cheek and tenderly wrapped her arms around his neck. "Oh, baby. C'mere." she consoled soothingly. She pulled him into her breast and slowly rocked him and comfortingly whispered "Ssshhh … It's okay now … ssshhh." Danny quietly wept into Whitney's chest; his body heaved and lurched in breathless, confusing contradictions of mourning and desire. She stroked his hair and ran her fingertips across his back. Soon, he was fast asleep, safe and content in Whitney's arms. Tonight, as the moon sailed across the sky, she would not let go.

Ghosts from the Past

With newspaper in hand, Butch walked into Pokey's diner a few minutes before eight a.m. and once again seated himself in the last booth with his back against the wall. The early morning sunshine bathed the table with excellent reading light. As he read, swirling steam from his cup of coffee rose into the sunbeam, casting transparent heat waves on the paper. After a while, he looked at his watch, curious as to when Danny and Whitney would make their appearance; half past eight. At around ten minutes to nine, he watched as Whitney's faded white compact pickup pulled in and parked next to his truck. He peered over the rim of his reading glasses and watched as the newly formed couple joyfully bounced themselves to the restaurant entrance.

    The front door swung open wide, giving the brass jingle bells a good jostling. Danny strutted in with his left arm slung across Whitney's shoulders and her right arm wrapped around his waist. The gleeful pair were all smiles as they approached the table. He suddenly pulled away from her, bent over and wiped out the bench. Bowing down, he extended his arm out to the seat and offered up his best rendition of Professor Henry Higgins, "Yo seet m' laideee?"

    "Aaooohh!" Whitney replied with her finest interpretation of Eliza Doolittle, "Hau so vay thotful auv ya gov'nah!"

With intentional, staggered bluntness, Butch mumbled, "I … am gonna … be … sick!" as the lovebirds joined him at the table.

"Yo!" Danny hollered over his right shoulder, holding his empty coffee cup high in the air, "Two coffee's please!"

"Nice to see you made it in okay last night!" Butch commented, not taking his eyes from his paper.

The waitress almost immediately appeared at Danny's side. "Two coffees please." he calmly and politely requested.

"You wan' those black, hon?"

"Two cream and two sugars," he replied and turned to Whitney, "How 'bout you, doll?"

"Oh, just two creams and two sugars please. Just … like … you!" she gushed.

"No way!" he shockingly declared with a whip of his head.

"Way!" she replied, just as energetic, then grabbed his arm and yanked him closer for a kiss.

"So are you two crazy cats goin' to the sock hop?" Butch interjected as the prepubescent adolescents bounced in their seats.

Danny finally acknowledged and greeted Butch, "Morning!" then reached across the table and playfully slapped him on his left shoulder.

"Yes, a good morning indeed!" he stated, sarcastically. The waitress reappeared and poured two fresh cups of coffee as Butch continued, "Miss Whitney, a pleasure to see you again! A good time was had by all with last night's activities, I assume?"

"Oh, Yeah!" they answered in unison as they opened each others sugar and creamers, entangling their arms.

Later, after the bulk of breakfast had been downed, Butch reluctantly addressed the reason for which they came to town. "Okay!" he started, "Going by what Danny said is supposed to happen, I figure that if you're in our headquarters at the time this is supposed to take place, then the so called 'magical spell' will be broken. It ain't gonna happen with forty troopers surrounding you." Whitney reached under the table and took Danny's hand as the mood and tone of the moment suddenly shifted.

"You really think so?" Danny asked, not completely sold on the simplicity of the idea, "Something's gotta happen though, right? I'm not trying to contest your theory, but I think there's gonna be more to this than what you and I bargained for."

Butch looked into Whitney's desperate eyes and confidently addressed her, "I think that at this time, right now … what we do will determine if what Danny has been saying will come true. What I have come to believe and understand over this past year and half is … you gotta have faith." Danny fought back a tear as Butch reached out and squeezed both of their hands, "We gotta have faith. The one thing we need to focus on, of all there is in this world that's good n' bad, in the past, in the future and all that there ever will be … is God. His love for us, and us for Him. That's it! Out of love comes Faith. Faith is seeing … and believing in … what others say can't be believed in or doesn't exist. If we keep our faith and disprove this prediction, then whatever was making you see this … I think will stop, because, man can't change or alter God's plan and God doesn't reveal his plans to man. So, this? I think is about to stop … because it's not from God. And I firmly believe that with having God by our side to see us through this, once it's over and done, we'll all start to live a whole new life!" Danny raised his arm over Whitney's right shoulder and tenderly squeezed her. Butch released their hands and wiped his eyes before encouraging Whitney, "You'll be fine!"

Danny rolled up his sleeves as Butch, again, reviewed the plans for the day. "Now you got my cell number? Right?" he asked, concernedly.

"Yeah!" Danny confirmed, looking through his duffle bag for his charger, "I just need to charge up on the way!"

"Okay, again," he restated, "We'll go to my house first so we can drop off the trucks, then we'll take my car to the station … and wait. Okay?"

In irritation they both blasted, "Okay!"

Butch climbed into his truck and waited for Whitney to back up first. Danny searched through his duffle bag once more for his phone charger, but was unable to find it. With a prompting honk of Butch's horn, Whitney pulled out of the parking lot as Danny frustratingly hissed, "Forget it … I can't find it!" Butch pulled out behind them, loaded down with Danny's belongings. Once he was a few blocks away from Pokey's,

Butch looked into his rearview mirror and watched as a Penguin Ice refrigerated truck pulled onto the road.

Dale followed from a little more than a mile back, keeping Butch's truck in sight. "Brooke!" he called out, slapping and twisting the steering wheel, "Don't you know I love you?" In his mind, Dale replayed the moment the gun went off, watching himself shoot Brooke over and over again. He could still see the blood splatter on the vinyl backseat from the bullet ripping through her left lung. Dale never forgot the shocked and sorrowful look that hung on her face as the bright red blood began to flow from the entry wound. "All I wanted was to be with you!" he shouted, "Why didn't you shut up when I told you to? You just had to keep yelling! Had to keep pushing!" Memories of her decapitation still haunted him; the way she fell out of the door just as he collided with Tommy Lee's car. "You never had faith in me! You never trusted me!" he screamed. He conjured up the faces and voices of his later victims; the way they pleadingly called his name, begging for mercy, just as Brooke did, before he raised his gun to snuff their young and promising lives.

Dale drove the same refrigerated truck as when he killed his first Brooke look alike near Alma in 1988, the second one in Athens in 1993 and Emory in 1999. It was easy for Dale to meet girls at the grocery stores, restaurants, bars, and hotels on his delivery route; he had his pick. He knew he still looked young enough to woo them and his body was always in peak condition from lifting the large bags of ice all day long. Between the muscles, the curly, jet-black hair and big hazel eyes, you'd be hard pressed to not notice him. The problem with getting to know Dale, unbeknownst to his victims, was his deep, hidden insatiable hunger to find a surrogate replacement for his lost love. Also a problem for Dale, was his inability to forgive himself for what he had done and to accept the responsibility for his actions. Try as he might, Dale just couldn't seem to find the inner strength to let go of Brooke, to forgive himself or to ask God for forgiveness and seek help; he was too afraid, bitter, and selfish.

As he followed Butch, Dale grew more and more restless. He focused on his first victim, Marnie, and how he felt upon seeing her give another man her attention. It was Marnie that sent him over the edge, setting him on his path for murder. Dale was soon oblivious to the road as he relived his time with Marnie. She was a little shorter than Brooke, but other than that, was the spitting image. He met her in the spring of 1988 while making a delivery to the Dairy Queen, just inside the Alma city limits. He was unloading his last dolly full of ice in the outside locker; she was clocking in for the late afternoon and early evening shift. Marnie made direct eye contact, smiled and said "hello." As he headed back to his truck, he looked back and caught her watching him. For the next few months, he made it a point to have lunch or dinner there when he knew she was working. As time went by, their conversations grew more intimate and lengthy. But, as the anniversary of Brooke's death drew near, Dale found himself consumed with conflicting thoughts of being attracted to Marnie and the guilt of what he had done to Brooke.

In the early evening of July twenty-third, 1988, Dale dropped by the Dairy Queen, unannounced, and saw Marnie leaning over the counter, speaking to an attractive, younger male customer. He stood outside the front entry as she flirted, unaware that she was being monitored. Her body language told him she was attracted to the young man: touching his arm when he spoke, tossing her hair as she laughed and playing with her necklace in her teeth. Jealous and enraged, Dale stormed back to his truck, still undetected. He stayed in the cab, watching from the cover of darkness under the metal awning, steeping in his bitterness. Almost an hour had passed by when he noticed both the boy and Marnie look at their watches. They made some small talk before the boy leaned over and kissed her on the cheek, then exited. He left with a wave from his car as he drove away. Dale watched as she excitedly hopped up and down with her fellow female coworkers, clapping her hands.

As closing time approached, Dale entered the restaurant with a drawn out "Hi!" to Marnie. "Hey yourself!" she replied flatly, wiping down the malt machine.

"What're you doin' tonight?" he asked, leaning across the counter.

"Uh … uh" she stumbled, searching for an excuse.

"I got some Shiner chilled in the truck?" he eerily suggested, "We could go out and talk for a while?" Marnie bit her lower lip as she glanced at her watch, looked outside, then back to Dale.

"Um … okay … but just for a while," she reluctantly consented, "I gotta get home. I got some stuff to do."

"Yeah, sure!" Dale eagerly agreed, knowing she lied to him.

He escorted Marnie to his truck, opened the passenger door and aggressively helped her into the cab. He slammed the door and stared at her as he rounded the driver's side front fender. Dale climbed inside the truck and leaned over to Marnie, smirking, "You ready for a night you'll never forget?" She pushed herself back against her door, uneasy with his tone and facial expression.

"You know, maybe I should … " she nervously spoke as Dale started the engine and quickly engaged the transmission, throwing gravel as he exited the dark parking lot.

"Sure is a pretty moon out tonight?" he said, peering up at the sky. Marnie remained quiet, looking out her window with her legs and arms crossed. "You know," he stated nonchalantly, "You're such a pretty girl!" She looked at him and faintly smiled as she fumbled with her watch band. Dale reached over and placed his hand on her left thigh, then slid his fingers down to her knee, "You kinda remind me of someone I used to know real good!" Uncomfortable with his touch, she pushed his hand away.

"You know, it really is late and I should be … " she frighteningly declared.

"Here we are!" Dale abruptly announced and slammed on the brakes. Marnie lunged out and locked her arms against the dash board to keep from flying forward. The heavy truck came to a screeching halt on the shoulder of the road. "C'mon!" he instructed as he quickly exited the truck and walked around to the passenger side. He yanked open the door and extended his hand, "The night is young, the moon is full, and the beer is cold!"

Marnie regrettably took his hand, turned her legs toward the door and placed her left hand on the door's arm rest. He gave a small tug and pulled her clumsily down to the ground. She began crying as he helped her up to her feet, grabbed her by the elbow, and briskly walked her to the back of the truck. "Dale, please … what's wrong?" she whimpered.

"What could possibly be wrong?" he asked sarcastically, throwing the latch open on the insulated, double metal doors. "You said you wanted a beer," he answered smartly as he jerked open the doors to the freezing cargo compartment. The door swung just inches away from Marnie's face and slammed against the outside trailer wall with a deep, echoing thud. She could hear the wind blowing through the mesquites, the crickets in the grass, a few birds chirping and in the distance, some coyotes howling. More over all of this, however, she could hear her heart beat. "C'mon, let's get a drink!" Dale urged with wave of his arm.

Tears streamed down her cheeks as she crouched and pleadingly sobbed, "Dale … please … I just want to go home!"

As he followed Butch, Dale remembered how he gathered Marnie in his arms and lifted her into the freezer compartment then climbed in with her. He pulled on a rope to close the door behind him, trapping her inside in the process. For a moment all was quiet, except for Marnie's heavy breathing and the deep, resonating sound of the slamming metal door. Two dull overhead lights suddenly flickered on and Marnie found herself standing between palettes of stacked bags of ice.

"Let's have one of those beers!" Dale happily suggested. He gruffly pushed her out of the way and lifted one bag of ice to expose the top of the dark longneck bottles. "Here, have one on me!" he instructed, handing her a bottle from the almost frozen six-pack. Shaking with fright and freezing temperatures, Marnie refused his offer. "Oh c'mon! We drove all this way! You gotta have a least one." he insisted, opening the bottle. She crossed her arms, trembling, and again shook her head no. "I said have a beer!" Dale demanded and grabbed her hair. He pulled her head backwards and forced the bottle into her mouth. She tried to push his hands away, but he was much too strong. She choked and violently spewed beer from the sides of her lips, spraying herself and Dale in dark brown foam.

"Guess you're not a beer drinker!" he exclaimed as he shattered the beer bottle on the floor and released Marnie's head. She fell to her knees as he pushed one door slightly open to take a peek outside. Quiet.

"Dale, please!" Marnie pleaded, "I want to go home! My mom is expecting me!" She covered her face and doubled over, wailing loudly. As he listened to her weep, Dale could only see Brooke, kicking and screaming in the backseat, begging to go home to her mother.

"You remember when I said you reminded me of someone?" he sternly asked, circling around her, "She said the very same things! She said she didn't want to be with me either! She'd rather go home to her momma!" Dale reached behind him and pulled his .38 revolver from the back of his pants. "Why is it … " he inquired, lowering the gun in front of him, "that both you and she didn't give me a chance? Didn't even try to finish things out with me? Huh?"

Marnie lightly gasped, "Momma!"

"All you had to do was let me love you!"

He remembered how strong he felt when Marnie looked up to him with her mouth open wide, weeping in silent anguish, her face twisted and disfigured with fear. "Maybe you and she can talk it over?" he coldly suggested.

"Dale, you don't have to do this!" she peeped, struggling to stand.

"Sure I do!" he contradicted as he raised the gun and cocked the hammer, "It's the only way I can make you and her understand!" Dale pulled the trigger and sent a bullet careening through the top of her left breast, knocking her backward on the stack of ice. He cautiously opened the door to take another peek outside; nothing moved but the wind in the mesquites. He tucked the gun into the back of his pants while stepping to look at Marnie. He waved his hand over her open eyes to see if she was still alive. "Well … " he said to the gradually cooling corpse, "your loss!"

He bent over and looked underneath her torso; bright red blood slowly oozed from the 1exit wound in her left scapula and began collecting in a burgundy puddle at the base of the ice bags. He grabbed the remaining beer, jumped out of the truck and closed the door behind him. Dale climbed in the truck cab, opened a beer and took a long sip. After almost an hour and a half and the remaining five beers, he climbed back into the storage area and tossed Marnie's corpse over his shoulder. He crossed the highway and snuck off into the dark, almost laughing out loud at how simple an undertaking killing her was. Surely at that hour, he thought, some animal would smell her and find her body. Just to make sure she wasn't discovered for as long as possible, he took Marnie to a thick, remote patch of mesquites with deep buffalo grass. He laid her on her back with her arms at her side, still looking out into space.

He then pulled down a large, sprawling limb from one of the trees and walked back to where he placed Marnie's body. He drug the branch by its base from the opposite direction in which he walked, pulling the grass back to its original position.

Once the body was disposed of, he pulled his truck forward onto the asphalt, ran back to the shoulder and drug the branch across the dirt.

Having made sure that all traces of tire marks were erased, he threw the tree limb into the rear of the truck, made a U-turn and took off down the road. Feeling he was then in the clear on the opposite side of Alma, he tossed the beer bottles and branch behind a dumpster then pulled into a coin operated power wash. He took the hose with him into the refrigerated compartment to blow out the frozen blood. He was safe. She was gone. Problem eradicated.

Whitney and Danny began to slow down as they approached a stop light a few blocks away from Butch's townhouse. Butch pulled up next to them in the left turning lane and rolled down his passenger window. Two cars back, Dale patiently waited and placed his .38 special in the seat next to him, rubbing the handle.

"What're ya doin?" Whitney hollered to Butch. Danny rolled his window down and sat on the ledge of the door.

"Gonna get some gas before we go to the storage room later." Butch answered.

"Can't ya get it later?" Danny yelled back, tossing his arms in the air, "Does it hafta be right now?"

"I'm scared, Danny!" she stated, grabbing his calf.

"It's okay, ya'll go ahead … " Butch instructed, "I'll be right behind you. Five minutes, that's it."

Danny climbed back into Whitney's truck. "Geez!" he snapped. The fold, hovering above Whitney's right shoulder suddenly turned from bright red to a dark purple and green. "Hey! It's … it's not red!" Danny shouted, "It's not red! It's green! It's back to green!"

"Huh?" Whitney replied in dismay and looked at her shoulder as if a bug was crawling on her shirt. "You're all green!" He again shouted, "Well, there's a little purple, but you're green!"

"Really? Green?" she hopped in her seat excitedly, "I'm green?" She lunged into Danny and squeezed him tightly with tears of joy filling her eyes.

Danny crawled out of the window and again sat on the door ledge and hollered, "Butch!" but he had already rolled up his window. "Butch!" he again yelled as Whitney honked her horn. Danny watched in horror as the green fold above Butch's right shoulder turned bright red. "Butch!"

he yelled once more as the left turn signal changed and Butch quickly rounded the corner.

Danny climbed back in the truck as their light also turned green. Whitney accelerated and let loose with a high pitched, "Woohoo!" while honking her horn.

"Oh, my God! Oh, my God! Oh, my God!" Danny chanted as he searched for his cell phone.

"What? What baby! What's wrong!?" she asked, her mood changing abruptly at the tone in Danny's voice. Danny found his phone and frantically dialed Butch's number

"C'mon, c'mon!" he mumbled, clenching his teeth.

"Danny, hun, what's wrong?" she again inquired, rubbing his left shoulder. "You're scarin' me! Is everything okay?"

"Butch! Butch!" he yelled, pounding the phone in frustration. The phone showed almost no tower signal strength and flashed the weak battery sign.

"What? What?" she repeated anxiously, "Tell me so I can help!"

"You can't help!" he screamed angrily. "He turned red!" Danny roared as tears began to flow, "Butch just turned red! You turned green! He's red!" Whitney started breathing heavily. Unbeknownst to her, Dale was still following one car behind her. "I can't reach him on my phone! The buildings are too tall and the battery is too weak!"

Dale accelerated and moved into the middle lane. As he pulled parallel to the car directly behind Whitney's truck, he swerved to his left, knocking the small passenger car into the oncoming traffic. Dale didn't stop, nor did Whitney or Danny notice what just happened behind them.

Dale laughed out loud and stepped on the gas, taunting Whitney as he prepared to smash into her rear bumper, "This is for you, baby!" Whitney screamed at the force of the impact as Danny lurched forward and struck his head against the windshield. Dale again accelerated and pulled up to Whitney's in an attempt to clip her.

In a white knuckled panic Whitney screamed, "Danny! Danny!" Blood slowly trickled from his forehead down onto his face.

Dale tapped Whitney's right rear, sending her careening across her two right lanes of traffic. Dale overcorrected his truck and fishtailed to the right. At one point, the remaining ice in the back of the truck shifted;

the sudden change in the vehicles rear center of gravity caused his truck to roll into the path of the oncoming vehicles. Whitney's truck slammed between two parked cars, coming to rest against a light post.

A passerby with a cell phone immediately called 911 to report the accident. Amazingly, Dale's and Whitney's trucks were the only ones wrecked, minus the sedan Dale rammed the block before and the cars that Whitney's truck plowed into. All other vehicles in both directions managed to avoid any type of collision.

As Butch pumped his gas a few blocks away, he heard of the accidents and the call for assistance on his police scanner. He quickly removed the pump handle from his tank, jumped in his truck and answered on his radio, "Ranger Two two nine nine responding! Ranger Two two nine nine responding! I need all available emergency personnel! I need S.W.A.T., ambulance and reinforcement personnel as well! This is a hostage situation! I repeat this is a hostage situation!"

As he raced to the scene of the accident, Butch began blaming himself for what had happened, "Man, why did I leave? Why did I leave? This wouldn't have happened if I hadn't of left!"

Butch reached the intersection and sedan that Dale rammed and flashed his badge to the officer directing traffic. He then noticed the crowd gathered farther down the road. He turned the corner, flicked his headlights and honked his horn, shouting, "Move outta the way!" as he desperately tried to pass through the now jam-packed street. Growing more and more flustered, he hopped the median and drove on the opposite side of the street.

He finally reached the overturned ice truck, stopped and exited his truck with his gun drawn. He pulled out his badge chain and hung it around his neck for all to see as he crouched down and cautiously approached the ice truck. He peered through the windshield and found the cab empty, but noticed an empty box of .38 rounds. "We have a missing, injured, and potentially armed driver!" he yelled to one of the police officers.

Butch spotted the roof of Whitney's truck through the crowd of onlookers and emergency personnel. As he hurriedly walked through the crowd, he was acutely aware that Dale could be lurking anywhere, ready to strike. He reached Whitney's truck and the EMT assisting her.

"Ma'am, I need to get you stabilized and out of the way." "I don't w to leave! I want to stay with Danny!" he heard Whitney say and ran around to the other side of the truck. Two hook and ladder trucks pulled up as he yanked another EMT out of the way and called out, "Danny! Can you hear me? Danny?" Danny's right arm, like his father's left arm in '78, was broken in three places; his face was streaked with trails of blood that flowed from the gash in his scalp. "Danny! Danny, c'mon! Listen to me," Butch quickly interrogated, "Is Whitney gonna be okay? Danny! What's gonna happen now?" Danny wearily raised his left eye lid to find that he could no longer see the red fold on Butch's shoulder. He looked up to the EMT and noticed that he, too, had no fold on his shoulder.

"It was red!" he groggily explained, "Now … I can't see! Whitney … "

Butch climbed on the hood of the truck to get a visual of where the medical assistant had taken Whitney.

"You were red … " Danny mumbled as the EMT turned his attention back to his wounds, "But now I don't see … "

"Whitney!" Butch yelled from atop the truck, growing frustrated that anything at any moment could happen.

From across the street he heard a faint, "Butch," and spied an arm waving over the crowd.

The paramedic helped Danny up and out of the truck as Butch turned and ordered, "I want a police escort with this man, now! No one gets near him! Understand?" He jumped off the hood and moved in the direction of Whitney's waving arm.

While passing through the crowd, Butch heard a shrill, mournful cry, "Brooke!" but couldn't see where it came from. He drew his gun and looked all about him. Just like the wreck in 1978, Dale managed to quickly mingle into the crowd and lose himself among the spectators. He ducked into one of the department stores on the opposite side of the street from where Whitney crashed her truck. He merely needed to wait for her to be exposed. With this many people, he rationalized, it would be near impossible for them to locate where a single shot came from. Dale limped out of the department store, envisioning the lifestyle Brooke once said she'd like to have: a little white house up north in mountains, maybe in California or Oregon near the ocean, with two children playing in the front yard, rolling and laughing in the thick, en grass. "Brooke!" he again called out, walking through the rows of onlookers. Butch heard the cry once more and started slowly backing up toward Whitney's position on the ambulance back bumper. Dale crossed under the yellow police tape between the two fire trucks and loudly called again, "Brooke!" then sat on the rear deck of one of the trucks. Tears welled up in his eyes as he spoke out to her, "I just wanted you to be with me!" He removed his gun from his pants and painfully confessed, "I wanted us to have our kid and make it outta here."

Peeking around the corner of the fire truck, Dale noticed Danny being led to one of the ambulances. He, too, started walking directly toward the ambulances with his gun in his right hand, tucked up under his left arm. "Brooke!" he shouted once more. To most of the police and emergency personnel, a person calling out for someone at the scene of an accident was nothing new, but to Butch, Danny, and Whitney, it was a sign.

Danny turned his head to see Dale as he again shouted, "Brooke!" He scoured the crowd for Butch, but could only see Whitney, sitting open and exposed on the ambulance rear bumper. "Brooke! I love you!" Dale yelled a mere twenty yards away. Upon hearing the name yelled once more, Butch stepped out from behind the ambulance door just in time to see Dale raise his gun and pull the trigger, firing off one round. Instead of striking Whitney, the bullet found its way to Butch's chest. Butch fell to the ground as the police opened fire on Dale. His body was riddled with speeding bullets that tore away at his flesh.

"No!" Danny screamed and watched Butch's body slump to the ground. For a moment, he was ten years old again, reliving the moment Tommy Lee was shot in front of his own eyes.

Whitney fell to the ground, clinging to Butch's arm as he gasped for breath. A paramedic rushed to his side and shouted, "He's alive! Get me a stretcher!" Whitney laid Butch's head in her lap and stroked his hair as she wept. Danny quickly hobbled to Butch's side as the paramedics tended to his wound. Danny lowered his knee into a puddle of Butch's blood that had dripped onto the asphalt.

"I'm sorry! I'm sorry!" he wept, clutching Butch's hand.

"This is kinda how we first met! Remember?" Butch asked, smiling wearily, "C'mon, what's to be sorry for? You gave me back my dad. You're my friend." Danny heard Dale screaming in pain as police and paramedics surrounded him. "I know that if your daddy were here right now

Butch bargained, reaching up to stroke his friends face, "he'd be proud of you ... 'cuz if you were my boy I'd be proud o' you!" "Hey girl!" he addressed Whitney with a wink, "You gotta take care o' my boy!" Butch turned his eyes back to Danny and asked, "You know I love ya, right?" Danny nodded his head as he and Whitney both began to sob heavily. "And you know ... " he started, but never finished his thought. Butch died with his hand in Danny's and his head on Whitney's lap.

The silence was broken by Dale's screams, "Brooke! Brooke, I love you!" As he looked over his shoulder at Dale and the care being administered to him, Danny's heart erupted, dark with rage. In his mind he saw the faces of his childhood friends, Tommy, Brooke and the faces of Dale's other victims. Danny reached over Butch's body and took the pearl-handled .9 millimeter from his hand. Whitney watched as Danny's face suddenly lost all expression.

"Danny?" she said, her voice filled with panic and concern. He looked at her with lifeless eyes, not saying a word. "Danny!" she firmly stated, "Stop this right now!" He turned away and painfully struggled to his feet.

Danny looked down at the gun, removed the safety and pulled back the barrel to load a bullet. A few officers noticed Danny walking toward Dale and the EMTs then spied the gun in his hand.

"Freeze!" one of them shouted and drew his gun, alerting the other officers who in turn drew their guns.

"Danny!" Whitney screamed, still holding Butch's head in her lap "Danny! Stop! Don't!" Danny kept walking toward the paramedics who abandoned Dale and fled for safety.

"Freeze!" they again demanded and shouted, "Drop the gun!" all the while pointing theirs. Danny, oblivious to their requests, rewound the images of himself sitting in the floorboard of his father's squad car and the knock on the window. He remembered his father, standing in the freezing rain, smiling and telling him that everything was okay, then his head disappeared.

Whitney removed Butch's head from her lap and clumsily rushed to Danny, begging, "Please, Danny, stop!" She wrapped her arms around his waist and struggled desperately to restrain him, but he was too focused and much too strong. He drug her behind him as he approached Dale.

The officers yelled at Whitney, "Ma'am, stay down!" but she too wouldn't listen.

Whitney jumped up in front of Danny as he stood over Dale. She threw her arms around his neck and whispered softly in his ear, "Danny, baby ... please ... don't do this. I love you!"

"Brooke!" Dale called out somewhat apologetically when he saw Whitney standing above him, "I just wanted us to be happy. I miss you so much!"

Danny slowly lowered his gun then tossed it to the side as Pastor Brock's words spoke to his heart, "Therefore let all bitterness, and wrath, and anger, and clamor, and evil speaking be put away from you, with all malice: And be ye kind one to another, tenderhearted, forgiving one another, even as God, for Christ's sake hath forgiven you!"

Danny tried to suppress his tears upon remembering the sermon and coming the realization of what he must do. He reached out for Whitney's hand and both squatted down over Dale, each taking one of his hands. Danny lowered his head, closed his eyes and began reciting, "Our father, who art in heaven, hallowed be Your name. Thy kingdom come, Thy will be done ... " Dale opened his eyes and looked lovingly upon Danny and Whitney. He smiled to himself, breathed a sigh of contentment and was gone.

And All Flesh Shall be Made New

It was Sunday morning and Pastor Cregan addressed his congregation, "If you'd please turn in your Bibles to the book of Ephesians, chapter ten, as we learn of God's instructions on how we are to prepare ourselves for spiritual battle." A whimpering infant temporarily disrupted the quiet, attentive congregation. Danny took his tiny baby boy, Cleo Lee, from Whitney's arms. The beautiful child always seemed to fall asleep faster when being rocked in his daddy's arms.

listen|imagine|view|experience

AUDIO BOOK DOWNLOAD INCLUDED WITH THIS BOOK!

In your hands you hold a complete digital entertainment package. Besides purchasing the paper version of this book, this book includes a free download of the audio version of this book. Simply use the code listed below when visiting our website. Once downloaded to your computer, you can listen to the book through your computer's speakers, burn it to an audio CD or save the file to your portable music device (such as Apple's popular iPod) and listen on the go!

How to get your free audio book digital download:

1. Visit www.tatepublishing.com and click on the e|LIVE logo on the home page.
2. Enter the following coupon code:
   4598-86e5-6024-1666-568e-5156-aabb-e67c
3. Download the audio book from your e|LIVE digital locker and begin enjoying your new digital entertainment package today!